'May be her best yet, though, to be honest, this is what I always tend to say after reading the latest Anne Tyler. I've now read it twice, and I may well read it again'

Craig Brown, *Mail on Sunday*

'Tyler writes with an apparent effortlessness which conceals great art. The Whitshank family is tragic, comic, absurd, absorbing – and lives on its illusions, as every family must. You'll shiver with recognition'

Helen Dunmore, *Stylist*

'One of the most accomplished writers working today… A must-read'

Good Housekeeping

'Her extraordinary gift for producing what seems less like fiction than actuality works wonders again. Characters all but elbow their way off the page with lifelikeness… Magnificent'

Sunday Times

'There is no limit to the superlatives that Tyler inspires'

Irish Times

'Every sentence is perfect in this witty story of family life'

Sun

'The extraordinary thing about her writing is the extent to which she makes one believe every word, deed and breath'

Observer

ANNE TYLER

Anne Tyler was born in Minneapolis, Minnesota, in 1941 and grew up in Raleigh, North Carolina. She is the Pulitzer Prize-winning author of *Breathing Lessons* and many other bestselling novels, including *The Accidental Tourist*, *Dinner at the Homesick Restaurant*, *Saint Maybe*, *Ladder of Years*, *A Patchwork Planet*, *Back When We Were Grownups*, *The Amateur Marriage*, *Digging to America* and *The Beginner's Goodbye*. In 1994 she was nominated by Roddy Doyle and Nick Hornby as 'the greatest novelist writing in English' and she has recently received the Sunday Times Award for Literary Excellence, which recognises a lifetime's achievement in books.

ALSO BY ANNE TYLER

ANNE TYLER

A Spool of
Blue Thread

VINTAGE

1 3 5 7 9 10 8 6 4 2

Vintage
20 Vauxhall Bridge Road,
London SW1V 2SA

Vintage is part of the Penguin Random House group of companies whose
addresses can be found at global.penguinrandomhouse.com.

Penguin
Random House
UK

First published in Vintage in 2015
First published in hardback by Chatto & Windus in 2015

www.vintage-books.co.uk

A CIP catalogue record for this book is
available from the British Library

ISBN 9780099598480

Printed and bound by CPI Group (UK) Ltd, Croydon, CR0 4YY

MIX
Paper from
responsible sources
FSC® C018179

Penguin Random House is committed to a sustainable future
for our business, our readers and our planet. This book is made
from Forest Stewardship Council® certified paper

PART ONE

Can't Leave Till the Dog Dies

1

Late one July evening in 1994, Red and Abby Whitshank had a phone call from their son Denny. They were getting ready for bed at the time. Abby was standing at the bureau in her slip, drawing hairpins one by one from her scattery sand-colored topknot. Red, a dark, gaunt man in striped pajama bottoms and a white T-shirt, had just sat down on the edge of the bed to take his socks off; so when the phone rang on the nightstand beside him, he was the one who answered. "Whitshank residence," he said.

And then, "Well, hey there."

Abby turned from the mirror, both arms still raised to her head.

"What's that," he said, without a question mark.

"Huh?" he said. "Oh, what the *hell*, Denny!"

Abby dropped her arms.

"Hello?" he said. "Wait. Hello? Hello?"

He was silent for a moment, and then he replaced the receiver.

"What?" Abby asked him.

"Says he's gay."

"*What?*"

"Said he needed to tell me something: he's gay."

"And you hung up on him!"

"No, Abby. *He* hung up on *me*. All I said was 'What the hell,' and he hung up on me. Click! Just like that."

"Oh, Red, how *could* you?" Abby wailed. She spun away to reach for her bathrobe—a no-color chenille that had once been pink. She wrapped it around her and tied the sash tightly. "What possessed you to say that?" she asked him.

"I didn't mean anything by it! Somebody springs something on you, you're going to say 'What the hell,' right?"

Abby grabbed a handful of the hair that pouffed over her forehead.

"All I meant was," Red said, "'What the hell *next*, Denny? What are you going to think up next to worry us with?' And he knew I meant that. Believe me, he knew. But now he can make this all *my* fault, my narrow-mindedness or fuddy-duddiness or whatever he wants to call it. He was *glad* I said that to him. You could tell by how fast he hung up on me; he'd been just hoping all along that I would say the wrong thing."

"All right," Abby said, turning practical. "Where was he calling from?"

"How would I know where he was calling from? He doesn't have a fixed address, hasn't been in touch all summer, already changed jobs twice that we know of and probably more that we *don't* know of . . . A nineteen-year-old boy and we have no idea what part of the planet he's on! You've got to wonder what's wrong, there."

"Did it sound like it was long distance? Could you hear that kind of rushing sound? Think. Could he have been right here in Baltimore?"

"I don't know, Abby."

She sat down next to him. The mattress slanted in her direction; she was a wide, solid woman. "We have to find him," she said. Then, "We should have that whatsit—caller ID." She leaned forward and gazed fiercely at the phone. "Oh, God, I want caller ID this *instant*!"

"What for? So you could phone him back and he could just let it ring?"

"He wouldn't do that. He would know it was me. He would answer, if he knew it was me."

She jumped up from the bed and started pacing back and forth, up and down the Persian runner that was worn nearly white in the middle from all the times she had paced it before. This was an attractive room, spacious and well designed, but it had the comfortably shabby air of a place whose inhabitants had long ago stopped seeing it.

"What did his voice sound like?" she asked. "Was he nervous? Was he upset?"

"He was fine."

"So *you* say. Had he been drinking, do you think?"

"I couldn't tell."

"Were other people with him?"

"I couldn't *tell*, Abby."

"Or maybe . . . one other person?"

He sent her a sharp look. "You are *not* thinking he was serious," he said.

"Of course he was serious! Why else would he say it?"

"The boy isn't gay, Abby."

"How do you know that?"

"He just isn't. Mark my words. You're going to feel silly, by and by, like, 'Shoot, I overreacted.'"

"Well, naturally that is what you would want to believe."

"Doesn't your female intuition tell you anything at all? This is a kid who got a girl in trouble before he was out of high school!"

"So? That doesn't mean a thing. It might even have been a symptom."

"Come again?"

"We can never know with absolute certainty what another person's sex life is like."

"No, thank God," Red said.

He bent over, with a grunt, and reached beneath the bed for his slippers. Abby, meanwhile, had stopped pacing and was staring once more at the phone. She set a hand on the receiver. She hesitated. Then she snatched up the receiver and pressed it to her ear for half a second before slamming it back down.

"The thing about caller ID is," Red said, more or less to himself, "it seems a little like cheating. A person should be willing to take his chances, answering the phone. That's kind of the general *idea* with phones, is my opinion."

He heaved himself to his feet and started toward the bathroom. Behind him, Abby said, "This would explain so much! Wouldn't it? If he should turn out to be gay."

Red was closing the bathroom door by then, but he poked his head back out to glare at her. His fine black eyebrows, normally straight as rulers, were knotted almost together. "Sometimes," he said, "I rue and deplore the day I married a social worker."

Then he shut the door very firmly.

When he returned, Abby was sitting upright in bed with her arms clamped across the lace bosom of her nightgown. "You are surely not going to try and blame Denny's problems on my profession," she told him.

"I'm just saying a person can be *too* understanding," he said. "Too sympathizing and pitying, like. Getting into a kid's private brain."

"There is no such thing as 'too understanding.'"

"Well, count on a social worker to think that."

She gave an exasperated puff of a breath, and then she sent another glance toward the phone. It was on Red's side of the bed, not hers. Red raised the covers and got in, blocking her view. He reached over and snapped off the lamp on the nightstand. The room fell into darkness, with just a faint glow from the two tall, gauzy windows overlooking the front lawn.

Red was lying flat now, but Abby went on sitting up. She said, "Do you think he'll call us back?"

"Oh, yes. Sooner or later."

"It took all his courage to call the first time," she said. "Maybe he used up every bit he had."

"Courage! What courage? We're his parents! Why would he need courage to call his own parents?"

"It's you he needs it for," Abby said.

"That's ridiculous. I've never raised a hand to him."

"No, but you disapprove of him. You're always finding fault with him. With the girls you're such a softie, and then Stem is more your kind of person. While Denny! Things come harder to Denny. Sometimes I think you don't like him."

"Abby, for God's sake. You know that's not true."

"Oh, you love him, all right. But I've seen the way you look at him—'Who *is* this person?'—and don't you think for a moment that he hasn't seen it too."

"If that's the case," Red said, "how come it's *you* he's always trying to get away from?"

"He's not trying to get away from me!"

"From the time he was five or six years old, he wouldn't let you into his room. Kid preferred to change his own sheets rather than let you in to do it for him! Hardly ever brought his friends home, wouldn't say what their names were, wouldn't even tell you what he did in school all day.

'Get out of my life, Mom,' he was saying. 'Stop meddling, stop prying, stop breathing down my neck.' His least favorite picture book—the one he hated so much he tore out all the pages, remember?—had that baby rabbit that wants to change into a fish and a cloud and such so he can get away, and the mama rabbit keeps saying how she will change too and come after him. Denny ripped out every single everlasting page!"

"That had nothing to do with—"

"You wonder why he's turned gay? Not that he *has* turned gay, but *if* he had, if it's crossed his mind just to bug us with that, you want to know why? I'll tell you why: it's the mother. It is always the smothering mother."

"Oh!" Abby said. "That is just so outdated and benighted and so . . . *wrong*, I'm not even going to dignify it with an answer."

"You're certainly using a lot of words to tell me so."

"And how about the father, if you want to go back to the Dark Ages for your theories? How about the macho, construction-guy father who tells his son to buck up, show some spunk, quit whining about the small stuff, climb the darn roof and hammer the slates in?"

"You don't *hammer* slates in, Abby."

"How about him?" she asked.

"Okay, fine! I did that. I was the world's worst parent. It's done."

There was a moment of quiet. The only sound came from outside—the whisper of a car slipping past.

"I didn't say you were the *worst*," Abby said.

"Well," Red said.

Another moment of quiet.

Abby asked, "Isn't there a number you can punch that will dial the last person who called?"

"Star sixty-nine," Red said instantly. He cleared his throat. "But you are surely not going to do that."

"Why not?"

"Denny was the one who chose to end the conversation, might I point out."

"His feelings were hurt, was why," Abby said.

"If his feelings were hurt, he'd have taken his time hanging up. He wouldn't have been so quick to cut me off. But he hung up like he was just *waiting* to hang up. Oh, he was practically rubbing his hands together, giving me that news! He starts right in. 'I'd like to tell you something,' he says."

"Before, you said it was 'I *need* to tell you something.'"

"Well, one or the other," Red said.

"Which was it?"

"Does it matter?"

"*Yes*, it matters."

He thought a moment. Then he tried it out under his breath. "'I need to tell you something,'" he tried. "'I'd like to tell you something.' 'Dad, I'd like to—'" He broke off. "I honestly don't remember," he said.

"Could you dial star sixty-nine, please?"

"I can't figure out his reasoning. He knows I'm not anti-gay. I've got a gay guy in charge of our drywall, for Lord's sake. Denny *knows* that. I can't figure out why he thought this would bug me. I mean, of course I'm not going to be thrilled. You always want your kid to have it as easy in life as he can. But—"

"Hand me the phone," Abby said.

The phone rang.

Red grabbed the receiver at the very same instant that Abby flung herself across him to grab it herself. He had it first, but there was a little tussle and somehow she was the one who ended up with it. She sat up straight and said, "Denny?"

Then she said, "Oh. Jeannie."

Red lay flat again.

"No, no, we're not in bed yet," she said. There was a pause. "Certainly. What's wrong with yours?" Another pause. "It's no trouble at all. I'll see you at eight tomorrow. Bye."

She held the receiver toward Red, and he took it from her and reached over to replace it in its cradle.

"She wants to borrow my car," she told him. She sank back onto her side of the bed.

Then she said, in a thin, lonesome-sounding voice, "I guess star sixty-nine won't work now, will it."

"No," Red said, "I guess not."

"Oh, Red. Oh, what are we going to do? We'll never, ever hear from him again! He's not going to give us another chance!"

"Now, hon," he told her. "We'll hear from him. I

promise." And he reached for her and drew her close, settling her head on his shoulder.

They lay like that for some time, until gradually Abby stopped fidgeting and her breaths grew slow and even. Red, though, went on staring up into the dark. At one point, he mouthed some words to himself in an experimental way. "'. . . need to tell you something,'" he mouthed, not even quite whispering it. Then, "'. . . like to tell you something.'" Then, "'Dad, I'd like to . . .' 'Dad, I need to . . .'" He tossed his head impatiently on his pillow. He started over. "'. . . tell you something: I'm gay.' '. . . tell you something: I *think* I'm gay.' 'I'm gay.' 'I think I'm gay.' 'I think I *may* be gay.' 'I'm gay.'"

But eventually he grew silent, and at last he fell asleep too.

Well, of course they did hear from him again. The Whitshanks weren't a *melodramatic* family. Not even Denny was the type to disappear off the face of the earth, or sever all contact, or stop speaking—or not permanently, at least. It was true that he skipped the beach trip that summer, but he might have skipped it anyhow; he had to make his pocket money for the following school year. (He was attending St. Eskil College, in Pronghorn, Minnesota.) And he did telephone in September. He needed money for textbooks, he said. Unfortunately, Red was the only one home at the time, so it wasn't a very revealing conversation.

"What did you talk about?" Abby demanded, and Red said, "I told him his textbooks had to come out of his earnings."

"I mean, did you talk about that last phone call? Did you apologize? Did you explain? Did you ask him any questions?"

"We didn't really get into it."

"Red!" Abby said. "This is classic! This is such a classic reaction: a young person announces he's gay and his family just carries on like before, pretending they didn't hear."

"Well, fine," Red said. "Call him back. Get in touch with his dorm."

Abby looked uncertain. "What reason should I give him for calling?" she asked.

"Say you want to grill him."

"I'll just wait till he phones again," she decided.

But when he phoned again—which he did a month or so later, when Abby was there to answer—it was to talk about his plane reservations for Christmas vacation. He wanted to change his arrival date, because first he was going to Hibbing to visit his girlfriend. His girlfriend! "What could I say?" Abby asked Red later. "I had to say, 'Okay, fine.'"

"What could you say," Red agreed.

He didn't refer to the subject again, but Abby herself sort of simmered and percolated all those weeks before Christmas. You could tell she was just itching to get things out in the open. The rest of the family edged around her warily. They knew nothing about the gay announcement— Red and Abby had concurred on that much, not to tell them without Denny's say-so—but they could sense that something was up.

It was Abby's plan (though not Red's) to sit Denny down and have a nice heart-to-heart as soon as he got home. But on the morning of the day that his plane was due in, they had a letter from St. Eskil reminding them of the terms of their contract: the Whitshanks would be responsible for the next semester's tuition even though Denny had withdrawn.

"'Withdrawn,'" Abby repeated. She was the one who had opened the letter, although both of them were reading it. The slow, considering way she spoke brought out all the word's ramifications. Denny had withdrawn; he *was* withdrawn; he had withdrawn from the family years ago. What other middle-class American teenager lived the way he did—flitting around the country like a vagrant, completely out of his parents' control, getting in touch just sporadically and neglecting whenever possible to give them any means of getting in touch with *him*? How had things come to such a pass? They certainly hadn't allowed the other children to behave this way. Red and Abby looked at each other for a long, despairing moment.

Understandably, therefore, the subject that dominated Christmas that year was Denny's leaving school. (He had decided school was a waste of money, was all he had to say, since he didn't have the least idea what he wanted to do in life. Maybe in a year or two, he said.) His gayness, or his non-gayness, just seemed to get lost in the shuffle.

"I can almost see now why some families pretend they weren't told," Abby said after the holidays.

"Mm-hmm," Red said, poker-faced.

Of Red and Abby's four children, Denny had always been the best-looking. (A pity more of those looks hadn't gone to the girls.) He had the Whitshank straight black hair and narrow, piercing blue eyes and chiseled features, but his skin was one shade tanner than the paper-white skin of the others, and he seemed better put together, not such a bag of knobs and bones. Yet there was something about his face—some unevenness, some irregularity or asymmetry— that kept him from being truly handsome. People who remarked on his looks did so belatedly, in a tone of surprise, as if they were congratulating themselves on their powers of discernment.

In birth order, he came third. Amanda was nine when he was born, and Jeannie was five. Was it hard on a boy to have older sisters? Intimidating? Demeaning? Those two could be awfully sure of themselves—especially Amanda, who had a bossy streak. But he shrugged Amanda off, more or less, and with tomboyish little Jeannie he was mildly affectionate. So, no warning bells there. Stem, though! Stem had come along when Denny was four. Now, that could have been a factor. Stem was just naturally good. You see such children, sometimes. He was obedient and sweet-tempered and kind; he didn't even have to try.

Which was not to say that Denny was bad. He was far more generous, for instance, than the other three put together. (He traded his new bike for a kitten when Jeannie's beloved cat died.) And he didn't bully other children, or throw tantrums. But he was so close-mouthed. He had these spells of unexplained obstinacy, where his face would grow set and pinched and no one could get through to him. It seemed to be a kind of *inward* tantrum; it seemed his anger turned in upon itself and hardened him or froze him. Red threw up his hands when that happened and stomped off, but Abby couldn't let him be. She just had to jostle him out of it. She wanted her loved ones happy!

One time in the grocery store, when Denny was in a funk for some reason, "Good Vibrations" started playing over the loudspeaker. It was Abby's theme song, the one she always said she wanted for her funeral procession, and she began dancing to it. She dipped and sashayed and dum-da-da-dummed around Denny as if he were a maypole, but he just stalked on down the soup aisle with his eyes fixed straight ahead and his fists jammed into his jacket pockets. Made her look like a fool, she told Red when she got home. (She was trying to laugh it off.) He never even glanced at her! She might have been some crazy lady! And this was when he was nine or ten, nowhere near that age yet when boys find their mothers embarrassing. But he had found Abby embarrassing from earliest childhood, evidently. He acted as if he'd been assigned the wrong mother, she said, and she just didn't measure up.

Now she was being silly, Red told her.

And Abby said yes, yes, she knew that. She hadn't meant it the way it sounded.

Teachers phoned Abby repeatedly: "Could you come in for a talk about Denny? As soon as possible, please." The issue was inattention, or laziness, or carelessness; never a lack of ability. In fact, at the end of third grade he was put ahead a year, on the theory that he might just need a bigger challenge. But that was probably a mistake. It made him even more of an outsider. The few friends he had were questionable friends—boys who didn't go to his school, boys who made the rest of the family uneasy on the rare occasions they showed themselves, mumbling and shifting their feet and looking elsewhere.

Oh, there were moments of promise, now and then. He won a prize in a science contest, once, for designing a form of packaging that would keep an egg from cracking no matter how far you threw it. But that was the last contest he entered. And one summer he took up the French horn, which he'd had a few lessons in during elementary school, and he showed more perseverance than the family had ever seen in him. For several weeks a bleating, blurting, fogged version of Mozart's Horn Concerto No. 1 stumbled through the closed door of his room hour after hour, haltingly, relentlessly, till Red began cursing under his breath; but Abby patted Red's hand and said, "Oh, now, it could be worse. It could be the Butthole Surfers," which was Jeannie's music of choice at the time. "I just think it's wonderful that he's found himself a project," she said, and whenever Denny paused a few measures for the orchestral parts, she would tra-la-la the missing notes. (The entire family knew the piece by heart now, since it blared from the stereo any time that Denny wasn't playing it himself.) But once he could make it through the first movement without having to go back and start over, he gave it up. He said French horn was boring. "Boring" seemed to be his favorite word. Soccer camp was boring, too, and he dropped out after three days. Same for tennis; same for swim team. "Maybe we should cool it," Red suggested to Abby. "Not act all excited whenever he shows an interest in something."

But Abby said, "We're his parents! Parents are *supposed* to be excited."

Although he guarded his privacy obsessively—behaved as if he had state secrets to hide—Denny himself was an inveterate snoop. Nothing was safe from him. He read his sisters' diaries and his mother's client files. He left desk drawers suspiciously smooth on top but tumbled about underneath.

And then when he reached his teens there was the drinking, the smoking, the truancy, the pot and maybe worse. Battered cars pulled up to the house with unfamiliar drivers honking and shouting, "Yo, Shitwank!" Twice he got in trouble with the police. (Driving without a license; fake ID.) His style of dress went way beyond your usual adolescent grunge: old men's overcoats bought at flea markets; crusty, baggy tweed pants; sneakers held together with duct tape. His hair was unwashed, ropy with grease, and he gave off the smell of a musty clothes closet. He could have been a homeless person. Which was so ironic, Abby told Red. A blood member of the Whitshank family, one of those enviable families that radiate clannishness and togetherness and just . . . specialness; but he trailed around their edges like some sort of charity case.

By then both boys were working part-time at Whitshank Construction. Denny proved competent, but not so good with the customers. (To a woman who said, flirtatiously, "I worry you'll stop liking me if I tell you I've changed my mind about the paint color," his answer was "Who says I ever liked you in the first place?") Stem, on the other hand, was obliging with the customers and devoted to the work— staying late, asking questions, begging for another project. Something involving wood, he begged. Stem loved to deal with wood.

Denny developed a lofty tone of voice, supercilious and amused. "Certainly, my man," he would answer when Stem asked for the sports section, and "Whatever you say, Abigail." At Abby's well-known "orphan dinners," with their assemblages of misfits and loners and unfortunates, Denny's courtly behavior came across first as charming and then as offensive. "Please, I insist," he told Mrs. Mallon, "have *my* chair; it can bear your weight better." Mrs. Mallon, a stylish divorcee who took pride in her extreme thinness, cried, "Oh! Why—" but he said, "*Your* chair's kind of fragile," and his parents couldn't do a thing, not without drawing even more attention to the situation. Or B. J. Autry, a raddled blonde whose harsh, cawing laugh made everyone wince: Denny devoted a whole Easter Sunday to complimenting her "bell-like tinkle." Though B. J., for one, gave as good as she got. "Buzz off, kid," she said finally. Red hauled Denny over the coals afterward. "In this house," he said, "we don't insult our guests. You owe B. J. an apology."

Denny said, "Oh, my mistake. I didn't realize she was such a delicate flower."

"Everybody's delicate, son, if you poke them hard enough."

"Really? Not me," Denny said.

Of course they thought of sending him to therapy. Or Abby did, at least. All along she had thought of it, but now she grew more insistent. Denny refused. One day during his junior year, she asked his help taking the dog to the vet—a two-person job. After they'd dragged Clarence into the car, Denny threw himself on the front seat and folded his arms across his chest, and they set off. Behind them, Clarence whimpered and paced, scritching his toenails across the vinyl upholstery. The whimpers turned to moans as the vet's office drew closer. Abby sailed past the vet and kept going. The moans became fainter and more questioning, and eventually they stopped. Abby drove to a low stucco building, parked in front and cut the engine. She walked briskly around to the passenger side and opened the door for Denny. "Out," she ordered. Denny sat still for a moment but then obeyed, unfolding himself so slowly and so grudgingly that he almost *oozed* out. They climbed the two steps to the building's front stoop, and Abby punched a button next to a plaque reading RICHARD HANCOCK, M.D. "I'll collect you in fifty minutes," she said. Denny gave her an impassive stare. When a buzzer sounded, he opened the door, and Abby returned to the car.

Red had trouble believing this story. "He just walked in?" he asked Abby. "He just went along with it?"

"Of course," Abby said breezily, and then her eyes filled with tears. "Oh, Red," she said, "can you imagine what a hard time he must be having, if he let me do that?"

Denny saw Dr. Hancock weekly for two or three months. "Hankie," he called him. ("I've got no time to clean the basement; it's a goddamn Hankie day.") He never said what they talked about, and Dr. Hancock of course didn't, either, although Abby phoned him once to ask if he thought a family conference might be helpful. Dr. Hancock said he did not.

This was in 1990, late 1990. In early 1991, Denny eloped.

The girl was named Amy Lin. She was the wishbone-thin, curtain-haired, Goth-costumed daughter of two Chinese-American orthopedists, and she was six weeks pregnant. But none of this was known to the Whitshanks. They had never heard of Amy Lin. Their first inkling came when her father phoned and asked if they had any idea of Amy's whereabouts. "Who?" Abby said. She thought at first he must have dialed the wrong number.

"Amy Lin, my daughter. She's gone off with your son. Her note said they're getting married."

"They're *what*?" Abby said. "He's sixteen years old!"

"So is Amy," Dr. Lin said. "Her birthday was day before yesterday. She seems to be under the impression that sixteen is legal marrying age."

"Well, maybe in Mozambique," Abby said.

"Could you check Denny's room for a note, please? I'll wait."

"All right," Abby said. "But I really think you're mistaken."

She laid the receiver down and called for Jeannie—the one most familiar with Denny's ways—to help her look for a note. Jeannie was just as disbelieving as Abby. "Denny? Married?" she asked as they climbed the stairs. "He doesn't even have a girlfriend!"

"Oh, clearly the man is bonkers," Abby said. "And so imperious! He introduced himself as 'Dr. Lin.' He had that typical doctor way of ordering people about."

Naturally, they didn't find a note, or anything else telltale—a love letter or a photograph. Jeannie even checked a tin box on Denny's closet shelf that Abby hadn't known about, but all it held was a pack of Marlboros and a matchbook. "See?" Abby said triumphantly.

But Jeannie wore a thoughtful expression, and on their way back down the stairs she said, "When has Denny *ever* left a note, though, for any reason?"

"Dr. Lin has it all wrong," Abby said with finality. She picked up the receiver and said, "It appears that you're wrong, Dr. Lin."

So it was left to the Lins to locate the couple, after their daughter called them collect to tell them she was fine although maybe the teeniest bit homesick. She and Denny were holed up in a motel outside Elkton, Maryland, having run into a snag when they tried to apply for a marriage license. By that time they had been missing three days, so the Whitshanks were forced to admit that Dr. Lin must not be bonkers after all, although they still couldn't quite believe that Denny would do such a thing.

The Lins drove to Elkton to retrieve them, returning directly to the Whitshank house to hold a two-family discussion. It was the first and only time that Red and Abby laid eyes on Amy. They found her bewilderingly unattractive—sallow and unhealthy-looking, and lacking any sign of spirit. Also, as Abby said later, it was a jolt to see how well the Lins seemed to know Denny. Amy's father, a small man in a powder-blue jogging suit, spoke to him familiarly and even kindly, and her mother patted Denny's hand in a consoling way after he finally allowed that an abortion might be wiser. "Denny must have been to their house any number of times," Abby told Red, "while you and I didn't realize Amy even existed."

"Well, it's different with daughters," Red said. "You know how we generally get to meet Mandy and Jeannie's young men, but I'm not sure the young men's parents always meet Mandy and Jeannie."

"No," Abby said, "that's not what I'm talking about. This is more like he didn't just meet her family; he *joined* it."

"Rubbish," Red told her.

Abby didn't seem reassured.

They did try to talk with Denny about the elopement once the Lins left, but all he would say was that he'd been looking forward to taking care of a baby. When they said he was too young to take care of a baby, he was silent. And when Stem asked, in his clumsy, puppyish way, "So are you and Amy, like, engaged now?" Denny said, "Huh? I don't know."

In fact, the Whitshanks never saw Amy again, and as far as they could tell, Denny didn't, either. By the end of the next week he was safely installed in a boarding school for problem teenagers up in Pennsylvania, thanks to Dr. Hancock, who made all the arrangements. Denny completed his junior and senior years there, and since he claimed to have no interest in construction work, he spent both summers busing tables in Ocean City. The only times he came home anymore were for major events, like Grandma Dalton's funeral or Jeannie's wedding, and then he was gone again in a flash.

It wasn't right, Abby said. They hadn't had him long enough. Children were supposed to stick around till eighteen, at the very least. (The girls hadn't moved away even for college.) "It's like he's been stolen from us," she told Red. "He was taken before his time!"

"You talk like he's died," Red told her.

"I *feel* like he's died," she said.

And whenever he did come home, he was a stranger. He had a different smell, no longer the musty-closet smell but something almost chemical, like new carpeting. He wore a Greek sailor's cap that Abby (a product of the sixties) associated with the young Bob Dylan. And he spoke to his parents politely, but distantly. Did he resent them for shipping him off? But they hadn't had a choice! No, his grudge must have gone farther back. "It's because I didn't shield him properly," Abby guessed.

"Shield him from what?" Red asked.

"Oh . . . never mind."

"Not from *me*," Red told her.

"If you say so."

"I'm not taking the rap for this, Abby."

"Fine."

At such moments, they hated each other.

And then Denny was off to St. Eskil—a miracle, in view of his checkered past and his C-minus average. Though you couldn't say college changed things. He was still the Whitshanks' mystery child.

Not even that famous phone call changed things, because they never did talk it out with him. They never sat him down and said, "Tell us: gay, or not gay? Just *explain* yourself, is all we ask." Other events followed too fast. He didn't stay long enough in one place. After Christmas he used his return ticket to go back to Minnesota, probably on account of the girlfriend, and worked for a month or two at some kind of plumbers' supply, or so they gathered when he sent Jeannie a visored cap for her birthday reading THOMPSON PIPES & FITTINGS. But the next they heard, he was in Maine. He got a job rebuilding a boat; he got fired; he said he was going back to school but apparently nothing came of that.

He had this way of talking on the phone that was so intense and animated, his parents could start to believe that he felt some urgent need for connection. For weeks at a time he might call every Sunday until they grew to expect it, almost depend on it, but then he'd fall silent for months and they had no means of reaching him. It seemed perverse that someone so mobile did not own a mobile phone. By now Abby had signed them up for caller ID, but what use was that? Denny was OUT OF AREA. He was UNKNOWN CALLER. There should have been a special display for him: CATCH ME IF YOU CAN.

He was living in Vermont for a while, but then he sent a postcard from Denver. At one point he joined forces with someone who had invented a promising software product, but that didn't last very long. It seemed jobs kept disappointing him, as did business partners and girlfriends and entire geographical regions.

In 1997, he invited the family to his wedding at a New York restaurant where his wife-to-be worked as a waitress and he was the chef. The what? How had *that* come about? At home he'd never cooked anything more ambitious than a can of Hormel chili. Everybody went, of course—Red and Abby and Stem and the girls and both the girls' husbands. In hindsight, there may have been too many of them. They outnumbered everyone else. But they were invited, after

all! He said he'd like all of them there! He had used that
intense tone of voice that suggested he *needed* them there.
So they rented a minivan and drove north to throng the
tiny restaurant, which was really more of a bar—a divey
little place with six stools at a wooden counter and four
round, dinky tables. Another waitress and the owner
attended, along with the bride's mother. The bride, whose
name was Carla, wore a spaghetti-strapped maternity dress
that barely covered her underwear. She was clearly older
than Denny (who was twenty-two at the time, way too
young to think of marrying). Her rough mat of hair was
dyed a uniform dense brown, like a dead thing lying on
her head, and her blue-glass-bead eyes had a hard look. She
seemed almost older than her own mother, a plump, bubbly
blonde in a sundress. Still, the Whitshanks did their best.
They circulated before the ceremony, asking Carla where
she and Denny had met, asking the other waitress whether
she was the maid of honor. Carla and Denny had met at
work. There wasn't going to be a maid of honor.

Denny behaved quite sociably, for Denny. He wore
a decent-looking dark suit and a red tie, and he spoke
cordially to everyone, moving from person to person but
returning between times to stand at Carla's side with one
hand resting on the small of her back in a proprietary way.
Carla was pleasant but distracted, as if she were wondering
whether she'd left a burner on at home. She had a New York
accent.

Abby made it her special project to get to know the bride's

mother. She chose the chair next to her when it was time to sit down, and the two of them began talking together in lowered tones, their heads nearly touching and their eyes veering repeatedly toward the bridal couple. This gave the rest of the Whitshanks some hope that once they were on their own again, they would learn the inside story. Because what was happening here, exactly? Was it a love match? Really? And when was that baby due?

The preacher, if that was the term for him, was a bike messenger with a license from the Universal Life Church. Carla commented several times on how he had "cleaned up real good," but if so, the Whitshanks could only imagine what he must have looked like before. He wore a black leather jacket—in August!—and a stubbly black goatee, and his boots were strung with chains so heavy that they clanked rather than jingled. But he took his duties seriously, asking the groom and the bride in turn if they promised to be loving and caring, and after they both said "I do," he laid his hands on their shoulders and intoned, "Go in peace, my children." The other waitress called out, "Yay," in a weak, uncertain voice, and then Denny and Carla kissed—a long and heartfelt kiss, the Whitshanks were relieved to see—after which the owner brought out several bottles of sparkling wine. The Whitshanks hung around a while, but Denny was so busy with other people that eventually they took their leave.

Walking toward the minivan, everybody wanted to know what Abby had found out from Carla's mother. Not much, Abby said. Carla's mother worked in a cosmetics store. Carla's father was "out of the picture." Carla had been married before but it hadn't lasted a minute. Abby said she had waited and waited for some mention of the pregnancy, but it never did come up and she hadn't liked to ask. Instead Lena—that was the mother's name—had complained at some length about the suddenness of the wedding. She could have done something nice if only she'd had some warning, she said, but she hadn't been informed until a week ago. This made Abby feel better, because the Whitshanks hadn't been informed till then, either. She had worried they'd been deliberately excluded. But then Lena went on to talk about Denny this, Denny that: Denny had bought his suit at a thrift shop, Denny had borrowed his tie from his boss, Denny had found them a cute one-bedroom above a Korean record store. So Lena knew him, evidently. She certainly knew him better than the Whitshanks knew Carla. Why was he always so eager to exchange his family for someone else's?

On the drive home, Abby was unusually subdued.

For nearly three months after the wedding, they didn't hear a word. Then Denny phoned in the middle of the night to say Carla had had her baby. He sounded jubilant. It was a girl, he said, and she weighed seven pounds, and they were calling her Susan. "When can we see her?" Abby asked, and he said, "Oh, in a while." Which was perfectly understandable, but when it was Denny saying it, you had to wonder how long he had in mind. This was the

Whitshanks' first grandchild, and Abby told Red that she couldn't bear it if they weren't allowed to be in her life.

But the surprise was, on Thanksgiving morning—and Denny most often avoided Thanksgiving, with its larger-than-ever component of orphans—he phoned to say he and Susan were boarding a train to Baltimore and could somebody come meet him. He arrived with Susan strapped to his front in a canvas sling arrangement. A three-week-old baby! Or not even that, actually. Too young to look like anything more than a little squinched-up peanut with her face pressed to Denny's chest. But that didn't stop the family from making a fuss about her. They agreed that her wisps of black hair were pure Whitshank, and they tried to uncurl one tiny fist to see if she had their long fingers. They were dying for her to open her eyes so they could make out the color. Abby pried her from the sling to check, but Susan went on sleeping. "So, how does it happen," Abby said to Denny, as she nestled Susan against her shoulder, "that you are here on your own?"

"I'm not on my own. I'm with Susan," Denny said.

Abby rolled her eyes, and he relented. "Carla's mother broke her wrist," he said. "Carla had to take her to the emergency room."

"Oh, what a pity," Abby said, and the others murmured sympathetically. (At least Carla wasn't "out of the picture.") "How will that work, though? Did she pump?"

"Pump?"

"Did she pump enough milk?"

"No, Mom, I brought formula." He patted the pink

vinyl bag hanging from his shoulder.

"Formula," Abby said. "But then her supply will go down."

"Supply of what?"

"Supply of breast milk! If you feed a baby formula, the mother's milk will dry up."

"Oh, Susan's a bottle baby," Denny said.

Abby had been reading books on how to be a good grandmother. The main thing was, don't interfere. Don't criticize, don't offer advice. So all she said was, "Oh."

"What do you expect? Carla has a full-time job," Denny said. "Not everyone can afford to stay home and loll around breast-feeding."

"I didn't say a word," Abby said.

There had been times in the past when Denny's visits had lasted just about this long. One little question too many and he was out the door. Perhaps remembering that, Abby tightened her hold on the baby. "Anyhow," she said, "it's good to have you here."

"Good to be here," Denny said, and everyone relaxed.

It was possible he had made some sort of resolution on the train trip down, because he was so easygoing on that visit, so uncritical even with the orphans. When B. J. Autry gave one of her magpie laughs and startled the baby awake, all he said was, "Okay, folks, you can check out Susan's eyes now." And he was very considerate about Mr. Dale's hearing problem, repeating one phrase several times over without a trace of impatience.

31

Amanda, who was seven months pregnant, pestered him with child-care questions, and he answered every one of them. (A crib was completely unnecessary; just use a bureau drawer. No need for a stroller, either. High chair? Probably not.) He made polite conversation about Whitshank Construction, including not only his father but Jeannie, who was a carpenter there now, and even Stem. He listened quietly, nodding, to Stem's inch-by-inch description of a minor logistical problem. ("So, the customer wants floor-to-ceiling cabinets, see, so we tear out all the bulkheads, but then he says, 'Oh, wait!' ")

Abby fed the baby and burped her and changed her miniature diaper, which was the disposable kind, but Abby refrained from so much as mentioning the word "landfill." It turned out that Susan had a chubby chin and beautifully sculptured lips and a frowning, slate-blue gaze. Abby passed her to Red, who made a big show of dismay and ineptness but later was caught pressing his nose to her downy head, drawing in a long deep breath of baby smell.

When Denny said he couldn't spend the night, they understood, of course. Abby packed up some leftover turkey for Carla and her mother, and Red drove Denny and the baby to the station. "Don't be a stranger, now," Red said when Denny got out, and Denny said, "Nope, see you soon."

Which he had said before, any number of times, and it hadn't meant a thing. This time, though, was different. Maybe it was fatherhood. Maybe he was beginning to recognize the importance of family. In any case, he came back for Christmas—just for the day, but still!—and he brought not only Susan but Carla. Susan was seven weeks old, and she'd made that forward leap into awareness of her surroundings, looking at people when they talked to her and responding with lopsided smiles that revealed a dimple in her right cheek. Carla was casually friendly, although she didn't seem to be trying all that hard. She wore jeans and a sweatshirt, so Abby, who *was* trying hard, stayed in her denim skirt instead of changing for dinner. She said, "Carla, may I offer you a glass of wine? So nice that you're not breast-feeding. You can drink whatever you want." Her daughters rounded their eyes at each other: Mom going overboard, as usual! But they were trying pretty hard themselves. They complimented every single thing about Carla they could think of, including the tattoo of her dog's name in the bend of her left arm.

The whole family agreed later that the visit had gone well. And since Denny started bringing Susan down every month or so after that, it appeared that he thought so too. (He didn't bring Carla, because he came on Carla's workdays. She worked now at a hamburger joint, he said; both of them had left the restaurant, but his own schedule was more flexible.) Susan learned to sit up; she began solid foods; she learned to crawl. Sometimes now Denny spent the night. He slept in his old room, with Susan next to his bed in the Portacrib that Abby had saved from her own children's era. By this time, Amanda's Elise had been born, and the family liked to imagine how the two little girls would grow up together as lifelong best friends.

Then Denny took offense at something his father said. It was summer and they were talking about the upcoming family beach trip. Denny said he and Susan could make it, but Carla had to work then. Red said, "How come *you* don't have to work?"

Denny said, "I just don't."

"But Carla does?"

"Right."

"Well, I don't get that. Carla's the mom, right?"

"So?"

Two other people were present—Abby and Jeannie—and both of them grew suddenly alert. They sent Red identical cautioning glances. Red didn't seem to notice. He said, "Do you *have* a job?"

"Is that any of your business?" Denny asked.

Then Red shut up, although clearly it cost him some effort, and it seemed that was the end of it. But when Abby asked for help hauling out the Portacrib, Denny said not to bother. He wasn't planning to spend the night, he said. He was perfectly civil, though, and he took his leave without any suggestion of a scene.

Three years passed before they heard from him again.

For the first several months, they did nothing. That was how deferential they were, how cowed by Denny's silences. But on Susan's birthday, Abby phoned him, using the number she'd made a note of the first time it had popped up on their caller ID. (Parents of people like Denny develop the wiles of secret agents.) Red lurked nearby, looking nonchalant. All Abby got, though, was a recorded voice saying the number had been disconnected. "It seems they've moved," she told Red. "But that's a *good* thing, don't you think? I bet they found a bigger place, with a separate bedroom for Susan." Then she called information and asked for a new listing for Dennis Whitshank, but there wasn't one. "How about Carla Whitshank?" she asked, sending a nervous glance toward Red. (After all, it was not unthinkable that they might be separated by now.) But after that she hung up and said, "I guess we're going to have to wait for *him* to get in touch."

Red merely nodded and wandered off to another room.

More months passed. Years passed. Susan must be walking, then talking. That mesmerizing stage when language develops exponentially from one day to the next, when children are little *sponges* for language: the Whitshanks missed every bit of it. At this point they had two other grandchildren—Jeannie's Deb was born shortly after Denny's last visit—but that just made it harder, watching those two grow up and knowing Susan was doing the same without any of them there to witness it.

Then 9/11 came along, and Abby just about lost her mind with worry. Well, the whole family felt some concern, of course. But as far as they knew, Denny didn't have any business inside the World Trade Center, so they told themselves he was fine. Yes, fine, Abby agreed. But you could see she wasn't convinced. She watched TV obsessively for two days, long after the rest of them had grown sick of the very sight of those towers falling and falling. She began thinking up reasons that Denny could have been there. You couldn't predict, with Denny; he'd held so many different kinds of jobs. Or maybe he'd just been walking by. She began to believe that she could sense he was in trouble. Something just felt wrong, she said. Maybe they should phone Lena.

"Who?" Red asked.

"Carla's mother. What was her last name?"

"I don't know."

"You *have* to know," Abby said. "Think."

"I don't believe we ever heard her last name, hon."

Abby started pacing. They were in their bedroom, and she was treading her usual path up and down the Persian runner, her nightgown flapping around her knees. "Lena Abbott . . . Adams . . . Armstrong," she said. "Lena Babcock . . . Bennett . . . Brown." (Sometimes the alphabet worked for her.) "We were introduced," she said. "Denny introduced us. He must have told us her last name."

"Not if I know Denny," Red said. "I'm surprised he introduced us at all, but if he did, he probably said, 'Lena, meet my folks.'"

Abby couldn't argue with that. She went on pacing.

Then she said, "The waitress. The other one."

"Well, I have *no* idea what her name was."

"No, me either, but she called Lena Mrs. Something, I remember that. I remember thinking she must be the shy type, if she wouldn't use Lena's first name even in this day and age."

She gave up pacing and went around to her side of the bed. "Oh, well, it will come to me by and by," she said. She prided herself on her phenomenal memory, but it sometimes operated on a delay. "It will float up in its own good time, if I just don't force it."

Then she lay down and smoothed her covers and ostentatiously closed her eyes, so Red got into bed himself and switched the lamp off.

In the middle of the night, though, she prodded his shoulder. "Carlucci," she said.

"Huh?"

"I can hear the waitress saying it. 'Mrs. Carlucci, can I get you a refill?' How could I have forgotten? Carla Carlucci: alliteration. Or something more than alliteration, but I don't know the term for it. It just now came to me when I got up to go pee."

"Oh. Good," Red said, turning onto his back.

"I'm going to try Information."

"Now?" He squinted at the clock radio. "It's two thirty a.m.! You can't phone her now."

"No, but I can get her number," Abby said.

Red went back to sleep.

In the morning she announced that there were three L. Carluccis in Manhattan, and she was going to call each one of them in turn. She had decided to start at seven. It was just after six at the moment; the Whitshanks were early risers. "Some folks might still be asleep at seven," Red said.

"Maybe so," Abby said, "but technically, seven is morning."

Red said, "Well, okay." Then he went downstairs and made a pot of coffee, although as a rule he'd be leaving for work now with a stop-off at Dunkin' Donuts.

At five till seven, Abby placed her first call. "Good morning, may I speak to Lena, please?" Then, "Oh, *I'm* sorry! I must have the wrong number."

She placed the second call. "Hello, is this Lena?" The briefest pause. "Well, excuse me. Yes, I *know* it's early, but—"

She winced. She dialed again. "Hello, Lena?"

She straightened. "Well, hi there! It's Abby Whitshank, down in Baltimore. I hope I didn't wake you."

She listened a moment. "Oh, I know what you mean," she said. "I keep telling Red, 'Sometimes I wonder why I go to bed at all, the little bit of sleep I manage.' Is it age, do you think? Is it the stress of modern times? Speaking of which, Lena, I was wondering. Are Carla and Susan and Denny okay? I mean, after last Tuesday?"

("Last Tuesday" was how people were still referring to it. Not till the following week would they start saying "September eleventh.")

"Oh, really," Abby said. "I see. Well, that's something, at least! That's comforting. And so you don't . . . Well, of course I can see that you wouldn't . . . Well, thank you so much, Lena! And please give my love to Carla and Susan . . . Hmm? . . . Yes, everyone here is fine, thanks. Thank you, now! Bye!"

She hung up.

"Carla and Susan are all right," she said. "Denny she *assumes* is all right, but she doesn't know for sure because he's moved to New Jersey."

"New Jersey? Where in New Jersey?"

"She didn't say. She said she doesn't have his number."

Red said, "Carla would, though. On account of Susan. You should have asked for Carla's number."

"Oh, what's the point?" Abby said. "We know he was nowhere near the towers. Isn't that enough? And I'm not willing to bet that even Carla has his number, if you want the honest truth."

Then she started loading the dishwasher, while Red stood gaping at her.

So: New Jersey. Another broken relationship. *Two* broken relationships, unless Denny had stayed in touch with Susan. Red said of course he had stayed in touch; wasn't he the most hands-on father they knew of? Abby said that didn't necessarily follow. Maybe Susan had been just another passing fancy, she said, like that half-baked software project of his.

This was not characteristic of Abby. She believed devoutly in people's capacity for change, sometimes to the exasperation of everyone else in the family. But now she seemed to have given up. When she phoned Jeannie and

Amanda with the news, she spoke in a toneless, emotionless voice, and she told Red he could just let Stem know when he saw him at work. "I'll get right on it," Red said, falsely hearty. "He'll be relieved."

"I don't know why," Abby said. "There was never any real danger."

The following morning, a Saturday, Amanda stopped by unannounced. Amanda was a lawyer, their hardest-nosed, most competent, most take-charge child. "Where's the number for this Lena person?" she asked.

Abby pulled it off the fridge door and handed it to her. (Of course she'd kept it.) Amanda sat down at the kitchen table and reached for the phone and dialed.

"Hello, Lena?" she said. "Amanda calling. Denny's sister. May I have Carla's phone number, please?"

The burble at the other end must have been some kind of protest, because Amanda said, "I have no intention of upsetting her, believe me. I just need to get in touch with my rascal of a brother."

That seemed to do the trick; she dipped her free hand in her purse and pulled out a memo pad with a tiny gold pen attached. "Yes," she said, and she wrote down a number. "Thank you very much. Goodbye."

She dialed again. "Busy," she told her parents. Abby groaned, but Amanda said, "*Naturally* it's busy; her mother's calling her with a heads-up." She drummed her fingers on the table a moment. Then she dialed once more. "Hi, Carla," she said. "It's Amanda. How've you been?"

Carla's answer didn't take much time, but even so, Amanda seemed impatient. "Good," she said. "Well, could I have my brother's number? I'm going to give him a piece of my mind."

While she wrote it down, Red and Abby hunched forward and stared at the pad, hardly breathing. "Thanks," Amanda said. "Bye." And she hung up.

Abby was already reaching for the pad, but Amanda pulled it away from her and said, "*I* am making this call." She dialed once more.

"Denny," she said, "it's Amanda."

They couldn't hear what his response was.

"Someday," Amanda said, "you're going to be a middle-aged man thinking back on your life, and you'll start wondering what your family's been up to. So you'll hop on a train and come down, and when you get to Baltimore it will be this peaceful summer afternoon and these dusty rays of sunshine will be slanting through the skylight in Penn Station. You'll walk on through and out to the street, where nobody is waiting for you, but that's okay; they didn't know you were coming. Still, it feels kind of odd standing there all alone, with the other passengers hugging people and climbing into cars and driving away. You go to the taxi lane and you give the address to a cabbie. You ride through the city looking at all the familiar sights—the row houses, the Bradford pear trees, the women sitting out on their stoops watching their children play. Then the taxi turns onto Bouton Road and right away you get a strange feeling. There are little signs of neglect at our house that Dad would never put up with: blistered paint and gap-toothed shutters. Mismatched mortar patching the walk, rubber treads nailed to the porch steps—all these Harry Homeowner fixes Dad has always railed against. You take hold of the front-door handle and you give it that special pull toward you that it needs before you can push down the thumb latch, but it's locked. You ring the doorbell, but it's broken. You call, 'Mom? Dad?' No one answers. You call, 'Hello?' No one comes running; no one flings open the door and says, 'It's you! It's so good to see you! Why didn't you let us know? We'd have met you at the station! Are you tired? Are you hungry? Come in!' You stand there a while, but you can't think what to do next. You turn and look back toward the street, and you wonder about the rest of the family. 'Maybe Jeannie,' you say. 'Or Amanda.' But you know something, Denny? Don't count on *me* to take you in, because I'm angry. I'm angry at you for leading us on such a song and dance all these years, not just these last few years but *all* the years, skipping all those holidays and staying away from the beach trips and missing Mom and Dad's thirtieth anniversary and their thirty-fifth and Jeannie's baby and not attending my wedding that time or even sending a card or calling to wish me well. But most of all, Denny, *most* of all: I will never forgive you for consuming every last little drop of our parents' attention and leaving nothing for the rest of us."

She stopped speaking. Denny said something.

"Oh," she said, "I'm fine. How have *you* been?"

*

So Denny came home.

The first time, he came alone. Abby was disappointed that he didn't bring Susan, but Red said he was glad. "It makes this visit different from those last ones," he said. "Like he's getting squared away with us first. He's not taking it for granted that he can just pick up where he left off."

He had a point. Denny did seem different—more cautious, more considerate of their feelings. He commented on little improvements around the house. He said he liked Abby's new hairstyle. (She had started wearing it short.) He himself had lost the boyish sharpness along his jaw, and he had a more settled way of walking. When Abby asked him questions—though she tried her best to ration them—he made an effort to answer. He wasn't what you'd call chatty, but he answered.

Susan was doing great, he said. She was attending preschool now. Yes, he could bring her to visit. Carla was fine too, although they were not together anymore. Work? Well, at the moment he was working for a construction firm.

"Construction!" Abby said. "Hear that, Red? He's working in construction!"

Red merely grunted. He didn't look as happy about this as he might have.

Notice all that was missing, though, from what Denny had told them. How much did he really have to do with his daughter? And when he said he and Carla were "not together," did he mean they were divorced? Just what were his living arrangements? Was construction his chosen career now? Had he given up on college?

Then Jeannie came over with little Deb, and Red and Abby left them alone, and by the end of her visit they knew more. He had a *lot* to do with Susan, Jeannie reported; he was very much involved in her life. Divorce was too expensive, for now. He shared half a house with two other guys but they were starting to get on his nerves. Sure, he would finish college. Someday.

But still, somehow, it wasn't enough information. Oh, always there seemed to be something else—something that surely, if they could ferret it out, would at last explain him.

He stayed a day and a half, that time. Then he left, but— here was the important part—they did have his cell phone number. That number they'd dialed was his cell phone number! This changed everything.

They allowed a strategic lapse of several weeks, and then Abby called him (Red hovering in the background) and invited him to bring Susan for Christmas. Denny said Carla would never allow Susan to be away on Christmas Day, but maybe *after* Christmas he'd bring her.

Red and Abby knew all about his maybes.

But he did it. He brought her. Christmas fell on a Tuesday that year, and he brought her down Wednesday and they stayed through Friday. Susan was a self-possessed four-year-old with a mass of brown curls and very large, very brown eyes. The eyes were a bit of a shock. Those were not Whitshank eyes! Nor were her clothes the rough-and-tumble play clothes that the Whitshank children wore. She arrived in a red velvet dress, with white tights and red Mary Janes. Well, perhaps on account of Christmas. But the next morning, when she came down to breakfast, she wore a ruffled white blouse and a red plaid taffeta pinafore very nearly as fancy. Jeannie said it made her kind of sad to think of Denny having to button all those tiny white buttons down the back of Susan's pinafore.

"Do you remember us?" they asked her. "Do you remember coming to visit us when you were just a baby?"

Susan said, slowly, "I think so," which of course could not be true. But it was nice of her to pretend. She said, "Did you have a different dog?"

"No, this is the same one."

"I thought you had a *yellow* dog," she said, and they traded unhappy glances. Who was it she was thinking of who had a yellow dog, and perhaps one not so slobbery and arthritic as old Clarence?

She was entranced with her cousins. (Aha! They could be the Whitshanks' bait: fairy child Elise and rowdy little Deb.) She seemed unfamiliar with card games but soon developed a passion for Go Fish. Also, it emerged that she knew how to read. They were surprised that Carla could have reared a precocious child, but maybe that was thanks to Denny. She liked to snuggle next to Abby and sound out the words to *Hop on Pop*, heaving a loud sigh of satisfaction whenever she finished a page.

By the time she left, she'd lost all her reserve. She stood in front of the train station holding Denny's hand, waving like a maniac and shouting, "Bye-bye! See you! See everybody soon! Bye-bye!"

So Denny brought her again, and then again. She had her own room now, the one that used to be the girls' room. She drank her cocoa from a mug reading SUSAN, and when it was time to set the table she knew where to find the alphabet plate that Denny had once used. And he, meanwhile, sat back and watched all this benignly. He was the most accommodating father. It seemed she had smoothed his edges down.

In 2002, shortly after Jeannie's Alexander was born, Denny came to stay with Jeannie and tend her children. At the time, this was puzzling. Abby had already done the usual grandmother stint—taken off work to keep Deb while Jeannie was in the hospital, and stopped by frequently afterwards to offer help with errands and laundry. But then all at once, there was Denny. And he remained there— slept on Jeannie and Hugh's pull-out couch for three solid weeks, pushed Deb in her stroller every afternoon to the playground, cooked the meals, met Abby at the door with a diaper draped over his shoulder and the baby in his arms.

It came to light only later that Jeannie had been going through some sort of postpartum depression. So, had she phoned Denny and asked him to come down and take care of her? Asked Denny and not Abby? Abby did her best to find out, using her most neutral, non-offended tone. Well,

Jeannie said, it was true that she had phoned him, but just to talk. And maybe he had heard something in her voice—well, of course he had, because she'd grown a little teary, she was ashamed to say—and he had told her he would be coming in on the next train.

This was both touching and distressing. Had Jeannie not realized she could call her own mother?

Well, but Abby had her job to go to, Jeannie said.

As if Denny himself didn't have a job.

Or, who knows? Maybe he didn't.

Red told Abby they should just be grateful that Denny had come to the rescue.

Abby said, "Oh, yes. Yes, I know that."

Things fell into more or less of a pattern. Denny never became particularly good at keeping in touch, but then, that was true of a lot of sons. The point was that he did keep in touch, and they did have that phone number for him, if not always his current address.

How shocking, Abby told Red, that they were willing to settle for so little. She said, "Would you have believed it? Sometimes whole days go by when I don't give him a thought. This is just not natural!"

Red said, "It's *perfectly* natural. Like a mother cat when her kittens are grown. You're showing very good sense."

"It's not supposed to work that way with humans," Abby told him.

At least they could be sure that Denny would never live far from New York City. Not as long as Susan lived there. Although he did travel now and then, because once he sent Alexander a birthday card from San Francisco. And another time, he shortened his Christmas visit because he was taking a trip to Canada with his girlfriend. This was the first they'd heard of the girlfriend, and the last. Susan stayed on alone that year. She was old enough—seven, but she seemed older. Her head was slightly big for her body, and her face was beautiful in the way that a grown woman's face is beautiful, her brown eyes large and weary, her lips full and soft and complicated. She showed no sign of homesickness, and when Denny came to collect her she greeted him equably. "How was Canada?" Abby dared to ask him.

He said, "Pretty good."

It was really very hard to visualize Denny's personal life.

Nor were they always entirely clear about his occupation. They did know that at one point, he had a job installing sound systems, because he volunteered his expertise when Jeannie's Hugh was wiring their den. Another time, he showed up wearing a hoodie with KOMPUTER KLINIK stitched on the pocket, and at Abby's request he offhandedly fixed her Mac, which had been acting a bit sluggish. But he always seemed free to come and go, and to stay as long as he liked. How do you reconcile that with a full-time job? When Stem got married, for instance, Denny came for a solid week to fulfill his best-man duties, and although Abby was thrilled about that (she fretted about her boys' not being close), she kept asking if he was sure this wouldn't cause him trouble at work. "Work?" he said. "No."

On one occasion, he visited for nearly a month with no explanation whatsoever. Everybody suspected that it involved some private crisis, since he arrived looking very seedy and not in the best of health. For the first time, they noticed faint lines at the corners of his eyes. His hair straggled unevenly over the back of his collar. But he didn't refer to any problems, and not even Jeannie dared ask. It was as if he had his family trained. They had become almost as oblique as Denny himself.

This stirred some resentment in them, from time to time. Why should they tiptoe around him? Why should they have to deflect the neighbors' questions about him? "Oh," Abby would say, "Denny is fine, thank you. Really fine! Right now he's working at . . . Well, I'm not sure exactly *where* he's working, but anyhow: he's just fine!"

Yet he did provide something that they counted on, somehow. He did leave a hole when he was absent. That first time that he skipped the beach trip, for instance, the summer he claimed to be gay: nobody knew that he wasn't coming. They kept waiting for him to phone and announce his arrival date, and when it grew clear that he wasn't going to, everyone experienced the most crushing sense of flatness. Even after they'd arrived at the cottage they always rented, and unpacked their groceries and made up the beds and settled into their usual beach routine, they couldn't shake the thought that he still might show up. They turned hopefully from their jigsaw puzzle when the screen door slammed in an evening breeze. They stopped speaking in mid-sentence when somebody out beyond the breakers started swimming toward them with that distinctive, rolling stroke that Denny always used. And halfway through the week . . . oh, here was the strangest part. Halfway through the week, Abby and the girls were sitting on the screen porch one afternoon shucking corn, and they heard Mozart's Horn Concerto No. 1 playing out back. They looked at each other; they rose from their chairs; they rushed through the house and out the door . . . and they saw that the music came from a car parked across the road. Someone was sitting in the driver's seat with all the windows rolled down (but still, he must be baking!) and his radio playing full-blast. A man in a tank top; not an item of clothing Denny would have been caught dead in. A heavyset man, if you judged by the girth of the elbow resting on the window ledge. Heavier than Denny could be even if he had done nothing but eat since the last time they had seen him. But still, you know how it is when you're missing a loved one. You try to turn every stranger into the person you were hoping for. You hear a certain piece of music and right away you tell yourself that he could have changed his clothing style, could have gained a ton of weight, could have acquired a car and then parked that car in front of another family's house. "It's him!" you say. "He came! We knew he would; we always . . ." But then you hear how pathetic you sound, and your words trail off into silence, and your heart breaks.

2

In the Whitshank family, two stories had traveled down through the generations. These stories were viewed as quintessential—as *defining*, in some way—and every family member, including Stem's three-year-old, had heard them told and retold and embroidered and conjectured upon any number of times.

The first story concerned their earliest known ancestor, Junior Whitshank, a carpenter much sought after in Baltimore for his craftsmanship and his sense of design.

If it seems odd to call a patriarch "Junior," there was a logical explanation. Junior's true name was Jurvis Roy, shortened at some point to J.R. and then re-expanded, accordion-like, to Junior. (This was a fact so little known that his own daughter-in-law had to ask his name when she was briefly contemplating making her firstborn a III if he turned out to be a boy.) But what was even odder was that Junior was not some distant great-great, but merely

Red Whitshank's father. And there was no evidence of his existence prior to 1926, which seemed an unusually recent year for the start of a family tree.

Where he came from was never documented, but the general feeling was that he might have hailed from the Appalachian Mountains. Maybe he had once said something to that effect. Or it could have been mere guesswork, based on the way he talked. According to Abby, who had known him since her girlhood, he had a thin, metallic voice and a twangy Southern accent, although he must have decided at some point that it would elevate his social standing if he pronounced his *i*'s in the Northern way. In the middle of his country-sounding drawl, Abby said, a distinct, sharp *i* would poke forth here and there like a brier. She didn't sound entirely charmed by this trait.

Junior's few photos revealed a face that was just a little too fine-boned—a look that people back then felt no compunction about referring to as "poor white trash." In coloring he was pure Whitshank, black-haired even in his sixties with very white skin and squinty blue eyes, and he had the rangy, gaunt Whitshank body. He wore a stiff dark suit every day of the year, Abby said, but here Red would interrupt to say that the suits were a later development, when all Junior had to do was tour his work sites checking on things. Most of Red's childhood memories featured his father in overalls.

At any rate, Junior's first recorded appearance in Baltimore was as the employee of a building contractor named Clyde

L. Ward. This came to light in a typewritten letter that was found among Junior's papers after his death, telling Whom It May Concern that J. R. Whitshank had worked for Mr. Ward from June of 1926 through January 1930 and had proved an able carpenter. But he must have been more than merely able, because by 1934, a tiny rectangle in the *Baltimore Post* was advertising the services of Whitshank Construction Co., "Quality and Integrity."

It was not the best era for starting a business, heaven knows, but apparently Junior flourished, first remodeling and then building from scratch various stately houses in the neighborhoods of Guilford, Roland Park, and Homeland. He acquired a Model B Ford pickup with an interlaced "WCC" painted on both doors above a telephone number—no mention of the company's full name or its function, as if everyone who counted surely must know, by now. In 1934 he had eight employees; in 1935, twenty.

In 1936, he fell in love with a house.

No, first he must have fallen in love with his wife, because he was married by then. He had married Linnie Mae Inman at some point. But he never had much to say about Linnie, whereas he had a great deal to say, *reams* to say, about the house on Bouton Road.

It was nothing but an architect's drawing the first time he laid eyes on it. Mr. Ernest Brill, a Baltimore textile manufacturer, had unfurled a roll of blueprints while standing in front of the lot where he and Junior had arranged to meet. And Junior glanced first at the lot (full

of birds and tulip poplars and sprinkles of white dogwood)
and then down at the drawing of the front elevation, which
showed a clapboard house with a gigantic front porch, and
the words that popped into his head were "Why, that's *my*
house!"

Not that he said this aloud, of course. "Hmm," he said
aloud. And "I see." And he took the blueprints from Mr.
Brill and studied the elevation. He turned to the sheets
beneath to look at the floor plans. He said, "Mm-hmm."

"What do you think?" Mr. Brill asked.

Junior said, "Well . . ."

It was not a grand house, of the sort that you might expect
a man like Junior to covet. It was more, let's say, a *family*
house. A house you might see pictured on a thousand-
piece jigsaw puzzle, plain-faced and comfortable, with the
Stars and Stripes, perhaps, flying out front and a lemonade
stand at the curb. Tall sash windows, a fieldstone chimney,
a fanlight over the door. But best of all, that porch: that
wonderful full-length porch. "It hit me," was how Junior
would put it later. "I don't know; it just hit me."

So he told Mr. Brill, "I reckon I could do it."

Why hadn't he simply built an identical house for
himself? Red's children used to ask. Copied the blueprints
and built his own? Red told them he couldn't say. Then he
said that maybe it had had something to do with the site.
Bouton Road was prime real estate, after all, and by 1936
most of the lots there had been bought up. In those days
of no air conditioning, houses in Baltimore wore thick,

dark awnings that shrouded the windows nearly to the sills from May to October of every year, but awnings wouldn't be needed with all those tulip poplars. Besides, the way the house would occupy that particular property, perched at the top of a long, gentle slope: where else could it show so well?

So Junior built the house for Mr. Brill.

He built better than he'd ever built anything in his life. He niggled over every pantry shelf and cabinet knob. He argued against any request that struck him as cutting corners or lacking in good taste. Because taste, really, was the secret of Junior's reputation. How he came by it nobody knew, but he had the most unerring nose for anything pretentious. No two-story columns for Junior! No la-di-da portes cochères, with their intimations of chauffeured limousines gliding up to let their passengers off! When Mr. Brill dared to broach the possibility of a U-shaped "carriageway" out front, Junior all but exploded. "Carriageway!" he said. "What in tarnation is that? You drive a Chrysler Airflow, not a coach-and-six!" (Or that was his report of the conversation, at least. He may very well have exaggerated his own outspokenness in the telling.) Then he went on to fantasize, at length and in loving detail, how visitors would approach the house. The driveway should run to the side, he said, for the sole use of the Brill family. Guests should park down on the street. Picture how they'd climb out of their cars, raise their eyes to the porch, start up the flagstone walk while Mr. and Mrs. Brill stood waiting on the porch steps to welcome them. Oh, and by the way, those steps should be wooden. It was wrong to have anything else. People thought of wooden steps as buckling or peeling, but when they were properly cared for there was nothing handsomer than a wide set of varnished treads (a bit of fine sand mixed into the varnish for traction) rising to a wooden porch floor as solid as a ship's deck. Such steps took work, took money, took vigilance. Such steps *signified*.

Mr. Brill said he completely agreed.

Junior spent almost a year on the house, using all his men plus some he brought in from outside. Then the Brills took possession, and he went into mourning. Ordinarily a talker—his customers tried to avoid running into him when they had any place urgent to get to—he fell into a deep silence, and moped, and took little interest in the job that followed the Brills' job. It was Junior himself who revealed all this, years later. (His wife was not very forthcoming.) "I just couldn't believe," he said, "that those folks got to live in my house."

Luckily, it turned out that the Brills lacked handyman skills. When the first frost came, they telephoned Junior to say that the heat wasn't working, and Junior had to drive over and bleed their radiators. He could have shown them how to do it themselves, but he didn't. He went around to every room with a radiator key, and when he was finished he slipped the key back into his pocket and told the Brills to call him again if they had any more trouble. Pretty soon he was stopping by on a more or less weekly basis. The windows—outsized—required special screens and storm windows with finicky hardware, and he was the one who arrived spring and fall to supervise their installation. Like a love-struck groomsman who hangs around the bride long after the wedding, he kept inventing excuses to pop in. He dropped off a can of touch-up paint and then half a box of leftover floor tiles. He double-checked a lock that he had oiled just the week before. He came and went at all hours, using his own keys if nobody was home. Any telltale sign of wear he discovered sent him into a tizzy—a chip in the plaster or a hairline crack in a bathroom sink. He behaved as if he'd merely lent the house out and the borrowers were mistreating it.

One of Red's earliest memories, dating from age three or so, was of clambering down from his father's truck while Mrs. Brill stood waiting on the back stoop, a cardigan clutched around her shoulders. "Don't you go running off again if you don't hear it first thing," she told his father in a shrill voice. "I just know it's going to get quiet the minute you step inside." That had been a squirrel in the attic, Red recalled. "She was a real nervous Nellie," he said. "She thought every animal she met was out to get her, and she was always smelling smoke, and she was scared to death of break-ins. Break-ins! On Bouton Road!" Most damning of all, she never really warmed to the house. She complained that it was too far from downtown, and she missed their old apartment with her ladies' club a stone's throw away. Granted, there was a ladies' club on Roland Avenue, but that wasn't quite the same thing.

What made it worse was that Mr. Brill traveled frequently on "bidness," as Junior called it, leaving Mrs. Brill with no protection but their two spoiled boys. (Junior attached the word "spoiled" to the Brill boys every time he mentioned them, although he never offered any concrete examples of spoiled behavior.) The boys were in their teens and weighed at least as much as Junior did, but it was Junior Mrs. Brill telephoned whenever she heard a noise in the basement.

And Red could just about bet that Junior wasn't paid for his trouble. The Brills took him for granted. They addressed him by his first name while they remained "Mr." and "Mrs." Mrs. Brill descended on him each Christmas just as she descended on her yard boy and her cleaning girl, arriving at his door in her puffy fur coat with a basket of store-bought preserves. Her car purred out front; she never stayed to visit, although she was always invited.

Junior lived in Hampden, mere blocks away from the Brills but a world apart in atmosphere. He and Linnie rented a two-bedroom house that sat several feet below the level of the street, which gave it a huddled look. They had two children: Merrick (a girl) and Redcliffe. Oho! this might lead some to say. Was it possible that the Whitshanks' mysterious family origins might have included some Merricks? Or Redcliffes? But no, those were just Junior's notion of names that sounded genteel. They implied illustrious forebears, perhaps on the mother's side. Oh, Junior was forever thinking up ways to look like quality. And yet he kept them in that sad little house in Hampden, which he didn't even bother fixing up although he could have done it better than anyone.

"I was biding my time," was how he explained it years later. "I was just biding my time, was all." And he went on changing the fuses in his beloved Bouton Road house, and tightening its hinges, and chasing off various birds and bats without the least sign of impatience.

One cold evening in February of 1942, Mrs. Brill arrived on the Whitshanks' front stoop with both of her boys in tow. None of them wore coats. Mrs. Brill had been crying. It was Linnie who opened the door to them, and she said, "What on earth . . . ?" Mrs. Brill grabbed Linnie's wrist. "Is Junior here?" she asked.

"I'm here," Junior said, appearing next to Linnie.

"The most awful thing," Mrs. Brill said. "Awful, awful, awful."

Junior said, "Why don't you come on in."

"I walked into the sunroom," she said, staying where she was. "I was planning to write some letters. You know my little writing desk where I conduct my correspondence. And there on the floor by my chair I saw this canvas bag, like a tool bag. That kind with the jaws that open? And it was open all the way, and I could make out these burglar tools inside."

"Huh," Junior said.

"Screwdrivers and a crowbar and—oh!" She slumped sideways toward one of her boys, who stood his ground and allowed it. "On top," she said, "a coil of rope."

Linnie said, "Rope!"

"Like what you would tie someone up with."

"Oh, my heavens!"

"Well, now," Junior said, "we're going to get to the bottom of this."

"Oh, would you, Junior? Please? I know I should have called the police, but all I could think was, 'I just have to get out of here. I have to get my boys out.' And I grabbed up the car keys and ran. I didn't know who else to turn to, Junior."

"Now, you did exactly right," Junior said. "I'm going to take care of everything. You stay here with Linnie, Mrs. Brill, and I'll have the cops make sure it's safe before you go back in."

Mrs. Brill said, "Oh, *I'm* not going back. That house is dead to me, Junior."

At this point, one of her sons said, "Aw, Ma?" (History's only recorded comment from either of the Brill boys.)

But she repeated, "Dead to me."

"We'll just see, why don't we," Junior said. And he reached for his jacket.

What did the two women talk about, once they were alone? Years later Jeannie asked that, but no one could give her an answer. Linnie herself had never said, apparently, and Merrick and Red had been so young—Merrick five and Red four—that they didn't remember. It almost seemed that when Junior left a scene, it had ceased to exist. Then he returned and everything started up again, brought to life by his whiny, thin voice and "He says to me . . ." and "Says I, I says . . ."

The police said to him, "Looks like a plain old workman's bag," and Junior said to them, "It sure does." He nudged it with the toe of his boot. "How to explain the rope, though," he added after a moment.

"Lots of times a workman needs rope."

"Well, you're right. Can't argue with that."

They all stood around a while, looking down at the bag.

"Thing is, *I'm* their workman, most often," Junior said.

"Is that a fact."

"But who can figure?"

And he turned up both palms, as if testing for rain, and raised his eyebrows at the police and shrugged, and they all agreed to drop it.

Then the conversation when Mr. Brill returned from his trip: "*You* buy the house?" Mr. Brill said. "Buy it and do what with it?"

"Why, live in it," Junior said.

"Live in it! Oh. I see. But . . . are you sure you'd be happy there, Junior?"

"Who wouldn't be happy there?" Junior asked his children years later, but what he said to Mr. Brill was, "One thing, I know it's well built."

Mr. Brill had the grace not to explain that this wasn't quite what he'd meant.

*

Red remembered growing up in that house as heaven. There were enough children on Bouton Road to form two baseball teams, when they felt like it, and they spent all their free time playing out of doors—boys and girls together, little ones and big ones. Suppers were brief, pesky interruptions foisted on them by their mothers. They disappeared again till they were called in for bed, and then they came protesting, all sweaty-faced and hot with grass blades sticking to them, begging for just another half hour. "I bet I can still name every kid on the block," Red would tell his own children. But that was not so impressive, because most of those kids had stayed on in the neighborhood as grown-ups, or at least come back to it later after trying out other, lesser places.

Red and Merrick were folded into that pack of children without hesitation, but their parents never seemed to blend in with the other parents. Maybe it was Linnie's fault; she was so shy and quiet. Noticeably younger than Junior, a thin, pale woman with lank, colorless hair and almost colorless eyes, she tended to shrink and wring her hands when somebody addressed her. It certainly wasn't Junior's fault, because he would go up and start talking to anyone. Talk, talk, talk people's ears off. Or was that the source of the problem, in fact? People were polite, but they didn't talk back much.

Well, never mind. Junior finally had his house. He tinkered endlessly with it. He put a toilet in the hall closet underneath the stairs, because almost as soon as they moved in he realized that one bathroom was not going to be sufficient. And he lined the guest room with cabinets for Linnie's sewing supplies, since they never had guests. For years they owned next to no furniture, having sunk every last penny into the down payment, but he refused to go out and buy just any old cheap stuff, no sir. "In this house, we insist on quality," he said. It was downright comical, the number of his sentences that started off with "In this house." In this house they never went barefoot, in this house they wore their good clothes to ride the streetcar downtown, in this house they attended St. David's Episcopal Church every Sunday rain or shine, even though the Whitshanks could not possibly have started out Episcopalian. So "this house" really meant "this family," it seemed. The two were one and the same.

One thing was a puzzle, though: despite Junior's reported loquaciousness, his grandchildren never formed a very clear picture of him. Who *was* he, exactly? Where had he come from? For that matter, where had Linnie come from? Surely Red had some inkling—or his sister, more likely, since women were supposed to be more curious about such things. But no, they claimed they didn't. (If they were to be believed.) And both Junior and Linnie were dead before their first grandchild turned two.

Also: was Junior insufferable, or was he likable? Bad, or good? The answer seemed to vary. On the one hand, his ambition was an embarrassment to all of them. They winced when they heard how slavishly he aped his social superiors. But when they considered his pinched circumstances, his nose-pressed-to-the-window wistfulness, and his dedication—his genius, in fact—they had to say, "Well . . ."

He was like anybody else, Red said. Insufferable *and* likable. Bad *and* good.

Nobody found this a satisfactory answer.

All right, so the first family story was Junior's: how the Whitshanks came to live on Bouton Road.

The second was Merrick's.

Merrick was her father's daughter, no doubt about it. At the age of nine, she had engineered her own transfer from public school to private, and while Red was stumbling through the University of Maryland with his mind fixed on his true calling—construction—Merrick was off at Bryn Mawr College, studying how to rise above her origins. On winter weekends, she went skiing with friends. In warmer weather, she sailed. She started using words like "divine" and "delicious" (not referring to food). Imagine her parents speaking that way! Already she had traveled a great distance from them.

Merrick's best friend from fourth grade on was Pookie Vanderlin, who attended Bryn Mawr also. And in the spring of 1958, when both girls were finishing their junior year, Pookie got engaged to Walter Barrister III, commonly known as Trey.

This Trey was a Baltimore boy, a graduate of Gilman

and Princeton who worked now in his family's firm, doing something with money. So over summer vacation, when Merrick and Pookie and their friends gathered on the Whitshanks' front porch to smoke Pall Malls and talk about how bored they were, Trey was often there as well. He seemed to keep a very loose schedule at the office. By the time Red got home from his summer job, at four p.m. or so—contractors' hours—he'd find Trey lounging on the porch with the others, a pristine white cardigan tied oh-so-casually around his shoulders and his feet encased in leather loafers with no socks (the first time Red had ever seen this practice, although unfortunately not the last). Later they'd all go out and do whatever they did in the evenings. Since Red was the one telling this story, there was no knowing what Merrick's friends did, but presumably they ate in some joint and then caught a movie, maybe, or went dancing. Late at night they would return to sit on the porch again. It was an unusually spacious porch, after all, so deep that they could stay dry there even during a rainstorm. Their voices would drift up clearly to the two front bedrooms—Red's bedroom and his parents'. Red often leaned out his window to call down, "Hey! Some of us have to get up in the morning, you know!" but his parents never uttered a word of protest. Junior was probably gloating: all those shiny-haired, nonchalantly graceful boys and girls on his porch, when their folks had never invited him and Linnie to *their* porches, not on a single occasion.

The young people were pairing off that summer. Senior

year was approaching, and this was back when girls tended to marry right after college. Merrick seemed to have not just one boy in attendance but two, neither of whom Red knew well. They were a few years older than he and they sort of resembled each other, so that he was always getting them mixed up. Besides which, he had trouble believing that anyone could be seriously attracted to his sister. Merrick was skinny and ungainly, with the Whitshanks' definite jaw that looked better on the men than on the women, and that summer she was wearing her hair in a dramatic new style, flaring out on the left side but pressed flat to her skull on the right, so that it looked as if she were perpetually being buffeted by a strong wind. But Tink and Bink, or whatever their names were, seemed quite taken with her. They called her "Bean," short for "Beanpole," and you could tell by their teasing that they were trying to win her favor.

Her father asked her, once, "Now, who is that blond fellow? With the crew cut?"

"Which one?" Merrick said.

"The one who was complaining about his golf game last night."

"Which *one*, Dad."

From this, Red gathered that neither young man had particularly impressed her. Also: that his parents, or at least his father, had been listening to those porch conversations with more interest than Red had realized.

Meanwhile, Pookie was getting down to the fine points of her wedding. It was less than a year away now, and an event of such scale took some planning. A date had been set, and a venue for the reception. The color scheme for the bridesmaids' dresses was under deliberation. Merrick had been asked to serve as maid of honor. She told her parents it was bound to be a bore, but her mother said, "Oh, now, I think it's nice of Pookie to choose you," and her father said, "I don't guess you realize that Walter Barrister the First founded Barrister Financial."

Red had started noticing that any time it was a girls-only gathering, Pookie had a tendency to speak of Trey belittlingly. She mocked the loving care he gave to the sheet of blond hair that fell over his forehead, and she referred to him habitually as "the Prince of Roland Park." "I can't come shopping tomorrow," she'd say, "because the Prince of Roland Park wants me to go to lunch with his mother." Partly, this could be explained by the fact that her crowd liked to affect a tone of ironic amusement no matter what they were discussing. But also, Trey sort of deserved the title. Even during high school he had driven a sports car, and the Barristers' house in Baltimore was only one of three that they owned, the others in distant resorts that advertised in the *New York Times*. Pookie said he was spoiled rotten, and she blamed it on his mother, "Queen Eula."

Eula Barrister was stick-thin and fashionable and discontented-looking. Any time Red saw her in church, he was reminded of Mrs. Brill. Mrs. Barrister ran that church, and she ran the Women's Club, and she ran her family, which consisted of just three people. Trey was her only child—her darlin' boy, she was fond of saying; her poppet. And Pookie Vanderlin was nowhere near good enough for him.

Over the course of the summer, Red heard long recitals of Pookie's tribulations with Queen Eula. Pookie was summoned to excruciating family dinners, to stiff old-lady teas, to Queen Eula's own beautician to do something about her eyebrows. She was chided for her failure to write bread-and-butter notes, or for writing bread-and-butter notes that weren't enthusiastic enough. Her choice of silver pattern was reversed without her say-so. She was urged to consider a wedding gown that would hide her chubby shoulders.

Over and over, Merrick gasped, like somebody on stage. "No! I can't believe it!" she would say. "Why doesn't Trey stick up for you?"

"Oh, *Trey*," Pookie said in disgust. "Trey thinks she hung the moon."

Not only that: Trey was inconsiderate, and selfish, and given to hypochondria. He forgot Pookie existed any time he ran into his buddies. And for once, just once in her life, she would like to see him make it through an evening without drinking his weight in gin.

"He'd better watch out, or he'll lose you," Merrick said. "You could have anyone! You don't have to settle for Trey. Look at Tucky Bennett: he just about shot himself when he heard you'd gotten engaged."

Often, Pookie delivered her recitals even though Red was present. (Red didn't count, in that group.) Then Red would ask, "How come you put up with it?" Or "You said *yes* to this guy?"

"I know. I'm a fool," she would say. But not as if she meant it.

That fall, when they were all back in college, Merrick fell into a pattern of coming home every weekend. This was unlike her. Red came home a lot himself, since College Park was so close, but gradually he realized that she was there even more often. She went with the family to church on Sunday, and afterwards she would stop out front to say hello to Eula Barrister. Even when Trey was not standing at his mother's elbow (which generally he was), Merrick would be eagerly nodding her head in her demure new pillbox hat, giving a liquid laugh that any brother would know to be false, hanging on to every one of Eula Barrister's prune-faced remarks. And in the evening, if Trey stopped by for a visit—as was only natural! Merrick said. He was marrying her best friend, after all!—the two of them sat out on the porch, although it was too cold for that now. The smell of their cigarette smoke floated through Red's open window. (But if it was so cold, his children would wonder years later, why was his window open?) "I've had it with her. I tell you," Trey said. "Nothing I do makes her happy. Everything's pick, pick, pick."

"She doesn't properly value you, it sounds like to me," Merrick said.

"And you should see how she acts with Mother. She claimed she couldn't help Mother sample the rehearsal-dinner menus because she had a term paper due. A term paper! When it's her wedding!"

"Oh, your poor mother," Merrick said. "She was only trying to make her feel included."

"How come *you* understand that, Bean, and Pookie doesn't?" Red slammed his window shut.

Junior told Red he was imagining things. After the situation blew up, after the truth came bursting out and nearly all of Baltimore stopped speaking to Trey and Merrick, Red said, "I knew this would happen! I saw it coming. Merrick planned it from the start; she stole him."

But Junior said, "Boy, what are you talking about? Human beings can't be stolen. Not unless they want to be."

"I swear, she started plotting last summer and damned if she didn't go through with it. She flattered Trey to his face and she ran him down to Pookie behind his back and she curtsied and kowtowed to his mother till I thought I was going to puke."

"Well, it's not like he was Pookie's property," Junior said.

Then he said, "And anyhow, he's Merrick's now."

And two lines deepened at the corners of his mouth, the way they always did when he had settled some piece of business exactly to his liking.

*

An outside observer might say that these weren't stories at all. Somebody buys a house he's admired when it finally comes on the market. Somebody marries a man who was once engaged to her friend. It happens all the time.

Maybe it was just that the Whitshanks were such a *recent* family, so short on family history. They didn't have that many stories to choose from. They had to make the most of what they could get.

Clearly they couldn't look to Red for stories. Red just went ahead and married Abby Dalton, whom he had known since she was twelve—a Hampden girl, coincidentally, from the neighborhood where the Whitshanks used to live. In fact, he and she lived in Hampden themselves, during the early days of their marriage. ("Why'd we even bother moving," his father asked him, "if you were going to head back down there the very first chance you got?") Then after his parents died—killed by a freight train in '67 when their car stalled on the railroad tracks—Red took over the house on Bouton Road. Certainly Merrick didn't want it. She and Trey had a much better place of their own, not to mention their Sarasota property, and besides, she said, she had never really liked that house. It didn't have en suite bathrooms, and when Junior had finally added one to the master bedroom, reconfiguring the giant cedar-lined storeroom back in the 1950s, she'd complained that she was jolted awake every time the toilet flushed. So there Red was, in the house he'd grown up in, where he planned to die one day. Not much of a story in that.

The neighborhood referred to it as "the Whitshank house" now. Junior would have been happy to know that. One of his major annoyances was that from time to time he'd been introduced as "Mr. Whitshank, who lives in the Brill house."

There was nothing remarkable about the Whitshanks. None of them was famous. None of them could claim exceptional intelligence. And in looks, they were no more than average. Their leanness was the rawboned kind, not the lithe, elastic slenderness of people in magazine ads, and something a little too sharp in their faces suggested that while they themselves were eating just fine, perhaps their forefathers had not. As they aged, they developed sagging folds beneath their eyes, which anyway drooped at the outer corners, giving them a faintly sorrowful expression.

Their family firm was well thought of, but then so were many others, and the low number on their home-improvement license testified to nothing more than mere longevity, so why make such a fuss about it? Staying put: they appeared to view it as a virtue. Three of Red and Abby's four children lived within twenty minutes of them. Nothing so notable about that!

But like most families, they imagined they were special. They took great pride, for instance, in their fix-it skills. Calling in a repairman—even one of their own employees—was looked upon as a sign of defeat. All of them had inherited Junior's allergy to ostentation, and all of them were convinced that they had better taste than the rest of the world. At times they made a little too much of the family quirks—of both Amanda and Jeannie marrying men named Hugh, for instance, so that their husbands were referred to as "Amanda's Hugh" and "Jeannie's Hugh"; or their genetic predisposition for lying awake two hours in the middle of every night; or their uncanny ability to keep their dogs alive for eons. With the exception of Amanda they paid far too little attention to what clothes they put on in the morning, and yet they fiercely disapproved of any adult they saw wearing blue jeans. They shifted uneasily in their chairs during any talk of religion. They liked to say that they didn't care for sweets, although there was some evidence that they weren't as averse as they claimed. To varying degrees they tolerated each other's spouses, but they made no particular effort with the spouses' families, whom they generally felt to be not quite as close and kindred-spirited as their own family was. And they spoke with the unhurried drawl of people who work with their hands, even though not all of them did work with their hands. This gave them an air of good-natured patience that was not entirely deserved.

Patience, in fact, was what the Whitshanks imagined to be the theme of their two stories—patiently lying in wait for what they believed should come to them. "Biding their time," as Junior had put it, and as Merrick might have put it too if she had been willing to talk about it. But somebody more critical might say that the theme was envy. And someone else, someone who had known the family intimately and forever (but there wasn't any such person), might ask why no one seemed to realize that another, unspoken theme lay beneath the first two: in the long run, both stories had led to disappointment.

Junior got his house, but it didn't seem to make him as happy as you might expect, and he had often been seen contemplating it with a puzzled, forlorn sort of look on his face. He spent the rest of his life fidgeting with it, altering it, adding closets, resetting flagstones, as if he hoped that achieving the perfect abode would finally open the hearts of those neighbors who never acknowledged him. Neighbors whom he didn't even like, as it turned out.

Merrick got her husband, but he was a cold, aloof man unless he was drinking, in which case he grew argumentative and boorish. They never had children, and Merrick spent most of her time alone in the Sarasota place so as to avoid her mother-in-law, whom she detested.

The disappointments seemed to escape the family's notice, though. That was another of their quirks: they had a talent for pretending that everything was fine. Or maybe it wasn't a quirk at all. Maybe it was just further proof that the Whitshanks were not remarkable in any way whatsoever.

3

On the very first day of 2012, Abby began disappearing. She and Red had kept Stem's three boys overnight so that Stem and Nora could go to a New Year's Eve party, and Stem showed up to collect them around ten o'clock the next morning. Like everyone else in the family, he gave only a token knock before walking on into the house. "Hello?" he called. He stopped in the hall and stood listening, idly ruffling the dog's ears. The only sounds came from his children in the sunroom. "Hello," he said again. He walked toward their voices.

The boys sat on the rug around a Parcheesi board, three stair-step towheads dressed scruffily in jeans. "Dad," Petey said, "tell Sammy he can't play with us. He doesn't add the dots up right!"

"Where's your grandma?" Stem asked.

"I don't know. Tell him, Dad! And he rolled the dice so hard, one went under the couch."

"Grandma *said* I could play," Sammy said.

Stem walked back into the living room. "Mom? Dad?" he called.

No answer.

He went to the kitchen, where he found his father sitting at the breakfast table reading the *Baltimore Sun*. Over the past few years Red had grown hard of hearing, and it wasn't till Stem entered his line of vision that he looked up from his newspaper. "Hey!" he said. "Happy New Year!"

"Happy New Year to you."

"How was the party?"

"It was good. Where's Mom?"

"Oh, somewhere around. Want some coffee?"

"No, thanks."

"I just made it."

"I'm okay."

Stem walked over to the back door and looked out. A lone cardinal sat in the nearest dogwood, bright as a leftover leaf, but otherwise the yard was empty. He turned away. "I'm thinking we'll have to fire Guillermo," he said.

"Pardon?"

"*Guillermo*. We should get rid of him. De'Ontay said he showed up hungover again on Friday."

Red made a clucking sound and folded his newspaper. "Well, it's not like there aren't plenty of other guys out there nowadays," he said.

"Kids behave okay?"

"Yes, fine."

"Thanks for looking after them. I'll go get their stuff together."

Stem went back into the hall, climbed the stairs, and headed toward the bedroom that used to be his sisters'. It was full of bunk beds now, and the floor was a welter of tossed-off pajamas and comic books and backpacks. He began stuffing any clothing he found into the backpacks, taking no particular notice of what belonged to which child. Then, with the backpacks slung over one shoulder, he stepped into the hall again. He called, "Mom?"

He looked into his parents' bedroom. No Abby. The bed was neatly made and the bathroom door stood open, as did the doors of all the rooms lining the U-shaped hall— Denny's old room, which now served as Abby's study, and the children's bathroom and the room that used to be his. He hoisted the backpacks higher on his shoulder and went downstairs.

In the sunroom, he told the boys, "Okay, guys, get a move on. You need to find your jackets. Sammy, where are your shoes?"

"I don't know."

"Well, look for them," he said.

He went back to the kitchen. Red was standing at the counter, pouring another cup of coffee. "We're off, Dad," Stem told him. His father gave no sign he had heard him. "Dad?" Stem said.

Red turned.

"We're leaving now," Stem said.

"Oh! Well, tell Nora Happy New Year."

"And you thank Mom for us, okay? Do you think she's running an errand?"

"Married?"

"*Errand*. Could she be out running an errand?"

"Oh, no. She doesn't drive anymore."

"She doesn't?" Stem stared at him. "But she was driving just last week," he said.

"No, she wasn't."

"She drove Petey to his play date."

"That was a month ago, at least. Now she doesn't drive anymore."

"Why not?" Stem asked.

Red shrugged.

"Did something happen?"

"I think something happened," Red said.

Stem set the boys' backpacks on the breakfast table. "Like what?" he asked.

"She wouldn't say. Well, not like an accident or anything. The car looked fine. But she came home and said she'd given up driving."

"Came home from where?" Stem asked.

"From driving Petey to his play date."

"Jeez," Stem said.

He and Red looked at each other for a moment.

"I was thinking we ought to sell her car," Red said, "but that would leave us with just my pickup. Besides, what if she changes her mind, you know?"

"Better she *doesn't* change her mind, if something happened," Stem said.

"Well, it's not as if she's old. Just seventy-two next week! How's she going to get around all the rest of her life?"

Stem crossed the kitchen and opened the door to the basement. It was obvious no one was down there—the lights were off—but still he called, "Mom?"

Silence.

He closed the door and headed back to the sunroom, with Red following close behind. "Guys," Stem said. "I need to know where your grandma is."

The boys were just as he'd left them—sprawled around the Parcheesi board, jackets not on, Sammy still in his socks. They looked up at him blankly.

"She was here when you came downstairs, right?" Stem asked. "She fixed you breakfast."

"We haven't had any breakfast," Tommy told him.

"She didn't fix you breakfast?"

"She asked did we want cereal or toast and then she went away to the kitchen."

Sammy said, "I never, ever get the Froot Loops. There is only two in the pack and Petey and Tommy always get them."

"That's because me and Tommy are the oldest," Petey said.

"It's not fair, Daddy."

Stem turned to Red and found him staring at him intently, as if waiting for a translation. "She wasn't here for breakfast," Stem told him.

"Let's check upstairs."

"I did check upstairs."

But they headed for the stairs anyway, like people hunting their keys in the same place over and over because they can't believe that isn't where they are. At the top of the stairs, they walked into the children's bathroom—a chaotic scene of crumpled towels, toothpaste squiggles, plastic boats on their sides in the bottom of the tub. They walked out again and into Abby's study. They found her sitting on the daybed, fully dressed and wearing an apron. She wasn't visible from the hall, but she surely must have heard Stem calling. The dog was stretched out on the rug at her feet. When the men walked in, both Abby and the dog glanced up and Abby said, "Oh, hello there."

"Mom? We've been looking for you everywhere," Stem said.

"*I'm* sorry. How was the party?"

"The party was fine," Stem said. "Didn't you hear us calling?"

"No, I guess I didn't. I'm so sorry!"

Red was breathing heavily. Stem turned and looked at him. Red passed a hand over his face and said, "Hon."

"What," Abby said, and there was something a little too bright in her voice.

"You had us worried there, hon."

"Oh, how ridiculous!" Abby said. She smoothed her apron across her lap.

This room had become her work space as soon as Denny

was gone for good—a retreat where she could go over any clients' files she'd brought home with her, or talk with them on the phone. Even after her retirement, she continued to come here to read, or write poems, or just spend time by herself. The built-in cabinets that used to hold Linnie's sewing supplies were stuffed with Abby's journals and random clippings and handmade cards from when the children were small. One wall was so closely hung with family photographs that there was no space visible between one frame and the next. "How can you *see* them that way?" Amanda had asked once. "How can you really look at them?" But Abby said blithely, "Oh, I don't have to," which made no sense whatsoever.

Ordinarily she sat at the desk beneath the window. No one had ever known her to sit on the daybed, which was intended merely to accommodate any excess of overnight guests. There was something contrived and stagey in her posture, as if she had hastily scrambled into place when she heard their steps on the stairs. She gazed up at them with a bland, opaque smile, her face oddly free of smile lines.

"Well," Stem said, and he exchanged a look with his father, and the subject was dropped.

What you do on New Year's you'll be doing all year long, people claim, and certainly Abby's disappearance set the theme for 2012. She began to go away, somehow, even when she was present. She seemed to be partly missing

81

from many of the conversations taking place around her. Amanda said she acted like a woman who'd fallen in love, but quite apart from the fact that Abby had always and forever loved only Red, so far as they knew, she lacked that air of giddy happiness that comes with falling in love. She actually seemed *un*happy, which wasn't like her in the least. She took on a fretful expression, and her hair—gray now and chopped level with her jaw, as thick and bushy as the wig on an old china doll—developed a frazzled look, as if she had just emerged from some distressing misadventure.

Stem and Nora asked Petey what had happened on the ride to his play date, but first he didn't know what play date they were talking about and then he said the ride had gone fine. So Amanda confronted Abby straight on; said, "I hear you're not driving these days." Yes, Abby said, that was her little gift to herself: never to have to drive anyplace ever again. And she gave Amanda one of her new, bland smiles. "Back off," that smile said. And "Wrong? Why would you think anything was wrong?"

In February, she threw her idea box away. This was an Easy Spirit shoe box that she had kept for decades, crammed with torn-off bits of paper she meant to turn into poems one day. She put it out with the recycling on a very windy evening, and by morning the bits of paper were lying all over the street. Neighbors kept finding them in their hedges and on their welcome mats—"moon like a soft-boiled egg yolk" and "heart like a water balloon." There was no question as to their source. Everyone knew about Abby's poems, not to mention her fondness for similes. Most people just tactfully discarded them, but Marge Ellis brought a whole handful to the Whitshanks' front door, where Red accepted them with a confused look on his face. "Abby?" he said later. "Did you mean to throw these out?"

"I'm done with writing poems," she said.

"But I liked your poems!"

"Did you?" she asked without interest. "That's nice."

It was probably more the *idea* Red liked—his wife the poet, scribbling away at her antique desk that he'd had one of his workmen refinish, sending her efforts to tiny magazines that promptly sent them back. But even so, Red began to wear the same unhappy expression that Abby wore.

In April, her children noticed that she'd started calling the dog "Clarence," although Clarence had died years ago and Brenda was a whole different color, golden retriever instead of black Lab. This was not Abby's usual absentminded roster of misnomers: "Mandy—I mean Stem" when she was speaking to Jeannie. No, this time she *stuck* with the wrong name, as if she were hoping to summon back the dog of her younger days. Poor Brenda, bless her heart, didn't know what to make of it. She'd give a puzzled twitch of her pale sprouty eyebrows and fail to respond, and Abby would cluck in exasperation.

It wasn't Alzheimer's. (Was it?) She seemed too much in touch for Alzheimer's. And she didn't exhibit any specific physical symptoms they could tell a doctor about, like seizures or fainting fits. Not that they had much hope of persuading her to see a doctor, anyhow. She'd fired her internist at age sixty, claiming she was too old now for any "extreme measures," and for all they knew he wasn't even in practice anymore. But even if he were: "Is she forgetful?" he might ask, and they would have to say, "Well, no more than usual."

"Is she illogical?"

"Well, no more than . . ."

There you had the problem: Abby's "usual" was fairly scatty. Who could say how much of this behavior was simply Abby being Abby?

As a girl, she'd been a fey sprite of a thing. She'd worn black turtlenecks in winter and peasant blouses in summer; her hair had hung long and straight down her back while most girls clamped their pageboys into rollers every night. She wasn't just poetic but artistic, too, and a modern dancer, and an activist for any worthy cause that came along. You could count on her to organize her school's Canned Goods for the Poor drive and the Mitten Tree. Her school was Merrick's school, private and girls-only and posh, and though Abby was only a scholarship student, she was the star there, the leader. In college, she plaited her hair into cornrows and picketed for civil rights. She graduated near the top of her class and became a social worker, what a surprise, venturing into Baltimore neighborhoods that none of her old schoolmates knew existed. Even after she married Red (whom she had known for so long that neither of them could remember their first meeting), did she turn ordinary? Not a chance. She insisted on natural childbirth, breast-fed her babies in public, served her family wheat germ and home-brewed yogurt, marched against the Vietnam War with her youngest astride her hip, sent her children to public schools. Her house was filled with her handicrafts—macramé plant hangers and colorful woven serapes. She took in strangers off the streets, and some of them stayed for weeks. There was no telling who would show up at her dinner table.

Old Junior thought Red had married her to spite him. This was not true, of course. Red loved her for her own sake, plain and simple. Linnie Mae adored her, and Abby adored her back. Merrick was appalled by her. Merrick had been forced to serve as Abby's Big Sister back when Abby had first transferred to her school. Even then she had felt that Abby was beyond hope of rescue, and time had proven her right.

As for Abby's children, well, naturally they loved her. It was assumed that even Denny loved her, in his way. But she was a dreadful embarrassment to them. During visits from their friends, for instance, she might charge into the room declaiming a poem she'd just written. She might buttonhole the mailman to let him know why she believed in reincarnation. ("Mozart" was the reason she gave. How could you hear a composition from Mozart's childhood and not feel sure that he had been drawing on several lifetimes' worth of experience?) Encountering anyone with even a hint of a foreign accent, she would seize his hand and gaze into his eyes and say, "Tell me. Where is home, for you?"

"Mom!" her children protested afterward, and she would say, "What? What'd I do wrong?"

"It's none of your business, Mom! He was hoping you wouldn't notice! He was probably imagining you couldn't even guess he was foreign."

"Nonsense. He should be *proud* to be foreign. I know I would be."

In unison, her children would groan.

She was so intrusive, so sure of her welcome, so utterly lacking in self-consciousness. She assumed she had the right to ask them any questions she liked. She held the wrongheaded notion that if they didn't want to discuss some intimate personal problem, maybe they would change their minds if she turned the tables on them. (Was this something she'd learned in social work?) "Let's put this the other way around," she would say, hunching forward cozily. "Let's say *you* advise *me*. Say I have a boyfriend who's acting too possessive." She would give a little laugh. "I'm at my wit's end!" she would cry. "Tell me what I should do!"

"Really, Mom."

They had as little contact as possible with her orphans — the army veterans who were having trouble returning to normal life, the nuns who had left their orders, the homesick Chinese students at Hopkins—and they thought Thanksgiving was hell. They snuck white bread into the house, and hot dogs full of nitrites. They cowered when they heard she'd be in charge of their school picnic. And most of all, most emphatically of all, they hated how her favorite means of connecting was commiseration. "Oh, poor you!" she would say. "You're looking so tired!" Or "You must be feeling so lonely!" Other people showed love by offering compliments; Abby offered pity. It was not an attractive quality, in her children's opinion.

Yet when she went back to work, after her last child started school, Jeannie told Amanda it wasn't the relief that she had expected. "I thought I would be glad," she said, "but then I catch myself wondering, 'Where's Mom? Why isn't she breathing down my neck?'"

"You can notice a toothache's gone too," Amanda said. "It doesn't mean you want it back again."

In May, Red had a heart attack.

It wasn't a very dramatic one. He experienced a few ambiguous symptoms on a job site, was all, and De'Ontay insisted on driving him to the emergency room. Still, it came as a shock to his family. He was only seventy-four! He had seemed so healthy; he climbed ladders the same as ever and carried heavy loads, and he didn't weigh a pound more than he had when he'd gotten married. But now Abby wanted him to retire, and both the girls agreed with her. What if he lost consciousness while he was up on a roof? Red said he would go crazy if he retired. Stem said maybe he could keep on working but quit going up on roofs. Denny was not on

87

hand for this discussion, but he most probably would have sided with Stem, for once.

Red prevailed, and he was back on the job shortly after being discharged from the hospital. He looked fine. He did say he felt a bit weak, and he admitted to getting tired earlier in the day. But maybe that was all in his head; he was observed several times taking his own pulse, or laying one palm in a testing way across the center of his chest. "Are you all right?" Abby would ask. He would say, "Of *course* I'm all right," in an irritated tone that he had never used in the past.

He had hearing aids now, but he claimed they were no help. Often he just left them sitting on top of his bureau—two pink plastic nubbins the size and shape of chicken hearts. As a result, his conversations with his customers didn't always go smoothly. More and more, he allowed Stem to deal with that part of the business, although you could tell it made him sad to give it up.

He was letting the house go, too. Stem was the first to notice that. While once upon a time the house was maintained to a fare-thee-well—not a loose nail anywhere, not a chink in the window putty—now there were signs of slippage. Amanda arrived with her daughter one evening and found Stem reinstalling the spline on the front screen door, and when she asked, offhandedly, "Problem?," Stem straightened and said, "He'd never have let this happen in the old days."

"Let what happen?"

"This screen was bagging halfway out of its frame!

And the powder-room faucet is dripping, have you noticed?"

"Oh, dear," Amanda said, and she prepared to follow Elise on into the house.

But Stem said, "It's like he's lost interest," which stopped her in her tracks.

"Like he doesn't care, almost," Stem said. "I said, 'Dad, your front screen's loose,' and he said, 'I can't keep on top of every last little thing, goddammit!'"

This was huge: for Red to snap at Stem. Stem had always been his favorite.

Amanda said, "Maybe this place is getting to be too much for him."

"Not only that, but Mom left a kettle on the stove the other day, and when Nora stopped by, the kettle was whistling full-blast and Dad was writing checks at the dining-room table, totally unaware."

"He didn't hear the *kettle*?"

"Evidently not."

"That kettle stabs my eardrums," Amanda said. "It may have been what turned him deaf in the first place."

"I'm beginning to think they shouldn't be living alone," Stem told her.

"Really. Shouldn't they."

And she walked past him into the house with a thoughtful look on her face.

The next evening, there was a family meeting. Stem, Jeannie, and Amanda just happened to drop in; no spouses and no children. Stem looked suspiciously spruced up, while

Amanda was as perfectly coiffed and lipsticked as always in the tailored gray pantsuit she'd worn to the office. Only Jeannie had made no effort; she wore her usual T-shirt and rumpled khakis, and her horsetail of long black hair was straggling out of its scrunchie. Abby was thrilled. When she'd seated them all in the living room, she said, "Isn't this nice? Just like the old days! Not that I don't love to see your families too, of course—"

Red said, "What's up?"

"Well," Amanda said, "we've been thinking about the house."

"What about it?"

"We're thinking it's a lot to look after, what with you and Mom getting older."

"I could look after this house with one hand tied behind my back," Red said.

You could tell from the pause that followed that his children were considering whether to take issue with this. Surprisingly, it was Abby who came to their aid. "Well, of course you can, sweetie," she said, "but don't you think it's time you gave yourself a rest?"

"A dress!"

His children half laughed, half groaned.

"You see what I have to put up with," Abby told them. "He will not wear his hearing aids! And then when he tries to fake it, he makes the most unlikely guesses. He's just . . . perverse! I tell him I want to go to the farmers' market and he says, 'You're joining the *army*?'"

"It's not my fault if you mumble," Red said.

Abby gave an audible sigh.

"Let's stick to the subject," Amanda said briskly. "Mom, Dad: we're thinking you might want to move."

"Move!" Red and Abby cried together.

"What with Dad's heart, and Mom not driving anymore . . . we're thinking maybe a retirement community. Wouldn't that be the answer?"

"Retirement community, huh," Red said. "That's for *old* people. That's where all those snooty old ladies go when their husbands die. You think we'd be happy in a place like that? You think they'd be glad to see us?"

"Of course they'd be glad, Dad. You've probably remodeled all their houses for them."

"Right," Red said. "And besides: we're too independent, your mom and me. We're the type who manage for ourselves."

His children didn't seem to find this so very admirable.

"Okay," Jeannie said, "*not* a retirement community. But how about a condo? A garden apartment, maybe, out in Baltimore County."

"Those places are made of cardboard," Red said.

"Not all of them, Dad. Some are very well built."

"And what would we do with the house, if we moved?"

"Well, sell it, I suppose."

"Sell it! Who to? Nothing has sold in this city since the crash. It would stay on the market forever. You think I'm going to vacate my family home and let it go to rack and ruin?"

"Oh, Dad, we'd never let it—"

"Houses need humans," Red said. "*You* all should know that. Oh, sure, humans cause wear and tear—scuffed floors and stopped-up toilets and such—but that's nothing compared to what happens when a house is left on its own. It's like the heart goes out of it. It sags, it slumps, it starts to lean toward the ground. I swear I can look at just the ridgepole of a house and tell if nobody's living there. You think I'd do that to this place?"

"Well, sooner or later *someone* will buy it," Jeannie said. "And meanwhile, I'll stop in and check on it every single day. I'll run the faucets. I'll walk through the rooms. I'll open all the windows."

"That's not the same," Red said. "The house would know the difference."

Abby said, "Maybe one of you kids would want to take it over! You could buy it from us for a dollar, or whatever way it's done."

This was met with silence. Her children were happily settled in their own homes, and Abby knew it.

"It's served us so well," she said wistfully. "Remember all our good times? I remember coming here when I was a girl. And then all those hours we spent on the porch when your father and I were courting. Remember, Red?"

He made an impatient, brushing-away gesture with one hand.

"I remember bringing Jeannie here from the hospital," Abby said, "when she was three days old. I had her wrapped like a little burrito in the popcorn-stitch blanket Grandma Dalton had crocheted for Mandy, and I walked in the door saying, 'This is your home, Jean Ann. This is where you'll live, and you're going to be so happy here!'"

Her eyes filled with tears. Her children looked down at their laps.

"Oh, well," she said, and she gave a shaky laugh. "Listen to me, nattering on like this about something that can't happen for years. Not while Clarence is alive."

Red said, "*Who?*"

"Brenda. She means Brenda," Amanda told him.

"It would be cruel to make Clarence move during his final days," Abby said.

No one seemed to have the energy to continue the discussion.

Amanda talked Red into hiring a housekeeper who would also be willing to drive. Abby had never had a housekeeper, not even when she worked, but Amanda told her she would soon get used to it. "You'll be a lady of leisure!" she said. "And any time you want to go someplace, Mrs. Girt will take you."

"I'd only want to go someplace to get away from Mrs. Girt," Abby said.

Amanda just laughed as if Abby had been joking, which she hadn't.

Mrs. Girt was sixty-eight years old, a heavyset, cheerful

woman who'd been laid off her job as a lunch lady and needed the extra income. She arrived at nine every morning, puttered around the house awhile, ineffectually tidying and dusting, and then set up the ironing board in the sunroom and watched TV while she ironed. There was not a whole lot of ironing required for two elderly people living on their own, but Amanda had instructed her just to keep herself occupied. Meanwhile, Abby stayed at the other end of the house, showing none of her usual interest in hearing every detail of a new acquaintance's life story. Any time Abby made the slightest sound, Mrs. Girt would pop out of the sunroom and ask, "You okay? You need something? You want I should drive you somewheres?" Abby said it was intolerable. She complained to Red that she didn't feel the house was her own anymore.

Still, she never asked *why*, exactly, this woman was felt to be necessary.

Two weeks into the job, Mrs. Girt forcibly removed a skillet from Abby's hands and insisted on making her an omelet, during which time the iron she had abandoned set fire to a dish towel in the sunroom. No serious harm was done except to the dish towel, which was plain terry cloth from Target and hadn't needed ironing in the first place, but that was the end of Mrs. Girt. Amanda said the next person they hired would have to be under forty. She suggested too that they might consider hiring a man, although she didn't say why.

But Abby said, "No."

"No?" Amanda said. "Oh. Okay. So, a woman."

"No man, no woman. Nothing."

"But, Mom—"

"I can't!" Abby said. "I can't stand it!" She started crying. "I can't have some stranger sharing my house! I know you think I'm old, I know you think I'm feeble-minded, but this is making me *miserable*! I'd rather just go ahead and die!"

Jeannie said, "Mom, stop. Mom, please don't cry. Oh, Mom, honey, we would never want you to be miserable." She was crying too, and Red was trying to move both girls out of the way so he could get to Abby and hug her, and Stem was walking around in circles rummaging through his hair, which was what he always did when he was upset.

So: no man, no woman, nothing. Red and Abby were on their own again.

Till the tail end of June, when Abby was discovered wandering Bouton Road in her nightgown and Red hadn't even noticed she was missing.

That was when Stem announced that he and Nora were moving in with them.

Well, certainly Amanda couldn't have done it. She and Hugh and their teenage daughter led such busy lives that their corgi had to go to doggie day care every morning. And Jeannie's family lived in the house Jeannie's Hugh had grown up in, with Jeannie's Hugh's mother relocated to the guest room. They'd have needed to uproot Mrs. Angell and bring her along—a ludicrous notion. While Denny, needless to say, was out of the question.

Really, Stem should have been out of the question, too. Not only did he and Nora have three very active and demanding boys, but they were devoted to their little Craftsman house over on Harford Road, which they spent every spare moment lovingly restoring. It would have been cruel to ask them to leave it.

But Nora, at least, was home all day. And Stem was that kind of person, that mild, accepting kind of person who just seemed to take it for granted that life wasn't always going to go exactly as he'd planned it. In fact, he kept thinking up new advantages to his proposal. The boys would see more of their grandparents! They could join the neighborhood swimming pool!

His sisters barely argued, once they'd absorbed the idea. "Are you sure?" they asked weakly. His parents put up more resistance. Red said, "Son, we can't expect you to do that," and Abby grew teary again. But you could see the wistfulness in their faces. Wouldn't it be the perfect solution! And Stem said, firmly, "We're coming. That's that." So it was settled.

They moved on a Saturday afternoon in early August. Stem and Jeannie's Hugh, along with Miguel and Luis from work, loaded Stem's pickup with suitcases and toy chests and a tangle of bikes and trikes and pedal cars and scooters. (Stem and Nora's furniture was left behind for the renters, a family of Iraqi refugees sponsored by Nora's church.)

Meanwhile, Nora drove the three boys and their dog over to Red and Abby's.

Nora was a beautiful woman who didn't know she was beautiful. She had shoulder-length brown hair and a wide, placid, dreamy face, completely free of makeup. Generally she wore inexpensive cotton dresses that buttoned down the front, and when she walked her hem fluttered around her calves in a liquid, slow-motion way that made every man in sight stop dead in his tracks and stare. But Nora never noticed that.

She parked her car down on the street like a guest, and she and the boys and the dog started up the steps toward the house—the boys and Heidi leaping and cavorting and falling all over themselves, Nora drifting serenely behind them. Red and Abby stood side by side waiting for them on the porch, because this was quite a moment, really. Petey shouted, "Hi, Grandma! Hi, Grandpa!" and Tommy said, "We're going to live here now!" They'd been very excited ever since they heard the news. Nobody knew how Nora felt about it. At least outwardly, she was like Stem: she seemed to take things as they came. When she reached the porch, Red said, "Welcome!" and Abby stepped forward and hugged her. "Hello, Nora," she said. "We're so grateful to you for doing this." Nora just smiled her slow, secret smile, revealing the two deep dimples in her cheeks.

The boys would sleep in the bunk-bed room. They raced up the stairs ahead of the grown-ups and threw themselves on the beds they always claimed when they stayed over.

Stem and Nora would occupy Stem's old room, diagonally across the hall. "Now, I've taken down all the posters and such," Abby told Nora. "You two should feel free to hang whatever you like on the walls. And I've emptied the closet and the bureau. Will that give you enough storage space, do you think?"

"Oh, yes," Nora said in her low, musical voice. It was the first time she had spoken since she'd arrived.

"I'm sorry the bed's not here yet," Abby said. "They can't deliver it till Tuesday, so I'm afraid you're going to have to make do with the twin beds until then."

Nora just smiled again and wandered over to the bureau, where she set down her pocketbook. "For supper I'm fixing fried chicken," she said.

Red said, "What?" and Abby told him, "Fried chicken!" At a lower volume, she said, "We love fried chicken, but you really don't have to cook for us."

"I enjoy cooking," Nora said.

"Would you like Red to go to the grocery store for you?"

"Douglas is bringing groceries in the truck."

Douglas was what she called Stem. It was his real name, which nobody in the family had used since he was two. They always looked blank for a moment when they heard it, but they could see why Nora might want a more grown-up name for her husband.

When she and Stem had announced that they were getting married, Abby had said, "Excuse me for asking, but will you be expecting . . . Douglas to join your church?" Just about all they knew about Nora was that she belonged to a fundamentalist church that was evidently a big part of her life. But Nora had said, "Oh, no. I don't believe in dative evangelizing." Abby had repeated this later to the girls: "She doesn't believe in 'dative evangelizing.'" As a result, they had assumed for a long time that Nora must not be very bright. Although she did hold a responsible job—medical assistant in a doctor's office—before her children were born. And on occasion she came up with unsettlingly perceptive observations. Or were those accidental? She mystified them, really. Maybe now that she was living with them, they could finally figure her out.

Red and Abby left her upstairs to deal with the boys, who were walloping each other with pillows while Heidi, a flibbertigibbet collie, danced around them, barking hysterically. They went down and sat in the living room. Neither of them had any chores to do. They just sat looking at each other with their hands folded in their laps. Abby said, "Do you think this is how it will be all the rest of our lives?"

Red said, "What?"

Abby said, "Nothing."

Stem and Jeannie's Hugh arrived at the back door with the truck, and everybody went to unload—even the little boys, even Abby—except for Nora. Nora took delivery of the first item Stem brought in, an ice chest full of groceries, and she drew from it an apron folded on the very top. It was the kind that Red and Abby's mothers wore in the 1940s, flowered cotton with a bib that buttoned at the back of the neck. She put it on and started cooking.

Over supper, there was a great deal of talk about accommodations. Abby kept wondering if one of the boys shouldn't be moved to her study. "Maybe Petey, because he's the oldest?" she asked. "Or Sammy, because he's the youngest?"

"Or me, because I'm in the middle!" Tommy shouted.

"That's okay," Stem told Abby. "They were sharing one room at home, after all. They're used to it."

"I don't know why it is," Abby said, "but these last few years the house has just always seemed the wrong size. When your father and I are alone it's too big, and when you all come to visit it's too small."

"We'll be fine," Stem said.

"Are you two talking about the dog?" Red asked.

"Dog?"

"Because I just don't see how two dogs can occupy the same territory."

"Oh, Red, of course they can," Abby said. "Clarence is a pussycat; you know that."

"Come again?"

"Clarence is on my bed right this minute!" Petey said. "And Heidi is on Sammy's bed."

Red overrode Petey's last sentence, perhaps not realizing Petey was speaking. "My father was opposed to letting a dog in the house," he said. "Dogs are hard on houses. Bad for the woodwork. He'd have made both those animals stay out in the backyard, and he'd have wondered why we owned them anyways unless they had some job to do."

The grown-ups had heard this too many times to bother commenting, but Petey said, "Heidi's got a job! Her job is making us happy."

"She'd be better off herding sheep," Red said.

"Can we get some sheep, then, Grandpa? Can we?"

"This chicken is delicious," Abby told Nora.

"Thank you."

"Red, isn't the chicken delicious?"

"I'll say! I've had two pieces and I'm thinking about a third."

"You can't have a third! It's full of cholesterol!"

The telephone rang in the kitchen.

"Now, who on earth can that be?" Abby asked.

"Only one way to find out," Red told her.

"Well, I'm just not going to answer. Everyone who's anyone knows it's the supper hour," Abby said. But at the same time, she was pushing back her chair and standing up. She had never lost the conviction that someone might be needing her. She made her way to the kitchen, forcing two of the little boys to scoot their chairs in as she passed behind them.

"Hello?" they heard. "Hi, Denny!"

Stem and Red glanced toward the kitchen. Nora placed a dollop of spinach on Sammy's plate, although he squirmed in protest.

"Well, nobody thought . . . What? Oh, don't be silly. Nobody thought—"

"What's for dessert?" Tommy asked his mother.

Stem said, "Ssh. Grandma's on the phone."

"Blueberry pie," Nora said.

"Goody!"

"Yes, of course we would have," Abby said. A pause. "Now, that is *not true*, Denny! That is simply not . . . Hello?"

After a moment, they heard the latching sound of the receiver settling back into its wall mount. Abby reappeared in the kitchen doorway.

"Well, that was Denny," she told them. "He's coming in tonight on the twelve-thirty-eight train, but he says just to leave the door unlocked and he'll catch a cab from the station."

"Huh! He'd damn well better," Red said, "because *I* won't be up that late."

"Well, maybe you should meet him, Red."

"Why's that?"

"I'll go," Stem told her.

"Oh, I think maybe your father, dear."

There was a silence.

"What was his problem?" Red asked finally.

"Problem?" Abby said. "Well, not a problem, exactly. He just doesn't understand why we didn't ask *him* to come stay."

Even Nora looked surprised.

"Ask Denny!" Red said. "Would he have done it?"

"He says he would have. He says he's coming now, regardless."

Abby had been standing in the doorway all this time, but now she made her way back to her chair and fell into it heavily, as if the trip had exhausted her. "He found out from Jeannie that you were moving in," she told Stem. "He thinks he should have been consulted. He says the house doesn't have enough bedrooms for you all; it should have been him instead."

Nora started reaching for people's plates and stacking them, not making a sound.

"What wasn't true?" Red asked Abby.

"Excuse me?"

"You said, 'That's not true, Denny.'"

"See how he does?" Abby asked Stem. "Half the time he's deaf as a post and then it turns out he's heard something all the way off in the kitchen."

"What wasn't true, Abby?" Red asked.

"Oh," Abby said airily, "*you* know. Just the usual." She placed her silverware neatly across her plate and passed the plate to Nora. "He says he doesn't know why we had Stem come when . . . *you* know. He says Stem is not a Whitshank."

There was another silence, during which Nora rose in one fluid motion, still without a sound, and bore the stack of plates out to the kitchen.

*

Actually, it *was* true that Stem was not a Whitshank. But only in the most literal sense.

People tended to forget the fact, but Stem was the son of a tile layer known as Lonesome O'Brian. Lawrence O'Brian, really; but like most tilers he was sort of standoffish, fond of working by himself and keeping his own counsel, and so Lonesome was the name everybody called him. Red always said Lonesome was the best tile man going, although certainly not the fastest.

The fact that Lonesome had a son seemed incongruous. People tended to look at the man—tall and cadaverously thin, that translucent kind of blond where you can see the plates of his skull—and picture him living like a hermit: no wife, no kids, no friends. Well, they were right about the wife and perhaps even the friends, but he did have this toddler named Douglas. Several times when his sitting arrangements fell through, he brought Douglas in to work with him. This was against the rules, but since the two of them never had any cause to be in a hard-hat area, Red let it pass. Lonesome would head straight to whatever kitchen or bathroom he was working on, and Douglas would scurry after him on his short little legs. Not once did Lonesome look back to see if Douglas was keeping up; nor did Douglas complain or ask him to slow down. They would settle in their chosen room, door tightly closed, not a peep from them all morning. At lunchtime they would emerge, Douglas scurrying behind as before, and eat their sandwiches with the other men, but somewhat to the side. Douglas was so young that he still drank from a spouted cup. He was a waifish, homely child, lacking the dimpled cuteness that you would expect in someone that age. His hair was almost white, cut short and prickly all over his head, and his eyes were a very light blue, pinkish around the rims. All his clothes were too big for him. They seemed to be wearing *him*; he was only an afterthought. His trousers were folded up at the bottoms several times over. The shoulders of his red jacket jutted out from his spindly frame, the elastic cuffs hiding all but his miniature fingertips, which were slightly powdered-looking like his father's—an occupational side effect.

The other men did their best to engage him. "Hey, there, big fellow," they'd offer, and "What you say, my man?" But Douglas only squinched himself up tighter against his father and stared. Lonesome didn't try to ease the situation the way most fathers would have—answering on his child's behalf or cajoling him into showing some manners. He would just go on eating his sandwich, a pathetic, slapped-together sandwich on squashed-looking Wonder Bread.

"Where's his mom?" someone new might ask. "She sick today?"

"Traveling," Lonesome would say, not bothering to raise his eyes.

The new man would send a questioning look toward the others, and they would glance off to the side in a way that meant "Tell you later." Then later one of them would fill him in. (There was no lack of volunteers; construction workers are notorious gossips.) "The kid there, his mom ran off when he was just a baby. Left Lonesome holding the bag, can you believe it? But any time anyone wants to know, Lonesome says she's just taking a trip. He acts like she's coming back someday."

Abby had heard about Douglas, of course. She pumped Red for his men's stories every night; it was the social worker in her. And when she heard that Lonesome claimed Douglas's mother was coming back, she said flatly, "Is that a fact." She knew all about such mothers.

"Well, apparently she *has* come back at least twice that people know of," Red said. "Stayed just a week or so each time, and Lonesome got all happy and fired the babysitter."

Abby said, "Mm-hmm."

In April of 1979, a crisp, early-spring afternoon, Red phoned Abby from his office and said, "You know Lonesome O'Brian? That guy who brings his kid in?"

"I remember."

"Well, he brought him in again today and now he's in the hospital."

"The child's in the hospital?"

"No, Lonesome is. He had some kind of collapse and they had to call an ambulance."

"Oh, the poor—"

"So do you think you could come by my office and pick up the kid?"

"Oh!"

"I don't know what else to do with him. One of the fellows brought him here and he's sitting on a chair."

"Well—"

"I can't talk long; I'm supposed to be meeting with an inspector. Could you just come?"

"Okay."

She hurried Denny into the car (he was four at the time, still on half-days at nursery school) and drove up Falls Road to Red's office, a little clapboard shack out past the county line. She parked on the gravel lot, but before she could step out of the car Red emerged from the building with a very small boy on one arm. You could see that the child felt anxious. He was keeping himself upright, tightly separate. It was the first time Abby had laid eyes on him, and although he matched Red's description right down to the oversized jacket, she was unprepared for his stony expression. "Why, hello there!" she said brightly when Red leaned into the rear of the car to set him down. "How are you, Douglas? I'm Abby! And this is Denny!"

Douglas scrunched back in his seat and gazed down at his corduroy knees. Denny, on his left, bent forward to eye him curiously, but Douglas gave no sign of noticing him.

"After my meeting I'm going to stop by Sinai," Red said. "See what's doing with Lonesome, and ask him how to get ahold of his sitter. So could you just—I appreciate this, Ab. I promise it won't be for long."

"Oh, we'll have a *good* time. Won't we?" Abby asked Douglas.

Douglas kept his eyes on his knees. Red shut the car door and stood back, holding one palm up in a motionless goodbye, and Abby drove off with the two little boys sitting silent in the rear.

At home, she freed Douglas from his jacket and fixed both boys a snack of sliced bananas and animal crackers. They sat at the child-size table she kept in one corner of the kitchen—Denny munching away busily, Douglas picking up each animal cracker and studying it, turning it over, looking at it from different angles before delicately biting off a head or a leg. He didn't touch the bananas. Abby said, "Douglas, would you like some juice?" After a pause, he shook his head. So far, she hadn't heard him speak a word.

She allowed both boys to watch the afternoon kiddie shows on TV, although ordinarily she would not have. Meanwhile, she let Clarence in from the yard—he was just a puppy at the time, not to be trusted alone in the house— and he raced to the sunroom and scrabbled up onto the couch to lick the boys' faces. First Douglas shrank back, but he was clearly interested, in a guarded sort of way, and so Abby didn't intervene.

When the girls came home from school, they made a big fuss over him. They dragged him upstairs to look through the toy chest, competing for his attention and asking him questions in honeyed voices. Douglas remained silent, eyes lowered. The puppy came along with them, and Douglas spent most of his time delivering small, awkward pats to the top of the puppy's head.

Around suppertime, Red arrived with a paper grocery

bag. "Some clothes and things for Douglas," he told Abby, setting the bag on the kitchen counter. "I borrowed Lonesome's apartment keys."

"How is he?"

"Mighty uncomfortable when I saw him. Turns out it's his appendix. While I was there they took him to surgery. He'll need to stay over one night, they said; he can come home late tomorrow. I did ask about the sitter, but it seems she's got some kind of leg trouble. Lonesome said he felt bad about saddling us with the boy."

"Well, it's not as if he's a bother," Abby said. "He might as well not be here."

At supper, Douglas sat on an unabridged dictionary Red had placed on a chair. He ate seven peas, total, which he picked up one by one with his fingers. The table conversation went on around him and above him, but there was a sense among all of them that they had a watchful audience, that they were speaking for his benefit.

Abby got him ready for bed, making him pee and brush his teeth before she put him in a pair of many-times-washed seersucker pajamas that she found in the grocery bag. Seersucker seemed too lightweight for the season, but that was her only choice. She settled him in the other twin bed in Denny's room, and after she'd drawn up the blankets she hesitated a moment and then planted a kiss on his forehead. His skin was warm and slightly sweaty, as if he'd just expended some great effort. "Now, you have a good, good sleep," she told him, "and when you wake up it'll be tomorrow and you can see your daddy."

Douglas still didn't speak, he didn't even change expression, but his face all at once seemed to open up and grow softer and less pinched. At that instant he was not so homely after all.

The next morning Abby had a neighbor drive carpool, because even back in those days, before the child-seat laws, she didn't feel right letting such a small boy bounce around loose with the others. Once they were on their own, she settled Douglas on the floor in the sunroom with a jigsaw puzzle from Denny's room. He didn't put it together, even though it consisted of only eight or ten pieces, but he spent a good hour quietly moving the pieces about, picking up first one and then another and examining it intently, while the puppy sat beside him alert to every movement. Then after she finished her morning chores Abby sat with him on the couch and read him picture books. He liked the ones with animals in them, she could tell, because sometimes when she was about to turn a page he would reach out a hand to hold it down so he could study it a while longer.

When she heard a car at the rear of the house, she thought it was Peg Brown delivering Denny from nursery school. By the time she got to the kitchen, though, Red was walking through the back door. "Oh!" she said. "What are *you* doing home?"

"Lonesome died," Red said.

"What?"

"Lawrence. He died."

"But I thought it was just his appendix!"

"I know," he said. "I went to his room but he wasn't there, and the guy in the next bed said he'd been moved to Intensive Care. So I went to Intensive Care but they wouldn't let me see him, and I was thinking I'd just leave and come back later when all at once this doctor walked out and told me they had lost him. He said they'd worked all night and they'd done what they could but they lost him: peritonitis."

Something made Abby turn her head, and she saw Douglas in the kitchen doorway. He was gazing up into Red's face. Abby said, "Oh, sweetheart." She and Red exchanged glances. How much had he understood? Probably nothing, if you judged by his hopeful expression.

Red said, "Son . . ."

"It won't come through to him," Abby said.

"But we can't keep it a secret."

"He's too young," Abby said, and then she asked Douglas, "How old are you, sweetheart?"

Neither of them really expected an answer, but after a pause, Douglas held up two fingers. "Two!" Abby cried. She turned back to Red. "I was thinking three," she said, "but he's two years old, Red."

Red sank onto a kitchen chair. "Now what?" he asked her.

"I don't know," Abby said.

She sat down across from him. Douglas went on watching them.

"You still have the keys, right?" she asked Red. "You'll have to go back to the apartment, look for papers. Find Lonesome's next of kin."

Red said okay and stood up again, like an obedient child.

Then Peg Brown honked out back, and Abby rose to let Denny in.

That evening when she was in Denny's room, getting Douglas ready for bed, Denny asked her, "Mama?"

"What."

"When is that little boy going home?"

"Very soon," she told him. He was hanging around her in a too-close, insistent way, still fully dressed because it wasn't quite his bedtime yet. "Go on downstairs," she told him. "Find yourself something to do."

"Tomorrow is he going?"

"Maybe."

She waited till she heard his shoes clopping down the stairs, and then she turned back to Douglas. He was sitting on the edge of the bed in his pajamas, looking very neat and clean. That night he'd had a bath, although she had let him skip it the night before. She sat down on the bed beside him and said, "I know I told you that you'd get to see your daddy today. But I was wrong. He couldn't come."

Douglas's gaze was fixed on some middle distance. He appeared to be holding his breath.

"He wanted to, very much. He wanted to see you, but he couldn't. He can't."

That was it, really—the most a two-year-old would be

able to comprehend. She stopped speaking. She placed an arm around him, tentatively, but he didn't relax against her. He sat separate and erect, with perfect posture. After a while she took her arm away, but she went on looking at him.

He lay down, finally, and she covered him up and placed a kiss on his forehead and turned out the light.

In the kitchen, Denny and Jeannie were bickering over a yo-yo, but Mandy looked up from her homework as soon as Abby walked in. "Did you tell him?" she asked. (She was thirteen, and more in touch with what was going on.)

"Well, as much as I could," Abby said.

"Did he say anything?"

"Nothing."

"Maybe he doesn't know how to talk."

"Oh, he has to know how," Abby said. "It's just that he's upset right now."

"Maybe he's retarded."

"But I know he understands me."

"Mom!" Jeannie broke in. "Denny says this is his yo-yo, when it's not. He broke his. Tell him, Mom! It's mine."

"Stop it, both of you."

The back door opened and Red stepped in, carrying another grocery bag. All he had said on the phone was to go ahead and eat without him, so Abby's first question was "What'd you find?"

He set the bag on the table. "The sitter's this ancient old lady," he told her. "Her number was Scotch-taped above the phone. By the sound of her, she was *way* too old to be in charge of a kid. She doesn't know if he has any relatives, and she doesn't know where his mother is and says she doesn't want to know. He's better off without her, she says."

"Weren't there any other numbers?"

"Doctor, dentist, Whitshank Construction."

"Not the mother? You'd think at least Lonesome would know how to reach her in case of emergency."

"Well, if she's traveling, Ab . . ."

"Ha," Abby said. "Traveling."

Red inverted the grocery bag over the table. More clothes fell out, and two plastic trucks, and a thin sheaf of papers. "Automobile title," he said, picking up one of the papers. "Bank statement," picking up another. "Douglas's birth certificate."

Abby held out her hand and he gave her the birth certificate. "Douglas Alan O'Brian," she read aloud. "Father: Lawrence Donald O'Brian. Mother: Barbara Jane Eames."

She looked up at Red. "Were they not married?"

"Maybe she just didn't change her name."

"January eighth, nineteen seventy-seven. So Douglas had it right; he's two. I don't know why I thought he was older. I guess it was because he . . . keeps so much to himself, you know?"

"So what do we do next?" Red asked. "I have no idea what we do."

"Call Social Services?"

"Oh, God forbid!"

Red blinked. (Abby used to work for Social Services.)

"Let me warm up your supper," Abby told him. And from the way she rose, all businesslike, it was clear that she was done talking for now.

The children went to bed one by one, youngest to oldest. Jeannie, as she was saying good night, asked, "Can we keep him?" But she seemed to realize she couldn't expect an answer. The other two didn't refer to him. And Red and Abby didn't, either, once they were alone, although Red did make an attempt, at one point. "You just know Lonesome had to have *some* kin out there," he said.

But Abby said, "I am so, so sleepy all of a sudden."

He didn't try again.

The next day was a Saturday. Douglas slept later than any of them, later than even Amanda who had reached that adolescent slugabed age, and Abby said, "Let him rest, poor thing." She fed the others breakfast, not sitting down herself but bustling between stove and table, and as soon as they'd finished eating she said, "Why don't you kids get dressed and then take Clarence on a walk."

"Let Jeannie and Denny do it," Amanda said. "I told Patricia she could come over."

"No, you go too," Abby said. "Patricia can come later."

Amanda started to speak but changed her mind, and she followed the others out of the room.

That left Red, who was reading the sports section over his second cup of coffee. When Abby sat down across from him, he glanced at her uneasily and then ducked behind his paper again.

"I think we should keep him," Abby said.

He slapped the paper down on the table and said, "Oh, *Abby*."

"We're the only people he's got, Red. Clearly. That mother: even if we managed to track her down, what are the odds she'd want him? Or take proper care of him if she did want him, or stick by him through thick and thin?"

"We can't go around adopting every child we run into, Ab. We've got three of our own. Three is all we can afford! *More* than we can afford. And you were going back to work once Denny starts first grade."

"That's okay; I'll go back when Douglas starts."

"Plus, we have no rights to him. Not a court in this land would let us keep that kid; he's got a mother somewhere."

"We just won't tell the courts," Abby said.

"Have you lost your mind?"

"We'll say we're just looking after him till his mother can come and get him. In fact, that really *is* what we'll be doing."

"And besides," Red said. "How do we know for sure he's even normal?"

"Of course he's normal!"

"Does he talk?"

"He's shy! He's feeling anxious! He doesn't know us!"

"Does he react?"

"*Yes*, he reacts. He's reacting just the way any child would who's had his world turned upside down with no warning."

"But it could be that something's wrong with him," Red said.

"Well, and what if it were? You'd just throw a child to the wolves if he's not Einstein?"

"And would he fit in with our family? Would he get along with our kids? Is he our kind of personality? We don't know the first damn thing about him! We don't know him! We don't *love* him!"

"Red," Abby said.

She rose to her feet. She was fully, crisply dressed, at nine thirty on a Saturday morning. Which was, come to think of it, not her usual weekend custom. Her hair was already pinned up in its topknot. She looked uncharacteristically imposing.

"He was sitting on the edge of the bed last night in his pajamas," she said, "and I saw the back of his neck, this fragile, slender *stem* of a neck, and it struck me all at once that there was nobody anywhere, any place on this planet, who would look at that little neck and just have to reach out and cup a hand behind it. You know how you just have to touch your child, sometimes? How you drink him in with your eyes and you could stare at him for hours and you marvel at how dear and impossibly perfect he is? And that will never again happen to Douglas. He has nobody left on earth who thinks he's special."

"Dammit, Abby—"

"Don't you curse at *me*, Red Whitshank! I need this! I

have to do this! I cannot see that little stem of a neck and let him go on alone in this world. I can't! I'd rather die!"

Mandy and Jeannie and Denny were standing in the kitchen doorway. At the same moment, both Red and Abby became aware of that. None of the three had dressed yet, and all of them wore the same wide-eyed look of alarm.

Then a soft, padding sound came from behind them, and when the children turned, Douglas walked up to stand at their center.

"I wet the bed," he told Abby.

They didn't adopt him. They didn't notify Social Services. They didn't even make an announcement to their friends. Everything went on as before, and Douglas went on being Douglas O'Brian—although, since Abby developed a habit of calling him "my little stem," he did acquire a nickname. And sometimes the neighbors referred to him as Stem Whitshank, but that was just absentmindedness.

Outsiders had the impression that he was only staying till his mother got her affairs sorted out. (Or was it some other relative? Stories differed.) But most people, after a while, just assumed he was one of the family.

In a matter of weeks he took to calling Red and Abby "Dad" and "Mom," but not because they told him to. He was merely echoing the other children, in the same way that he echoed Abby and addressed even grown-ups as "sweetheart," till he got old enough to know better.

He grew more talkative, though so gradually that nobody could recall what specific day he became a normal, chattery youngster. He wore clothes that fit him, and he slept in a room of his own. It had once been Jeannie's room, but they moved Jeannie in with Mandy because Stem certainly couldn't continue sharing with Denny. Denny was sort of prickly about Stem. It all worked out, though. Mandy more or less put up with Jeannie's presence, and Jeannie was thrilled to be living in a teenager's room with cosmetics crowding the bureau top.

Above Stem's bed hung a framed black-and-white photo of Lonesome holding a Budweiser, snapped by one of Red's workmen the day they finished a building project. Abby believed very strongly that Stem should be encouraged to cherish his memories of his father. Of his mother too, if he'd *had* any memories, but he didn't seem to. The reason his mother had gone away was, she was unhappy, Abby always told him. It wasn't that she hadn't loved him. She loved him very much, as he would see if she ever came back. And Abby showed him the page in the phone book where his own name was listed year after year, "O'Brian Douglas A," along with the Whitshanks' number so his mother could easily find him. Stem listened to all this closely, but he said nothing. And in time it seemed he lost his memories of even his father, because when Abby asked Stem on his tenth birthday whether he ever thought about him, he said, "I maybe remember his voice."

"His voice!" Abby said. "Saying what?"

"I think he used to sing me a song when I was going to sleep. Or *some* guy did."

"Oh, Stem, how nice. A lullaby?"

"No, it was about a goat."

"Oh. And nothing else? No recollection of his face? Or something you two did together?"

"I guess not," Stem said, without sounding too concerned about it.

He was an old soul, Abby told people. He was the kind of person who adapted and moved on, evidently.

He went through school without a fuss, earning only average grades but fulfilling all his assignments. You could imagine him as the butt of school bullies, since he was small for his age in the early years, but actually he did fine. It may have been his friendly expression, or his general unflappability, or his tendency to assume the best in people. At any rate, he got along. He graduated from high school and went straight into Whitshank Construction, where he'd been working part-time ever since he was old enough; he said he didn't see the need for college. He married the only girl he had ever shown any real interest in, had his children one-two-three, seemed never to look around and wonder if he might be better off someplace else. In this last respect, he was the one most like Red. Even his walk was Red's— loping, leading with his forehead—and his lanky frame, though not his coloring. You could say that he looked like a Whitshank who'd been left out to bleach in the open too long: hair not black but light brown, eyes not sapphire but light blue. Faded, but still a Whitshank.

More of a Whitshank than Denny was, Denny had remarked when he heard that Stem had joined the firm.

Although once, back when Denny was a teenager still living at home, he'd asked Abby, "What's this kid *doing* here? What did you think you were up to? Did you ever consider asking our permission?"

"Permission!" Abby said. "He's your brother!"

Denny said, "He is not my brother. He is not remotely related to me, and for you to tell me he is is like . . . like those pretend-to-be liberals who claim they never notice whether a person is black or white. Don't they have eyes? Don't *you*? Were you so keen on doing good in the outside world that you didn't stop to wonder if this would be good for *us*?"

Abby just said, "Oh, Denny."

Oh, Denny.

4

On Sunday morning the study door was closed—Denny's door—and everyone tried to keep the little boys from making too much noise. "Go play in the sunroom," Nora told them when they'd finished breakfast. "Quietly, though. Don't wake your uncle." But even on their best behavior, exaggeratedly tiptoeing as they left the kitchen, they seemed to radiate disruption. They jostled and elbowed and poked one another and tripped over their own pajama cuffs, while Heidi ran frenzied circles around them. On the floor in the corner, Brenda raised her head to watch them leave and then groaned and settled her chin on her paws again.

Red was sleeping late too, so the others had no way of knowing how things had gone at the train station. "I tried to stay awake till the two of them got home," Abby said, "but I must have nodded off. I can't seem to read in bed anymore! I should have sat up for them downstairs. Another cup of coffee, Nora?"

"I can do that, Mother Whitshank. You sit still."

It was going to be a while, evidently, before the two women settled just who was in charge of what. This morning Abby had put out toast and cereal as usual, and then Nora had come down and scrambled an entire carton of eggs without so much as a by-your-leave.

Stem was in his pajamas and Abby in her bathrobe, but Nora wore one of her dresses, white cotton with navy sprigs, and sandals that showed her smooth, tanned feet. For breakfast she had eaten more than all the rest of them put together, but so slowly and so gracefully that it seemed she hardly ate at all.

"I was thinking," Abby said, "we might invite the girls and their families to lunch. I know they'll want to see Denny."

"Could we make it a late lunch?" Nora asked. "The children and I have church."

"Oh, certainly. Yes, we could start at . . . one o'clock, would you say? I believe I'll do a rolled roast."

"If you put the roast in the oven for me," Nora said, "I can see to the rest of the meal when I get back."

"Well, I'm still able to manage a simple family meal, Nora."

"Yes, of course," Nora said serenely.

Stem said, "I'll pick up whatever you need in the way of groceries."

"Oh, Dad can do that," Abby told him.

"Mom. That's what I'm here for."

"Well . . . but go to Eddie's, then, where you can charge it to our account."

"Mom."

Luckily for Abby, Red walked in at that moment. (Abby disliked money discussions.) He was wearing his ratty old bathrobe and his mules that made a whisk-broom sound, and he was carrying his Fred Flintstone glass that he used for his nighttime water. "Morning, all," he said.

"Well, hi!" Abby said, sliding her chair back, but Nora was already up and fetching the coffeepot. "Did Denny get in all right?" Abby asked.

"Yep," Red said, sitting down.

Stem said, "Train on schedule?"

Either Red didn't hear him or he felt the question wasn't worth answering. He reached for the platter of scrambled eggs.

"There's toast," Abby told him. "Whole wheat."

He dished out a large pile of eggs and passed the platter to Nora, who took another helping.

"If I have to see that statue one more dad-blamed time," he said, "I'm going to hire myself a wrecking ball. It's embarrassing! Other cities' train stations have fountains, or hunks of metal or something. We have a giant tin Frankenstein with a heart that pulses pink and blue."

"How was Denny?" Abby asked him.

"Fine, as far as I could tell." He peered into the cream pitcher. "Is there more cream?"

Nora rose and went to the fridge.

"All we talked about was the Orioles," he said, giving in at last to his audience. "Neither one of us believes they can keep this up till postseason."

"Oh."

"He brought three bags with him."

"Three!"

"I asked him," Red said, stirring his coffee. "I asked why so much luggage, and he said it was summer clothes and winter clothes."

"Winter!"

"Winter took most of the room, he said. Thicker material."

"How'd he carry all that?" Stem asked.

"Boarding, he used a redcap, he told me. But getting off again . . . Have you tried finding a redcap in Baltimore? After midnight? He managed okay, though. If I'd known, I would have parked the car and come inside the station."

"Winter clothes!" Abby said to herself in a trailing voice.

"Good eggs," Red told her.

"Oh, Nora made those."

"Good eggs, Nora."

"Thank you."

"I guess I should empty the study closet," Abby said. "But already I've had to find space for the things from the bunk-room closet, and the one in Stem and Nora's room." She was looking a little panicked.

"Relax," Red told her, without looking up from his eggs.

"I *hate* it when you tell me to relax!"

Nora said, "I can empty that closet."

"You wouldn't know where to put things."

"Nora's a whiz at organizing storage space," Stem said.

"Yes, I'm sure she is, but—"

"Hey, everybody," Denny said, walking into the kitchen. He was wearing paint-stained khakis and a String Cheese Incident T-shirt, and his hair was very shaggy, fringing the tops of his ears. (As a rule, the men in the family were fanatic about keeping their hair short.) He seemed healthy, though, and cheerful. Abby said, "Oh, sweetheart! It's so good to see you!" and she rose to hug him. He returned her hug briefly and then bent to pet Brenda, who had struggled to her feet and shambled over to nuzzle him. Stem lifted one hand from where he sat, and Nora smiled and said, "Hello, Denny."

"Any breakfast left?"

"There's plenty," Abby said. Nora stood up again to fetch the coffeepot.

"Where're the kids?" Denny asked when he was seated.

"In the sunroom," Abby said. "I hope they didn't wake you."

"Never heard a thing."

"How was your trip?"

"Not too bad." He helped himself to the eggs.

"You could have waited till this morning, you know. The train's empty on Sunday mornings."

"It was empty last night," he said.

Stem asked, "You still working with those kitchen people?"

"Naw, I quit that job."

"So what are you doing now?"

"I'm *here* now," Denny said, and he sent Stem a level gaze.

Nora said, "If you'll excuse me, I have to get the boys ready for church."

Denny transferred his gaze to her for a moment, and then he picked up his fork and started eating.

The little boys were thrilled to hear that Denny was awake. They swarmed back into the kitchen and climbed all over him and pelted him with questions and demands—had he brought his baseball glove? would he take them down to the creek?—while Heidi barked and jittered around them and tried to insert herself into their midst. Denny shrugged them away good-naturedly and promised they'd do something later, and then Nora herded them upstairs, Stem following close behind with Sammy on his back, and Red went off to the sunroom with the morning paper.

That left just Abby and Denny. As soon as they were alone, she poured herself another cup of coffee and sat down again. "Dennis," she said.

"Oh-oh."

"What?"

"Gotta watch out if you're calling me 'Dennis,'" he said. He spooned some jam onto his plate.

"Denny, I know what Jeannie must have told you. How I'm so dithery nowadays I need a keeper."

"She didn't say that."

"Well, *whatever* she said, I just want to explain my side of it." He cocked his head.

"This thing that got them all worried," she said, "I mean the reason Stem and Nora thought they should move in with us: it wasn't the way it sounds. I didn't . . . wander off and get lost like some mental defective or something. What happened was, it was the night of that terrible storm, the one they're calling a 'derecho,' remember that? Oh, Lord, 'derecho,' 'El Niño' . . . all these words we throw around these days. Tell me that's not global warming! But anyhow, this storm knocked over one of the Ellises' giant trees, right on the line between our two properties. That's not to mention the hundreds of other trees, as well as shutting down half the city's electrical power, including ours."

"Bummer," Denny said. He bit into his toast.

"You should have seen that tree, Denny. It looked like a huge stalk of broccoli lying on its side, only with roots. And the hole it left! A hole as deep as a basement. You can understand why a person would be curious about it."

"What are you saying: you went out to look at the hole?"

"Well, probably."

"Probably?"

"I mean, yes, I'm pretty sure that's what I did."

"Mom. It was a storm the strength of a hurricane. You must remember if you went out in it."

"I do remember. I mean, I remember I *was* out in it; I just don't remember *going* out. See, sometimes my mind skips across a few minutes, like a needle on a record. I'll be doing something ordinary, but then all at once it's later, you know? Maybe five or ten minutes later; I'm not sure. And there's a completely empty gap between the last minute and the current minute. It's not like when you phase out doing some routine chore but you're still aware that time has passed. This is more like . . . waking after surgery."

"That sounds like a mini stroke or something," Denny said. "Or maybe a seizure."

"Well, *I* don't know."

"Have you mentioned it to a doctor?"

"Absolutely not."

"But it could be there's some easy fix."

"No fix I'd want at my age," Abby said. "And besides, it doesn't happen very often. Not often at all."

"So, okay, you're telling me you just found yourself out in a rainstorm, looking down into a hole."

"Well, it wasn't a rainstorm anymore. The rain had stopped. But otherwise, yes, that's it exactly. And I was in my nightgown and slippers, and I didn't have my house key. Well, why should I? Usually, that lock is set on manual. Oh, I *despise* an automatic lock! It must have been your father's doing; he's always going around fiddling with things. And then naturally he couldn't hear me when I called; he was sound asleep by then, and you can see how deaf he's grown. I called, I knocked . . . I couldn't ring the doorbell, of course, because the power was out, and anyhow he doesn't hear the doorbell most of the time. I even tried throwing pebbles at our bedroom windows, but that doesn't work as well in real life as it does in books. So finally I thought, well, I would just settle in the hammock and wait till morning. It wasn't so bad, really. It was kind of nice. All the lights were out, the streetlights and people's house lights, and the only sounds were the leaves dripping and the tree frogs peeping. I curled up in the hammock and went to sleep, and in the morning when I woke it was still too early for your dad to be up, so I figured I'd walk down the block a ways to see the damage. The whole neighborhood was a disaster zone, Denny! Enormous trunks and branches lying clear across the street, electrical lines draped everywhere, a car smushed in front of the Browns' place . . . And that's when Sax Brown saw me, when I went to check the smushed car to make sure nobody was trapped inside. Oh, I know what it must have looked like: I was half a block from home in a nightgown with a muddy hem. Not very confidence-inspiring!" And she gave a little laugh.

Denny said, "Okay . . ."

"But it's no reason to call in the nursemaids."

"No, it doesn't sound like it," Denny said.

"Oh, good."

"It sounds more like, say, a confluence of circumstances outside of your control. I can certainly relate to *that*."

"So you agree that none of you needs to be here," Abby said. "Not that I don't love having you, of course, each and every one of you. But I certainly don't *need* you."

"Why didn't you tell Stem all this?"

"Stem? Well, I did. I tried to. I tried to tell everyone."

"Why don't you ask *him* to leave? Why ask me and not him?"

"Oh, sweetheart, I'm not asking you to leave. I hope you'll stay as long as you like. I'm just saying I don't need a babysitter. *You* understand that. Stem just . . . doesn't. He's more on your father's wavelength, you know? He and Dad put their heads together sometimes and develop these *notions*, you know what I mean?"

"I know exactly what you mean," Denny said.

But then just as Abby was sitting back in her seat with an expression of relief, her forehead finally losing its tightness, he said, "Same old same old," and stood up and walked out of the kitchen.

It was a piece of bad luck that one of Abby's orphans showed up for Sunday lunch. Atta, her name was, and some complicated last name—a recent immigrant in her late fifties or so, overweight and putty-skinned, wearing a heavy, belted dress and stockings that looked like Ace bandages. (It was ninety-two degrees out, and stockings had not been seen in Baltimore for months.) The first anybody knew of her, she was standing outside the front screen door rat-tat-tatting and calling, "Hello? I have come to the right place?"

"Khello" was how she pronounced it, and "have" sounded like "khev."

"Oh, my goodness!" Abby said. She was descending the stairs behind Stem, both of them carrying stacks of papers they were hoping to find space for in the sunroom. "Atta, isn't it? Why, how nice to . . ."

She turned to pile her papers on top of Stem's, and then she opened the screen door for Atta. "I am early?" Atta asked as she clomped in. "I think not. You said twelve thirty."

"No, of course not. We're just . . . This is my son Stem," Abby said. "Atta's new to Baltimore, Stem, and she doesn't know a soul yet. I met her at the supermarket."

"How do you do," Stem said. He wasn't able to shake hands, but he nodded at Atta over his armload of papers. "Excuse me; I'll just go set these down someplace."

"Come and have a seat," Abby told Atta. "Did you have any trouble finding us?"

"Of course not. But you did say twelve thirty."

"Yes?" Abby said uncertainly. Maybe the problem was her outfit; she was wearing a sleeveless blouse with a chain of safety pins dangling from the tip of one breast, and wide aqua pants that stopped just below the knee. "We're pretty informal here," she said. "We tend not to dress up much. Oh, here's my husband! Red, this is Atta. She's come to have Sunday lunch with us."

"How do you do," Red said, shaking hands. In his other hand he carried a screwdriver. He'd been fiddling with the cable box again.

"I do not eat red meat," Atta told him in a loud, flat voice.

"Oh, no?"

"In my own country I eat meat, but here they put hormones." ("Khormones.")

"Huh," Red said.

"Sit down, both of you," Abby told them, and then, as Stem re-emerged from the sunroom, "Stem, sit down and keep Atta company while I go see to lunch."

Stem sent her a look of distress, but Abby gave him a brilliant smile and left the room.

In the kitchen, Nora stood at the counter slicing tomatoes. "What am I going to do?" Abby asked her. "We have an unexpected guest for lunch and she doesn't eat red meat."

Without turning, Nora said, "How about some of that tuna salad Douglas got at the grocery?"

"Oh, good idea. Where's Denny?"

"He's playing catch with the boys."

Abby went to the screen door and looked out. In the backyard, Sammy was chasing a missed ball while Denny stood waiting, idly pounding his glove. "Maybe I'll just let him be," Abby said, and then she said, "Oh, my," on a long, sighing breath and went to the fridge for the iced tea.

In the living room, Atta was telling Red and Stem what was wrong with Americans. "They act extremely warm and open," she said, "extremely hello-Atta-how-are-you, but then, nothing. I have not one friend here."

"Oh, now," Red said, "I'm sure you'll have friends by and by."

"I think I will not," she said.

Stem asked, "Will you be joining a church?"

"No."

"Because Nora, my wife, she belongs to a church, and they've got a whole committee just to welcome new arrivals."

"I will not be joining a church," Atta said.

A silence fell. Red finally said, "I didn't quite catch that last bit."

Stem and Atta looked at him, but neither spoke.

"*Here* we are!" Abby caroled, breezing in with a tray. She set it on the coffee table. "Who'd like a glass of iced tea?"

"Oh, thanks, hon," Red said in a heartfelt way.

"Has Atta been telling you about her family? She has the most unusual family."

"Yes," Atta said, "my family was exceptional. Everybody envied us." She plucked a packet of NutraSweet from a bowl and held it close to her eyes, her lips twitching slightly as she read the fine print. She replaced the packet in the bowl. "We came from a distinguished line of scientists on both sides, and we had many intellectual discussions. Other people wished they could be members."

"Isn't that unusual?" Abby said, beaming.

Red sank lower in his chair.

At lunch, there was such a crowd that the grandchildren had to eat in the kitchen—all but Amanda's Elise, age fourteen, who considered herself an adult. Twelve people sat in the dining room: Red and Abby, their four children and the children's three spouses, Elise, Atta, and Mrs. Angell, Jeannie's live-in mother-in-law. The dinner plates were practically touching, with the silverware bunched between them, and people kept saying, "I'm sorry; is this your glass or mine?" Abby, at least, seemed to find the situation exhilarating. "What a *multitude!*" she told her children. "Isn't this fun?" They eyed her morosely.

Earlier there had been a little huddle in the kitchen, where most of them had retreated soon after being introduced to Atta. When Abby made the mistake of walking in on them, they drew apart to glare at her. "Mom, how *could* you?" Amanda asked, and Jeannie said, "I thought you'd promised to stop doing this."

"Doing what?" Abby asked. "Honestly, if you all can't show a little hospitality toward a stranger . . ."

"This was supposed to be just family! You're never satisfied with just family! Aren't we ever enough for you?"

By now, though, things had settled down to a simmer. Amanda's Hugh was making his usual production of the carving (he had taken a special course, after which he always insisted on doing the honors), although Red kept muttering, "It's *boneless*, for God's sake; what's the big deal?" Nora glided in and out of the kitchen, quieting the children and mopping up spills, while Mrs. Angell, a sweet-faced woman with a puff of blue-white hair, did her best to draw Atta into conversation. She inquired about Atta's work, her native foods, and her country's health-care system, but Atta slammed each question to the ground and let it lie there like a dead shuttlecock. "Will you be applying for American citizenship?" Mrs. Angell asked at one point. "Decidedly not," Atta said.

"Oh."

"Atta has been finding Americans unfriendly," Abby told Mrs. Angell.

"My heavens! I never heard *that* before!"

"Oh, they *pretend* to be friendly," Atta said. "My colleagues ask, 'How are you, Atta?' They say, 'Good to see you, Atta.' But do they invite me home with them? No."

"That's shocking."

"They are, how do you say? Two-faced," Atta said.

Jeannie leaned across the table to ask Denny, "Remember B. J. Autry?"

Denny said, "Mm-hmm."

"I just suddenly thought of her; I don't know why."

Amanda snickered, and Stem gave a groan. *They* knew why. (B. J., with her strident voice and her grating laugh, had been one of their mother's more irksome orphans.) Denny, though, studied Jeannie for a moment without smiling, and then he turned to Atta and said, "I think you've made a mistake."

"Oh?" she said. " 'Two-faced' is an incorrect term?"

"In this situation, yes. 'Polite' would more accurate. They're trying to be polite. They don't much like you, so they don't invite you to their homes, but they're doing their best to be nice to you, and so that's why they ask how you are and tell you it's good to see you."

Abby said, "Oh! Denny!"

"What."

"And also," Atta told him, apparently unfazed, "they say, 'Have a nice weekend, Atta.' How should I do *that*? This is what I should ask them."

"Right," Denny said. He smiled at his mother. She sat back in her chair and gave a sigh.

"Behold!" Amanda's Hugh crowed, spearing a slice of beef with his carving fork. "See this, Red?"

"Eh?"

"This slice has your name on it. Observe the paper-thinness."

"Oh, okay, thank you, Hugh," Red said.

Amanda's Hugh was famous in the family for asking, once, why there seemed to be a diploma under the azalea bushes. He'd been referring to the white PVC drainage pipe leading from the basement sump pump. The family never got over it. ("Seen any diplomas out in the shrubbery lately, Hugh?") They liked him well enough, but they marveled at how astonishingly impractical he was, how out of touch with matters they considered essential. He couldn't even replace a wall switch! He was trim and model-handsome and accustomed to admiration, and he kept seizing on new careers and then abandoning them in a fit of impatience. Currently, he owned a restaurant called Thanksgiving that served only turkey dinners.

Jeannie's Hugh, by contrast, was a handyman who worked at the college Jeannie'd gone to. The other girls had had their hearts set on pre-med students, but evidently one look at unassuming Hugh, with his sawdust-colored beard and his tool belt slung low around his hips, had made Jeannie feel instantly at home. Now, here was someone she could relate to! They married during her senior year, causing some discomfort among the college administrators.

At the moment, he was asking Elise all about her ballet, which was considerate of him. (She'd been left out of the conversation up till then.) "Is it on account of ballet that you're wearing your hair so tight?" he asked, and Elise said, "Yes, Madame O'Leary requires it," and sat up taller—a reed-thin, ostentatiously poised child—and touched the little doughnut on the tippy-top of her head.

"But what if you were frizzy-haired and couldn't make it stay in place?" he asked. "Or what if you were one of those people whose hair will only grow so long?"

"No exceptions are made," Elise told him severely. "We have to have a chignon."

"Well, shoot!"

"And also these flowing skirts," Amanda told him. "They tie them on over their leotards. Everyone expects tutus, but tutus are just for performances."

Abby said, "Oh, Jeannie, remember when Elise was just born and we dressed her in a tutu?"

"Do I!" Jeannie said. She laughed. "She had three of them, remember? We dressed her in one tutu after the other."

"Your mom had asked us to babysit," Abby told Elise. "It was the first time she was leaving you and she felt safer starting with family. So we told her, 'Go on! Go!' and the instant she was gone we stripped you down to your diaper and started trying clothes on you. Every single piece of clothing you'd gotten at your baby shower."

"*I* never knew that," Amanda said, while Elise looked pleased and self-conscious.

"Oh, we'd been dying to get our hands on all those cunning outfits. Not just the tutus but a darling little sailor dress and a bikini swimsuit and then—remember, Jeannie?—navy-ticking coveralls with a hammer loop."

"Of course I remember," Jeannie said. "I was the one who gave them to her."

"Well, we were sort of punch-drunk," Abby explained to Atta. "Elise was the first grandchild."

"Or else not," Denny said.

"What, sweetie?"

"You seem to be forgetting that Susan was the first grandchild."

"Oh! Well, of course. Yes, I just meant the first grandchild who was close; I mean geographically close. I wouldn't forget Susan for the world!"

"How *is* Susan?" Jeannie asked.

"She's good," Denny said.

He ladled gravy over his meat and passed the tureen to Atta, who squinted into it and passed it on.

"What's she doing with her summer?" Abby asked.

"She's in some kind of music program."

"Music, how nice! Is she musical?"

"I guess she must be."

"Which instrument?"

"Clarinet?" Denny said. "Clarinet."

"Oh, I figured maybe French horn."

"Why would you figure that?"

"Well, *you* used to play French horn."

Denny sliced into his meat.

"What's Susan doing over the summer?" Red asked.

Everyone looked at him.

"Clarinet, Red," Abby said finally.

"Eh?"

"Clarinet!"

"My grandson in Milwaukee plays the clarinet," Mrs. Angell said. "It's hard to listen to him without giggling, though. Every third or fourth note comes out as this terrible squawk." She turned to Atta and said, "I have thirteen grandchildren, can you believe it? Do you have grandchildren, Atta?"

"How would that be possible?" Atta demanded.

Another silence fell, this one heavy and muffling, like a blanket, and they all turned their attention to the food.

After lunch Atta took her leave, carrying with her the remains of the store-bought sheet cake they'd served for dessert. (She'd barely touched the tuna salad—"Mercury," she had announced—but it seemed she had quite a sweet tooth.) Elise joined the other children in the backyard, but everyone else went out onto the porch. Even Nora had been persuaded to leave the kitchen cleanup till later, and Red chose to nap in the mildew-smelling hammock at the south end of the porch rather than up in his room.

"Why are Dad's arms so splotchy?" Denny asked his sisters in a low voice. The three of them were sharing the porch swing.

But it was Abby who answered, sharp-eared as always. She broke off a conversation with Mrs. Angell to call, "It's the blood thinner he's on. It makes him subject to bruising."

"And since when has he started napping?"

"The doctors ordered him to do that. He's supposed to nap even on weekdays, but he doesn't."

Denny was quiet a moment, absently kicking the swing back and forth and watching a gray squirrel skitter beneath a bush. "Interesting how nobody told me about his heart attack," he said. "I didn't know a thing till last night. If I hadn't happened to phone Jeannie, I might not ever have known."

"Well, it's not as if you could have made any difference," Amanda said.

"Thanks heaps, Amanda."

Abby stirred protestingly in her rocker.

"Hasn't it been just the loveliest summer?" Mrs. Angell asked in a lilting voice.

Since in fact it had been a very hot summer, wracked by violent storms, it was obvious that she was merely trying to change the subject. Abby reached over to pat her hand. "Oh, Lois," she said, "you always look on the bright side."

"But I enjoy the heat, don't you?"

"Yes," Abby said, "but I can't help thinking of those poor souls down in the inner city with no means of keeping cool."

The Whitshanks themselves kept cool only with ceiling fans and a cleverly rigged attic fan and high, old-fashioned ceilings. Every now and then Red talked about installing air conditioning, but he said it didn't sit right with him to disturb the bones of the house. Even the porch had ceiling fans, three of them, spaced out along its length—beautiful old fans with varnished wooden blades that matched the varnished porch ceiling and floor and the honey-colored porch swing and the wide front steps. (Junior's choices, all of them, and Junior's decision to set the lacy windowless transoms above every ground-floor doorway to let the breezes flow through.) And then the tulip poplars, of course: they provided shade, although Abby often complained about too *much* shade. Nothing would grow beneath them; the lawn was mostly packed earth with a few hardy sprigs of crabgrass poking forth, and the only plants that bloomed along the north edge of the lot were the hostas, with their miserly buds and their giant, monstrous leaves.

"What are the Nelson kids up to?" Jeannie asked, her eyes on the Nelsons' house across the street.

"I'm not sure," Abby said. "Nowadays, you ask people about their children and you can see they wish you hadn't.

They say, 'Well, our son just graduated from Yale but at the moment he's, um . . .' and then it turns out he's bartending or brewing cappuccinos, and more often than not he's moved back home again."

"He's lucky if he's found a job at all," Amanda's Hugh said. "I've had to start laying off some of my wait staff."

"Oh, dear, is the restaurant not doing well?"

"It seems nobody's eating out anymore."

"But now Hugh has this *better* idea," Amanda said. "He's thought up a whole new business, provided he can find backers."

"Really," Abby said. She frowned.

"Do Not Pass Go," Hugh said.

"What?"

"That would be the name of my company. Catchy, right?"

"But what would it . . . do?"

"It's a service for anxious travelers," Hugh said. "Anxious to excess, I mean. You probably have no idea these people exist, since none of you ever travel, but I've seen a few, believe me. My own cousin, for one; my cousin Darcy. She packs so far ahead of time she has nothing left to wear. She packs *everything*, for every possible eventuality. She thinks her house mysteriously senses that she's about to leave it; she says that just hours before a trip it will spring a leak or develop a sewage backup or a malfunction in the burglar alarm. The instructions she writes for the dog sitter are practically novels. She starts to suspect her cat has diabetes.

143

So what I'm thinking is, for people like Darcy we would do all the prep work. *Way* more than what travel agents do. She gives us the dates and the destination, and 'Say no more,' we tell her. We not only reserve her flight and her hotel; we pack her suitcases three days ahead and ship them off express; no checked baggage. We arrange for the trip to the airport and the driver at the other end, the museum tickets and the tour guides and the tables at all the best restaurants. But that's only the beginning! We have the pet care covered, the house-maintenance service on call (I need to talk to Red about that), we've lined up an English-speaking doctor just blocks from her hotel, and we've scheduled a hair appointment for halfway through the trip. Three hours before her flight we ring her doorbell. 'It's time,' we say. 'Oh,' she might tell us, 'but the thing of it is, my mother has developed congestive heart failure and might go at any minute.' 'Yes, *this*,' we say, and we whip out a cell phone, 'this is your cell phone with European capabilities, and your mother has the number and so does her assisted-living facility, and we've purchased travel insurance that guarantees your immediate flight home in case of any medical emergency.'"

Denny laughed, but none of the others did.

"That would have to be a very rich traveler," Jeannie's Hugh said.

"Well, I admit it's not going to be cheap."

"Very rich and very crazy, both at once. Wrapped up in one single person. How many of those could be living here in Baltimore?"

"Sheesh, man! Way to encourage a guy!"

"Oh, but I love the *name*," Abby said hastily. "Did you think it up yourself, Hugh?"

"I did."

"And is it . . . When you say 'Do Not Pass Go,' do you mean . . .?"

"You don't have to wade through all the usual planning and fuss at the start, is what I mean."

"*I* see. So it's got nothing to do with jail."

"Jail! God, no."

"And what about your restaurant?" Jeannie asked.

"I'm going to sell it."

"Oh, will anyone want to buy it?"

"Sheesh, people!"

"I was only wondering," Jeannie said.

Mrs. Angell said, "Have you all noticed that lately the birds have started sounding more conversational? It's like they're talking, these days, not singing. Can you hear?"

They took a moment to listen.

"Maybe on account of the heat," Abby suggested.

"I worry they've given up music. Turned to prose."

"Oh, I can't believe they'd do *that*," Abby said. "More likely they're just tired. They've decided to let the crickets take over."

"When my California grandchildren come every summer to visit," Mrs. Angell said, "they always ask, 'What is that *noise*?' 'What noise?' I say. They say, 'That chirping and that whirring, that scritch-scritch-scritching noise.' 'Oh,' I say, 'I believe you must be talking about the crickets or the locusts or whatever. Isn't it funny? I don't even hear them.' 'But they're *deafening*!' they say. 'How can you not hear them?' "

And once she had spoken it seemed they all heard them, although no one had before—the steady racket of them. They made a rhythmic, jingling sound, like the chink-chink of old-fashioned sleigh bells.

Amanda said, "Well, I, for one, think Hugh's idea is brilliant."

"Thank you, hon," Hugh told her. "I'm glad *you* believe in me."

Mrs. Angell said, "Well, of course! We all do! And how about you, Denny?"

"Do I think Hugh is brilliant?"

"What are you working at, I meant."

"Well, nothing," Denny told her. "I'm down here helping my folks out." He tipped his head back against the back of the swing and laced his fingers across his chest.

"It's so nice having him home," Abby told Mrs. Angell.

"Oh, I can imagine!"

"You still with that kitchen outfit?" Jeannie's Hugh asked him.

"Not anymore," Denny said. Then he said, "I've been substitute teaching."

Abby said, "*What?*"

"Substitute teaching. Well, this past spring I was."

"Don't you need a college degree for that?"

"No, as a matter of fact. Although I have one."

Everyone looked at Abby, waiting for her next question. It didn't come. She sat staring across at the Nelsons' house with something tense and set about her mouth. Finally, Jeannie asked it: "You've finished college?"

"Yes," Denny said.

"How did you *do* that?"

"Same way anyone does it, I guess."

They looked again at Abby. She stayed silent.

"Well, you never did much like building things," Stem said after a moment. "I remember from back when you were working with Dad in the summers."

"I've got nothing against building things; I just couldn't stand the customers," Denny said, sitting up straight again. "All those trendy homeowners wanting wine cellars in their basements."

"Wine cellars! Ha!" Stem said. "And dog-washing stations in their garages."

"Dog-washing stations?"

"Lady up in Ruxton."

Denny snorted.

"Mother Whitshank?" Nora asked. "Can I get you anything? A little more iced tea?"

"No, thanks," Abby said shortly.

The grandchildren were migrating now from the backyard to the front, and Sammy even invaded the porch, climbing the steps to throw himself in his mother's lap and complain about his brothers. "*Some*body needs his nap," Nora told him, but she sat on limply, gazing out over Sammy's head to where the other children were debating the rules of their game. "The bushes by the house are safe, but not the ones in the side yard," one was saying.

"But the ones in the side yard are the best places! You can hide underneath them."

"So why would we use them as safes?"

"Oh."

Jeannie's son, Alexander, was It, which was painful to watch because he was the first Whitshank in known history to show a tendency toward pudginess. When he ran, he cast his legs out clumsily and paddled the air with both hands. Ironically, his sister, Deb, was the family's best athlete—a wiry girl with muscular, mosquito-bitten legs—and she beat him to the biggest azalea bush and sang out, "Ha-ha! Safe!"

"Can somebody please call Heidi?" Alexander asked the grownups. "She keeps getting in my way."

Heidi was nowhere near him—she was racing around the perimeter with her usual exuberance—but Stem whistled and she came bounding up the porch steps. "Down, girl," he said. He tousled her mane affectionately, and she gave a resigned whimper and curled herself at his feet.

"Brenda must be getting old," Denny told his sisters. "She'd have been out here chasing Heidi, once upon a time."

Jeannie said, "It kills me to think she's old. Can you imagine this house without a dog?"

"Easily," Denny said. "Dogs are hell on houses."

"Oh, Denny."

"What? They scratch the woodwork, they scuff the floors . . ."

Amanda made a *tch*-ing sound of amusement.

"What's so funny?" he asked her.

"Listen to you! You sound like Dad. You're the only one of us who doesn't have a dog, and Dad claims he wouldn't have one, either, if it were up to him."

"Oh, that's just talk," Abby told them. "Your dad loves Clarence as much as we do."

Her four children exchanged glances.

In the hammock, Red groaned and sat up. "*What* are you saying?" he asked, rummaging through his hair.

"Just talking about how you love dogs, Dad," Jeannie called.

"I do?"

Amanda tapped Denny's wrist. "When will we be seeing Susan?" she asked him.

"Well, she can't visit till we've got a room free to put her up in," Denny said.

Till Stem and his family moved out, was his implication, but Amanda sidestepped that by saying, "She could always share the bunk room with the little boys. Would she mind?"

"Or wait for the beach trip," Jeannie suggested. "That's coming up very soon, and the beach house has tons of beds."

Denny let the subject drop. His eyes followed the children playing in the yard—Petey tussling with Tommy,

Elise pulling them apart and chiding them in her thin, bossy voice.

"Think I'm going to have to call the Petronelli brothers and have them repair the front walk again," Red said, ambling down the porch to join them. On his way, he grabbed a rocker by one of its ears. He set it next to Abby.

"Every time I come here, you're doing something to that walk," Denny told him.

"The trouble goes back to your grandfather's time. He wasn't happy with how it was laid."

"It did seem he was always fiddling with it," Abby said.

"One of my first memories after we moved in was, he had all the mortar ripped out and the stones reset. But still he wasn't satisfied. He claimed it was graded wrong."

"What's that got to do with *now*, though?" Stem asked. "It's been graded several times over, since then. In order to fix that walk once and for all, you'd have to cut down all the poplars with their roots that burrow beneath it, and I don't see you doing that."

"Oh, you men, stop talking shop!" Abby said. "It's too nice a day for that. Isn't it, Lois?"

"Goodness, yes," Mrs. Angell said. "It's a *lovely* day. I believe I feel a bit of a breeze starting up."

It was true that the leaves had begun rustling overhead, and Heidi's petticoats of fur were stirring on her haunches.

"Weather like this always takes me back to the day I fell in love with Red," Abby said dreamily.

The others smiled. They knew the story well; even Mrs. Angell knew it.

Sammy was sound asleep against his mother's breast. Elise was spinning and spinning under a dogwood tree, with her head tipped back and her arms flung out.

"It was a beautiful, breezy, yellow-and-green afternoon . . ." Abby began. Which was the way she always began, exactly the same words, every single time. On the porch, everybody relaxed. Their faces grew smooth, and their hands loosened in their laps. It was so restful to be sitting here with family, with the birds talking in the trees and the crosscut-sawing of the crickets and the dog snoring at their feet and the children calling, "Safe! I'm safe!"

5

On Monday, Denny slept till almost eleven. "Will you look at Mr. Sleepyhead!" Abby said when he finally came downstairs. "What time did you get to bed?"

He shrugged and took a box of cereal from the cupboard. "One thirty?" he said. "Two?"

"Oh, no wonder, then."

"If I stay up late enough, I have some hope of sleeping through," he said. "All those middle-of-the-night thoughts swarming in on me; I hate that."

"Your dad gets up and reads when that happens," Abby told him.

Denny didn't bother answering her. The Whitshanks held two opposing opinions about what to do with their wakeful hours, and they had long ago argued the subject into the ground.

After breakfast, as if to make up for lost time, he became a whirlwind of activity. He vacuumed the whole downstairs, oiled the hinges on the backyard gate, and trimmed the backyard hedge. He skipped lunch to scrub the charcoal grill, and then he borrowed Abby's car and drove to Eddie's to buy steaks to barbecue for supper. Abby told him to charge the steaks to her account, and he didn't argue.

The house seemed invisibly partitioned between Nora and Abby—Nora busying herself in the kitchen or tending her children, Abby up in her bedroom or reading in the living room. They were courteous to each other but wary, clearly trying not to get in each other's way. The only time all day that they engaged in a real conversation was when Denny was at the grocery store. Nora, carrying Sammy upstairs for his afternoon nap, met Abby coming down the stairs with a stack of papers. "Oh, Mother Whitshank," Nora said. "Is that something I can help you with?"

"No, thank you, dear," Abby said. "I just thought while Denny was out of the house I'd collect the last of my things from his room. Though heaven knows where I'll put them."

"Couldn't you pack them into a box and store them in the back of his closet?"

"Oh, no, I don't think so."

"I could bring up a box from the basement. I saw some near the washing machine."

"I don't think so," Abby said more firmly, and then she sighed and patted the spiral-bound notebook on the top of her stack. "I never feel quite comfortable leaving my belongings where Denny can get at them," she said.

"Oh," Nora said. She hitched Sammy higher on her hip, but she didn't continue up the stairs.

"I know he doesn't mean any harm, but I have poems and private journals and little thoughts I've jotted down. I'd feel silly if anyone saw them."

"Well, of course," Nora said.

"So I figured I'd haul it all to the sunroom and do some pruning. Then I'll see if Red will lend me one of his desk drawers."

"I'd be happy to bring down what's left," Nora said.

"Oh, I think I've got everything, dear."

And the two of them went their separate ways.

For supper they had Denny's grilled steaks and Nora's homemade succotash. Nora cooked in a sort of country style; succotash wasn't something the rest of them were accustomed to. And she did that modern thing of preparing a whole different dish for the children when they wouldn't eat their steaks. She went out to the kitchen without complaint and fixed macaroni and cheese from a box. Abby told the boys, "Oh, your poor mother! Isn't she nice to get up from her meal and make you something special," which was her way of saying that her own children used to eat what was set before them. But the boys had heard this before, and they just gazed at her expressionlessly. Only Red seemed to read her meaning. "Now, hon," he told her. "That's how things are done these days."

"Well, I know that!"

The boys had spent the latter part of the afternoon at

the neighborhood pool with Nora, and they were pink-faced and slick-haired and puffy-eyed. Sammy's head kept drooping over his plate; he hadn't slept during his nap. "Early bedtime for all of you," Stem told them.

"Can't we play catch with Uncle Denny first?" Petey asked.

Stem glanced over at Denny.

"Fine with me," Denny said.

"Yippee!"

"How was work today?" Abby asked Red.

Red said, "Work was a pain in the ass. Got this lady who's—"

"Excuse me," Abby said, and she stood up and went out to the kitchen, calling, "Nora, *please* come eat your supper! Let me do the macaroni."

Red rolled his eyes and then, taking advantage of her absence, reached for the butter and added a giant dollop to his succotash.

"I knew that lady was trouble when she brought out her four-inch binder," Stem told Red.

"Pick, pick, pick," Red agreed. "Niggle, niggle, niggle."

Nora emerged from the kitchen with a saucepan and a serving spoon, Abby following. "Great succotash, Nora," Red said.

"Thank you."

She dished macaroni onto Tommy's plate, then Petey's, then Sammy's. Abby resettled herself in her chair and reached for her napkin. "So," she told Red. "You were saying?"

"Pardon?"

"You were saying about work?"

"I forget," Red said huffily.

"He was saying about Mrs. Bruce," Stem told her. "Lady who's getting her kitchen updated."

"I warned her about that grout," Red said. "I told her more than once, I said, 'Ma'am, you go for that urethane grout and you're adding on two days' work time. Cleanup is a bitch.'"

Then he said, "Oh, pardon me," because Nora was sending him a sorrowful look from under her long, heavy lashes.

"Cleanup's hell," he said. "I mean, difficult. Major hazing problem. Didn't I tell her that, Stem?"

"You told her."

"And what does she do? Goes for urethane. Then throws a hissy fit over how much time the guys are taking."

He paused a moment and frowned, perhaps wondering if the word "hissy" were something Nora could object to.

"I don't know why you put up with people like that," Denny said.

"Comes with the territory," Red said.

"I wouldn't stand for it."

"*You* might not," Red told him, "but we don't have that luxury. Half our men were idle for the first two weeks in April. You think that's any picnic? We take what jobs we can get, nowadays, and thank our lucky stars."

"You were the one who was griping," Denny said.

"I was explaining how work *is*, is all. But what would you know about that?"

Denny bent over his steak and sliced off a piece in silence.

"Well!" Abby said. "I don't know when I've eaten such a lovely meal, Nora."

"Yes, it's good, sweetheart," Stem said.

"Denny grilled the steaks," Nora said.

"Good steaks, Denny."

Denny said nothing.

"Now can we play catch?" Tommy asked him.

Stem said, "Let him finish his supper, son."

"No, I'm done," Denny said. "Thanks, Nora." And he pushed back his chair and stood up, even though most of his steak remained and he had barely touched his succotash.

On Tuesday, Denny slept till noon. Then he mopped all the bathroom floors and the floor in the kitchen. He swept the front porch, wiped down the porch furniture, and tightened a loose baluster he discovered in the porch railing. He repaired the clasp on a string of Abby's beads and swapped out the battery in a smoke detector. Later that afternoon, while Nora and the children were at the pool, he put together an elaborate vegetable lasagna to serve for supper that night. Nora had been planning to serve hamburgers and corn on the cob, as she told him when she returned, but Denny said they could have those the next night.

"Or we could have your lasagna the next night," Nora said, "because hamburgers and corn on the cob ought to be eaten fresh."

"Oh, you two!" Abby cried. "Neither one of you needs to trouble yourself about supper. I'm capable of *that* much."

"My lasagna should be eaten fresh too," Denny said. "Look. Nora. I'm just trying to keep busy here. I don't have enough to do."

"There's a reason for that," Abby announced to the room at large. "Too many people are trying to help!"

But she might as well have been a gnat. Neither one of them so much as glanced at her; they were too busy facing each other down.

Supper that night was hamburgers and corn on the cob. Halfway through the meal, Denny asked, in a tone of detached curiosity, "Stem, did it ever occur to you that you may have married your mother?"

"Married my mother?" Stem asked. "Which mother?"

"They both claim to be oh so accommodating, but you notice how—" Denny broke off. "Huh?" he said. "*Which* mother!"

He sat back and stared at Stem.

Nora continued placidly spreading butter on her ear of corn. Stem said, "Nora is very accommodating. I'd like to know how many other women would be willing to pack up and leave their homes behind the way she has."

"Oh," Abby wailed, "but we didn't *ask* her to do that! We wouldn't ask it of any of you!"

Nora said, "Of course you wouldn't, Mother Whitshank. We volunteered. We wanted to do it. Think of all Douglas owes you."

"Owes?" Abby said. She looked stung.

All at once Red came alive at the head of the table and said, "What? *What's* going on?" He glanced from face to face, but Abby made a dismissive downward gesture with one hand, so he didn't pursue it.

On Wednesday, Denny got up at ten thirty, so maybe he was inching into a halfway normal schedule. He vacuumed all the bedrooms and folded a load of laundry that Nora had put in the dryer, completely mixing up which clothes belonged to which person. Then he replaced a button on one of Abby's blouses, leaving a spill of spools and crochet hooks on the shelf in the linen closet where Abby kept her sewing box. After that he played Crazy Eights with the little boys. When Abby told him she was heading off for her pottery class, he offered to drive her, but she said she always hitched a ride with Ree Bascomb. "Suit yourself," Denny said, "but I'm just sitting here twiddling my thumbs; you might as well make use of me."

"You're *very* useful, dear," Abby said. "It's just that Ree and I have been riding together forever. But I appreciate the thought."

"Can I borrow your computer while you're gone?" Denny asked.

"My computer," Abby said. A panicked look crossed her face.

"I'd like to get online."

"Well, you aren't . . . you won't read my e-mail or anything, will you?"

"No, Mom. Who do you take me for?"

She didn't seem reassured.

"I just wanted to connect to the outside world, for once," Denny said. "I'm kind of isolated here."

"Oh, Denny, haven't I been saying? You ought not to *be* here!"

"How welcoming," Denny said.

"Oh, you know what I mean. I'm not an old lady, Denny. I don't need to have my hand held. This is all so unnecessary!"

"Is that so," Denny said.

And then, as if her words had jinxed things, that afternoon she had one of her blank spells.

She had promised to be back from her pottery class around four. They didn't start worrying till five. Red and Stem were home by then, and Red was the one who said, "Don't you figure your mom should be here now? I know she and Ree get to talking, but still!"

"Do you have Ree's phone number?" Denny asked.

"It's on the speed dial. Maybe one of you all could call. I'm not so good on the phone these days."

All three men looked at Nora. "I'll do it," she said.

She went to the phone in the sunroom, and Red tagged after her. Stem and Denny stayed seated in the living room.

"Hello? Mrs. Bascomb?" they heard her say. "This is Nora, Abby Whitshank's daughter-in-law. Do you happen to have her there with you?"

There was a pause, and then she said, "I see. Well, thank you so much! . . . Yes, I'm sure she will. Goodbye." The receiver clicked into its cradle. "They got back to Mrs. Bascomb's an hour ago," she said, "and Mother Whitshank set out for home straightaway."

"Damn! Sorry," Red said. "I've told her and told her, I said, 'Make Ree take you all the way to our door.' She knows she's not supposed to walk home by herself. Shoot, I bet she walked over there, too."

Stem and Denny exchanged glances. The distance was barely a block and a half; it was news to both of them that Abby couldn't be trusted to manage it.

"Maybe she stopped by a friend's house on the way back," Nora said.

"Nora," Red said. "People in this neighborhood do not *stop by*."

"I didn't know that," Nora said.

They returned to the living room, and Denny stood up from his chair. "Okay," he said. "Stem, you walk up Bouton toward Ree's. I'll head in the other direction in case she somehow bypassed the house."

"I'm coming too," Red said.

"Fine."

The three of them left. Nora stepped onto the porch to watch after them, her arms folded across her chest.

Stem took off toward Ree Bascomb's in his long, loping stride, while Red and Denny turned in the opposite direction. Red's pace was more laborious. Always before, he'd been a man in a hurry; now he trudged. They hadn't even reached the third house before they heard Stem call out, "Found her!" Or Denny heard. Red continued plodding on. Denny touched his sleeve. "He found her," he said.

"Eh?" Red turned.

"Stem found her."

They started back, passing home. They could see Stem up at the far end of the block, facing the Lincolns' house, but they couldn't see Abby. Denny walked faster, letting Red drop behind.

Abby was sitting on the brick steps leading to the Lincolns' front walk, with a colorful pottery object resting on her lap. She seemed fine, but she was making no attempt to rise. "I'm so sorry!" she told Denny and Red when they reached her. "I don't know how to explain it. I was just sitting here; that was the first thing I knew. I was sitting on these steps and I thought, 'Am I coming, or am I going?' I honestly couldn't tell. It was so *unsettling*!"

"But you had your pottery," Stem pointed out.

"My what?"

She looked down at it—a charming little clay house, no bigger than a box of notecards. The exterior was a vivid yellow, and the roof was red. A snarl of green pottery tendrils spread across one end of the roof to give a suggestion of leafy boughs.

"My pottery," she said wonderingly.

"So you must have been coming, right? Coming home from pottery class."

"Oh. Right," Abby said. Then she cupped the house in both hands and held it up to them. "My very best work so far!" she said. "See?"

"Good job, hon," Red told her.

And all three men nodded too vigorously, beaming too brightly, like parents admiring a piece of art that a child has brought home from nursery school.

Because of the way the house on Bouton Road was designed, a person could stand at the upstairs hall railing and hear everything that was said in the entrance hall below. The Whitshank children—and sometimes Red as well—used to do this whenever the doorbell rang, lurking invisibly overhead until they could be certain that it wasn't just one of Abby's orphans.

But Merrick, of course, had been a child in that house herself once upon a time, so when she dropped by on Thursday evening, she peered overhead the instant Abby let her in. "Who is that?" she called out. "I know you're up there."

After a pause, Denny appeared at the top of the stairs. "Hi, Aunt Merrick," he said.

"Denny? What are *you* doing home? Hello, Redcliffe," she added, because Red had stepped forward too now, his hair still damp from his after-work shower.

"Hey there," he said.

Abby said, "How nice to see you, Merrick," and gave her a peck on the cheek, craning around the cardboard carton in Merrick's arms.

"Abby," Merrick said neutrally. Then, "Why, hello, cutie!" because Heidi had just bounded in, panting and grinning. Merrick was always much nicer to dogs than to humans. "Who is *this* sweetie pie?" she asked Abby.

"That's Heidi."

"Don't tell me poor old Brenda finally died."

"No . . ." Abby said.

"Well, how do you do, Miss Heidi?" Merrick said, and she shifted her carton to one hip in order to stroke Heidi's long nose.

Not counting the carton, Merrick was the picture of elegance—an angular, hatchet-faced woman, her too-black hair cut as short as a boy's, wearing slim white pants and an Asian-looking tunic. "We're about to leave for a cruise," she told Abby, "and after that I'm going on to the Florida place, so I've brought you all the goodies from my fridge."

"Hmm," Abby said. Merrick was forever foisting her dribs and drabs of leftovers on the family. She disapproved of waste. "Well, bring them in," Abby said, and she led Merrick toward the kitchen. Red and Denny, who had made their way down the stairs as slowly as possible, trailed them at a distance.

"How long are you here for?" Merrick asked Denny.

"I've come to help out," he said.

This didn't exactly answer her question, but before she could press him, Abby broke in to say, "What have you been up to, Merrick? We haven't seen you all summer!"

"You know I hate to come here in hot weather," Merrick said. "It's barbaric, not to have air conditioning in this day and age." She set the carton on the kitchen table with a thump. "Why, Norma," she said.

Nora barely turned from the pot she was stirring. "Nora," she said coolly.

"Does this mean Stem is here, too?" Merrick asked Abby. "Stem *and* Denny, both at the same time?"

"Yes, isn't that lovely?" Abby said in a sort of cheerleader tone.

"Wonders never cease."

"He's upstairs showering just now. I'm sure he'll be down in a minute."

"Why is he showering *here*?"

Abby was saved from having to answer this by Red's sudden "Excuse me?"

"Why here, I said."

"Why what here?"

"Honestly, Redcliffe. Give up and get a hearing aid."

"I have a hearing aid. I have two."

"Get some that work, then."

The three little boys arrived on the back porch, piling against a screen that was already starting to bulge. They yanked the door open and tumbled inside, breathless and overheated-looking. "Is it supper yet?" Petey asked.

"Boys, you remember your Great-Aunt Merrick," Abby said.

"Hi," Petey said uncertainly.

"How do you do," Merrick said, extending her hand. He studied it a moment and then raised his own hand to give her a high five, which didn't quite work out. He ended up accidentally slapping the backs of her fingers. His brothers didn't attempt even that much. "We're hungry!" one of them said. "When's supper?"

"It's all ready," Nora told them. "Go wash up and we can sit down."

"What: *now*?" Merrick asked. "Don't I get a drink?"

Everyone looked at Abby. Abby said, "Oh. Would you like one?"

"I don't suppose you have any vodka," Merrick said happily.

There was a moment when it seemed that Abby might say no, but then some sort of hostess instinct must have kicked in, and she said, "Of course." (They had it because of Merrick.) Red and Denny slumped. "Will you see to the drinks, dear?" Abby asked Denny. "Let's the rest of us go to the living room."

As she and Red and Merrick left the kitchen, Petey was

heard to say, "But we're starving!" and Nora murmured something in reply.

"I haven't had a chance to sit down all day," Merrick told Abby as they crossed the hall. "It's exhausting, getting ready for a trip."

"Where are you off to?"

"We're taking a cruise down the Danube."

"How nice."

"Wouldn't you know, Trey is being a bore about it. He'd rather go golfing somewhere. Oh! Brenda! There you are! God, she looks dead, the poor darling. What happened to Father's clock?"

Abby glanced from Brenda, stretched out on the cooling hearthstones, to the clock on the mantel above. A crack ran across the glass of its case. "There was a little mishap with a baseball," she said. "Won't you have a seat?"

"Boys are so hard on houses," Merrick said, folding herself into an armchair. She had been shadowed by Heidi, who settled expectantly at her knee. "And why are there so many of them? Did I count three?"

"Oh, yes," Abby said. "There are three, all right."

"Was the third one planned?" Merrick asked. "Oh. Stem. Hello. Had you *planned* on a third child?"

"Not really," Stem said cheerfully. He gave off the scent of Dial soap as he crossed the room to a chair. "How're you doing, Aunt Merrick?"

"I'm exhausted, I was just saying," Merrick told him. "It seems preparing for a trip gets more tiring every year."

"Why not stay home, then?"

"What!" she said in horror. Then she sat up straighter; Denny was bringing the drinks. In one hand he held a tumbler tinkling with ice and filled to the brim with vodka, and in the other a glass of white wine. Three cans of beer were tucked perilously under his left arm. "*Here* we go," he said. He placed the tumbler on the lamp table next to her. He crossed to give Abby the wine and then handed a can of beer each to Red and Stem, after which he sat down on the couch with the third can and popped the tab. "Cheers," he said.

Merrick took a deep swig of her drink and breathed out a long "Ah." She asked Denny, "Is Sarah here too?"

"Who's Sarah?"

"Sarah your daughter."

"Susan, you mean."

"Susan, Sarah . . . Is *Susan* here too?"

"She's coming down for the beach trip."

"Oh, God, not that everlasting beach trip," Merrick said. "You're like lemmings about that beach! Or spawning salmon, or something. Don't you all ever think about vacationing any place else?"

"We *love* the beach," Abby told her.

"Really," Merrick said, and she drew her sharp purple fingernails languidly across the top of Heidi's head. "Sometimes it amazes me that our ancestors had the gumption to make it to America," she told Red.

"Excuse me?"

"America!" she shouted.

Red looked confused.

"Mother and Father never traveled at all, if you'll remember," she told him.

"Well, you have certainly made up for that," Red said. "You seem to need more than one house, even."

"What can I say? I hate winter."

"In my opinion," Red said, "going to Florida for the winter is kind of like . . . not paying your dues. Not standing fast for the hard part."

"Are you calling Baltimore summers the *easy* part?" Merrick asked. Then, as if to prove her point, she said "Whew!" and left off petting Heidi to bat a hand in front of her face. "Can somebody turn that fan up a notch?"

Stem rose and gave the fan cord a tug.

"*I* can see why you might want two houses," Denny spoke up. "Or even more than two. I get that. I bet sometimes when you wake in the morning you don't know where you are for a moment, am I right? You're completely disoriented."

"Well . . . I guess," Merrick said.

"Before you open your eyes you think, 'Why does it feel like the light is coming from my left? I thought the window was on my right. Which house is this, anyway?' Or you get out of bed at night to go pee and you walk into a wall. 'Whoa!' you say. 'Where's the bathroom gone?' "

Merrick said, "Well . . ." and Abby took on a worried look. Evidently Denny was having one of his unexpectedly confiding moments.

"I *love* that feeling," he said. "You don't know your place in the world; you're not pegged; you're not nailed into this one single same old never-ending spot."

"I suppose," Merrick said.

"You think that might be the reason people travel?" he asked. "I'll bet it could be. Is that why *you* travel?"

"Oh, well, it's more like I'm just trying to get as far as possible from Trey's mother," Merrick said. She swirled the ice in her glass. "The old bat just celebrated her ninety-ninth birthday," she told Red. "Can you believe it? Queen Eula the Immortal. I swear, I think she's staying alive just to spite me. It's not only that she's a pill herself; I blame her for making Trey such a pill. She spoiled that man rotten, I tell you. Gave him every little thing he ever wanted: the Prince of Roland Park."

Red put a hand to his forehead and said, "This is so *eerie*! Is it déjà vu? Why do I feel like I've heard this someplace before?"

"And the older he gets, the worse he gets," she went on obliviously. "Even when he was young he was a hopeless hypochondriac, but now! Believe me, it was a dark day in the universe when the Internet started letting people research their medical symptoms."

She might have gone on (she usually did), but at that moment Petey came into the room. "Grandma," he said, "can we have the last of that fudge ripple?"

"What: before supper?" Abby asked.

"We're already eating our supper."

"Yes, you can have it. And take Heidi when you go, will you? She's sneezing again."

It was true that Heidi had started sneezing—a whole fit of sneezes, light but spattery. "Gesundheit," Merrick told her. "What's the trouble, honeybunch? Coming down with something?"

"She does this all day long," Abby said. "You wouldn't suppose sneezing would be such an irritation, but it is."

Petey said, "Mom thinks it's on account of she's allergic to Grandma's rugs."

"Well, I wouldn't bring her to visit, then, poor baby," Merrick said.

"She's got to visit. She lives here."

"Heidi lives here?"

"She lives here with us."

"*You* live here?"

"Yes, and Sammy's allergic, too. All night he breathes dramatically."

Merrick looked at Abby.

"Take Heidi to the kitchen, Petey," Abby said. "Yes," she told Merrick, "they've moved in to help out; isn't that nice?"

"Help out with what?"

"Well, just . . . you know. We're getting older!"

"I'm getting older too, but I haven't turned my house into a commune."

"To each his own, I guess!" Abby sang out merrily.

"Wait," Merrick said. "Is there something someone's not telling me? Has one of you been diagnosed with some terminal disease?"

"No, but after Red's heart attack—"

"Red had a heart attack?"

"You knew that. You sent him a fruit basket in the hospital."

"Oh," Merrick said. "Yes, maybe I did."

"And I'm not so spry either, lately."

"This is ridiculous," Merrick said. "Two people get a bit wobbly and their entire family moves in with them? I never heard of such a thing."

Denny cleared his throat. "Actually," he said, "Stem is not here on a permanent basis."

"Well, thank heaven."

"*I* am."

Merrick looked at him, waiting for him to go on. The others stared down at their laps.

"I'm the one who's staying," Denny said.

Stem said, "Well, not—"

"Oh, for God's sake, why is *anyone* staying?" Merrick asked. "If your parents are really so decrepit—and I must say I find that hard to believe; they're barely in their seventies—they should move to a retirement community. That's what other people do."

"We're too independent for a retirement community," Red told her.

"Independent? Bosh. That's just another word for selfish.

It's stiff-backed people like you who end up being the biggest burdens."

Stem rose to his feet. "Well," he said, "I guess Nora must be fretting about her supper getting cold," and he stood waiting in the center of the room.

Everyone looked at him in surprise. Finally Merrick said, "Oh, *I* see. Clear that tiresome woman out of here; she tells too many home truths." But she was standing up as she spoke, draining the last of her drink as she moved toward the front hall. "I know, I know," she said. "I see how it is."

The others rose to follow her. "Here," Merrick said at the door, and she thrust her empty glass at Abby. "And by the way," she told Denny. "You're supposed to have a life by now. You're only putting things off, scurrying back home on the slightest excuse."

She left, clicking across the porch with a brisk, energetic stride, like someone triumphant in the knowledge that she had set everybody straight.

"What is she *talking* about?" Denny asked after a moment.

Abby said, "Oh, you know how she is."

"I can't abide that woman."

Ordinarily Abby would have tut-tutted, but now she just sighed and headed for the kitchen.

The men went into the dining room and settled at the table, none of them speaking, although Red did say, as he dropped onto his chair, "Ah, me." They waited in a kind of drained silence. From the kitchen they could hear the burble of the little boys' voices and a clatter of utensils. Then Nora emerged through the swinging door, carrying a casserole. Abby came behind with a salad. "You should see Merrick's leftovers," she told the men. "A smidgen of store-bought pasta sauce in the bottom of a jar. A wedge of Brie completely hollowed out inside the rind. And . . . what else, Nora?" she asked.

"A cold broiled lamb chop," Nora said, setting the casserole on the table.

"A lamb chop, yes, and a Chinese take-out carton of rice, and one single, solitary pickle in a bottle of scummy brine."

"We should put her in touch with Hugh," Denny said.

"Hugh?" Abby asked.

"Amanda's Hugh. Do Not Pass Go. She could call him before every trip."

"Oh, you're right," Abby said. "They're made for each other!"

"He'd tell her he knows a soup kitchen that's *dying* to have her leftovers, and he'd come by her house and collect them and take them off to the trash."

This made the others laugh—even Nora, a little. Red said, "Oh, now. You folks," but he was laughing too.

"What?" Tommy asked. He'd cracked open the door from the kitchen. "What's so funny?"

None of them wanted to say; they just smiled and shook their heads. To a child, they must have looked like some happy, cozy club that only grown-ups could belong to.

*

It took a total of five vehicles to carry them all to the beach. They could have managed with fewer, but Red insisted, as usual, on driving his pickup. How else could they bring everything they needed, he always asked—the rafts and boogie boards, the sand toys for the children, the kites and the paddle-ball racquets and the giant canvas shade canopy with its collapsible metal frame? (In the old days, before computers, he used to include the entire *Encyclopaedia Britannica*.) So he and Abby made the three-hour trip in the pickup, while Denny drove Abby's car with Susan in the passenger seat and the food hampers in the rear. Stem and Nora and the three little boys came in Nora's car, and Jeannie and Jeannie's Hugh started out separately from their own house with their two children, though not with Hugh's mother, who always spent the beach week visiting Hugh's sister in California.

Amanda and Amanda's Hugh and Elise traveled on a whole different day—Saturday morning instead of Friday afternoon, since Amanda always had trouble getting away from her law office—and they stayed in a different cottage, because Amanda's Hugh couldn't tolerate what he called the hurly-burly.

None of the dogs came. They were all boarding at Penpals.

The house the Whitshanks rented every summer stood right on the beach—a comparatively uncrowded stretch of the Delaware coast—but it wasn't what you'd call luxurious. The walls were tongue-and-groove, painted a depressing pea-soup green; the floorboards were so splintery no one dared go barefoot; the kitchen dated from the 1940s. But it was big enough for all of them, and far homier than the glittering new mansions with giant Palladian windows that had popped up elsewhere along the shore. Besides, Red could always use a few fix-it jobs to keep him occupied. (He wasn't a natural vacationer.) Even before Abby and Nora had unpacked the food, he had happily catalogued half a dozen minor household emergencies. "Will you look at this outlet!" he said. "Practically dangling by a thread!" And off he went to the truck for his tools, with Jeannie's Hugh not far behind.

"The next-door people are back," Jeannie called, stepping in from the screen porch.

Next door was almost the only house as unassuming as theirs was, and the people she was referring to had been renting it for at least as long as the Whitshanks had been renting theirs. Oddly enough, though, the two families never socialized. They smiled at each other if they happened to be out on the beach at the same time, but they didn't speak. And although Abby had once or twice debated inviting them over for drinks, Red always voted her down. Leave things as they were, he told her: less chance of any unwelcome intrusions in the future. Even Amanda and Jeannie, on the lookout during the early days for playmates, had hung back shyly, because the next-door people's two daughters always brought friends of their own, and besides, they were slightly older.

So for all these years—thirty-six, now—the Whitshanks had watched from a distance while the slender young parents next door grew thicker through the middle and their hair turned gray, and their daughters changed from children to young women. One summer in the late nineties, when the daughters were still in their teens, it was noticed that the father of the family never once went down to the water, spending the week instead lying under a blanket in a chaise longue on their deck, and the summer after that, he was no longer with them. A muted, sad little group the next-door people had been that year, when always before they had seemed to enjoy themselves so; but they did come, and they continued to come, the mother taking her early-morning walks along the beach alone now, the daughters in the company of boyfriends who metamorphosed into husbands, by and by, and then a little boy appearing and later a little girl.

"The grandson has brought a friend this year," Jeannie reported. "Oh, that makes me want to cry."

"Cry! What for?" Hugh asked her.

"It's the . . . circularity, I guess. When we first saw the next-door people the daughters were the ones bringing friends, and now the grandson is, and it starts all over again."

"You sure have given these folks a lot of thought," Hugh said.

"Well, they're *us*, in a way," Jeannie said.

But you could see Hugh found that hard to understand.

On the Friday that the Whitshanks arrived, only the

men and the children went down to the water. The women were busy unpacking and making beds and organizing supper. But by Saturday, when Amanda and her family showed up, they'd all settled into their routine of a full morning on the beach, and lunch at the house in their sandy swimsuits, and then afternoon on the beach again. The canvas canopy sheltered the white-skinned Whitshank grown-ups, but the in-laws sat brazenly in the sun. Stem's three little boys challenged the breakers to bowl them over but then ran away at the last minute, shrieking with laughter, while Stem stood guard at the water's edge with his arms folded. Amanda's Elise, storky and pale in a tutu-like swimsuit, stayed high and dry on a corner of the blanket underneath the canopy, but Susan and Deb spent most of their time diving through the waves. Susan was fourteen this summer—Elise's age, but she seemed to have more in common with thirteen-year-old Deb. Both she and Deb were children still, although Deb was a skinny little thing while Susan was more solidly built, waistless and nearly flat-chested but with something almost voluptuous about her full lips and her large brown eyes. The two of them had a bedroom to themselves this year. Elise used to bunk with them rather than in her parents' cottage, but not any longer. (She'd gotten stuck up, Deb and Susan claimed.) Alexander was mostly on his own as well—too young for the girls and too sedentary for Stem's boys. Mostly he stayed seated at the water's edge, letting the surf froth up and then ebb around his soft white legs, except for when

his father coaxed him into a game of paddle ball or a ride
on a raft.

Elsewhere on the beach, teenagers built giant sand castles,
and mothers dipped their babies' bare feet in the foam, and
fathers threw Frisbees to their children. Seagulls screamed
overhead, and a little plane flew up and down the coastline,
trailing a banner that advertised all-you-can-eat crabs.

Amanda and Amanda's Hugh didn't seem to be getting
along. Or Amanda wasn't getting along; Hugh appeared
cheerfully unaware. Anything he said to her she answered
shortly, and when he invited her to take a walk on the
beach, she said, "No, thanks," and turned the corners of
her mouth down as she watched him set off on his own.

Abby, sitting next to Amanda but outside the canopy,
under the sun, said, "Oh, poor Hugh! Don't you think
you should go with him?" (She was eternally monitoring
her daughters' marriages.) But Amanda didn't answer, and
Abby gave up and went back to her reading. A stack of
trashy magazines had been discovered beneath the TV,
no doubt left behind by a previous renter, and they had
passed through the hands of her granddaughters and then
her daughters and ended up with Abby herself, who was
leafing through one now and tsk-ing over the silliness. "All
this excitement about could so-and-so be pregnant," she
told her daughters, "and I don't even know who so-and-so
is! I've never heard of her." In her skirted pink swimsuit,
her plump shoulders glistening with suntan lotion and her
legs lightly dusted with sand, she looked something like a

cupcake. She hadn't ventured into the water at all so far, and neither had Red. In fact, Red was wearing his work shoes and dark socks. Evidently this was the year when the two of them were declaring themselves to be officially old.

"I remember when I first met him, I thought he was a jerk," Amanda told Denny. She must have been referring to Hugh. "I had that apartment on Chase Street with a garbage chute at the end of the hall, and I kept finding bags of garbage just sitting on the floor around the chute, not sent down the way they should have been. And poking out of the bag I'd see beer bottles and chili cans, things that should have been put in the recycling bin. It made me furious! So one day I taped a sign to a bag: WHOEVER DID THIS IS A PIG."

"Oh, Amanda! Honestly," Abby said, but Amanda didn't seem to hear her. "I don't know how he knew it was me," she told Denny, "but he must have. He knocked on my door and he was holding my sign. 'Did you write this?' he said, and I said, 'I most certainly did.' Well, he put on this big charm act. Said he was terribly sorry, it wouldn't happen again, he didn't know the recycling rules and he hadn't sent the bag down the chute because it wouldn't fit, blah blah— as if that were any excuse. But I admit, he won me over. You know what, though? I should have paid attention. There it was, all spelled out for me from the beginning: This is a man who thinks he's the only person on the planet. How much clearer could it have been?"

"So, *now* does he recycle?" Denny asked.

"You're missing the point," Amanda said. "I'm talking about his nature, the very nature of the man. It's all about what's expedient, for him. He's just arranged to sell the restaurant to someone for next to nothing, for a song, merely because he's bored and he wants to go into something new. Can you believe it?"

"I thought you approved of the something new," Denny said. "I thought you said it was brilliant."

"Oh, I was just being supportive. Besides, it's not the something new I mind; it's the way he goes about getting rid of the old. He didn't even consult me! Just took the very first offer he got, because he wants what he wants when he wants it."

Abby touched Amanda's arm. She sent a meaningful glance toward Elise, but Amanda said, "*What*," and turned away again. And Elise just then stood up in one long graceful movement and began walking toward the water, as if nothing the grown-ups said could have anything to do with her.

"*I* didn't know that was how you met," Abby said. "That's kind of like a movie! Like a Rock Hudson–Doris Day movie where they start out hating each other. I thought you met in the elevator or something."

"The man is impossible," Amanda said, as if Abby hadn't spoken.

"You can see why he'd jump at the chance to sell, though," Denny said. "I don't guess it's easy unloading a place that serves nothing but turkey."

"Well, it's not *married* to turkey. It could serve other things. And it's got tons of equipment, ovens and such, that are worth a lot of money."

"Oh," Abby said, "poor Hugh. Men don't handle failure well at all."

"Mom. Please. Enough with the 'poor Hugh.'"

"Want to take a walk, Ab?" Red asked suddenly. It wasn't clear whether he'd been listening to what was being said. Maybe he really did feel like a walk just then. At any rate, he heaved himself to his feet and stepped over to give Abby a hand up. She was still shaking her head as they started off down the beach.

"Now they'll have a long talk about what a bad wife I am," Amanda said, watching them go.

"Dad walks so slowly these days," Jeannie said. "Look at him. He's so stiff."

"How does he manage at work?" Denny asked her.

"I don't notice it so much at work. It's not as if he does anything physically demanding there anymore."

They watched their parents meet up with Nora, who was returning from a walk of her own. She exchanged a few words with them and then continued toward Stem and her children, floating ethereally through a group of teenage boys tossing a football at the water's edge. A black tie-on skirt fluttered and parted over her modest one-piece swimsuit, and her dark hair lifted from her shoulders in the breeze. The teenage boys halted their game to follow her with their eyes, one of them cradling the football under his arm.

"The unwitting femme fatale," Denny murmured, and Amanda gave a little hiss of amusement.

"Is Elise having any fun?" Jeannie asked Amanda. "It doesn't seem she's joining in much this year."

"I have no idea," Amanda said. "I'm only her mother."

"I guess ballet has kind of taken her away from things."

Amanda didn't answer. The three of them were silent a moment, their gazes fixed on a nearby toddler in a swim diaper who was pursuing a committee of gulls. The gulls strutted ahead of him at a dignified pace, gradually speeding up although they pretended not to notice him.

"How about Susan?" Jeannie asked Denny. "Is she having a good time?"

"She's having a great time," he said. "She really likes coming here. These are the only cousins she's got."

"Oh, does Carla not have any siblings?"

"Just an unmarried brother."

Jeannie and Amanda raised their eyebrows at each other.

"How *is* Carla these days?" Amanda asked after a moment.

"Fine as far as I know."

"Do you see much of her?"

"No."

"Do you see *anybody*?"

"Do I see anybody?"

"You know what I mean. Any women."

"Not really," Denny said. And then, just when it seemed the conversation was finished, he added, "Face it, I'm hardly a catch."

"Why not?" Jeannie asked.

"Well, I kind of come across as a deadbeat. I mean, it's not as if I've been blazing an impressive career path all these years."

"Oh, that's ridiculous. *Lots* of women would fall for you."

"No," Denny said, "when you think about it, things haven't changed much since the days when parents were trying to marry their daughters off to guys with titles and estates. Women still want to know what you *do* when they meet you. It's the first question out of their mouths."

"So? You're a teacher! Or a substitute teacher, at least."

"Right," Denny said.

A little girl ran past them toward the water—the granddaughter of the next-door people. Reflexively, Denny and his sisters half turned to watch the next-door people threading from their house to the beach, carrying towels and folding chairs and a Styrofoam cooler. They arrived at a spot some twenty feet distant from the Whitshanks. The grown-ups unfolded their chairs and settled in a straight row facing the ocean, while the grandson and his friend went down to where the little girl was bounding into the surf.

"Have we ever found out for sure that they come for just the one week?" Amanda asked. "Maybe they're here all summer."

"No," Jeannie said, "we saw them arrive that time, remember? With their suitcases and their beach equipment."

"Maybe they stay on, then, after we leave."

"Well, maybe. I guess they could. But I like to think

that they go when we do. They have the same conversation we always have: next year, should they make it *two* weeks? But by the end of their vacation they say, 'Oh, one week is enough, really.' And so they come for the same week year after year, and fifty years from now we'll be saying"—here Jeannie's voice changed to an old-lady whine—" 'Oh, look, it's the next-door people, and the grandson's got a grandson now!' "

"They've brought their lunch today," Denny said. "We could check out their menu."

Jeannie said, "What if we marched over there, right this minute, and introduced ourselves?"

"It would be a disappointment," Amanda said.

"How come?"

"They would turn out to have some boring name, like Smith or Brown. They'd work in, let's say, advertising, or computer sales or consulting. *Whatever* they worked in, it would be a letdown. They'd say, 'Oh, how nice to meet you; we've always wondered about you,' and then we'd have to give *our* boring names, and our boring occupations."

"You really think they wonder about us?"

"Well, of course they do."

"You think they like us?"

"How could they not?" Amanda asked.

Her tone was jokey, but she wasn't smiling. She was openly studying the next-door people with a serious, searching expression, as if she weren't so sure after all. Did they find the Whitshanks attractive? Intriguing? Did they admire their large numbers and their closeness? Or had they noticed a hidden crack somewhere—a sharp exchange or an edgy silence or some sign of strain? Oh, what was their *opinion*? What insights could they reveal, if the Whitshanks walked over to them that very instant and asked?

It was the custom for the men to do the dishes every evening while they were on vacation. They would shoo the women out—"Go on, now! Go! Yes, we know: put the leftovers in the fridge"—and then Denny would fill the sink with hot water and Stem would unfurl a towel. Meanwhile Jeannie's Hugh, one of those thorough, conscientious types, reorganized the whole kitchen and scrubbed down every surface. Red might carry a few plates in from the dining room, but soon, at the others' urging, he would settle at the kitchen table with a beer to watch them work.

Amanda's Hugh wasn't around for this. Her little family ate most of their suppers in town.

On their final evening, Thursday, the cleanup was more extensive. Every leftover had to be dumped, and the refrigerator shelves had to be emptied and wiped down. Jeannie's Hugh was in his element. "Throw it out! Yes, that too," he said when Stem held up a nearly full container of coleslaw. "No point hauling it all the way back to Baltimore." The three of them slid a glance toward Red, who shared his sister's horror of waste, but he was thumbing through one of the trashy magazines and he failed to notice.

"What's the plan for tomorrow?" Denny asked. "We leaving at crack of dawn?"

Hugh said, "Well, *I* should, at least. I've got half a dozen messages on my cell phone." He meant messages from the college. "Lots of stuff to see to in the dorms."

"So," Denny told Stem, "that means fall is coming."

"Pretty soon," Stem said. He returned a not-quite-clean plate to the sink.

"You don't want to wait too long to move back home," Denny told him, "or the kids will have to switch schools."

Stem was drying another plate. He stopped for a second, but then he went on drying. "They've already switched," he said. "Nora registered both of the older boys last week."

"But it makes more sense for you to move back, now that I'm staying on."

Stem laid the plate on a stack of others.

"You're not staying," he said.

"What?"

"You'll be leaving any time now."

"What are you talking about?"

Denny had turned to look at him, but Stem went on wiping plates. He said, "You'll pick a fight with one of us, or you'll take offense at something. Or one of those calls will come in on your phone from some mysterious acquaintance with some mysterious emergency, and you'll disappear again."

"That's bullshit," Denny told him.

Jeannie's Hugh said, "Oh, well now, guys . . ." and Red looked up from his magazine, one finger marking his place.

"You just say that because you *wish* I weren't staying," Denny told Stem. "I'm well aware you want me out of the way. It's no surprise to me."

"I don't want you out of the way," Stem said. They were facing each other squarely now. Stem was gripping a plate in one hand and the towel in the other, and he spoke a little more loudly than he needed to. "God! What do I have to do to convince you I'm not out to *get* you? I don't want anything that's yours. I never have! I'm just trying to be a help to Mom and Dad!"

Red said, "What? Wait."

"Well, isn't that just like you," Denny told Stem. "Spilling over with selflessness. Holier than God Almighty."

Stem started to say something more; he drew in a breath and opened his mouth. Then he made a despairing noise that sounded like "Aarr!" and without even seeming to think about it, he wheeled toward Denny and gave him a violent shove.

It wasn't an attack, exactly. It was more an act of blind frustration. But Denny was caught off balance. He staggered sideways, dropping the plate he held so that it shattered across the floor, and he tried to right himself but fell anyhow, his head grazing the edge of the table before he landed in a sitting position.

"Oh," Stem said. "Gosh."

Red stood up, slack-mouthed, with his magazine dangling from one hand. Hugh was hovering in front of the fridge and saying, "Guys. Hey, guys," and gripping his washrag in a useless sort of way.

Denny began struggling to his feet. His left temple was bleeding. Stem bent to offer him a hand, but instead of accepting it, Denny lunged at him from a half-standing position and butted Stem in the sternum. Stem buckled and fell backwards, slamming against a cabinet. He sat up again, but he looked groggy, and he raised a hand tentatively to the back of his head.

All at once the kitchen was full of fluttering women and shocked, wide-eyed children. There seemed to be a multitude of them, way more than could be accounted for. Abby was saying, "What *is* this? What's happened?" and Nora was leaning over Stem, trying to help him up. "Keep him sitting," Jeannie told her. "Stem? Do you feel dizzy?" Stem went on holding his head, with an uncertain look on his face. Shards of the plate lay all around him.

Denny stood backed against the sink. He seemed bewildered, more than anything. "I don't know what came over him!" he said. "He just went from zero to sixty!" Blood was traveling down the side of his face, darkening the olive green of his T-shirt.

"Look at you," Jeannie told him. "We've got to get you to an emergency room. The two of you."

"*I* don't need an emergency room," Denny said, at the same time that Stem said, "I'm okay. Let me up."

"They both have to go," Abby said. "Denny needs stitches and Stem might have a concussion."

"I'm *fine*," Stem and Denny said in chorus.

"Let's at least put you on the couch," Nora told Stem. She didn't seem all that perturbed. She helped him to his feet, this time without Jeannie's objecting, and guided him out of the room. All the children followed dumbly except for Susan, who was standing very close to Denny and stroking his wrist. Tears were streaming down her cheeks. "What are you crying about?" Denny asked her. "This is nothing. It doesn't even hurt." She nodded and swallowed, tears still streaming. Abby put an arm around her and said, "He's okay, honey. Head wounds always bleed a lot."

"Out," Jeannie said. "Everyone out of the kitchen while I check the damage. Get me the first-aid kit, Hugh. It's in the downstairs bathroom. Susan, I need paper towels."

Red had sunk back onto his chair at some point, but Abby touched his shoulder and said, "Let's go to the living room."

"I don't understand what happened," he told her.

"Me neither, but let's leave Jeannie to take care of things."

She helped him up, and they moved toward the door. Only Susan remained. She handed Jeannie a roll of paper towels. "Thanks," Jeannie said. She tore off several sheets and dampened them under the faucet. "First we're going to clean the wound and see if it needs stitches," she told Denny. "Sit down."

"I do not need stitches," he said. He lowered himself to

a chair. She leaned over him and pressed the wad of damp towels to his temple. Susan, meanwhile, sat down in the chair next to his and picked up one of his hands. "Hmm," Jeannie said. She peered at Denny's cut. She refolded the paper towels and dabbed again at his temple.

"Ouch," he said.

"Hugh? Where's that first-aid kit?"

"Coming right up," Jeannie's Hugh said as he entered the kitchen. He handed her what appeared to be a fisherman's metal tackle box.

Jeannie said, "Go tell the others not to let Stem fall asleep, hear? *Leave* that," because Hugh was stooping to pick up shards of the plate. "We need to make sure he doesn't go into a coma." She had always been the type who grew authoritative in a crisis. Her long black ponytail almost snapped as she flicked it out of her way.

Hugh left. As soon as he was gone, Denny said, "I swear this was not my fault."

"Really," Jeannie said.

"Honest. You've got to believe me."

"Susan, find me the Neosporin."

Susan raised her eyes to Jeannie's face but went on sitting there.

"Ointment. In the first-aid kit," Jeannie told her. She folded the paper towels yet again. They were almost completely red now. Susan let go of Denny's hand to reach for the kit. Her blouse had a brushstroke of blood smeared across one shoulder.

"We were just doing the dishes," Denny said, "peaceful as you please. Then Stem flies off the handle because I say he can move home now."

"Yes, I can just imagine," Jeannie said.

"What is that supposed to mean?"

She tossed the paper towels into the garbage bin and accepted the Neosporin from Susan. "Hold still," she told Denny. She applied a dab of ointment. He held still, gazing up at her steadily. She said, "When are you going to drop all this, Denny? Get over it! Give it up!"

"Give what up? He was the one who started it!"

"Don't you think everyone's got some kind of . . . injury? Stem himself, for instance! Couldn't I feel jealous too, if I put my mind to it? Dad favors Stem *way* over me, even though I'm a really good worker. He's always talking about Stem taking charge of the business someday, as if I didn't exist, as if I couldn't do every single thing a man can do once somebody shows me how. But guess what, Denny: the fact is that nobody has to show Stem how. He was just, seems like, *born* knowing how. He can figure things out without being told. He honestly does deserve to be in charge."

Denny made an impatient snorting noise that she ignored. "Butterfly bandages," she told Susan. "If you can find me some of those, we're in business."

Susan rooted through the first-aid kit, which didn't seem well organized. She tossed aside scissors, tweezers, rolls of gauze, a bottle of vinegar for jellyfish stings, and came up with a box of butterfly bandages.

"Great," Jeannie said. She shook several out onto the table, then picked up one and tore open the wrapping. "A few of these should do the trick," she told Denny. "Hold still, please."

"It's not his being in charge I mind," Denny said. "*I* sure don't want to be in charge. It's that Dad isn't satisfied with the rest of us. His own three children! You said it yourself: you should be the one taking over the business. You're a Whitshank. But oh, no, Dad had to go hunting outside the family for someone."

"He didn't go hunting," Jeannie said. She drew back to study the bandage she had applied, and then she reached for another. "He didn't *choose* to have Stem join the family. It just happened."

"All my life, Dad has made me feel I didn't quite measure up," Denny said. "Like I'm . . . lame; I'm lacking. Listen to this, Jeannie: when I was working in Minnesota one summer, I had a boss who thought I had a really good eye. We were putting in cabinets, and I would come up with these design plans that he said were fantastic. He asked if I'd ever considered going into furniture making. *He* thought I had real talent. Why doesn't Dad ever feel that way?"

"And then what?" Jeannie asked.

"What do you mean, what?"

"What happened with the furniture making?"

"Oh, well . . . I forget. I think we moved on to the boring part, then. Baseboards or something. So I quit, by and by."

Jeannie sighed and collected the bandage wrappings

from the table. "Okay, Susan," she said. "You can help your dad to the living room now."

But just as Denny was getting to his feet, Stem walked in, with Nora close behind. By the looks of him, he'd recovered from the blow to his head. He seemed himself again, only paler and more rumpled. "Denny," he said, "I want to apologize."

"He is very, very sorry," Nora put in.

"I should not have lost my temper, and I want to pay for your String Cheese Incident T-shirt."

Denny made a little puffing sound of amusement, and Abby, who had come into the room behind them—of course she had to be part of this, falling all over herself to set her family to rights—said, "Oh, Stem, that's no problem; I'm sure we can treat it with OxiClean," which made Denny laugh aloud.

"Forget it," he told Stem. "Let's just say it never happened."

"Well, that's very generous of you."

"Fact is, I'm kind of relieved to find out you're human," Denny said. "Till now I didn't think you had a competitive bone in your body."

"Competitive?"

"Let's shake on it," Denny said, holding out his hand.

Stem said, "Why do you say I'm competitive?"

Denny let his hand drop. "Hey," he said. "You just assaulted me for saying I should be the one to help out with Mom and Dad. You don't call that competitive?"

"God *damn*!" Stem said.

Nora said, "Oh! Douglas."

Stem socked Denny in the mouth.

It wasn't an expert blow—it landed clumsily, a bit askew—but it was enough to send Denny tumbling back onto his chair. Blood bubbled up instantly from his lower lip. He gave a dazed shake of his head. Abby shrieked, "Stop! Please stop!" and Jeannie said, "Oh, for heaven's sake," and Susan started crying again and biting her knuckles. The others appeared in the doorway so instantaneously that it almost seemed they'd been lying in wait for this. Stem was looking surprised. He stared down at his fist, which was scraped across the knuckles. He shifted his gaze to Denny.

"Out," Jeannie ordered everyone.

Then she said, in a weary tone of voice, "First we're going to clean the wound and see if it needs stitches."

6

Abbey felt nervous at first about the appointment with Dr. Wiss, but then she thought, "I can do this, because I'm so familiar with my mother's Wiss pinking shears." And the exact, clunky weight of those shears instantly came to her mind, along with the too-thick handle loop that pressed uncomfortably against the bone at the base of her thumb, and the initial balkiness as the heavy teeth began chewing into the fabric.

But wait. Really, the one kind of Wiss had nothing to do with the other.

It was Nora who made the appointment. She had called her pastor for the name of a gerontologist, and then she phoned Dr. Wiss's office without consulting Abby. Meddlesome! She must have discussed it first with Red, though, because when Abby complained to him he didn't seem surprised, and he told her it wouldn't hurt to hear what a doctor had to say.

Abby was finding that Nora had started to get on her nerves. Why, for instance, did she persist in calling Abby "Mother Whitshank"? It made Abby sound like an old peasant woman in wooden clogs and a headscarf. Abby had offered all her children's spouses a choice of "Mom" or "Abby" when they first joined the family. "Mother Whitshank" hadn't so much as crossed her lips.

Also, Nora stacked the plates on top of each other when she was clearing the table, instead of carrying one in each hand as Abby had been taught was polite. All the plates arrived in the kitchen with food stuck to their backs. Yet she criticized Abby's housekeeping! Or that was her implication, at least, when she blamed the dust in the rugs for Sammy's allergies. And she cooked fatty fried foods that were bad for Red's heart, and she was much too lax with her children, and that queen bed she had requested completely filled Stem's little room, barely allowing space for a person to edge around it.

Oh, well, this was just roommate-itis, Abby told herself. It was rubbing elbows at too-close quarters; that was why she felt so irritable.

She told herself this several times a day.

She also reminded herself that some of our connections are brand-new connections, unrelated to our past incarnations—new experiences to broaden our horizons. Maybe Nora's role in Abby's life was to deepen and enrich Abby's soul; could that be true?

It wasn't as if Abby were a difficult mother-in-law. Why,

look at how well she got along with Amanda's Hugh! A challenge, as Amanda herself admitted, but Abby found him entertaining. And Jeannie's Hugh, of course, was a sweetheart. Some of Abby's friends had a terrible time with their children-in-law. Daughters-in-law more than sons-in-law, all of them agreed. Some were not on speaking terms. Abby was doing way better than they were.

If only she didn't feel so pushed aside. So extraneous, so unnecessary.

She had always assumed that when she was old, she would have total confidence, finally. But look at her: still uncertain. In many ways she was more uncertain now than she had been as a girl. And often when she heard herself speaking she was appalled at how chirpy she sounded—how empty-headed and superficial, as if she'd somehow fallen into the Mom role in some shallow TV sitcom.

What on earth had happened to her?

Her appointment with Dr. Wiss wasn't till November. (Long waiting line of problem oldsters, evidently.) Everything might have changed by November. Maybe her minor little inconsequential glitches—her "brain jumping the track," as she thought of it—would have disappeared on their own. Or maybe she would be dead! No, shelve that thought.

It was only mid-September now. Still summery, the leaves barely starting to turn, the mornings crisp but not truly cold. She could sit out on the porch after breakfast in just a sweater, gently toeing the swing back and forth and watching the parents and children walk past on their way to school. You could tell it was early in the school year because the children were so nicely dressed. Another month and they would be making less effort. And some of the older children would have shed their parents, although Petey and Tommy were too young for that, of course. They had set out with Nora several minutes ago—Sammy leaning forward in his stroller like a sea captain watching for landfall, Heidi prancing in front on her ridiculous great long leash. Three little towheads glimmering away through the trees; so non-Whitshank-like. Although Stem had been a towhead, so it was only to be expected.

The boys seemed to have settled easily into the neighborhood, zipping their scooters up and down the sidewalk out front and bringing playmates in for snacks. They told her that the other children called their house "the porch house." Abby liked that. She could remember her own first sight of the house, back when she was a freckle-faced middle-schooler from Hampden and snooty Merrick Whitshank was her designated Big Sister. That enormous, wonderful porch glimpsed from the street, Merrick and two teenaged friends lounging in this very swing so casually, so stylishly, wearing rolled-up blue jeans and gaily patterned neckerchiefs tied in jaunty knots. "Oh, Gawd, it's the midgets," Merrick had drawled, because Abby had two of her classmates with her, Little Sisters to Merrick's two friends. They were supposed to spend a companionable, fun-filled Saturday afternoon learning the words to the school song and baking cookies together. But that part Abby couldn't remember now—just her awe at the sight of this porch and the impressive flagstone walk leading up to it. Oh, and Merrick's mother: sweet Linnie. (Or Mrs. Whitshank, as Abby called her then.) It had probably been Linnie who supervised the cookie baking, because Abby couldn't picture Merrick doing that.

Linnie Mae Whitshank was pale and subdued, dressed in a wan flowered shift that could have been bought in a country store, but something about the tracery of smile lines at the corners of her eyes told Abby she might be taking in more than she let on. Long after the Big Sister charade had petered out, Abby thought of Linnie fondly. And then years later, when Abby started dating Red's friend Dane, there was Linnie, as openhearted as ever, stepping out on the porch night after night to offer homemade lemonade to all the neighborhood gang. Sometimes Junior put in an appearance, too—"Why, hey there! Boys. Girls." He'd hang around talking, talking, telling the girls they looked mighty pretty this evening and rehashing Colts games with the boys, till Linnie touched his sleeve and said, "Come away, now, Junior. Time to leave these young folks to their socializing."

Both of them dead and gone now; oh, my. Wiped off the face of the earth by a freight train, leaving not even bodies to mourn, just two closed caskets, and no one but the police to break the news. So unsatisfying, so inconclusive.

That bothered Abby more than it did Red. Red was of the opinion that instantaneous death was a mercy, but Abby wanted goodbyes. She would have liked to say, "Linnie, you were a good, good woman, and I've always felt sorry you led such a lonely life."

Abby had been visited, lately, by thoughts of all the people whose deaths she had been present for. Two grandparents, her mother, her beloved older brother who'd died young. Not her father, though. For her father, she had arrived just minutes too late. But she had hoped, as she bent and laid her face against his, that there was some lingering vestige of him that would register her presence. Even now, sitting on the porch and gazing down at Bouton Road, she felt her eyes tear up at the memory of his dear, whiskery cheek already cooling. We should all go out *attended* by someone! That was what she wanted for herself, certainly: Red's large hand enclosing hers as she lay dying. But then she reflected that this meant he would be without her when his own time came, and she couldn't endure the thought of that. How would Red survive, if she were the one to go first?

He always held her whole hand, rather than interlacing his fingers with hers. When she was in her early teens, hearing from her more forward friends about the boys who reached for their hands at the movies, it was that enfolding clasp that she had envisioned, and the first date who surreptitiously threaded his fingers through hers had convinced her that hand-holding was not all it was cracked up to be. Till Red.

Maybe she and Red could die at the same time. Say, on a plane. They could have a few minutes' warning, a pilot's announcement that would give them a chance to trade last words. Except that they never flew anywhere, so how was *that* going to happen?

"The trouble with dying," she'd told Jeannie once, "is that you don't get to see how everything turns out. You won't know the ending."

"But, Mom, there *is* no ending," Jeannie said.

"Well, I know that," Abby said.

In theory.

It was possible that in her heart of hearts, she was thinking that the world couldn't go on without her. Oh, weren't human beings self-deluding! Because the plain fact was that no one needed her anymore. Her children were grown up, and her clients had vanished into thin air the moment she retired. (And anyhow, toward the last it had seemed that her clients' needs were bottomless—that society was falling apart faster than she could patch it together. She was getting out just in time, she had felt.) Even her "orphans," as her family called them, were all but gone. B. J. Autry was dead of drugs and old Mr. Dale of a stroke, and the various foreign students had either returned to their own countries or else assimilated so successfully that they cooked Thanksgiving dinner for themselves now.

In the past, she had been at the center of things. She'd known everybody's secrets; everyone confided in her. Linnie had told her—swearing her to silence—that she and Junior were their families' black sheep; and Denny had told her (offhandedly, when she marveled at Susan's brown eyes) that Susan was not his. Nothing she heard had Abby relayed to anybody else, not even to Red. She was a woman of her word. Oh, people would have been amazed at all she knew and didn't say!

"You owe your job to me," she could have said to Jeannie. "Your father was dead set against having a woman on the construction site, but I persuaded him." What a temptation to let *that* slip! But she didn't.

And now she was so unnecessary that her children thought she should move to a retirement community—she and Red both, neither one of them nearly old enough yet. Thank God that had come to nothing. It was worth putting up with Nora, even, in order to dodge the retirement community. It had even been worth putting up with Mrs. Girt. Or almost worth it.

Abby felt bad now about Mrs. Girt. They had let her go without a thought! And she'd probably had some very sad story. It wasn't at all like Abby to pass up a chance to hear someone's sad story. "Amanda," she had said recently, "did we give that Mrs. Girt any severance pay?"

"Severance pay! She was with you nine days!"

"Still," Abby said, "she meant well. And *you* all meant well to arrange for her; I hope you don't think I'm ungrateful."

"Well, since both you and Dad were dead set against a retirement community, for some reason . . ."

"But you can see our side of it, can't you? Why, I bet

those places have social workers to deal with the inmates. We'd be the objects of social work! Can you imagine?"

To which Amanda had said, "The 'inmates'? And the 'objects,' Mom? Goodness. What does that say about your attitude to your own profession, all these years?"

Amanda could be so sharp-edged, sometimes.

Of the two girls, Jeannie was easier. (Abby knew she should stop calling them "the girls," but it would feel so silly to say "the women" and "the men.") Jeannie was biddable and unassuming; she lacked Amanda's acidity. She didn't confide in Abby, though. It had been such a blow when Jeannie had asked Denny to help out during that bad spell after Alexander was born. She could have asked Abby. Abby was right there in town! And then Denny: why had he never mentioned that he had finished college? He must have been taking courses for years, working them in around his various jobs, but he hadn't said a thing, and why not? Because he wanted her to go on worrying about him, was why. He didn't want to let her off the hook. So when he sprang it like that—just announced it after lunch that day: yes, he had his degree—it had felt like a slap in the face. She knew she should have been pleased for him, but instead she had felt resentful.

One thing that parents of problem children never said aloud: it was a relief when the children turned out okay, but then what were the parents supposed to do with the anger they'd felt all those years?

Although Denny might *not* be okay, even now. Abby

wasn't entirely at ease about him. Shouldn't he be looking for work? Maybe substitute teaching? Or even *really* teaching! He surely couldn't be thinking that helping out around the house was enough of an occupation, could he? Or that the odd bits of money she slipped him—a couple of twenties any time he ran an errand for her, never requesting change—could be called a living wage.

Yesterday, she had asked him, "How about your other belongings? You must have more than what you brought down. Did you put them into storage?"

"Oh, that's no problem," he'd said. "They're stashed in my old apartment."

"So you still have to pay rent?"

"Nah. It's just one room above a garage; my landlady doesn't care."

This was puzzling. What kind of landlady didn't charge rent unless her tenant was physically present? Oh, so much of his life seemed . . . irregular, somehow.

Or maybe it was perfectly regular, and Abby had just been sensitized by too many past experiences with Denny—too many evasions and semi-truths and suspect alibis.

Last week she'd knocked on his bedroom door to ask if he could take her to buy some greeting cards, and she'd thought she heard him tell her to come in, but she was mistaken; he was talking on his cell phone. "You know I do," he was saying. "How'm I going to make you believe me?" and then he'd looked over at Abby and his expression had altered. "What do you want?" he had asked her.

"I'll just wait till you're off the phone," she had said, and he'd told his caller, "I've got to go," and snapped his phone shut too quickly.

If it was a girl he'd been speaking to—a woman—Abby was truly glad. Everyone should have someone. Still, a part of her couldn't help feeling hurt that he hadn't mentioned this person. Why did he have to turn everything into such a mystery? Oh, he just took an active pleasure in going against the grain! No, the current, she meant. Going against the current. It was like a hobby for him.

Sometimes it seemed to her that with all her fretting over Denny, she had let her other children slip through her fingers unnoticed. Not that she had neglected them, but she certainly hadn't screwed up her eyes and *focused* on them the way she had focused on Denny. And yet it was Denny who complained of feeling slighted!

While she was flipping through her mail the other day, she'd grown gradually aware that he was speaking to her. "Hmm?" she'd said absently, slitting an envelope. Then, " 'Wealth management,' " she had said, biting off the words. "Don't you hate that phrase?" and Denny had said, "You're not listening, dammit."

"I'm listening."

"When I was a kid," he told her, "I used to daydream about kidnapping you just so I could have your full attention."

"Oh, Denny. I paid you a *lot* of attention! Too much, your dad always says."

He just cocked his head at her.

Not only had she paid him attention, but she had secretly taken more pleasure in him than in any of the others. He was so full of life, so fierce. (In fact, he sometimes brought Dane Quinn to mind—her renegade ex-boyfriend, killed these many years ago in a one-car accident.) And he could delight her with his unexpected slants of vision. Last month, rolling up the supposedly dusty rug in the little boys' room, he had paused to ask, "Did you ever think how conceited those Oriental rug weavers are, to believe they have to *try* and make a mistake so as not to compete with God? Like they would have done it perfectly otherwise, if they hadn't forced themselves to mess up!" Abby had laughed aloud.

Maybe when he was grown, she remembered thinking during his childhood, he would finally tell her what used to make him so angry. But then when he was grown she had asked him, and he had said, "I don't know, to be honest."

Abby sighed and watched a schoolboy walk past, bowed low beneath an overstuffed backpack.

This porch was not just long but deep—the depth of a smallish living room. In her early years here, when she was a gung-ho young housewife, she had ordered an entire suite of wicker furniture varnished the same honey-gold as the swing—a low table, a settee, and two armchairs—and arranged them in a circular "conversational group" at one end of the porch. But nobody wanted to sit facing away from the street, and so gradually the chairs had migrated to either side of the settee and people once again sat in a straight line gazing outward, not at each other, like passengers on a steamship deck. Abby thought that summed up her role in this family. She had her notions, her ideas of how things ought to be, but everyone proceeded as he or she liked, regardless.

She looked down through the trees and saw a flash of white: Heidi's mane feathering as she pranced homeward, followed by Nora wheeling the stroller in her sashaying, aimless way. Without even thinking about it, Abby bounded up from the swing like a much younger woman and slipped into the house.

The front hall still smelled of coffee and toast, which ordinarily struck her as cozy but today made her feel claustrophobic. She headed straight for the stairs and climbed them swiftly. She was out of sight by the time she heard the thump-thump of Sammy's stroller being hauled up the porch steps.

Her study door—Denny's door now—was shut, and a heavy silence lay behind it. His schedule had not reset itself as she had first imagined it might. He was still the last one to bed every night and the last one up in the morning, emerging at ten or eleven o'clock in his battle-weary outfit of olive-drab T-shirt and none-too-clean khakis, his face creased from his pillow and his hair hanging limp and greasy. Oh, Lord.

"Who said, 'You're only ever as happy as your least happy child?'" she'd asked Ree in last week's pottery class.

"Socrates," Ree answered promptly.

"Really? I was thinking more along the lines of Michelle Obama."

"Actually I don't know who said it," Ree admitted, "but believe me, it goes a whole lot farther back than Michelle."

You wake in the morning, you're feeling fine, but all at once you think, "Something's not right. Something's *off* somewhere; what is it?" And then you remember that it's your child—whichever one is unhappy.

She circled the hall to close the door to the little boys' room, a distracting welter of clothes and towels and parts of toys. Legos would bite the soles of your feet if you ventured in without your shoes on. She backtracked to her own room, stepped inside, and shut the door soundlessly behind her.

The bed was still unmade, because she'd wanted to get downstairs and eat a peaceful breakfast before Nora and the little boys came down. (Oh, the exhausting enthusiasm of small children hurling themselves into each new day!) Now she pulled up the covers and hung her bathrobe, and she folded Red's pajamas and tucked them beneath his pillow. On workdays Red dressed in the dark, and he always left a mess behind.

This was the room that had seen the fewest occupants: just Mr. and Mrs. Brill, then Junior and Linnie, then Red and Abby. The armoire in the corner was the Brills', in fact, because it had been too massive for the downtown apartment they'd moved to. And the other furniture was Junior and Linnie's, although the decorative objects were Abby's—the framed color print from her childhood showing a guardian angel hovering behind a little girl, and her mother's glass-slipper pincushion stuffed with velvet, and the little Hummel fiddler boy Red had given her when they were courting.

She heard Nora's voice downstairs, low and unintelligible, and a crowing sound from Sammy. A moment later there was a scratching at her door. She opened her door and Clarence slipped in. "I know, sweetie," Abby said. "It's very noisy down there." He circled on the rug a few times and then lay down. Good old Clarence. Brenda. Whoever. Abby did know this was Brenda if she bothered to stop and think about it.

"It's like when you're drifting off to sleep and a gear sort of slips in your head," she would tell Dr. Wiss. "Have you ever had that happen? You're having this very clear thought, but then all at once you're on this totally *other* illogical, unconnected thought and you can't trace it back to the first one. It's just tiredness, I imagine. I mean, once about five or ten years ago—oh, long before I was old—I had to drive home alone from the beach late at night to keep an appointment the next morning, and I suddenly found myself in this very scary neighborhood in Washington, D.C. And I could swear I'd managed to do it without crossing the Bay Bridge! I don't know *how* I did it. To this day I don't know. I was tired, was all. That was all it was."

Or last December, when the McCarthys had invited her and Red to a Christmas concert along with a bunch of their other friends, and she had been so chatty and confiding with the man who happened to be seated next to her but then discovered, by and by, that he was a total stranger, had nothing to do with the McCarthys and no doubt thought she was a lunatic. Just a skip in the record, that was. You can see how it might happen.

"And time," she would tell Dr. Wiss. "Well, *you* know about time. How slow it is when you're little and how it speeds up faster and faster once you're grown. Well, now it's just a blur. I can't keep track of it anymore! But it's like time is sort of . . . balanced. We're young for such a small fraction of our lives, and yet our youth seems to stretch on forever. Then we're old for years and years, but time flies by fastest then. So it all comes out equal in the end, don't you see."

She heard Nora climbing the stairs. She heard her say, "No, silly-billy. Cookies are for dessert." Her footsteps proceeded at a stately pace toward the boys' room, followed by Sammy's little sneakers.

Was there something wrong with Abby, that she didn't fall all over herself to spend every waking minute with her grandchildren? She did love them, after all. She loved them so much that she felt a kind of hollowness on the inner surface of her arms whenever she looked at them—an ache of longing to pull them close and hold them tight against her. The three little boys were such a clumped-together tangle, always referred to as a single unit, but Abby knew how different each was from the next. Petey was the worrier, bossing his brothers around not out of meanness but from a protective, herding instinct; Tommy had his father's sunny nature and his peacemaking skills; and Sammy was her baby, still smelling of orange juice and urine, still happy to cuddle up and let her read to him. And then the older ones: Susan so serious and dear and well-behaved—was she all *right?*— and Deb who was Abby herself at that age, a wiry knot of inquisitiveness, and poor clumsy, effortful Alexander who could wrench her heart, and finally Elise who was just so different from Abby, so completely *other*, that Abby felt privileged to be granted this close-up view of her.

But it was easier, somehow, to reflect on them all from a distance than to be struggling for room in their midst.

The upstairs hall was quiet again. Abby turned her doorknob by degrees, opened the door a bare minimum, and slipped out. The dog shoved the door wider open with his nose and plodded after her, snuffling noisily and causing Abby to wince and glance toward the boys' room.

Down the stairs to the front door she went, and out onto the porch. Then she stopped short, struck by an idea. She reached back into the house for the leash that hung on a hook just inside. Clarence made a glad moaning sound and shambled onto the porch behind her, while somewhere in the depths of the house Heidi gave a yelp of envy. Eat your heart out, Heidi. Abby was not a fan of overexcitable dogs.

She paused on the flagstone walk to clip the leash to Clarence's collar. This was the old-fashioned, short kind of leash, not the permissive retractable kind that people nowadays favored. Strictly speaking, Clarence didn't need a leash; he was so slow and stodgy and mindlessly obedient. But he did have a willful streak when it came to very small dogs. They seemed to bring out all the old feistiness of his puppy days. He never could resist pouncing on a toy terrier.

"We're not going far," Abby told him. "Don't get your hopes up." From the stiff-jointed way he moved, she suspected he wasn't up to more than a block or two in any case.

They turned to the left when they reached the street— the opposite direction from Ree's house. Not that Abby wouldn't love to see Ree, but after Abby's little lapse that time, Ree would have been distressed to find her walking alone. And Abby loved walking alone. Oh, it felt so good to set out like this, free as a bird, no "What'll we do about Mom?" hanging unspoken over her head! She hoped she wouldn't run into anybody she knew.

Sometimes on her walks it would strike her that of all her original family, she was the only one left. Who would ever have dreamed that she'd be traveling through the world without them? She thought again of the framed picture in her bedroom: the solitary child threading a path beneath giant, looming trees, the guardian angel following protectively behind. Except that Abby didn't believe in angels, and hadn't since she was seven. No, she was truly on her own.

She used to have at least one of her children with her

everywhere she went. It was both comforting and wearing. "Hand? Hand?" she used to say before she crossed a street. It came to her so clearly now: the stiff-armed reach out to her side with her palm facing backward, the confident expectation of some trusting little hand grabbing hers.

Clarence eyed a squirrel but kept on heeling, not even tempted. "I agree," Abby told him. "Squirrels are beneath you." Then she gave a testing pat to the cushiony space above her breasts. Had she thought to hang the house key around her neck before she set out? No, but never mind; the lock was set to manual. And there was always Nora to let her back in if need be.

Another secret she knew, but this wasn't something anyone had told her: it had occurred to her just recently that the song Stem remembered his father's singing him to sleep with could very well have been "The Goat and the Train." Burl Ives used to sing that on a children's record she had owned when she was small. Should she suggest it to Stem? It could be a transporting moment for him, hearing that song again after all these years. But he might think she was tactlessly reminding him that he was not a Whitshank. Or maybe her reason for keeping silent was more selfish. Maybe she just wanted him to forget that she wasn't his first and only mother.

He and Denny had treated each other with artificial politeness ever since their fight at the beach. You would think they were barely acquainted. "Denny, are you going to want that last piece of chicken?" Stem would ask, and

Denny would say, "Be my guest." They didn't fool her for a minute. They could have been two strangers in a waiting room, and she was beginning to lose hope that that would ever change.

Oh, always lately it seemed that some crisis arose at the beach house. No wonder she dreaded vacations! Not that she ever let on.

"What's gone wrong with us?" she'd asked Red on the ride home from this year's trip. "We used to be such a happy family! Weren't we?"

"Far as I can recall," Red had answered.

"Remember that time we all got the giggles at the movies?"

"Well, now . . ."

"It was a Western, and the hero's horse was staring straight at us, head-on, chewing oats, with these two little balls of muscle popping out at his jaws when he chomped down. He looked so silly! Remember that? We burst out laughing, all of us at once, and the rest of the audience turned toward us just mystified."

"Was I there?" Red asked her.

"You were there. You were laughing too."

Maybe the reason he'd forgotten was that he took their happiness for granted. He didn't fret about it. Whereas Abby . . . oh, she fretted, all right. She couldn't bear to think that their family was just another muddled, discontented, *ordinary* family.

"If you could have one single wish," she had asked Red

one night in bed when neither of them could sleep, "what would it be?"

"Oh, I don't know."

"I would wish wonderful lives for our children," Abby said.

"Yeah, that's good."

"How about you?"

"Oh," he said, "maybe that Harford Contractors would go bankrupt and quit underbidding me."

"Red! Honestly!"

"What?"

"How can you not put your children's welfare first?" Abby asked him.

"I do put it first. But you already took care of that with *your* wish."

"Huh," Abby said, and she had flounced over to her left side so she was lying with her back to him.

He was getting old, too. She wasn't the only one! He wore reading glasses that slipped down his nose and made him look like his father. And that "Eh?" of his when he hadn't heard right: where had *that* come from? It was almost as if he were acting a part. He thought that was how a person was supposed to sound at his age. And sometimes what he said landed oddly off the mark—"scarlet teenager," for instance, referring to a red bird he saw perched on their feeder. Which probably had to do with his hearing, again, but still, she couldn't help worrying. She saw the way salesclerks treated him lately, how condescendingly, speaking to him too loudly and using words of fewer syllables. They took him for just another doddery old man. It made her chest ache when she saw that.

Didn't anyone stop to reflect that the so-called old people of today used to smoke pot, for heaven's sake, and wear bandannas tied around their heads and picket the White House? When Amanda chided her for saying that something was "cool" ("I hate it when the older generation tries to copy the younger," she had said), did she not realize that "cool" had been used in Abby's time, too, not to mention long before?

She didn't mind *looking* old. It wasn't a real concern of hers. Her face had grown slightly puffy and her body had softened and slumped, but when she studied the family album she thought that her younger self seemed unappealingly puny by comparison—pinched and tight, almost starved-looking. And Red seemed downright frail in those photos, with his Adam's apple poking forth too sharply from his too-long neck. He weighed no more now than he had then, but somehow he gave the impression of greater solidity.

Abby had a little trick that she used any time Red acted like a cranky old codger. She reminded herself of the day she had fallen in love with him. "It was a beautiful, breezy, yellow-and-green afternoon," she'd begin, and it would all come back to her—the newness of it, the whole new world magically opening before her at the moment when she first realized that this person that she'd barely noticed all these years was, in fact, a treasure. He was *perfect*, was how she'd put it to herself. And then that clear-eyed, calm-faced boy would shine forth from Red's sags and wrinkles, from his crumpled eyelids and hollowed cheeks and the two deep crevices bracketing his mouth and just his general obtuseness, his stubbornness, his infuriating belief that simple cold logic could solve all of life's problems, and she would feel unspeakably lucky to have ended up with him.

"I bought a goat," she sang as she walked. "His name was Jim." Then she broke off, because she caught sight of someone approaching up ahead. But he turned left at the corner, so Abby resumed singing. "I bought him for . . ." Clarence trudged next to her in silence, every now and then accidentally or maybe deliberately bumping against her knee.

Wasn't it interesting how song lyrics stayed in your memory so much longer than mere prose! Not just the songs of her teens—"Tom Dooley" and "Michael, Row the Boat Ashore"—but ditties from her childhood, "White Coral Bells" and "Good Morning, Merry Sunshine" and "We're Happy When We're Hiking," and her mother singing something that began "I'll come down and let you in," and even jump-rope chants—"Johnny over the ocean, Johnny over the sea . . ." Anything that rhymed, it seemed. Rhyme imprinted things in your brain. Dental appointments should be put into rhyme, and important anniversaries. In fact, all of life's more meaningful events! If you came across any gap, all you had to do was start singing as much as you could remember—embark on the first line, confidently—and the missing part would arrive in your head just in the nick of time.

Abby used to worry about becoming forgetful, because her maternal grandfather had ended up with dementia. But that wasn't turning out to be her particular problem. She had a better memory than most of her friends, they all agreed. Why, just last week Carol Dunn had phoned, but when Abby answered she had heard only silence. "Hello?" she'd said again, and Carol had said, "I forget who I dialed." "This is Abby," Abby said, and Carol said, "Oh, hi, Abby! How are you? Gosh, I'd forget my own head if it wasn't—but anyhow, you aren't who I meant to call," and she had hung up.

Or Ree, who kept losing the names of things. "Next summer I think I'll plant some of those . . . Maryland flowers," she said, and Abby said, "Black-eyed Susans?"

"Yes, right." It always seemed to be Abby who had to fill in the blanks. She should tell Dr. Wiss that.

"In some ways," she should tell him, "my memory's better now than it was when I was young. The most surprising details suddenly show up again! Tiny things, infinitesimal things. The other day I all at once recalled the exact turn of the wrist that I used to give the handle of the CorningWare saucepan I got for a wedding present. I got a whole set of CorningWare with one interchangeable handle that you twisted to lock into place. That was almost fifty years ago! I used those for only a little while; they kept scorching things on the bottom. Who else could remember that?"

She might suddenly smell again the bitter, harsh, soul-dampening fumes of the chopped onions and green peppers her mother fried up most evenings as the base for her skillet dinners, back when Abby was a toddler whining with hunger and tiredness and just general five p.m. blues. She might hear the long-ago humming in the wires that the number 29 streetcar made when it sped down Roland Avenue without having to stop. And out of nowhere she pictured her childhood dog, Binky, who used to sleep with both paws folded over his nose to keep himself warm on cold nights. It was exactly like a time trip. She was bobbing along in a time machine gazing out the window at one scene after another in no particular order. At one *story* after another. Oh, there'd been so many stories in her life! The Whitshanks claimed to have only two; she couldn't imagine why. Why select just a certain few stories to define yourself? Abby had a wealth of them.

For years, she had been in mourning for the way she had let her life slip through her fingers. Given another chance, she'd told herself, she would take more care to experience it. But lately, she was finding that she had experienced it after all and just forgotten, and now it was returning to her.

What street was this? She hadn't been paying attention.

She stopped at the curb and gazed around her, and Clarence sat down on his haunches. To her left was the

Hutchinsons' house, with that beautiful huge magnolia tree that always seemed freshly enameled. She was surprised that she had walked this far; she'd thought Clarence would have protested by now. She made a clucking sound and he rose with a groan, the weight of the world on his shoulders, his head sagging so that it nearly touched the ground. "We'll take you home," she told him, "and you can have a nice long nap."

Just then, though—how could this happen?—a little mosquito of a chihuahua minced past on the sidewalk across the street. No owner anywhere to be seen, and no leash and not even a collar. Clarence sprang up instantaneously, as if his weariness had all been for show, and with a startlingly loud roar he leapt forward, yanking the leash from Abby's hand. Somehow she had time to see his entire life streaming by: his soft, pudgy belly and giant paws when he was a pup, his old fondness for playing fetch with tennis balls gone soppy with spit, his pure, delirious joy when the children used to come home from school. "Clarence!" she shrieked, but he paid no attention, so she tore after him into the street, while something she couldn't quite place—something huge and sleek and metallic that she hadn't been expecting— came speeding toward her.

"Oh!" she thought. "Why, this must be—"

And then no more.

7

Whitshanks didn't die, was the family's general belief. Of course they never said this aloud. It would have seemed presumptuous. Not to mention that some non-Whitshank would have been sure to point out that after all, Junior and Linnie had died. But that had been so long ago; Red was the only one left alive with any firsthand memory of it. (Nobody counted Merrick.) And Red was not himself right now. He was just a shell of himself. He walked around in his slippers, unshaven, with a vacant look in his eyes. For one whole day it appeared that he had lost his powers of speech, till it was discovered that he'd once again neglected to put his hearing aids in.

Abby died on a Tuesday, and on Wednesday she was cremated as she had always said she wanted to be; but the funeral wouldn't be held until the following Monday. This was so they could collect themselves and figure out what a funeral entailed, exactly. None of them had had any experience with such things except for Nora, and she came from such a different background that she really couldn't be much help.

Putting the funeral off for so long might have been a mistake, though, because it meant they were all suspended in a kind of limbo. They hung around the house drinking coffee, answering the telephone, sighing, bickering, accepting covered dishes from the neighbors, trading comical Abby stories that somehow made them end up crying instead of laughing. Both of the Hughs were there, because their wives required support. Stem fielded the occasional work-related call on his cell phone, but Red didn't even bother asking what the issue was. The grandchildren went to school as usual but gathered at the house in the afternoons, looking awed and stricken, while little Sammy, stuck at home all day with the grown-ups, seemed to be going slightly crazy. He gave up using his potty—an iffy business in the best of times—and started throwing spectacular tantrums. When Nora asked him, in a too-calm voice, what was troubling him, he said he wanted Clarence. This made everyone stir uneasily. "Brenda, you mean," Nora told him. "Brenda has gone to be with Jesus."

"I want him to come back from Jesus."

"Her," Nora said. "You want *her* to come back. But she's happier where she is."

"She was old, buddy," Stem said.

An embarrassed silence fell over the room. Luckily, though, Sammy failed to make the obvious connection. He hadn't mentioned Abby once, although she used to spend hours at a time reading him his favorite, unutterably boring dinosaur book over and over and over.

She'd been singing, Louisa Hutchinson said. Louisa was the one who had rushed out to the street when she heard the crash, and then called 911 and later had phoned the family. Thank heaven, because Abby hadn't been carrying any identification. "She walked toward our house singing," Louisa said, "and I went to our front window and I said to Bill, I said, '*Somebody's* in a good mood.' I don't know as I'd ever heard Abby singing before."

"Singing!" Jeannie and Stem said at exactly the same time. Then Jeannie asked, "What was the song?"

"Something about a goat; I don't know."

Jeannie looked at Stem. He shrugged.

Louisa said, "The dog lay so far from where Abby lay, I guess he must have been thrown. The driver found him, poor woman. The driver was beside herself. She found him lying close to where her car had knocked the lamppost over. I'm just thankful Abby didn't have to see him."

"Her," Jeannie said.

"Pardon?"

"The dog was a her."

"Oh, I'm sorry."

"She was old," Jeannie said. "The dog, I mean. She'd had a good long life."

"Still, though," Louisa said.

Then she held up the casserole she'd brought and told

them it was gluten-free, in case anybody cared.

And how did it happen, pray tell, that Abby had chanced to be off serenading the neighborhood with none of the family any the wiser? Amanda was the only one who came right out and asked, once Louisa was gone, but no doubt the others were wondering too. They sat around the living room listlessly, with the light coming in all wrong—sunshine filtering through the rear windows on a weekday morning, when most of the family should have been at work. "Don't look at *me*," Denny told Amanda. "I wasn't even up yet"—interrupting Nora, who was wearing a troubled expression and had started to speak also.

"I've asked myself and asked myself," Nora said. "You don't know how many times I've asked. When the boys and I left for school, she was sitting on the porch. When I came back she was gone. But Brenda was in the house still, so where was Mother Whitshank? Was she up in her room? Was she in the backyard? How did she leave for a walk without my knowing?"

"Well, you couldn't keep an eye on her every single minute," Jeannie said.

"I should have, though! It turns out I should have. I am so, so sorry. The two of us had a very special bond, you know. I'm never going to forgive myself."

"Hey," Stem said. "Hon."

Which was about as far as Stem could ever go when it came to offering comfort. Nora seemed grateful, however. She smiled at him, her eyes brimming.

"We're not mind readers," Denny said. "She should have *told* us she wanted a walk. She had no business taking off like that!"

Oh, everybody was true to form—Denny angry, Nora remorseful, Amanda looking for someone to blame. "How could she have told you," Amanda asked Denny, "when you were snoring away in bed?"

"Whoa!" he said, and drew back in his chair, holding up both hands.

"Anybody would think you'd worn yourself out with hard work," Amanda said.

"Well, it's not as if *you've* been over here slaving away."

"Stop it, both of you," Jeannie said. "We're getting off the subject."

"What *is* the subject?" Amanda's Hugh asked.

"I have this really, really awful feeling that Mom wanted us to play 'Good Vibrations' at her funeral."

"*What?*" Hugh said.

"She used to say as much. Didn't she, Mandy?"

Amanda couldn't answer because she had started crying, so Denny stepped in. He said, "I don't know if she meant that literally, though."

"We need to find her instructions. I remember she wrote some."

"Dad?" Stem asked. "Do you know where her instructions could be?"

Red was staring into space, both of his hands on his knees. He said, "Eh?"

"Mom's instructions for her funeral. Did she tell you where she put them?"

Red shook his head.

"We should check her study," Stem told the others.

"They wouldn't be in her study," Nora said. "She cleared out those shelves when Denny moved in. She said she was going to borrow some desk space from Father Whitshank."

"Oh!" Red said. "She did. She asked if she could put her stuff in one of my drawers."

Amanda sat up straighter and dabbed her nose with a tissue. "We'll look there," she said briskly. "And, Jeannie, I'm sure she didn't really want 'Good Vibrations.' Not when it came right down to it."

"You must not know Mom, then," Jeannie said.

"*My* only fear is, she's requested 'Amazing Grace.'"

"I like 'Amazing Grace,'" Stem said mildly.

"So did I, till it got to be a cliché."

"It's not a cliché to *me*."

Amanda raised her eyes to the ceiling.

At lunchtime they just foraged in the fridge instead of cooking. "I can't find a thing in here but casseroles," Denny complained, and Amanda said, "Isn't it interesting: people never seem to bring liquor when somebody dies, have you noticed? Why not a case of beer? Or a bottle of really good wine? Just these everlasting casseroles, and who eats casseroles nowadays?"

"I eat casseroles," Nora told her. "I serve them several times a week."

Amanda sent Denny a guilty glance and said no more.

"I was thinking when I woke up this morning about the next-door people," Jeannie said musingly. "The people at the beach. They'll tell each other next summer, they'll say, 'Oh, look at that! They don't have their mother anymore!'"

"Will we still *go* to the beach?" Stem wondered.

"Of course we'll go," Amanda told him. "Mom would expect us to. It would *kill* her if we didn't go!"

There was a silence. Then Jeannie gave a wail and buried her face in her hands.

Nora stood up and walked around the table, Sammy straddling her hip, to stroke Jeannie's shoulder. Sammy hung out at an angle and gazed down at her with interest. "There, there," Nora told her. "This will get easier, I promise. God never gives us more than we can handle."

Jeannie only cried harder.

"Actually, that's not true," Denny said in an informative tone of voice. He was leaning back against the fridge with his arms folded.

Nora glanced at him, still smoothing Jeannie's shoulder.

"He gives people more than they can handle every day of the year," Denny told her. "Half of the world is walking around just . . . *destroyed*, most of the time."

The others turned to Nora for her reaction, but she didn't seem to take offense. She just said, "Douglas, could you find Sammy's juice cup, please?"

Stem rose and left the room. The others stayed as they were. There was something disjointed about all of them, something ragged and out of alignment.

Stem was the one who searched Red's desk for the funeral instructions, while Red just watched from the couch with his hands resting slack on his knees. It turned out that Abby had taken over his bottom drawer. Her papers filled it to the brim—her poems and journals, letters from needy orphans and old friends, photos of long-ago classmates and her parents and various strangers.

All of these Stem leafed through in a desultory way and then handed over to Red, who took longer with them. The photos alone consumed several minutes. "Why, there's Sue Ellen Moore!" he said. "I haven't thought of her in years." And he gazed lingeringly at a laughing young Abby hanging on to the arm of a sullen boy smoking a cigarette. "I fell for her the first time I saw her," he told Stem. "Oh, she was always talking about the day she fell for *me*, I know. 'It was a beautiful, breezy, yellow-and-green afternoon,' she'd say, but that was when she was almost grown, she *was* grown, whereas I, now . . . I had been mooning over Abby all along. That's my friend Dane you see her with there; Dane was the one she liked first."

A desiccated violet flattened in waxed paper made him first frown in perplexity and then smile, but without saying why, and he spent some time studying a typewritten list of what must have been New Year's resolutions. "'I will make myself count to ten before I speak to the children in anger,'" he read out. "'I will remind myself daily that my mother is getting old and will not be with us forever.'" The folder of Abby's poems, though, he laid aside without a glance, as if fearing he would find them too painful, and he didn't so much as crack open any of her little black-and-red bound journals.

Some of the items were mystifying. A wrinkled, flattened Hershey's-bar wrapper; a piece of tree bark in a tiny brown paper bag; a yellowing two-page newsletter from a nursing home in Catonsville. "'Five Tasks for Dying,'" Stem read aloud from the newsletter.

"For dieting?"

"Dying."

"Oh, what's it say?"

"Nothing to do with a funeral service," Stem said, passing it over. "Telling people you love them, telling them goodbye . . ."

"Just—please, God—don't let her ask for a 'celebration,'" Red said. "I don't much feel like celebrating just now." He let the newsletter drop unread onto the couch beside him. Stem didn't seem to have heard him, though. He was studying a sheet of onionskin covered with blurred typewriting—a carbon copy, obviously; the one and only item in an unmarked manila envelope.

"Found it?" Red asked.

"No, just . . ."

Stem went on reading. Then he raised his head. His lips had gone white; he had a drawn, almost dehydrated look. "Here," he said, and he handed the paper to Red.

"'I, Abigail Whitshank,'" Red read out, "'hereby agree that—'" He stopped. His eyes went to the bottom of the page. He cleared his throat and continued, "'—hereby agree that Douglas Alan O'Brian will be raised like my own child, with all attendant rights and privileges. I promise that his mother will be granted full access to him whenever she desires, and that she may reclaim him entirely for her own as soon as her life circumstances permit. This agreement is contingent upon his mother's promise that she will never, ever, for any reason, reveal her identity to her son unless and until she assumes permanent responsibility for him; nor will I reveal it myself.'" He cleared his throat again. He said, "'Signed, Abigail Dalton Whitshank. Signed, Barbara Jane Autry.'"

"I don't understand," Stem said.

Red didn't answer. He was staring down at the contract.

"Is that *B. J.* Autry?" Stem asked.

Red still didn't speak.

"It is," Stem said. "It's got to be. Barbara Jane Eames, she started out, and then at some point she must have married someone named Autry. She was right there in front of us all along."

"I guess she found your listing in the phone book," Red said, looking up from the contract.

"Why didn't you tell me?" Stem demanded. "You had an obligation to tell me! I don't care what you promised!"

"*I* didn't promise," Red said. "I knew nothing about this."

"You had to know."

"I swear it: your mom never said word one."

"You're claiming she knew the truth all these years and kept it from her own husband?"

"Evidently," Red said. He rubbed his forehead.

"That's not possible," Stem told him. "Why on earth would she do that?"

"Well, she . . . maybe she was worried I would make her give you up," Red said. "I'd tell her she would have to hand you over to B. J. And she was right: I would have."

Stem's jaw dropped. He said, "You'd have handed me over."

"Well, face it, Stem: this was a *crazy* arrangement."

"But still," Stem said.

"Still what? You were B. J.'s legal offspring."

"I guess it's a good thing she's not around anymore, then," Stem said bitterly. "She died, right?"

"Yes, I seem to remember she did," Red said.

"You 'seem to remember,'" Stem said, as if it were an accusation.

"Stem, I swear to God I had no knowledge of any of this. I barely knew the woman! I can't even figure how your mom could get a lawyer to go along with it."

"She didn't get a lawyer. Look at the language. Oh, she *tried* to sound legal—'attendant rights and privileges,' 'unless and until'—but what lawyer writes 'never, ever'?

What official document is a single paragraph long? She cooked it up herself, she and B. J. between them. They didn't even have it notarized!"

"I have to say," Red said, looking down at the contract again, "I'm a little bit . . . annoyed by this."

Stem gave a humorless snort.

"Sometimes your mother could be . . . I mean, Abby could be . . ." Red trailed off.

"Look," Stem said. "Just promise me this. Promise you won't tell people."

"What, not tell *anyone*? Not even Denny and the girls?"

"No one. Promise you'll keep it quiet."

"How come?" Red asked him.

"I just want you to."

"But you're grown now. It couldn't change anything."

"I mean this: I need you to forget you ever saw it."

"Well," Red said. And he leaned forward and handed it over.

Stem folded the contract and put it in his shirt pocket.

It emerged that not even Red's bottom desk drawer had provided quite enough space for Abby's papers. Where her funeral directive showed up, finally, was the cupboard beneath the window seat, interleaved with programs from other people's funerals—her parents' and her brother's and a "ceremony of remembrance" for someone named Shawanda Simms whom none of the rest of the family had heard of. And no, she did not request "Good Vibrations," or "Amazing Grace," either, for that matter. She wanted "Sheep May Safely Graze" and "Brother James's Air," both to be sung by only the choir, thank goodness; and then the congregation should join in on "Shall We Gather at the River?" Friends and/or family could give testimonials, supposing they cared to (this wording struck her daughters as pathetically tentative), and Reverend Stock could say something brief and—if it wasn't asking too much—"not too heavy on the religion."

The mention of Reverend Stock threw everyone into a tizzy. First, they couldn't even think who he was. Then Jeannie figured out that he must be the pastor at Hampden Fellowship—the little church that Abby had gone back to from time to time, having belonged to it in her childhood. But the Whitshanks' official place of worship, at least on Christmas Eve and Easter, was St. David's, and St. David's was what Amanda had booked for eleven o'clock Monday morning. Did it really, really make any difference? she wondered aloud. Red said it did. Perhaps reasoning that Nora was their expert on religious matters, he commissioned her to place the necessary calls to St. David's and to Reverend Stock. Nora went off to the sunroom phone and came back some time later to report that Reverend Stock had retired several years ago, but Reverend Edwin Alban was saddened to hear of their loss and would pay a visit that afternoon to discuss the particulars. Red blanched at the mention of a visit, but he thanked her for arranging it.

By now, everybody in the family was unraveling around the edges. The three little boys kept waking at night and crossing the hall to climb into bed with Stem and Nora. Stem forgot to cancel an appointment with a Guilford woman who was thinking of adding a major extension to her house. Jeannie and Amanda got into a quarrel after Amanda said that while Alexander might indeed have held a special place in Abby's heart, it was only to be expected because "Alexander is so . . . you know." "He's so what? What?" Jeannie had demanded, and Amanda had said, "Never mind," and made a big show of clamping her mouth shut. Not ten minutes later, Deb gave Elise a black eye for claiming that their grandma had once confided that she loved Elise the best. "Now, how to amuse them today?" Red asked—a line from a Christopher Robin poem that Abby used to quote whenever some new family catastrophe arose. Then he got a stricken look, no doubt at the sound of Abby's merry voice echoing in his head. Meanwhile Denny, true to form, started spending long periods shut away in his room doing no one knew what, although occasionally he could be heard talking on his cell phone. But to whom? It was a mystery. Even Heidi was acting up. She kept raiding the garbage container under the kitchen sink and leaving disgusting knots of chewed foil beneath the dining-room table.

"You girls have to tell me if I start looking seedy," Red told his daughters. "I don't have your mother around anymore to keep me up to par." But as the week wore on, and his shirts developed food stains and he never got out of those slippers, he shrugged off any suggestion they made. "You know, Dad," Jeannie said, "I believe those pants of yours are ready for the rag bag," and he said, "What are you talking about? I've just now got them properly broken in." When Amanda offered to take his suit to the cleaner's in preparation for the funeral, he told her there was no need; he'd be wearing a dashiki. "A *what*?" Amanda asked him. He turned and walked out of the sunroom, leaving his daughters staring at each other in dismay. A few minutes later he came back carrying a blousy sort of smock in a teal blue so brilliant, so electrically vibrant, that it was painful to the eyes. "Your mother made this for our wedding," he said, "and I thought it would be appropriate if I wore it to her funeral."

"But, Dad," Amanda said, "your wedding was in the sixties."

"So?"

"Maybe in the sixties people wore these, although I can't quite . . . but that was almost half a century ago! All the seams are fraying, just look. There's a rip under one arm."

"So we'll fix it," Red said. "It'll be just as good as new."

Amanda and Jeannie exchanged a look, which Red caught. He turned abruptly to Denny, who was lounging on the couch cycling through TV channels. "This is *easy* to fix," Red told him, holding up the dashiki on its wire hanger. "Right? Am I right?"

Denny said "Huh?" and flicked his eyes over. "Oh, sure, I can fix that," he said. "If I can find the same color thread."

The girls groaned, but Denny stood up and took the dashiki from Red and left the room. "Thanks," Red called after him. Then he turned back to his daughters and said, "I've got some corduroys I could wear with it, kind of a light gray. Gray goes good with blue, doesn't it?"

"Yes, Dad," Amanda said.

"At our wedding I wore bell-bottoms," he said. "Your grandma Dalton had a conniption."

There'd been no photos of their wedding, because Abby had claimed that a photographer would ruin the mood. So Amanda and Jeannie perked up, and Jeannie asked, "What did Mom wear?"

"This long sort of flowy, I forget what they call it," Red said. "A Kaplan?"

"A caftan?"

"That's it." His eyes filled with tears. "She looked nice," he said.

"Yes, I bet she did."

"I know I can't ask, 'Why me?'" he said. The tears were running down his face now, but he didn't seem to realize it. "We had forty-eight good years together. That's way more than a lot of folks get. And I know I should be glad she went first, because she never could have managed without me. She couldn't even fix a leaky spigot!"

"Right, Dad," Jeannie said, and she and Amanda were crying too now.

"But sometimes I just have to ask anyhow. You know?"

"Yes, Dad. We know."

*

Carla wasn't happy about letting Susan miss school for the funeral. Everybody heard Denny arguing with her on the phone. "She was my mother's favorite grandchild," he said. "You're telling me the kid can't skip one measly math test for her sake?" In the end it was agreed that she could come but not stay over, in order to be back in school on Tuesday morning. So immediately after breakfast on the morning of the funeral Denny drove down to the train station to meet her. The child he returned with was a much more solemn, more dignified version of the Susan who'd gone to the beach with them. She wore a charcoal knit dress with a demure white collar, and black tights and black suede pumps. Some sort of training bra appeared to be crumpled around her chest. Stem's three boys eyed her shyly at first and wouldn't speak, but she herded them into the sunroom and in a few minutes chattery voices began drifting toward the kitchen, where the grown-ups were still sitting around the breakfast table.

Red wore floppy gray corduroys and his dashiki, which was even more startling off its hanger. The sleeves ballooned extravagantly over elasticized cuffs, giving him a buccaneer air, and the slit at the neck was deep enough to expose a whisk broom of gray chest hair. But Nora said, "Oh, didn't Denny do a nice job of mending!" and Red looked satisfied, not appearing to notice that she hadn't said a word about the overall effect.

When the doorbell rang and Heidi started barking,

they all gathered themselves together. That would be Ree Bascomb's maid, who had agreed to babysit the three boys. Once she'd been given her instructions, they all filed out the back door—Stem and Nora, Red, Denny and Susan—and climbed into Abby's car. Denny drove. Red sat next to him. During the ten-minute trip to the church Red said nothing at all, just gazed out the side window. In the rear, Nora made small talk with Susan. How was school this year? How was her mother? Susan answered politely but briefly, as if she felt it would be disrespectful not to keep her mind on the funeral. Denny drummed his fingers on the steering wheel every time they stopped for a light.

In Hampden, the rest of the world was enjoying an ordinary Monday morning. Two heavyset women stood talking to each other, one of them trailing a wheeled cart full of laundry. A man pushed a bundled-up baby in a stroller. The weather had started out cool but was rapidly growing warmer, and some people wore sweaters but a girl emerging from a liquor store was in short shorts and rubber flip-flops.

The church turned out to be a small, unassuming white cube topped with more of a cupola than a steeple, squeezed between a ma-and-pa grocery store and a house already decorated to the nines for Halloween. They might have missed it altogether if not for the signboard in front. HAMPDEN FELLOWSHIP was spelled out across the top of the frame, with WELCOME HOME PRIVATE SPRINKLE in movable type below. There wasn't even a parking lot, or not one that Denny could locate. They had to park on the street. As they were piling out of the car, Jeannie and Hugh drew up behind them with their two children and Hugh's mother. Then Amanda and *her* Hugh walked up with Elise, who was wearing patent-leather heels and a shiny, froufrou dress so short she could have been a cocktail waitress. A patch of pancake makeup nearly hid her black eye. All it took was the sight of each other for Jeannie and Amanda to dissolve in torrents of tears, and they stood on the sidewalk hugging while Mrs. Angell clucked sympathetically and clasped her purse to her bosom. She wore a pretty flowered hat that looked very churchlike. In fact all of them were dressed in their best today except for Red, whose dashiki hem flared below his Orioles jacket.

Eventually, they climbed the two front steps and entered a low-ceilinged white room lined with dark pews. It had the deep chill of a place that had sat through an autumn night without heat, although a furnace could be heard now rumbling somewhere below. A wooden lectern faced them, with a plain dark cross on the wall behind it, and off to one side a woman with dyed red hair was playing "Sheep May Safely Graze" on an upright piano. (Reverend Alban had already explained that his choir members were working folk and would not be able to sing on a weekday.) The pianist didn't look in their direction but continued plinking away while they threaded up the aisle and settled in the second row. Possibly they could have chosen the first row, but there was unspoken agreement that that would have felt too show-offy.

A tall vase of white hydrangeas stood in front of the lectern. Where had *those* come from? The Whitshanks hadn't ordered flowers, and they had specified in the *Sun* that they didn't want any sent—just donations to the House of Ruth, if people were so inclined. Abby had been odd about flowers. She liked them growing outside, unpicked. Jeannie whispered, "Maybe they're from someone's yard," which would have been preferable, at least, to flowers from a florist, but Amanda, sitting next to her, whispered, "Isn't it too late in the year?" They could have spoken in normal tones, but they were all a little self-conscious. None of them felt entirely certain about funeral etiquette—whom to greet, where to look, who should be handed discreet envelopes of cash at the end of the service. Twice just this morning, Amanda had phoned Ree Bascomb for advice.

The children sat at the far end, with Susan in the middle because she was from away and therefore the most interesting. Red was on the aisle, at Amanda's insistence. She had pointed out that friends might like to stop by his pew and say a few words to him. Since this was exactly what Red feared, he sat hunch-shouldered with his head lowered, like a bird in the rain, and stared fixedly at his knees.

Reverend Alban entered from a side door near the piano. Eddie, he'd asked them to call him. He was a very blond, disconcertingly young man in a black suit, his skin so fair that you could see the blood coursing beneath it. First he bent over Red and pressed Red's right hand between both of his own, and then he asked Amanda if she had the list of people who would be speaking. At the time of his visit to the house they hadn't yet decided on the speakers, but now Amanda handed him a sheet of paper and he ran his eyes down it and nodded. "Excellent," he said. "And how do you pronounce this one? E-lyce?"

"E-leece," Amanda said firmly, and Jeannie stiffened next to her. It didn't seem a good sign that he had had to ask. He slipped the paper inside his jacket and went to sit on a straight-backed chair beside the lectern.

Guests had begun trickling into the pews behind them. The Whitshanks heard footsteps and murmurs, but they went on facing forward.

Reverend Alban—Eddie—had admitted during his visit to the house that he hadn't known Abby personally. "I've only pastored at Hampden three years," he'd said. "I'm sorry we didn't have a chance to get acquainted. I'm sure she was a very nice lady."

The word "lady" had made them all go steely-faced and wary. This man had no *idea* of Abby! He was picturing some old biddy in orthopedic shoes. "She was not but seventy-two," Jeannie told him with her chin out.

But he himself was so young, that must have sounded old to him. "Yes," he'd said, "it always feels too soon. But the Lord in his wisdom . . . Tell me, Mr. Whitshank, do you have any wishes of your own for the service?"

"Me? Oh, no," Red had said. "No, I'm not . . . I don't . . . we haven't thrown a lot of funerals in this family."

"I understand. Then might I suggest—"

"It's true my parents passed away, but I mean, that was so sudden. Their car stalled on the railroad tracks. I guess I was in shock; I really don't remember too much about the funeral."

"That must have been—"

"Now that I look back on it, I don't feel like I really took it in. I feel like it sort of slipped by me. And it all seems so long ago, although truth to tell it was only back in the sixties. *Modern* times! We'd sent men into space by then. Why, my folks lived long enough to see aluminum-frame window screens, and clip-on fake mullions and flush doors and fiberglass bathtubs."

"Just fancy that," Reverend Alban had said.

So what with one thing and another, his visit hadn't settled much. None of the family knew what to expect when he rose to stand at the lectern, finally, and the piano fell silent.

"Let us pray," he .told the congregation. He held up both arms and everyone rose; pews creaked all through the room. He closed his eyes, but the Whitshanks kept theirs open—all but Nora. "Heavenly Father," he intoned in a hollow-sounding voice, "we ask you this morning to comfort us in our bereavement. We ask you to . . ."

"That Atta woman's here," Jeannie whispered to her husband.

"Who?"

"The orphan who came to lunch last month, remember?"

Apparently, in the process of rising for the prayer, Jeannie had contrived to cast a backward glance at the congregation. Now she glanced again and said, "Oh! And there's the driver of the car. She's got somebody with her; could be her husband."

"Poor gal," Hugh said.

The driver of the car that killed Abby had paid a visit to the house the day after the accident, all upset, and apologized a dozen times even though it was common knowledge that it hadn't been her fault. She kept saying that she would see that sweet dog till her dying day. "There are a *lot* of people here," Jeannie whispered, but then a look from Amanda hushed her.

Abby had not specified a Bible reading, but Reverend Alban provided one anyhow—a long passage from Proverbs about a virtuous woman. It was okay. At least, the family found nothing offensive in it. Then they were asked to sing a hymn called "Here I Am, Lord" that none of them was familiar with. Evidently Reverend Alban had felt the need of more musical selections than Abby had suggested. But that was okay too. Jeannie said later that it made her envision Abby arriving in heaven all brisk and bustly and social-worky: "Here I am, Lord; what needs doing?"

Abby *had* specified a poem. An Emily Dickinson poem, "If I Can Stop One Heart from Breaking," which Amanda read aloud at the lectern, after first welcoming everybody and thanking them for coming. She was the only one of Red and Abby's children who had wanted to speak. Denny claimed he wasn't good at such things; Jeannie had worried she would break down; Stem had simply said no without giving any reason.

However, Merrick had volunteered. Merrick! That was unexpected. She had flown in from Florida as soon as she heard the news and come directly to the house, prepared to roll up her sleeves and take over. Amanda had managed to fend her off, but no one could deny her when she begged to say a few words at the service. "I knew Abby longer than anyone did," she had said. "Longer even than Red!" And that was how she began her speech, standing not behind the lectern but beside it, as if to give the congregation the full benefit of her stark black dress with the asymmetrical hemline. "I knew Abby Dalton since she was twelve years old," she said. "Since she was a scrappy little Hampden girl whose father owned one of those hardware stores where you walk in off the street and say, 'Oh, my God! I'm so sorry! I seem to be in somebody's basement!' Shovels and rakes and wheelbarrows crowded up close together, coils of rope and lengths of chain hanging down from this really low ceiling you could practically bump your head on, and a tabby cat sound asleep on a sack of grass seed. But you know what? Abby turned out to be the livest wire in our whole school. She wasn't held back by her origins! She was a *firecracker*, and I'm proud to say she was my closest, dearest friend." Then her chin began to quiver, and she pressed her fingertips to her lips and shook her head and hurried back to her seat, which happened to be next to her mother-in-law.

All the other Whitshanks looked at each other with their eyes wide—even Red.

Next came Ree Bascomb, bless her heart, tiny and sprite-like in her cap of bouncy white curls. She started talking while she was still walking up the aisle. "I was actually *at* a hardware store once with Abby," she said. "Not her father's, of course. I didn't know her back then. I got to know her when we were young mothers going stir-crazy at home, and sometimes we'd just take off together, hop into one or the other's car and throw the kids in the backseat and drive somewhere just to be driving. So one day we were at Topps Home and Garden because Abby wanted a kitchen fire extinguisher, and while the man was ringing it up she said, 'Do you mind hurrying? It's kind of an emergency.' Just being silly, you know; she meant it as a joke. Well, he didn't get it. He said, 'I have to follow procedures, ma'am,' and she and I just doubled up laughing. We were *crying* with laughter! Oh, I don't think I'll ever again laugh as hard as I laughed with Abby. I'm going to miss her so much!"

She stepped away from the lectern dry-eyed, smiling at the Whitshanks as she passed them, but hers was the speech that made Jeannie and Amanda grow teary all over again.

"Thank you," Reverend Alban said. "And now we'll hear from Elise Baylor, Mrs. Whitshank's granddaughter."

Elise had an index card with her. She teetered up to the lectern on her strappy high heels, gazed out at the congregation with a dazzling smile, and cleared her throat.

"When me and my cousins were little," she said, "Grandma would call us on the phone and say, 'It's Saturday! Let's have Camp Grandma!' And we'd all go over to her house and she would do handicrafts with us—pressed flowers and pot holders and Popsicle-stick picture frames—or she'd read to us from these storybooks about children from other lands. I mean, some of those books were boring but parts were, like, sort of interesting. I'm going to remember my grandma for as long as I live."

Deb and Susan glared at her—it must have been the "*my* grandma" that irked them—while Alexander took on the sullen expression of a boy trying not to cry. Elise gave the congregation a triumphant look and clopped back to her seat.

"Thank you, all," Reverend Alban said. He nodded to the pianist, who pivoted hastily toward the piano and started on a rendition of "Brother James's Air." It seemed a peculiarly lighthearted tune for the occasion. Amanda's Hugh absentmindedly tapped one foot to the beat, till Amanda leaned forward and sent a meaningful frown down the row to him.

At the end of the piece, Reverend Alban rose and approached the lectern again. He placed his fingertips together. "I didn't know Mrs. Whitshank," he said, "and therefore I don't have the memories that the rest of you have. But it has occurred to me, on occasion, that our memories of our loved ones might not be the point. Maybe the point is *their* memories—all that they take away with them. What if heaven is just a vast consciousness that the dead return to? And their assignment is to report on the experiences they collected during their time on earth. The hardware store their father owned with the cat asleep on the grass seed, and the friend they used to laugh with till the tears streamed down their cheeks, and the Saturdays when their grandchildren sat next to them gluing Popsicle sticks. The spring mornings they woke up to a million birds singing their hearts out, and the summer afternoons with the swim towels hung over the porch rail, and the October air that smelled like wood smoke and apple cider, and the warm yellow windows of home when they came in on a snowy night. 'That's what *my* experience has been,' they say, and it gets folded in with the others—one more report on what living felt like. What it was like to be alive."

Then he raised his arms and said, "Page two thirty-nine in your hymnals: 'Shall We Gather at the River?,'" and everybody stood up.

"I don't understand," Red said to Amanda, under cover of the music. "*Where* did he say she went?"

"To a vast consciousness," Amanda told him.

"Well, that does sound like something your mother might do," he said. "But I don't know; I was hoping for someplace more concrete."

Amanda patted his hand, and then she pointed to the next line in the hymn book.

*

Ree Bascomb had warned them earlier that people would surely show up at the house right after the service. Whether or not they were invited, she said, there they'd be, expecting food and drink. So at least the family was prepared when the first caller rang the doorbell. Without so much as a pause to catch their breaths, they were back to murmuring thank-yous and accepting hugs and allowing their hands to be clasped. Ree's maid offered trays of little sandwiches delivered that morning by the caterer. A trio of Middle Eastern men, more formally dressed than Abby's own sons, watched in shocked silence as Stem's three boys chased each other around the legs of the grown-ups, and a tiny old woman whom nobody knew asked several people whether there were any of those biscuits that Abby used to make.

When Denny said his goodbyes before driving Susan to the train station, it was clear that he assumed the guests would be gone by the time he got back. But no, there they still were when he returned. Sax Brown and Marge Ellis were arguing about Afghanistan. Elise had got hold of a glass of white wine; she was pinching the stem daintily between her thumb and index finger with all her other fingers splayed out, and her makeup had worn thin and her black eye was re-emerging. Ree Bascomb's maid was serving crudités in her stocking feet now, and Ree herself, who had maybe had a tad too much to drink, stood with an arm looped around the waist of somebody's teenage son. Red looked exhausted. His face was gray and sagging. Nora was trying to make him sit down, but he stayed stubbornly upright.

Then suddenly the guests were gone, all of them at once, as if they had heard some secret dog whistle. The living room held no one but family, and it seemed too bright, like outdoors after a daytime movie. A decimated cheese board rested on an ottoman, and cracker crumbs littered the rug, and someone's forgotten shawl was slung across the back of a chair. Ree Bascomb's maid tinkled glassware in the kitchen. The toilet flushed in the powder room, and Tommy returned to the living room still hitching up his pants.

"Well," Red said. He looked around at everyone.

"Well," Amanda echoed.

They were all standing. They were all empty-handed. They had the look of people waiting for their next assignment, but there wasn't one, of course. It was over. They had seen Abby off.

It seemed there should be something more—some summing up, some account to deliver. "You wouldn't believe what Merrick said," they wanted to report. And "You'd have laughed to see Queen Eula. No sign of Trey, wouldn't you know, because he had an important meeting, but Queen Eula came. Can you imagine? Remember how she always used to swear you were a Communist?"

But wait. Abby was dead. She would never hear about any of this.

8

It could be argued that with Abby gone, there was no further need for anyone to stay on in the house with Red. He was more or less able-bodied, after all, and he went right back to work the morning after the funeral. That afternoon, though, he came home early and slipped upstairs to bed, and if Nora hadn't walked into his room with a stack of folded laundry he might have lain there undiscovered for who knows how long, one hand clamped to his chest and a line of either pain or worry crimping his forehead. He said it was nothing, just a tired spell, but he didn't object when Nora insisted on Denny's driving him to the emergency room.

In fact it *was* nothing—indigestion, the doctors decided six hours later, and he was sent home along with all four of his children, the other three having assembled at the hospital as soon as Nora phoned them. Still, it started his daughters thinking.

They had agreed, till then, that there would be plenty of time to sort out the household arrangements. Let things settle a bit, they told each other. But the rest of that week, both girls seemed to be on Bouton Road more often than they were at home—and generally without their husbands and children, as if to show that they meant business. They would wander in on some errand, Jeannie wanting Abby's recipe box or Amanda bringing grocery-store cartons to sort Abby's clothes into, and then they would hang around engaging one or another person in pointed conversation.

"You know we can't depend on Denny in any permanent way," Amanda told Nora, for instance. "He might promise us the moon, but one day he'll up and leave us. I'm surprised he's lasted this long." Then Denny walked into the kitchen and she broke off. Had he heard? But even after he'd set his cup in the sink and walked out again, Nora made no reply. She slid cookies off a baking sheet, her expression pleasant and noncommittal, as if Amanda had been talking just to hear herself talk.

And Stem! Maybe it was grief, but he'd become very quiet. "Underneath," Jeannie tried telling him once, "I think Dad has always assumed that you and Nora would live here forever. Inheriting the house, I mean, after he's gone." Then she sent a guilty look toward Denny, who was sitting next to Stem on the couch flicking through TV channels, but Denny merely grimaced. Even he knew it was Stem that Red would have pinned his hopes on. As for Stem himself, he didn't seem to have heard her. He kept his eyes fixed on the screen, although there was nothing to watch just then but commercials and more commercials.

After Sunday lunch, while Red was upstairs napping, Amanda told the others, "It's not like Dad needs a real caretaker. I grant you that. But someone should make sure every morning that he's made it through the night, at least."

"A simple phone call could establish that much," Stem said.

Jeannie and Amanda raised their eyebrows at each other. It was a remark they would have expected from Denny rather than Stem.

Stem wasn't looking at either of them. He was watching the children playing a board game on the rug.

Denny said, "Ah, well, maybe sooner or later Dad will find himself a lady friend."

"Oh! Denny!" Jeannie said.

"What?"

"Yes, he could do that," Amanda said equably. "Part of me wishes he would, by and by. Some nice, nurturing woman. Though another part of me says, 'But what if it's someone who's not our type? Someone who wears the back of her collar up or something?'"

"Dad would *never* fall for a woman who wore the back of her collar up!" Jeannie said.

Then Red's footsteps could be heard on the stairs, and everybody fell silent.

Later that same afternoon, when the girls had collected their families and were saying goodbye at the door, Red asked Amanda if he should let their lawyer know about Abby's death. "Goodness, yes," Amanda said. "Haven't you already done that? Who *is* your lawyer?" and Red said, "I have no idea; it was years ago we made our wills. Your mother was the one who took care of that stuff."

Stem made a sudden, sharp sound that resembled a laugh, and everybody looked at him.

"It's like that old joke," he told them. "The husband says, 'My wife decides the little things, like what job I take and which house we buy, and I decide the big things, like whether we should admit China to the U.N.'"

Jeannie's Hugh said, "Huh?"

"Women are the ones in charge," Stem told him. "Make no mistake about it."

"Isn't China *already* in the U.N.?"

But then Nora stepped in to say, "Don't worry, Father Whitshank, I'll track down your lawyer's name," and the moment passed.

On Monday, while Red was at work, Amanda arrived with more cartons. You'd think she didn't have a job. She was dressed in business clothes, though, so she must have been on the way to her office. "Tell me the truth, Nora," she said as soon as she had set the cartons in a corner of the dining room. "Can you imagine you and Stem staying on here forever?"

"You know we would never leave Father Whitshank if he really needed assistance," Nora said.

"So, do you think he *does* need assistance?"

"Oh, Douglas should be the one to answer that."

Amanda's shoulders slumped, and she turned without a word and walked out.

In the front hall she met up with Denny, who was coming down the stairs in his stocking feet. "Sometimes," she told him, "I wish Stem and Nora weren't so . . . virtuous. It's wearing, is what it is."

"Is that a fact," Denny said.

Red told his sons that he'd heard somewhere that after a man's wife dies, he should switch to her side of the bed. Then he'd be less likely to reach out for her in the night by mistake. "I've been experimenting with that," he told them.

"How's it working?" Denny asked.

"Not so very well, so far. Seems like even when I'm asleep, I keep remembering she's not there."

Denny passed Stem the screwdriver. They were taking all the screens down, preparing to put the storm windows in for the winter, and Red was supervising. Not that he really needed to, since the boys had done this many times before. He was sitting on the back steps, wearing a huge wool cardigan made by Abby during her knitting days.

"Last night I dreamed about her," he said. "She had this shawl wrapped around her shoulders with tassels hanging off it, and her hair was long like old times. She said, 'Red, I want to learn every step of you, and dance till the end of the night.'" He stopped speaking. He pulled a handkerchief from his pocket and blew his nose. Denny and Stem stood with a screen balanced between them and looked at each other helplessly.

"Then I woke up," Red said after a minute. He stuffed the handkerchief back in his pocket. "I thought, 'This must mean I miss having her close attention, the way I've always been used to.' Then I woke up again, for real. Have either of you ever done that? Dreamed that you woke up, and then found you'd still been asleep? I woke up for real and I thought, '*Oh*, boy. I see I've still got a long way to go with this.' Seems I haven't quite gotten over it, you know?"

"Gosh," Stem said. "That's hard."

"Maybe a sleeping pill," Denny suggested.

"What could *that* do?" Red asked.

"Well, I'm just saying."

"You think every one of life's problems can be solved by taking a drug."

"Let's lean this against that tree," Stem told Denny.

Denny nodded, tight-lipped, and swung around to back toward a poplar tree with the screen.

That evening, Ree Bascomb brought over an apple crumble and stayed to have a piece with them. "There's rum in it, is why I waited till I thought the little boys would be in bed," she said. Actually, the little boys were not in bed, although it was nearly nine. (They didn't seem to have a fixed bedtime, as Abby had often remarked in a wondering tone to her daughters.) But they were occupied with some sort of racetrack they'd constructed to run through the living room, so the grown-ups moved to the dining room—Ree, Stem and Nora, Red and Denny—where Ree set squares of apple crumble on Abby's everyday china and passed them around the table. She knew Abby's house as well as she knew her own, she often said. "You don't have to lift a finger," she told Nora, although Nora had already started a pot of decaf and rustled up cream and sugar, mugs and silverware and napkins.

Ree sat down at the table and said, "Cheers, everybody," and picked up her fork. "They say sweets are helpful in times of sadness," she said. "I've always found that to be true."

"Well, this was nice of you, Ree," Red said.

"I could use some sweets myself tonight. I don't know if you've heard, but on top of everything else now, Jeeter's died."

"Oh, what a pity," Nora said. Jeeter was Ree's tabby cat, going on twenty years old. Everyone in the neighborhood knew him.

Red said, "My God!" He set his fork down. "How in the world did that *happen*?" he asked.

"I just stepped out on the back stoop this morning and there he was, lying on the welcome mat. I hope he hadn't been waiting there all night, poor thing."

"My Lord! That's awful! But surely they're going to investigate the cause of death," Red said. He looked shattered. "These things don't just come about for no reason."

"They do if you're old, Red."

"Old! He wasn't even in nursery school yet!"

"What?" Ree said.

Everyone stared at him.

"I remember when he was born! It wasn't but two or three years ago!"

"What are you *talking* about?" Ree asked.

"Why, I'm . . . Didn't you say Peter died? Your grandson?"

"*Jeeter*, I said," Ree told him, raising her voice. "Jeeter, my cat. Good gracious!"

"Oh," Red said. "Excuse me. My mistake."

"I did wonder why you'd turned into such a cat person, all at once."

"Ha! Yes," he said, "and *I* wondered how you could act so offhand about your only grandchild passing." He gave an embarrassed chuckle and picked up his fork again. Then he peered across the table at Nora. She had her napkin pressed to her mouth, and her shoulders were heaving and she was making a slight squeaking sound. It seemed at first she might be choking, till it emerged that the tears streaming down her face were tears of laughter. Stem said, "Hon?" and the others stared at her. None of them had ever seen Nora get the giggles before.

"Sorry," she said when she could speak, but then she clapped her napkin to her mouth again. "I'm *sorry!*" she said between gasps.

"Glad to know you find me so amusing," Red said stiffly.

"I apologize, Father Whitshank."

She lowered the napkin and sat up straighter. Her face was flushed and her cheeks were wet. "I think it must be stress," she said.

"Of course it is," Ree told her. "You've all been through a world of stress! I should have thought before I came traipsing over here with my piddly little news."

"No, really, I—"

"Funny, I never noticed before how the two names rhymed," Ree said thoughtfully. "Peter, Jeeter."

Red said, "You were *nice* to come, Ree, and the crumble's delicious, honest." He didn't seem to realize that he hadn't taken a bite of it yet.

"I used Granny Smith apples," Ree told him. "All the other kinds fall apart, I find."

"These are not falling apart in the least."

"Yes, they're great," Denny said, and Stem chimed in with a not-quite-intelligible murmur. His eyes were still on Nora, although she seemed to have composed herself.

"Well!" Ree said. "Now that we've got the fun and games out of the way, let's talk about you all. What are your plans, everybody? Stem? Denny? Will you be staying on with your dad?"

It could have been an awkward moment—people were bracing for it around the table, clearly—except that Red said, "Nah, they'll be moving out shortly. I'm going to get myself an apartment."

"An apartment!" Ree said.

The others grew very still.

"Well, the kids have their regular lives, after all," Red said. "And there's no point in me rattling around alone here. I'm thinking I could just rent something, one of those streamlined efficiencies that wouldn't need any upkeep. It could have an elevator, even, in case I get old and doddery." He gave one of his chuckles, as if to imply how unlikely that was.

"Oh, Red, that's so adventurous of you! And I know just the place, too. Remember Sissy Bailey? She's moved into this new building in Charles Village, and she loves it. You remember she had that big house on St. John's, but now, she says, she doesn't have to give a thought to mowing the lawn, shoveling the snow, putting up the storm windows . . ."

"The boys were putting up our storm windows just this afternoon," Red said. "Do you know how many times I've been through that, in my life? Put them up in the fall, take them down in the spring. Put them up, take them down. Put them up, take them down. Is there no *end*? you have to ask."

"Very, very sensible to ditch all that," Ree said. She sent a bright look around the table. "Don't you all agree?"

After a brief hesitation, Denny and Stem and Nora nodded. None of them wore any expression whatsoever.

*

Amanda said it was sort of like when you're playing tug of war and the other side drops the rope with no warning. "I mean, it's almost a letdown," she said.

And Jeannie said, "Of course we want to take him off our worry list, but has he thought this through? Moving to some teeny modern place without crown moldings?"

"He's acting too meek," Amanda said. "This is too easy. We need to find out what's behind it."

"Yes, you have to wonder why he's in such a hurry."

They were talking to each other on their cell phones— Jeannie against a background of electric drills and nail guns, Amanda in the quiet of her office. Shockingly, no one had let them know right away about Red's announcement. They'd had to hear it the next morning. Stem happened to mention it at work, while he and Jeannie were dealing with a cabinetry issue.

"You did tell him we should talk this over," Jeannie had said immediately.

"Why would I tell him that?"

"Well, Stem?"

"He's a grown-up," Stem said, "and he's doing what you've hoped for all along. Anyhow: whatever he does, Nora and I are leaving."

"You are?"

"We're just waiting till her church can find a new home for our tenants."

"But you never said! You never discussed this with us!"

"Why should I discuss it?" Stem asked. "I'm a grown-up, too."

Then he rolled up his blueprints and walked out.

"It's like Stem's a different person lately," Jeannie told Amanda on the phone. "He's almost *surly*. He was never like this before."

"It must have to do with Denny," Amanda said.

"Denny?"

"Denny must have said something to hurt his feelings. You know Denny's never gotten over Stem moving back home."

"What could he have said to him, though?"

"What could he have said that he hasn't *already* said, is the question. Whatever it was, it must have been a doozie."

"I don't believe that," Jeannie said. "Denny's been on fairly good behavior lately."

But as soon as she hung up, she phoned him. (Wasn't it typical that even now, when he was living on Bouton Road again, she had to call his cell phone if she wanted to talk to him?)

It was past ten in the morning, but he must not have been fully awake yet. He answered in a muffled-sounding voice: "What."

"Stem says Dad is going to move to an apartment," Jeannie told him.

"Yeah, seems like he is."

"Where did *that* come from?"

"Beats me."

"And Stem and Nora are just waiting till their tenants find a new place and then they're leaving too."

Denny yawned aloud and said, "Well, that makes sense."

"Did you say anything to him?"

"To Stem?"

"Did you say anything that made him want to leave?"

"Dad's moving, Jeannie. Why *wouldn't* Stem leave?"

"But he was leaving in any case, he said. And he's been acting so different these days, so grumpy and short-tempered."

"He has?" Denny said.

"Something's eating him, I tell you. It sounds like he didn't even try to talk Dad out of this."

"Nope. None of us did."

"You mean you think it's okay? Dad giving up on the house his own father built?"

"Sure."

"You'll be out of a home, you know," Jeannie said. "We'll have to sell. I don't see you affording the taxes on an eight-room house on Bouton Road; you don't even have a job."

"Right," Denny said, not appearing to take offense.

"So will you go back to New Jersey?"

"Most likely."

Jeannie was quiet a moment.

"I don't understand you," she said finally.

"Okay . . ."

"You live here; you live there; you move around like it doesn't matter *where* you live. You don't seem to have any friends; you don't have a real profession . . . Is there anyone you really care about? I'm not counting Susan; our children are just . . . extensions of our own selves. But do you care how you worried Mom and Dad? Do you care about *us*? About me? Did you say something hurtful to Stem that's made him mad at everyone?"

"I never said a word to Stem," Denny said.

And he hung up.

"I feel awful," Jeannie told Amanda. They were on the phone again, although this time Amanda had answered in a hurried, impatient tone. "What *now*?" she had asked, sounding more like Denny than she knew.

"I really let Denny have it," Jeannie told her. "I accused him of being mean to Stem and giving grief to Mom and Dad and not working and not having any friends."

"So? What part of that isn't true?"

"I asked if he even cared about us. Well, specifically me."

"A reasonable question, I'd say," Amanda told her.

"I shouldn't have asked that."

"Get over it, Jeannie. He deserved every word."

"But asking if he cared about me, when here he quit his job that time and fell behind on his rent so he could come and help out because I was afraid I was going to smash my baby's head in!"

There was a silence.

"I didn't know that," Amanda said finally.

"You don't remember that Denny came and stayed with me?"

"I didn't know you were afraid you'd smash Alexander's head in."

"Oh. Well, forget that part."

"You could have told *me* that. Or Mom. She was a social worker, for God's sake!"

"Amanda, forget it. Please."

There was another silence. Then Amanda said, "But anyhow. The rest of what you said, Denny had coming to him. He *was* mean to Stem. And he did give Mom and Dad grief; he made their lives a living hell. And he *is* unemployed, and if he's got any friends we certainly haven't met them. And I'm not so sure he cares the least little bit about us! You told me yourself he sounded kind of unhappy when he telephoned that night before he came home. Maybe he was just looking for some *excuse* to come home."

"I still feel awful," Jeannie said.

"Listen, I hate to run, but I'm late for an appointment."

"Go, then," Jeannie said, and she stabbed her phone to end the call.

Denny and Nora were in the kitchen, cleaning up after supper. Or Nora was cleaning up, because Denny had done the cooking. But he was still hanging around, picking up random objects here and there on the counter and looking at the bottoms of them and setting them down.

Nora had been talking about Sissy Bailey's apartment. She had taken Red to see it earlier that afternoon. But he had claimed he could poke a hole in the walls with his index finger, so on Saturday a friend of the family who was a real-estate agent . . .

Denny said, "Is Stem pissed off about something?"

"Excuse me?" Nora said.

"Jeannie says he's in a bad mood."

"Why don't you ask him?" Nora said. She angled one last saucepan into a tiny space in the dishwasher.

"I thought maybe you could tell me."

"Is it so hard to just go talk to him? Do you dislike him that much?"

"I don't dislike him! Geez."

Nora closed the dishwasher and turned to look at him. Denny said, "What, you don't believe me? We get along fine! We've always gotten along. I mean, it's true he can be kind of a goody-goody, like 'See how much nicer I am than anybody else,' and he talks in this super-patient way that always sounds so condescending, and legend has it he behaves so well when his life doesn't work out perfectly although face it, how often has Stem's life not worked out perfectly? But *I* have no problem with Stem."

Nora smiled one of her mysterious smiles.

"Okay," Denny said. "I'll just ask him myself."

"Thanks for making supper," Nora told him. "It was delicious." He raised one arm and let it drop as he walked out.

In the sunroom the evening news was on, but Red was the only one watching. "Where's Stem?" Denny asked.

"Upstairs with the kids. I think somebody broke something."

Denny went back out to the hall and climbed the stairs. Children's voices were tumbling over each other in the bunk room. When he entered, the little boys were snaking that racetrack of theirs across the floor while Stem sat on a lower bunk, studying two parts of a bureau drawer.

"What have we here?" Denny asked him.

"Seems the guys mistook the bureau for a mountain."

"It was Everest," Petey told Denny.

"Ah."

"Could you hand me that glue?" Stem said.

"You really want to use glue on it?"

Stem gave him a look.

Denny passed him the bottle of carpenter's glue on the bureau. Then he leaned against the door frame, arms folded, one foot cocked across the other. "So," he said. "Sounds like you're moving out."

Stem said, "Yep." He squirted glue on a section of dovetailing.

"I guess you're pretty set on it."

Stem raised his head and glared at Denny. He said, "Don't even think about telling me I owe him."

"Huh?"

The little boys glanced up, but then they went back to their racetrack.

"I've done my bit," Stem told Denny. "You stay on yourself, if you think somebody ought to."

"Did I say that?" Denny asked him. "Why would *anybody* stay on? Dad's moving."

"You know perfectly well he's just hoping we'll talk him out of it."

"I don't know any such thing," Denny said. "What is it with you, these days? You've been behaving like a brat. Don't tell me it's just about Mom."

"*Your* mom," Stem said. He set the glue bottle on the floor. "She wasn't mine."

"Well, fine, if you want to put it that way."

"*My* mom was B. J. Autry, for your information."

Denny said, "Oh."

The little boys went on playing, oblivious. They were staging spectacular wrecks on an overpass.

"And all along, Abby knew that," Stem said. "She knew and she didn't tell me. She didn't even tell Dad."

"I still don't see why you're going around in a snit."

"I'm in a snit, as you call it, because—"

Stem broke off and stared at him.

"You knew, too," he said.

"Hmm?"

"This doesn't surprise you a bit, does it? I should have guessed! All that snooping you used to do: of course! You've known for years!"

Denny shrugged. He said, "It's immaterial to *me* who your mom was."

"Just promise me this," Stem said. "Promise you won't tell the others."

"Why would I tell the others?"

"I'll kill you if you tell."

"Ooh, scary," Denny said.

By now the little boys were taking notice. They'd stopped playing, and they were gaping at Stem. Tommy said, "Dad?"

"Go downstairs," Stem told him. "The three of you."

"But, Dad—"

"Now!" Stem said.

They stumbled to their feet and left, looking back at him as they went. Sammy was still clutching a plastic tow truck. Denny winked at him when he walked past.

"Swear to it," Stem told Denny.

"Okay! Okay!" Denny said, holding up both hands. "Uh, Stem, are you aware how fast that glue dries? You might want to fit those pieces together."

"Swear on your life that you will never let on to a soul."

"I swear on my life that I will never let on to a soul," Denny repeated solemnly. "I don't get it, though. Why do you care?"

"I just do, all right? I don't have to give you a reason," Stem said. But then he said, "I read someplace that even brand-new babies recognize their mothers' voices. Did you know that? They learn them in the womb. From the moment they're born, it's their mothers' voices they prefer. And I thought, 'Gosh, I wonder what voice *I* preferred, back then.' It seemed kind of sad to me that there was some voice I'd been craving all my life but never got to hear, at least not past the first little bit. And now look: it was B. J. Autry's voice—that gravelly rasp of hers and that trashy way of talking. When you think of how *Abby* talks, I mean talked! I should have belonged to Abby."

"So?" Denny said. "And eventually you did. Happy endings all around."

"But you remember how the family mocked B. J. behind her back. They'd wince when she gave that laugh of hers; they'd make faces at each other when she was holding forth about something. 'Oh, you know me; I just say it like it is,' she'd say. 'I tell it like I see it; I'm not one to mince my words.' As if that were something to brag about! And then everybody would share these secret glances, all round the table. So now I think, 'God, I'd die of shame if they found out she was my mother.' But I'm ashamed of feeling ashamed of her, too. I start thinking that the family had no *right* to act so snooty about her. I don't know what to think! Sometimes it's like I'm mourning what I missed out on: my real mother was sitting right there at our dining-room table and I never had an inkling, and it makes me mad as hell at Abby for not telling me— for that stupid, stupid contract. She wouldn't allow my own mother to tell me I was her son! And if B. J. had ever wanted me back, oh, Abby was happy to hand me over. 'Here you are, then'—easy come, easy go. And Dad: can you believe him? He told me *he* would have handed me over from the outset."

"You talked to Dad about this?"

"Well, guess what," Stem said, not appearing to hear

him. "B. J. never did want me back, as it turned out. She looked straight across the table at me and she didn't want me. She hardly ever *saw* me. She could have seen me any time, as often as she cared to, but she only came around now and then, two or three times a year."

"So what? You didn't even like her. You just said you hated her voice."

"Still, she was my mother. One woman in the world who thinks you're special—doesn't every kid deserve that?"

"You had that. You had Abby."

"Well, sorry, but that wasn't enough. Abby was *your* mom. I needed my own."

"You don't think Abby thought you were special?" Denny asked.

Stem was silent. He stared down at the drawer in his hands.

"Come *on*," Denny said. "She thought even the back of your neck was special. If she hadn't, you'd have led a very different life, believe me. You'd have been shunted around who knows where, rootless, homeless, stuck in foster care someplace, and you'd probably have turned into one of those misfit guys who have trouble keeping a job, or staying married, or hanging on to their friends. You'd have felt out of place wherever you went; there'd be nowhere you belonged."

He stopped. Something in his voice made Stem look up at him, but then Denny said, "Ha! You know what this proves."

"What."

"You're just following the family tradition, is all, the wish-I-had-what-somebody-else-has tradition—till they *do* have it. Like old Junior with his dream house, or Merrick with her dream husband. Sure! This could be the family's third story. 'Once upon a time,'" Denny intoned theatrically, "'one of us spent thirty years craving his real mother's voice, but after he found it, he realized he didn't like it half as much as his fake mother's voice.'"

Stem gave a thin, unhappy smile.

"Damn. You're more of a Whitshank than I am," Denny said.

Then he said, "That glue's bone-dry by now; didn't I warn you? You'll have to scrape it off and start over."

And he straightened up from the door frame and went back downstairs.

The family's real-estate friend dated from the days when Brenda had still been spry enough to be taken for a run now and then in Robert E. Lee Park. Helen Wylie used to walk her Irish setter there, and she and Abby had struck up a conversation. So when she arrived on Saturday morning—a breezy, sensible woman in corduroys and a barn jacket—no extensive instructions were needed. "I already know," she told Red straight off. "What you want is something solidly built. Prewar, I'm thinking. You were crazy to even consider something in that new building!

You want a place that you won't be ashamed to show to your contractor buddies."

"Well, you're right," Red said. Although he didn't have any contractor buddies, at least none that would be paying social calls.

"Let's go, then," Helen told Amanda. Amanda was the one who had gotten in touch with her, and she would be coming along. Even Red had admitted that he could use some help on this.

The first apartment was near University Parkway—old but well kept, with gleaming hardwood floors. The landlord said the kitchen had been remodeled in 2010. "Who did your work?" Red asked. He screwed up his face when he heard the name.

The second place was a third-floor walk-up. Red was only slightly winded by the time he reached the top of the stairs, but he didn't argue when Amanda pointed out that this wouldn't be a good long-term proposition.

The third place did have an elevator, and it was of an acceptable age, but so many dribs and drabs of belongings were crammed inside that it was hard to get any real sense of it. "I'll be honest," the super said. "The previous tenant died. His kids will have his stuff moved out within the next two weeks, though, and I'm going to get it cleaned then and give it a fresh coat of paint."

Amanda sent Helen a dispirited glance, and Helen turned the corners of her mouth down. A mole-colored cardigan sagged on the back of a rocker. A mug sat on the cluttered coffee table with a teabag tag trailing out of it. But Red seemed unfazed. He walked through the living room to the kitchen and said, "Look at this: he had everything arranged so he didn't have to get up from the table once he'd sat down to breakfast."

Sure enough, the rickety-looking card table held a toaster, an electric kettle, and a clock radio, all aligned against the wall, with a day-by-day pill organizer in the center where most people would have placed a vase of flowers. In the bedroom, Red said, "There's a TV you can watch from the bed." The TV was the heavy, old-fashioned kind, deeper than it was wide, and it stood on the low bureau across from the foot of the bed. "Watch the late news and then go straight to sleep," Red noted approvingly, although no TV had ever been seen in his bedroom on Bouton Road. But maybe that had been Abby's choosing. "This seems like a real convenient place for a guy making do on his own," Red said.

Amanda said, "Yes, but . . ." and she and Helen exchanged another glance.

"But picture it minus the furnishings," Helen suggested. "The TV and such will be gone, remember."

"I could put *my* set there, though," Red said.

"Of course you could. But let's focus on the apartment itself. Do you like the layout? Is it spacious enough? The rooms seem a little small to me. And what about the kitchen?"

"Kitchen is good. Reach across the table, grab your toast

straight out of the toaster. Take your heart pills. Turn on the weather report."

"Yes . . . The floor is linoleum, did you notice?"

"Hmm? Floor looks fine. I think my folks had a kitchen floor like that in our first house."

And that settled it. As Amanda told the others later, it appeared to be a question of imagination. Red's imagination: he had none. He just seemed glad that someone else had arranged things so he wouldn't need to.

Well, it did make things easier for his children. And they could always do some refurbishing after he'd moved in.

Helen was going to handle the house sale as well. She came in with them after the apartment tour to discuss the arrangements for that, with Stem and Denny joining in. "Such a comfortable old place this is," she said, looking around the living room. "And of course the porch is a huge draw. It's going to be a pleasure to show."

Everyone except Red looked encouraged. Red was gazing toward a nearby newspaper as if he wished he could be reading it.

"But it *is* still a sluggish market," Helen said. "And what I've learned is, buyers in these times expect perfection. We'll want to spruce the place up some."

"Spruce it up?" Red said. "What more could they possibly ask for? Every downstairs room but the kitchen's got double pocket doors."

"Oh, yes, I love the—"

"And it's not often you see an entrance hall like ours, two-story. Or these open transoms with the handsawed fretwork."

"But it isn't air-conditioned," Helen said.

Red said, "Oh, God," and he slumped in his seat.

"These days—" Helen said.

"Yeah, yeah."

"It won't be so hard," Denny told him. "They've got these mini-duct systems now where you won't need to tear up the walls."

Red said, "Who do you think you're talking to? I know all about those systems."

Denny shrugged.

"Also," Helen said. She cleared her throat. She said, "This would be your choice entirely, but you might want to consider his-and-her master bathrooms."

Red raised his head. He said, "Consider *what*?"

"I wouldn't bring it up except you do own a contracting firm, so it wouldn't be such an expense. That master bathroom you have now is gigantic. You could easily divide it in two, with a shower stall in between that's accessible from both sides. I just saw the most dazzling shower stall, with river-pebble flooring and multiple rainmaker nozzles."

Red said, "When my father built this house, it had only the one bathroom off the upstairs hall."

"Well, that was back in the—"

"Then he added the downstairs powder room after we moved in, and we thought we were something special."

"Yes, you certainly need a—"

"The master bathroom itself he didn't put in till my sister and I were in high school. What he'd say if he heard about his-and-hers, I can't even begin to imagine."

"It's customary, though, in the finer homes these days. As I'm sure you must have learned in your business."

"He himself grew up with just a privy," Red said. He turned to the others. "I bet you didn't know that about your grandfather, did you?"

They did not. They knew next to nothing about their grandfather, in fact.

"Well, a privy," Helen said with a laugh. "That would be a hard sell!"

"So we'll forget about the his-and-hers," Red told her. "Now, how long do you expect it will take to find a buyer?"

"Oh, once you've installed the air conditioning, and maybe upgraded your kitchen counters—"

"Kitchen counters!"

But then he clamped his lips tightly, as if reminding himself not to be difficult.

"It does seem the market's started looking up," Helen said. "There was a time there when places were languishing for a year or more, but lately I've been averaging, oh, just four to six months, with our more desirable properties."

"In four to six months it will go to seed," Red told her.

"You know it's not good for a house to sit empty. It will molder; it will get all forlorn; it will break my heart."

Amanda said, "Oh, Dad, we would never let that happen. We'll come and, I don't know, throw family picnics here or something."

Red just gazed at her miserably, his eyes so empty of light that he seemed almost sightless.

"Be honest," Jeannie said to Amanda. "Does any little part of you feel relieved that Mom died so suddenly?"

"You mean on account of her lapses," Amanda said.

"They would only have gotten worse; we can be pretty sure of that. Whatever they were. And Dad would be trying to look after her, and so would Nora; and Denny would have thought of some excuse to leave by then."

"But maybe it was just, oh, a circulation problem or something, and the doctors could have fixed it."

"That's not very likely," Jeannie said.

They were up in Red's bedroom on a rainy Sunday afternoon, packing cartons while the others watched a baseball game downstairs. Both of them wore scruffy clothes, and Amanda's chin was smudged with newspaper ink.

All week they had been packing, any free moment they could find. Separate islands of belongings had begun rising here and there in the house as people put in their requests: Abby's crafts supplies and her sewing machine in the upstairs hall for Nora, the good china packed in a barrel in the dining room for Amanda. (Red would keep the everyday china, which they were leaving in the cupboard until just before moving day.) Color-coded stickers dotted the furniture—a few pieces for Red's apartment, a few more for Stem and Jeannie and Amanda, and the vast majority for the Salvation Army.

Jeannie and Amanda dragged a filled carton between them out to the hall, where one of the boys could come get it later. Then Jeannie unfolded another carton and ran tape across the bottom flaps. "If I know Mom," she said, "she'd have refused any surgery anyhow."

"It's true," Amanda said. "Her advance directive basically asked us to put her out on an ice floe if she developed so much as a hangnail." She was collecting framed photos from the top of Abby's bureau. "I'm going to pack these up for Dad," she told Jeannie.

"Will he have space for them?"

"Oh, maybe not."

She studied the oldest photo—a snapshot of the four of them laughing on the beach, Amanda barely a teenager and the rest of them still children. "We look like we were having such a good time," she said.

"We *were* having a good time."

"Well, yes. But things could get awfully fraught, now and then."

"At the funeral," Jeannie said, "Marilee Hodges told me, 'I always used to envy you and that family of yours. The bunch of you out on your porch playing Michigan poker for toothpicks, and your two brothers so tall and good-looking, and that macho red pickup your dad used to drive with the four of you kids rattling around in the rear.'"

"Marilee Hodges was a ninny," Amanda said.

"Goodness, what brought *that* on?"

"It was hell riding in that truck bed. I doubt it was even legal. And I believe children should have their own rooms. And Mom could be so insensitive, so clueless and obtuse. Like that time she sent Denny for psychological testing and then told all of us his results."

"I don't remember that."

"Supposedly one of those inkblot thingies showed he'd been disappointed in his early childhood by a woman. 'What woman could that have been?' Mom kept asking us. 'He didn't know any women!'"

"I don't remember a thing about it."

"It was pretty clear she loved him best," Amanda said, "even though he drove her crazy."

"You're just saying that because you've got only one child," Jeannie told her. "Mothers don't love children best; they love them—"

"—differently, is all," Amanda finished for her. "Yes, yes, I know." Then she held up a photo of Stem at age four or five. "Would Nora like this, do you think?"

Jeannie squinted at it. "Put it in her box," she suggested.

"And what do I do with this one of Denny?"

"Does he have a box?"

"He says he doesn't want anything."

"Start a box for him anyhow. I bet wherever he lives is nothing but bare walls."

"I asked him yesterday," Amanda said, "whether he had let his landlady know that he was coming back, and all he said was, 'We're working on that.'"

"'Working on that'! What is *that* supposed to mean?"

"He's so darn secretive," Amanda said. "He pokes and pries into *our* lives, but then he gets all paranoid when we ask about his."

"I think he's mellowing, though," Jeannie told her. "Maybe losing Mom has done that. When I was taking down the wall of photos in his room, I asked him, 'Should I just chuck these?' All those photos of the Daltons, those chunky aunts from the forties with their shoulder pads and thick stockings. But Denny said, 'Oh, I don't know; that seems kind of harsh, don't you think?' I said, 'Denny?' I actually knocked on the side of his head with my knuckles. 'Knock knock,' I said. 'Is that *you* in there?'"

"Good," Amanda said promptly. "Let's give him these." And she reached for a sheet of newspaper and started wrapping a photo.

"Denny's getting nicer and Stem is getting crankier," Jeannie said. "And Dad! He's being impossible."

"Oh, well, Dad," Amanda said. "It's like you can't say anything right to him." She placed the wrapped photo in the carton Jeannie had just set up. "He's been fretting about the house so," she said. "How long it will take to sell it, how people might not appreciate it . . . So I asked him, I said, 'Should we try and get in touch with the Brills?'"

"The Brills," Jeannie repeated.

"The original-owner Brills. The ones who had the house built in the first place."

"Yes, I know who they *are*, Amanda, but wouldn't they be dead by now?"

"Not the sons, I don't imagine. The sons were only in their teens when Dad was a little boy. So I said, 'What if all these years the sons have been pining over this house and wishing they still lived here?' You remember what one of them said when their mother said they were moving. 'Aw, *Ma*?' he said. Well, you would think I'd suggested lighting a match to the place. 'What are you *thinking*?' Dad asked me. 'Where did you get such a damn-fool notion as that? Those two spoiled Brill boys are not *ever* getting their hands on this house. Put it right out of your mind,' he said. I said, 'Well, sorry. Gee. My mistake entirely.'"

"It's grief," Jeannie told her. "He's just lost the love of his life, bear in mind."

"Which loss are you talking about—Mom or the house?"

"Well, both, I guess."

"Huh," Amanda said. "I never heard before that grief makes people bad-tempered."

"Some it does and some it doesn't," Jeannie said.

They had reached that stage of packing where it seemed they'd created more mess than they had cleared out. Several half-filled cartons sat open around the room—the photos in a carton for Denny, blankets in a carton for Red, a mass of Abby's sweaters in a carton for Goodwill. With each sweater there had been a debate—"Don't you want to take this? You would look good in this!"—but after holding it up for a moment, one or the other of them would sigh and let it fall into the carton with the rest. The rug was linty, the floor was strewn with cast-off hangers and dry-cleaner's bags, and a hard gray light from the stripped windows gave the room a bleak and uncared-for look.

"You should have heard Dad's reaction when I told him he should maybe leave this bed behind and take a single," Amanda said.

"Well, I can understand: he wants the bed that he's used to."

"You haven't seen his apartment, though. It's dinky."

"It's going to feel weird to visit him there," Jeannie said.

"Yes, last night I had this peculiar moment when I was saying goodbye to him. He asked, 'Don't you want to take some leftovers with you?' *Mom's* thing to ask! 'It'll save you from cooking supper,' he said, 'one of the nights this week.' Oh, Lord, isn't it strange how life sort of . . . closes up again over a death."

"Even the little boys have adjusted," Jeannie said. "That's kind of surprising, when you think about it—that children figure out so young that people die."

"It makes you wonder why we bother accumulating, accumulating, when we know from earliest childhood how it's all going to end."

Amanda was looking around at the accumulation as she spoke—at the cartons and the stacked pillows and the tied-up bales of old magazines and the lamps with their shades removed. And that was nothing compared with the clutter elsewhere in the house—the towers of faded books teetering on the desk in the sunroom, the rolled carpets in the dining room, the stemware tinkling on the buffet each time the little boys stampeded past. And out on the front porch, waiting to go to the dump, the miscellaneous items that no one on earth wanted: a three-legged Portacrib, a broken stroller, a high chair missing its tray, and a string-handled shopping bag full of cracked plastic toys with somebody's small, clumsy pottery house perched on top, painted in kindergarten shades of red and green and yellow.

PART TWO

What a World, What a World

9

It was a beautiful, breezy, yellow-and-green morning in July of 1959, and Abby Dalton was standing at her front window watching for her ride. She wanted to run out before he could honk his horn. Her mother had a rule that boys should ring the doorbell and step inside the house and hold a polite conversation before they could carry Abby off, but try telling Dane Quinn that! He wasn't much of a one for small talk.

If her mother complained later, Abby would say, "Oh, didn't you hear him ring?" Her mother wouldn't quite believe her, but she would probably let it pass.

Abby was dressed in the new style she'd come home from college with this spring—a flowery, translucent skirt with a black knit leotard, and black nylon stockings even though the morning was already warming up. The stockings gave her a beatnik look, she hoped. (These were her only pair, and when she took them off at the end of the day she knew she'd find startling black splotches here and there on her legs where she had colored in the holes with a felt-tip marker.) Her long fair hair was streaked lighter in places from half a summer's worth of sun, and her eyes were heavily outlined with a black Maybelline eyebrow pencil but her lips were pale, which her mother said just made it seem she had forgotten something. Dane wasn't given to compliments—and that was fine; Abby could understand that—but occasionally, when she slid into his car, he would rest his eyes on her for a moment longer than usual, and she was thinking he might do that this morning. She had taken extra care getting ready, dampening her hair to comb it straight and dabbing a drop of vanilla on the insides of her wrists. Some days it was almond extract or rosewater or lemon oil, but today was most definitely a vanilla day, she'd decided.

She heard her mother's footsteps crossing the upstairs hall and she turned, but the footsteps stopped and her mother said something to Abby's father. He was shaving at the bathroom sink with the door open; it was Sunday and he'd slept late, for him. "Did you remember to . . . ?" her mother asked, and then something, something. Abby relaxed and turned back to the window. The Vincents from next door were getting into their Chevy. A good thing they were leaving: Mrs. Vincent was the kind of woman who would have asked Abby's mother, seemingly in innocence, "Now, who was that fella I saw Abby tearing out of the house to meet? Young folks nowadays are so . . . informal-like, aren't they?"

All Abby had told her mother was that she was hitching a ride with Dane to help set up for Merrick Whitshank's wedding. She had made it sound like a chore, not a date. (Although it *was* a date, in her mind. She and Dane were still at that early stage where even tagging along with him on some humdrum errand, hanging around his edges like a puppy tied outside a grocery store, made her feel especially chosen.) So far, Dane and her mother had come face-to-face only twice, and it hadn't gone well. Her mother just had a tendency to take against people, sometimes. She wouldn't say anything outright, but Abby always knew.

The Vincents drove away and a panel truck pounced on their space. Parking was very tight on this block. Almost no one had a garage. What could have been the Daltons' garage—the basement area at street level, opening onto the sidewalk—was Abby's father's hardware store. If Dane were to ring the doorbell for her, he would have had to park who-knows-where and walk from there to her house. So honking was just sensible, really.

Her mother was complaining about something, in her mild way. "... asked you a dozen times if I've asked once," she was saying, and Abby's father offered some muted response—"Sorry, hon," maybe, or "... told you I would get to it." Abby's cat marched purposefully down the stairs, each paw landing *plop*, *plop*, *plop*, as if he were offended. He leapt into the armchair near Abby and curled up and gave a disgusted sniff.

Some oppressive quality in the room—its small size,

or its overstuffed furniture, or its dimness compared to the sunlight out on the street—made Abby feel suddenly desperate to get away. Although she loved her home, really. And loved her family, too, and had thought she couldn't wait to finish her freshman year and come back to where she was cherished and made much of and admired. But all this summer she had felt so itchy and impatient. Her father told corny jokes and then laughed louder than his audience, "Haw! Haw!" with his mouth wide open, and her mother had this habit of humming a tiny fragment of some hymn every few minutes or so, just a couple of measures under her breath, after which, presumably, the hymn continued playing silently in her head until a few more notes emerged a moment later. Had she always done that? It would have perked things up if Abby's brother were around, but he was away lifeguarding at a Boy Scout camp in Pennsylvania.

Oh, and here came Dane! His two-tone Buick, blue and white, slowed for the stop sign at the corner. Already she could hear the pounding thrum of his radio. She grabbed her purse and tore open the screen door and rushed out lickety-split, so that by the time he'd double-parked in front of the Laundromat across the street she was flying down the stairs at the side of the house and there was no need for him to honk. His arm was dangling out his window— tanned skin, subtly muscled, glinting with gold hairs, she knew—and his face was turned toward her but she couldn't read his expression because cars kept passing between them. (All of a sudden there was traffic, as if his presence had enlivened the neighborhood.) She waited for a driver who made way too much of a production about having to veer around him, and then she darted across, causing another driver to brake and tap his horn. She circled the Buick's front end and opened the passenger door and hopped in with a flounce of her skirt. "Johnny B. Goode" was the song that was playing. Chuck Berry, hammering away. She set her purse on the seat between them and turned to meet Dane's gaze.

He tossed his cigarette stub out the window and said, "Hey, you."

"Hey, you."

Last night they had been all over each other but today they were playing it cool, evidently.

He shifted gears and started driving, his left arm still trailing out the window, his right wrist resting casually across the top of the steering wheel. "You look like you're still asleep," Abby told him.

In fact, he always looked that way. He kept his eyes so narrowed that it wasn't clear what color they were, and his pale-blond hair was too long and hanging over his face.

"I wish I *were* asleep," he said. "Last thing I wanted to hear was that alarm on a Sunday morning."

"Well, it's nice of you to do this."

"It's not nice so much as I need the money," he said.

"Oh, they're paying you?"

"What'd you think: I'd be getting up this early out of the goodness of my heart?"

But he just liked to sound tough, was all. He and Red were old friends, and she knew he was glad to help out.

Although it was probably true that he was short of cash. A few weeks back he'd been fired from his job. His family was well off—better off than hers, at least—but lately he'd been taking her on the kind of dates that didn't cost much: eating hamburgers at a drive-in or sitting around with their friends in somebody's parents' rec room or going to a movie. He would watch any movie that was showing, especially Westerns and tacky horror shows that made him laugh, though she was less enthusiastic because they couldn't really talk in the movies. Should she offer to pay her own way from now on? But the little she earned from her summer job was meant to pad out her scholarship. And besides, he might be insulted. He was prickly, she had learned.

They were leaving Hampden now. The houses grew farther apart; the lawns were bigger and greener. Dane said, "I don't guess I happened to mention that my dad's given me the boot."

"The boot?"

"Kicked me out of the house."

"Oh, my goodness!"

"I've been staying with my cousin. He's got an apartment on St. Paul."

Dane didn't often volunteer any personal details. She grew very still. (The radio had switched to "Good Golly, Miss Molly," and Dane's reedy, drawling voice was hard to distinguish from Little Richard's.) "I needed to get out of

292

there anyhow," he was saying. "Me and Pop were fighting a lot."

"Oh, what about?"

Dane unhooked his sunglasses from the rearview mirror and set them on his nose. They were the wraparound kind and she couldn't see his eyes at all now.

"Well," she said finally, "that can happen, in families."

It wasn't till they were waiting for the light at Roland Avenue that she ventured to break the silence again. "What is it you're helping to do today, anyhow?" she asked him.

"We're cutting up a tree."

"A tree!"

"Yesterday some of Mr. Whitshank's work crew took it down and today we're cutting it up. He wants the yard to look good for the wedding."

"But the wedding's at the church. And the reception's some place downtown."

"Maybe so, but the photographer's coming to the house."

"Oh," she said, still not seeing.

"Mr. Whitshank's got this whole, let's say, image in his head. He told us all about it. Can that guy ever talk! He can talk your ear off. He wants two photos. He wants Merrick coming down the stairs in her wedding dress with her bridesmaids ringed around the upstairs hall above her; that's the first photo. And then he wants her on the flagstone walk out front holding her bouquet with her bridesmaids spread in a V behind her. That's the second photo. The photographer's going to stand in the street with a wide-angle lens that takes in the whole house. Except this tulip poplar was smack in the way of the left-hand flank of bridesmaids and that's why it had to go."

"He's killing a perfectly good poplar tree for the sake of a photograph?"

"He says it was already dying."

"Hmm."

"Merrick and her bridesmaids have to get dressed at crack of dawn on her wedding day because taking those two photos is going to use up so much time," Dane said. "Mrs. Whitshank says he'll make Merrick late for her own wedding."

"And those full-length skirts! They'll get all leafy and twiggy!"

"Mr. Whitshank claims they won't. He's laying white carpet down the whole walk, and then extra on the sides near the house where the bridesmaids are going to stand."

Abby looked at Dane with her mouth open. Behind his dark glasses, he gave no hint what he thought of this plan.

"I'm surprised Merrick's going along with it," she told him.

"Oh, well, you know Mr. Whitshank," Dane said.

Abby didn't, in fact, know Mr. Whitshank at all. (*Mrs. Whitshank* was the one she was fond of.) She had the impression, though, that he was a man of strong opinions.

They passed the church where the wedding would take place in six more days. People were heading toward it in clusters, perhaps for Sunday school or an early service—the women and girls in pastels and flower-laden hats and white gloves, the men and boys in suits. Abby looked for Merrick, but she didn't see her. It was Dane's church too, not that he ever seemed to attend.

Abby had known Dane, at least by sight, since her early teens, but they hadn't gotten together till this past May, her first week home from college. She'd run into Red Whitshank one evening in the ticket line at the Senator, and he had two of his friends with him, one of them Dane Quinn. And Abby was with two of *her* friends; it had all worked out very neatly. Possibly Red had been hoping to sit next to her in the theater (it was common knowledge that he had a little crush on her), but she took one glance at Dane, at his forbidding scowl and his defensively hunched shoulders, and then stepped between him and her friend Ruth like the most brazen hussy (as Ruth said teasingly later). Something just came over her; she felt *pulled* to him. She liked his edginess, his wariness, his obvious grudge against the universe. Not to mention his good looks. Well, everyone knew his story. He'd been a standard-issue Gilman boy who went on to Princeton, like his father and both grandfathers before him, but just this past September—the start of his junior year— his mother had up and left his father and gone to live in Hunt Valley with the man who boarded her quarter horse. And as soon as Dane heard about it, he'd dropped out of school and come home. First he moped around the house but eventually, at his father's insistence, he got a job of some sort at Stephenson Savings & Loan. (Bertie Stephenson had been his father's college roommate.) He never talked about his mother; he iced over at any mention of her, but that just proved to Abby how deeply hurt he must be. Abby had a special fondness for people who tried to hide the damage. He became her newest worthy cause. She flung herself at him, worked to bring him out of himself, zeroed in on him at every gathering, wouldn't take no for an answer. But no *was* his answer, at first. He stood around separate from the others and drank too much and smoked too much and made sullen one-word responses to her most sympathetic remarks. Then one evening—on Red Whitshank's front porch, as it happened—he turned on her almost threateningly and backed her against the wall and said, "I want to know why you keep hanging around me."

She could have offered any number of good reasons. She could have said it was because of his obvious unhappiness, or her conviction that she could make a difference in his life. But what she said was, "Because of that up-and-down groove between your nose and your upper lip."

He said, "What?"

"Because your hair falls down all shaggy as if you're a little bit crazy."

He blinked and took a step back. "I don't know what you mean," he said.

"You don't have to know what I mean," she told him, and then, completely out of character, she moved toward him and raised her face to him and saw him begin to believe her.

Now it was more or less accepted that they were a couple,

although she could tell that their friends were surprised. She didn't explain herself to them. She became, in a way, a little like Dane; she grew cagey and evasive. She began to notice how stodgy their friends were, and although she had assumed, till now, that her ultimate goal in life was a husband and four children and a comfortable house with a yard, all at once she began biting off the words "domestic" and "suburban" with her eyebrows raised and the corners of her mouth turned down. "Who wants to go to the Club for dinner?" someone would say, and Dane would say, "Gosh, the Club, what an unspeakable thrill." Everybody would look sideways at Abby, but she would just smile tolerantly and take another sip of her Coke. She was the only one who knew him, she was saying—who divined that he was nowhere near as bad as he pretended to be.

Although every now and then, for a flash of a second, she wondered if his badness was precisely what attracted her. Not that he was *really* bad, but there was something risky about him, something contrary and outrageous. After he was fired, for instance, he had left the building with twenty-four boxes of staples. Fifty-seven thousand six hundred staples; later he'd done the math. (His glee when he told her this had made her smile.) And he didn't even own a stapler! He had once driven out to where his mother was living with Horse Guy, as Dane called him, and duct-taped all the doors shut in the middle of the night. *That* escapade had made Abby laugh aloud. "Why in the world . . . ?" she had asked, but he either couldn't or wouldn't explain; it was almost the only time he had let the word "mother" cross his lips, and maybe he already regretted it.

Also his drinking, while it was deplorable, lent him a certain shambling, reckless, juvenile-delinquent quality that touched her heart even while she was shaking her head over him. You could see this boy coming half a block away and know him by his rolling walk, his hands jammed in his pockets, his face half hidden by his shank of hair and his back a brooding C shape. Oh, it wasn't only the disadvantaged who needed compassion! He was leading a life just as hard, in some ways, as the lives of those poor little Negro children she was tutoring this summer. He could shoot a splinter of sadness straight through her.

She looked over at his profile, the slant of his cheek below the dark glasses, and sent him a small, warm smile even though he didn't see it.

"But. So. Anyhow. I was saying," he said, lifting his arm to signal a turn. "About my cousin."

"Your cousin," she repeated.

"George. The one I'm staying with."

"Oh, have I met him?"

"No, he's older. He's got a career and all. He's going away next weekend to visit his girlfriend in Boston."

The Buick tilted slightly as it swerved onto Bouton Road, and Abby grabbed her purse before it could slide off the seat.

"I'll have the place to myself," Dane said. He parked in front of the Whitshanks' and took his key from the ignition. The music stopped short but he went on sitting there, gazing through the windshield. "I was thinking you could come over Friday evening. Maybe tell your mom you were spending the night with a friend."

She had foreseen that something like this would arise, sooner or later. It was where they'd been heading all along. It was where she *wanted* to head.

So she couldn't explain what she said next. "Oh," she said. "I don't know," she said.

He turned and looked at her, although his expression was still a blank behind the dark glasses. "Don't know what?" he asked her.

"I'm not sure what friend I could tell her, and besides, I might be busy that night, I might have to do something with my parents; I'm not sure."

She wasn't handling this very smoothly. She was cross with herself for sounding so flustered. "I'll have to see," she told him, and she yanked open her door and all but fell out of the car in her haste to leave the moment behind.

Walking in front of him toward the house, though, she was conscious of her slim waist, and the sway of her skirt, and the swing of her hair down her back. He must have been thinking about this ahead of time. He must have consciously decided he wanted her, and imagined how it would be. The knowledge made her feel mysterious and desirable and grown-up.

Red Whitshank and another friend of his, Ward Rainey, stood talking with two workmen at the lower edge of the lawn. One of the workmen had a chainsaw, and Red and the other workman were carrying axes. All around them, in a massive tangle, lay thick branches and cross sections of trunk. That tulip poplar must have been gigantic. (And nowhere near dying, if you judged by all the green leaves.) The remainder of the trunk, some ten feet tall, still towered near the front porch, as flat-topped and perfectly cylindrical as an architectural column.

". . . figure when Mitch gets here he can tell us how much he wants left," Red was saying, and the man with the chainsaw said, "Well, I can't see as he'll want *any* left, because he's not going to haul it out roots and all, is he? That would leave too big of a hole."

"What, you're thinking he'll bring in a stump grinder?"

"Seems like that would make more sense."

Abby called, "Hi, everybody."

They turned, and Red said, "Hi, Abby! Hi, Dane."

"Red," Dane said, impassively.

Abby had always thought Red's looks didn't go with his name. He should have had red hair and that pinkish skin that went with it; he should have been freckled and doughy. Instead, he was all black-and-white, lean and lanky, with a boyishly prominent Adam's apple and wrist bones as distinct as cabinet knobs. Today he was wearing a T-shirt that was more holes than fabric, and khakis with dirty knees. He could have been one of his father's workmen. "These here are Earl and Landis," he was saying. "They're the guys who took this thing down."

Earl and Landis nodded without smiling, and Ward lifted a palm.

"You took it down just the two of you?" Abby asked the men.

"Naw, Red helped plenty," Earl said.

"Only with the muscle power," Red told her. "It was Earl and Landis who knew how not to take everything else with it."

"Laid her in place like a baby," Landis said with satisfaction.

Abby lifted her eyes to study the canopy of leaves above them. So many trees remained that she couldn't detect any change in the filtering of the light, but still, the loss of the poplar seemed a pity. The cross sections strewn about looked perfectly sound, and the sap filled the air with a scent as vital and sharp as fresh blood.

The men had returned to the subject of stump removal. Earl was of the opinion that they ought to just go ahead and cut the last of the trunk level with the ground, while Landis suggested waiting for Mitch. "Meantime we can strip these branches," he said, and he set a foot on the nearest branch and gave one of its shoots an experimental tap with his axe. Abby liked hearing workmen discuss logistics. It made her feel like a small child again, sitting on her father's counter swinging her feet and breathing in the smells of metal and machine oil.

Earl yanked the cord of his chainsaw and set up a deafening roar. He lowered the blade to the thickest part of a branch while Ward bent to grab another branch and haul it out of the way. "I don't guess you brought an axe," Red shouted to Dane.

Dane, who was lighting a cigarette, shook out his match and said, "Now, how would I ever have gotten my hands on an axe?"

"I'll fetch another from the basement," Red said. He propped his own axe against a dogwood. "Come on, Ab, I'll take you up to the house."

"You're sure I can't do something here?" she asked. It seemed a shame to go off and leave Dane.

But Red said, "You can help my mom fix lunch, if you like."

"Oh. Okay."

Dane cocked an eyebrow at her in a silent goodbye, and then she and Red turned to climb the flagstone walk. Leaving behind the din of the chainsaw, she felt as if her ears had gone numb. "You really think this will take until lunchtime?" she asked Red.

"Oh, longer than that," he said. "We're lucky if we're done before dark."

She supposed that was just as well. She would have more time to reassemble her composure in front of Dane. By evening she'd be a whole different person, self-possessed and mature.

They arrived at the porch steps, but instead of leaving her there, Red came to a stop. "Say," he said. "I was wondering. You want a ride to the wedding?"

"I'm not sure I'm going to the wedding," Abby said.

She had about decided not to, in fact. The invitation (on paper so thick it had required two postage stamps) had come as a surprise; she and Merrick weren't close. Besides, Dane wasn't invited. Merrick barely knew Dane. So Abby had been meaning for weeks now to send her regrets.

But Red said, "You aren't going? Mom was counting on it."

Abby wrinkled her forehead.

"I was, too," he told her. "Because who else will I know in that crowd?"

She said, "Don't you have to be an usher or something?"

"It never even came up," he said.

"Well, thank you, Red. You're nice to offer. I'll let you know if I decide to go, okay?"

He hesitated a moment, as if there were more he wanted to say, but then he smiled at her and split off toward the rear of the house.

Crossing the porch in three long strides, tall and craggy as Abraham Lincoln and dressed not all that differently from Lincoln, Junior Whitshank inclined his head a quarter-inch in Abby's direction and then swiftly descended the steps. "Morning, young lady," he said.

"Good morning, Mr. Whitshank."

"Merrick's not up yet, I don't believe."

"Well, I was looking for Mrs. Whitshank."

"Mrs. Whitshank is in the kitchen."

"Thanks."

Mr. Whitshank veered off the flagstone walk toward where the men were working. Abby, gazing after him, wondered where on earth he bought his shirts. They were white, always, and unfashionably high in the collar, so that a tall band of white encased his skinny neck. She often had the feeling that he might be modeling himself after some ideal—some illustrious figure from his past that he had admired. But his narrow black trousers looked empty in the seat, and the Y of his suspenders accentuated the weary, burdened posture of an ordinary laboring man.

"Mitch here yet?" she heard him call, and a murmur of answers rose above the buzz of the chainsaw like bees humming in a log.

Abby climbed the steps, crossed the porch, opened the screen door, and tootled, "Yoo-hoo!" It was something Linnie Whitshank would have done. Automatically, Abby seemed to have switched to Mrs. Whitshank's language and to her tone of voice—thin and fluty.

"Back here!" Mrs. Whitshank called from the kitchen.

Abby loved the Whitshanks' house. Even on a hot July day it was cool and dim, with the ceiling fan revolving high above the center hall and another fan gently stirring in the dining room. A folded tablecloth had been placed at one end of the table with a clutch of silverware resting on top, waiting to be distributed. She continued through to the kitchen, where Mrs. Whitshank stood at the sink rinsing okra pods. Mrs. Whitshank was slight and frail-looking, but an incongruously deep, low bosom filled out the top of her gingham housedress. Her pale hair hung limply almost to her shoulders. It was a young girl's hairstyle, and her face when she turned to Abby seemed young as well—unlined and plain and guileless. "Hey, there!" she said, and Abby said, "Hi."

"Don't you look pretty today!"

"I came to see how I could help," Abby said.

"Oh, honey, you don't want to spoil those nice clothes. Just sit and keep me company."

Abby pulled a chair out from the kitchen table and settled on it. She had learned not to argue with Mrs. Whitshank, who was a force of nature when it came to cooking and would only find Abby a hindrance.

"How's that tree coming along?" Mrs. Whitshank asked her.

"They're starting to cut up the branches now."

"Did you ever hear of such a thing? Bringing down a whole poplar for the sake of a photograph."

"Photy-graph," she pronounced it. She had a country way of talking, and unlike her husband, she made no attempt to alter it.

"Dane says the tree was already dying, according to Mr. Whitshank," Abby said.

"Oh, sometimes Junior will just get this sort of *vision* about how he wants things to be," Mrs. Whitshank told her. She shut off the faucet and wiped her hands on her apron. "He's already bought frames for the photos, isn't that something? Two big frames, wooden. I asked him, I said, 'You going to hang those over the mantel?' He said, 'Linnie Mae.'" She made her voice go deep and gruff. "Said, 'People don't hang family photos in their living rooms.' I said, 'I didn't know that.' Did you know that?"

"My mom's got photos all *over* the living room," Abby said.

"Well, then. See there?"

Mrs. Whitshank took a bottle of milk from the refrigerator and poured some into a bowl. "I'm fixing okra and sliced tomatoes," she told Abby. "And fried chicken, with some of my biscuits. Oh, later on you might help with the biscuits, now that you know how. And peach cobbler for dessert."

"That sounds delicious."

"Did Red tell you he would give you a ride to the wedding?"

"He did," Abby said, "but I'm not sure yet if I'm going."

She felt embarrassed now about waiting so long to make up her mind. If her mother had known, she would have been horrified. But all Mrs. Whitshank said was, "Oh, I wish you would! I need someone to prop me up."

Abby laughed.

"Merrick had me buy this yellow dress at Hutzler's," Mrs. Whitshank said. "It makes me look like I've got the jaundice, but Merrick was real set on it. She's like her daddy; she takes these notions." She was spooning cornmeal into a second bowl.

Abby said, "I'm just afraid I wouldn't know anybody. Merrick's crowd is all older than me."

"Well, I won't know them, either," Mrs. Whitshank said. "It'll be her college friends, mostly—not many from around here."

"Who all in your family is coming?" Abby asked.

"What do you mean?"

"I mean, grandparents? Aunts and uncles?"

"Oh, we don't have any of those," Mrs. Whitshank said.

She didn't sound very regretful about it. Abby waited for her to elaborate, but she was measuring out salt now.

"Well, I told Red I appreciate the offer," Abby said finally. "It's good to know I've got a ride if I need one."

Really she should just say yes and be done with it. She wasn't sure what was stopping her. It was only half a Saturday, a tiny chunk of her life.

The Saturday after she spent the night with Dane. *If* she spent the night.

She imagined how he might say, "Aw, you don't want to leave me all by myself, the morning after we . . ."

After we . . .

She looked down at her skirt and smoothed it across her knees.

"How's your job going?" Mrs. Whitshank asked her. "You still liking those little colored kids?"

"Oh, I'm loving them."

"I hate to think of you going down into that neighborhood, though," Mrs. Whitshank said.

"It's not a bad neighborhood."

"It's a *poor* neighborhood, isn't it? The people there are poor as dirt, and they'd as lief rob you as look at you. I swear, Abby, sometimes you don't show good sense when it comes to knowing who to be scared of."

"I could never be scared of those people!"

Mrs. Whitshank shook her head and dumped the colander of okra onto a cutting board.

"Oh, what a world, what a world," Abby said.

"How's that, honey?"

"That's what the wicked witch says in *The Wizard of Oz*. Did you know that? They're showing a revival downtown and I went to see it last night with Dane. The witch says, 'I'm melting! Melting! Oh, what a world, what a world,' she says."

"I remember the part about 'I'm melting,'" Mrs. Whitshank said. "I took Red and Merrick to see that movie when they were little bitty things."

"Yes, well, and then she talks about 'what a world.' I told Dane afterward, I said, 'I never heard that before! I had no idea she said that!'"

"Me neither," Mrs. Whitshank said. "In a way, it sounds kind of pitiful."

"Exactly," Abby said. "All at once I started feeling sorry for her, you know? I really believe that most people who seem scary are just sad."

"Oh, Abby, Lord preserve you," Mrs. Whitshank said with a gentle laugh.

*

Loud, sharp heels clopped down the stairs and through the front hall. The clops crossed the dining room and Merrick appeared in the kitchen doorway, wearing a red satin kimono and red mules topped with puffs of red feathers. Giant metal curlers encased her head like some sort of spaceman's helmet. "Gawd, what time is it?" she asked. She pulled out a chair and sat down next to Abby and took a pack of Kents from her sleeve.

"Good morning, Merrick," Abby said.

"Morning. Is that okra? Ick."

"It's for lunch," Mrs. Whitshank told her. "We've got all those men out front who are going to need feeding."

"Only Mom believes it's impolite to make your workmen bring their own sandwiches," Merrick told Abby. "Abby Dalton, are you wearing *hose*? Aren't you melting?"

"I'm melting!" Abby wailed in a wicked-witch voice, and Mrs. Whitshank laughed but Merrick just looked annoyed. She lit a cigarette and let out a long whoosh of smoke. "I had the most awful dream," she said. "I dreamed I was driving a little too fast on this winding mountain road and I missed a curve. I thought, 'Oh-oh, this is going to be bad.' You know that moment when you realize it's just got to, got to happen. I went sailing over the edge of a cliff, and I squeezed my eyes tight shut and braced for the shock. But the funny thing was, I kept sailing. I never landed."

Abby said, "That's a terrible dream!" but Mrs. Whitshank went on placidly slicing okra.

"I thought, 'Oh, now I get it,'" Merrick said. "'I must already be dead.' And then I woke up."

"Was the car a convertible?" Mrs. Whitshank asked.

Merrick paused, with her cigarette suspended halfway to her mouth. She said, "Pardon?"

"The car in your dream. Was it a convertible?"

"Well, yes, as a matter of fact."

"If you dream you're in a convertible it means you're about to make a serious error in judgment," Mrs. Whitshank said.

Merrick sent Abby a look of exaggerated astonishment. "I wonder what error you could possibly be thinking of," she said.

"But if the car is *not* a convertible, it would signify you're going to get some sort of promotion."

"Well, what a coincidence, I dreamed about a convertible," Merrick said. "And the whole world knows you're dead set against this wedding, so don't waste your breath, Linnie Mae."

Merrick often addressed her mother as "Linnie Mae." The twisted sound of the name in her mouth somehow managed to imply all of her mother's shortcomings—her twangy voice, her feed-sack-looking dresses, her backwoods pronunciations like "supposably" and "eck cetera" and "desk-es." Abby felt bad for Mrs. Whitshank, but Mrs. Whitshank herself didn't appear to take offense. "I'm just saying," she said mildly, and she slid a handful of okra spokes into the bowl of milk.

Merrick took a deep drag of her cigarette and blew smoke toward the ceiling.

"Anyhow!" Abby told Merrick. "I bet it was one of those dreams you were really glad to wake up from, wasn't it?"

Merrick said, "Mm-hmm," with her eyes on the fan blades spinning above her.

Then a girl's voice called, "Mare? Hello?" and Merrick straightened and called, "In the kitchen."

The screen door slammed, and a moment later Pixie Kincaid and Maddie Lane arrived in the kitchen, both wearing Bermuda shorts, Maddie carrying a powder-blue Samsonite vanity case. "Merrick Whitshank, you're still in your bathrobe!" Pixie said.

"I didn't get home from the party till after three in the morning."

"Well, neither did we, but it's almost ten! Did you forget we're practicing your makeup today?"

"I remember," Merrick said. She stubbed out her cigarette. "Come on upstairs and let's do this."

"Hi, Mrs. Whitshank," Pixie said belatedly. "Hi, um, Abby. See you later." Maddie just gave a little wave like a windshield wiper. Then the three of them walked out, Merrick's heels clattering. A sudden quiet descended.

"I guess Merrick must be feeling kind of tense these days," Abby said after a moment.

"Oh, no, that's just how she is," Mrs. Whitshank said cheerfully. She had finished slicing the okra. She stirred the slices around in the milk, using a slotted spoon. "She was a snippy little girl and now she's a snippy *big* girl," she said. "Nothing much I can do about it." She began transferring the okra slices to the cornmeal mixture. "Sometimes," she said, "it seems to me there's just these certain types of people that come around and around in our lives, know what I mean? Easy types and hard types; we run into them over and over. Merrick's always put me in mind of my granny Inman. Disapproving kind of woman; tongue like a rasp. She never did think much of me. *You*, now, you're a sympathizer, same as my aunt Louise."

"Oh," Abby said. "Yes, I see what you're saying. It's kind of like reincarnation."

Mrs. Whitshank said, "Well . . ."

"Except it's within one single lifetime instead of spread out over different lifetimes."

"Well, maybe," Mrs. Whitshank said. Then she said, "Honey, you want to do something for me?"

"Anything," Abby said.

"Fetch that pitcher of water from the icebox and those paper cups on the counter and take them out to the men, will you? I know they must be dying of thirst. And tell them lunch will be early; I'll bet they're wondering."

Abby stood up and went to the refrigerator. Her stockings were sticking damply to the backs of her legs. It might not have been the best idea to wear them on a day like today.

As she was crossing the front hall, she overheard Mr. Whitshank talking on the phone in the sunroom. "This afternoon? What the hell?" he was saying. "Goddammit,

Mitch, I've got five men out there waiting on you to tell them how to do that tree stump!" Abby made her footsteps lighter, thinking he might be embarrassed that she'd caught him using swear words.

Outside, the air hit her face like a warm washcloth, and the porch floorboards gave off the smell of hot varnish. But the soft, fresh breeze—unusual for this time of year—lifted the damp wisps along her hairline, and the water pitcher she was hugging chilled the insides of her arms.

Landis had gotten hold of a second chainsaw from somewhere, and he and Earl were slicing the thickest branches into fireplace-size logs. Dane and Ward were hacking off the thinner branches and dragging them to a huge pile down near the street, while Red had set up a chopping block and was splitting the logs into quarters. They all stopped work when Abby arrived. Earl and Landis killed their chainsaws and a ringing silence fell, so that her voice sounded shockingly clear: "Anybody want water?"

"I wouldn't say no," Earl told her, and they set down their tools and came over to her. Ward had taken his shirt off, which made him look like an amateur, and he and Dane were deeply flushed. Red, of course, had been working this hard the whole summer, but even he had rivulets of sweat running down his face, and Earl and Landis were so drenched that their blue chambray shirts were almost navy.

She distributed paper cups and then filled them while the men held them out, and they emptied them in one gulp and held them out again before she'd finished the first round. It wasn't till halfway through the third round that anyone said more than "Thanks." Then Red asked, "Did Dad get ahold of Mitch, do you know?"

"I think he's on the phone with him now."

"I still say we just go ahead and take the whole thing down," Earl told Red.

"Well, I don't want Mitch showing up and saying we made his job harder."

Dane and Abby were looking at each other. Dane's hair was damp, and he gave off a wonderful smell of clean sweat and tobacco. Abby had a sudden, worrisome thought: she didn't own any nice underwear. Just plain white cotton underpants and white cotton bras with the tiniest pink rosebud stitched to the center V. She looked away again.

"Hello?"

It was a beefy man in a seersucker suit, parting the azalea hedge that bordered the lawn next door. Twigs crackled under his chalk-white shoes as he walked toward them. "Say, there," he said when he reached them. He had his eyes fixed specifically on Red.

"Hi, Mr. Barkalow," Red said.

"Wonder if you realize what time your men started work this morning."

Landis was the one who answered. "Eight o'clock," he said.

"Eight o'clock," Mr. Barkalow repeated, still looking at Red.

Landis said, "That's when me and Red and Earl here started. The rest of them showed up later."

"Eight o'clock in the morning," Mr. Barkalow said. "A *Sunday* morning. A weekend. Does that strike you as acceptable?"

"Well, it seems okay to me, sir," Red said in a steady voice.

"Is that right. Eight o'clock on a Sunday morning seems a fine time to run a chainsaw."

He had ginger eyebrows that bristled out aggressively, but Red didn't seem intimidated. He said, "I figured most folks would be—"

"Morning, there!" Mr. Whitshank called.

He was striding toward them down the slope of the lawn, wearing a black suit coat that must have been put on in haste. The left lapel was turned wrong, like a dog's ear flipped inside out. "Fine day!" he said to Mr. Barkalow. "Good to see you out enjoying it."

"I was just asking your son, Mr. Whitshank, what he considers to be an acceptable hour to run a chainsaw."

"Oh, why, is there a problem?"

"The problem is that today is Sunday; I don't know if you're aware of it," Mr. Barkalow said.

He had transferred his bushy-browed glare to Mr. Whitshank, who was nodding emphatically as if he couldn't agree more. "Yes, well, we certainly wouldn't want to—" he said.

"It is *perverse* how you people love to make a racket

315

while the rest of us are trying to sleep. You're hammering on your gutters, you're drilling out your flagstones . . . Only yesterday, you sawed an entire tree down! A perfectly healthy tree, might I add. And always, always it seems to happen on a weekend."

Mr. Whitshank suddenly grew taller.

"It doesn't *seem* to happen on a weekend; it *does* happen on a weekend," he said. "That's the only time we honest laboring men aren't busy doing you folks' work for you."

"You ought to thank your lucky stars I don't report you to the police," Mr. Barkalow said. "They're bound to have ordinances dealing with this kind of thing."

"Ordinances! Don't make me laugh. Just because you all like to lie abed till noon, you and that spoiled son of yours with his big fat—"

"When you think about it," Red broke in, "it doesn't really matter if there are ordinances or there aren't."

Both men looked at him.

"What matters is, we seem to be waking our neighbors. I'm sorry about that, Mr. Barkalow. We certainly never intended to discommode you."

"'*Discommode*'?" his father repeated in a marveling voice.

Red said, "I wonder if we could settle on an hour that's mutually agreeable."

"'Mutually *agreeable*'?" his father echoed.

"Oh," Mr. Barkalow said. "Well."

"Does, maybe, ten o'clock sound all right?" Red asked him.

"Ten o'clock!" Mr. Whitshank said.

"Ten?" Mr. Barkalow said. "Oh. Well, even ten is . . . but, well, I guess we could tolerate ten if we were forced to."

Mr. Whitshank looked up at the sky as if he were begging for mercy, but Red said, "Ten o'clock. It's a deal. We'll make sure to abide by that in the future, Mr. Barkalow."

"Well," Mr. Barkalow said. He seemed uncertain. He glanced again at Mr. Whitshank, and then he said, "Well, okay, then. I guess that settles it." And he turned and walked off toward the hedge.

"*Now* see what you've done," Mr. Whitshank told Red. "Ten o'clock, for God's sake! Practically lunchtime!"

Red handed his paper cup to Abby without comment.

Landis said, "Uh, boss?"

"What is it," Mr. Whitshank said.

"Did you get the word from Mitch?"

"He's coming by this afternoon with his brother-in-law's stump grinder. He says take the trunk on down."

"So, cut it low to the ground?"

"Low as you can get it," Mr. Whitshank said, and by then he had already turned away and was halfway up the hill again, as if he'd washed his hands of all of them. The hem of his suit coat hung unevenly, Abby noticed—sagging at the sides and hitching up at the center, as if it belonged to a much older and shabbier man.

She circulated among the others, collecting their paper cups in silence, and then she started back up the hill herself.

*

"Sometimes Junior thinks the neighbors might be looking down their noses at him," Mrs. Whitshank said when she heard about the scene in the yard. "He's a little bit sensitive that way."

Abby didn't say so, but she could see his side of it. During her years as a scholarship student she'd had a few dealings herself with Mr. Barkalow's type—so entitled, so convinced that there was only one way to live. No doubt all his sons played lacrosse and all his daughters were preparing for their debutante balls. But she shook that thought away and folded the sheet of dough on the counter a second time and a third. ("Fold, fold, and fold again" were Mrs. Whitshank's instructions when she'd taught Abby how to make her biscuits. "Fold till when you slap the dough, you hear it give a burp.")

"Anyhow," Abby said, "Red got them to compromise. It all worked out in the end."

"Red is not so quick to take offense," Mrs. Whitshank said. She drew a large bowl from the refrigerator and removed the dish towel that covered it. "I think it's because he grew up here. He's used to people like the Barkalows."

The bowl contained pieces of chicken in a liquid white batter. Mrs. Whitshank lifted them out one by one with canning tongs and laid them on a platter to drain. "It's like he's comfortable with both sorts," she said. "With the neighbors and with the work crew. I know if he had his way, though, he'd quit college right this minute and go on the work crew full-time. It's only on account of Junior that he's sticking it out till graduation."

"Well, it never hurts to have a diploma," Abby said.

"That's what Junior tells him. He says, 'You want the option of something better. You don't want to end up like me,' he says. Red says, 'What's wrong with ending up like you?' He says the trouble with college is, it's not practical. The *people* there aren't practical. 'Sometimes they strike me as silly,' he says."

Abby had never heard Red talk about college. He was two years ahead of her and they seldom ran into each other on campus. "What are his grades like?" she asked Mrs. Whitshank.

Mrs. Whitshank said, "They're okay. Well, so-so. That's just not how his mind works, you know? He's the kind that, you show him some gadget he's never laid eyes on before and he says, 'Oh, I see; yes, this part goes into that part and then it connects with this other part . . .' Just like his daddy, but his daddy wants Red to be different from him. Isn't that always how it is?"

"I bet Red was one of those little boys who take the kitchen clock apart," Abby said.

"Yes, except he could put it back together again, too, which most other little boys can't. Oops, watch what you're doing, Abby. I *see* how you're twisting that glass!"

She meant the glass that Abby was using to cut out the biscuits. "Clamp it straight down on the dough, remember?" she said.

"Sorry."

"Let me fetch you the skillet."

Abby wiped her forehead with the back of her hand. The kitchen was heating up, and she was swathed in one of Mrs. Whitshank's bib aprons.

If it was true, Abby thought, that she represented a recurring figure in Mrs. Whitshank's life—the "sympathizer"— it was equally true that Mrs. Whitshank's type had shown up before in Abby's life: the instructive older woman. The grandmother who had taught her to knit, the English teacher who had stayed late to help her with her poems. More patient and softer-spoken than Abby's brisk, efficient mother, they had guided and encouraged her, like Mrs. Whitshank saying now, "Oh, those are looking good! Good as any I could have made."

"Maybe Red could join his dad's company full-time after college," Abby said. "Then it could be Whitshank and *Son* Construction. Wouldn't Mr. Whitshank like that?"

"I don't think so," Mrs. Whitshank said. "He's hoping the law for Red. Law or business, one. Red's got a fine head for business."

"But if he wouldn't be happy . . ." Abby said.

"Junior says happiness is neither here nor there," Mrs. Whitshank told her. "He says Red should just make up his *mind* to be happy."

Then she stopped hunting through the utensil drawer and said, "I'm not trying to make him sound mean."

"Of course not," Abby said.

"He only wants what's best for his family, you know? We're all he's got."

"Well, of course."

"Neither one of us has to do with our own families, anymore."

"Why is that?" Abby asked.

"Oh, just, you know. Circumstances. We kind of fell out of touch with them," Mrs. Whitshank said. "They're clear down in North Carolina, and besides, my side were never in favor of us being together."

"You mean you and Mr. Whitshank?"

"Just like Romeo and Juliet," Mrs. Whitshank said. She laughed, but then she sobered and said, "Now, here is something you might not know. Guess how old Juliet was when she fell in love with Romeo."

"Thirteen," Abby said promptly.

"Oh."

"They taught us that in school."

"They taught Merrick that, too, in tenth grade," Mrs. Whitshank said. "She came home and told me. She said, 'Isn't that ridiculous?' She said that after she heard that, she couldn't take Shakespeare seriously."

"Well, I don't know why not," Abby said. "A person can fall in love at thirteen."

"Yes! A person can! Like me."

"You?"

"I was thirteen when I fell in love with Junior," Mrs. Whitshank said. "That's what I'm trying to tell you."

"Oh, goodness, and here you are now, married to him!" Abby said. "That's amazing! How old was Mr. Whitshank?"

"Twenty-six."

Abby took a moment to absorb this. "He was twenty-six when you were thirteen?"

"Twenty-six years old," Mrs. Whitshank said.

Abby said, "Oh."

"Isn't that something?"

"Yes, it is," Abby said.

"He was this real good-looking guy, a little bit wild, worked at the lumberyard but only just sometimes. Rest of the time he was off hunting and fishing and trapping and getting himself into trouble. Well, you see the attraction. Who could resist a boy like that? Especially when you're thirteen. And I was a kind of *developed* thirteen; I developed real early. I met him at a church picnic when he came with another girl, and it was love at first sight for both of us. He started up with me right then and there. After that, we would sneak off together every chance we got. Oh, we couldn't keep our hands off each other! But one night my daddy found us."

"Found you where?" Abby asked.

"Well, in the hay barn. But he found us . . . you know." Mrs. Whitshank fluttered a hand in the air. "Oh, it was awful!" she said merrily. "It was like something out of a movie. My daddy held a gun to his neck. Then Daddy and my brothers ran him out of Yancey County. Can you believe it? Law, I think back on that now and it feels like it happened to somebody else. 'Was that *me*?' I say to myself. I didn't lay eyes on him again for close onto five years."

Abby had slacked off on the biscuit cutting. She was just standing there staring at Mrs. Whitshank, so Mrs. Whitshank took the glass from her and stepped in to finish up, making short work of it: clamp-clamp.

"But you kept in touch," Abby said.

"Oh, no! I had no idea where he was." Mrs. Whitshank was laying the biscuits in the greased skillet, edge to edge in concentric circles. "I stayed faithful to him, though. I never forgot him for one minute. Oh, we had one of the world's great love stories, in our little way! And once we got back together again, it was like we'd never parted. You know how that happens, sometimes. We took up right where we left off, the same as ever."

Abby said, "But—"

Had it never crossed Mrs. Whitshank's mind that what she was describing was . . . well, a crime?

Mrs. Whitshank said, "I don't know why I'm telling you, though. It's supposed to be a secret. I've never even told my own children! Oh, especially my own children. Merrick would make fun of me. Promise *you* won't tell them, Abby. Swear it on your life."

"I won't tell a soul," Abby said.

She wouldn't have known what words to use, even. It was all too extreme and disturbing.

*

323

Mr. and Mrs. Whitshank and Red, Earl and Landis, Ward, Dane and Abby: eight people for lunch. (Merrick would not be eating with them, Mrs. Whitshank said.) Abby traveled around the table doling out knives and forks. The Whitshanks' silverware was real sterling, embossed with an Old English *W*. She wondered when they had acquired it. Not at the time of their wedding, presumably.

Her parents just had dime-store cutlery, not all of it even matching.

Suddenly she felt homesick for her bustling, sensible mother and her kindly father with his shirt pocket full of ballpoint pens and mechanical pencils.

All the dining-room windows were open, the curtains wafting inward on the breeze, and she could see out to the porch where Pixie and Maddie sat in the swing with their backs to her, talking in soft, lazy voices. Merrick's makeup session must be finished; Abby heard the shower running upstairs.

She went to the kitchen for plates, and as she returned, one of the chainsaws roared to life again. Till then, she hadn't noticed the silence. The noise was so close that she bent to peer out a window and see what was going on. Apparently the men were tackling what remained of the trunk. Landis stood to the left, watching, while Earl stooped low with his saw. He was working on the far side of the tree, nearly out of her angle of vision, probably cutting a notch so it would fall away from the house, but Abby couldn't be sure from where she stood. She always worried men would get crushed doing that, although these two certainly looked as if they knew what they were doing.

She set the plates around and then counted out napkins from the sideboard and laid one beside each fork. She returned to the kitchen and asked Mrs. Whitshank, "Shall I pour the iced tea now?"

"No, let's wait a bit," Mrs. Whitshank said. She was standing at the stove frying chicken. "Go sit on the porch and cool off, why don't you? I'll call you when it's time."

Abby didn't argue. She was glad to leave the hot kitchen. She untied her apron and draped it over the back of a chair, and then she went out to the porch and settled in one of the rockers some distance from Pixie and Maddie. She looked for Dane and found him hauling a huge leafy branch down toward the pile near the street. His hair took on an almost metallic sheen when he stepped into a shaft of sunshine.

What would she tell her mother? "I'm going to spend the night at Ruth's," she could say, except that then her mother might phone her at Ruth's; it had been known to happen. And even if Abby dared to ask Ruth to cover for her, there was the problem of Ruth's parents.

Red was tossing split logs into a wheelbarrow. Ward was mopping his forehead with his balled-up shirt. Earl killed the chainsaw just as Merrick stepped onto the porch and said, "Whew," letting the screen door slam behind her. "Feels like I've washed a rubber mask off my face," she told Pixie and Maddie. She was eating from a bowl of cornflakes.

She walked over to a cane-bottomed chair, hooked it with one foot, and pulled it closer to the swing and sat down. Her hair was still in curlers but she had on Bermudas now and a sleeveless white blouse.

"We were just wondering who the James Dean was," Pixie told her.

"The who? Oh, that's Dane."

"He's *gaw*-juss."

"If next Saturday's like today," Merrick said, "my foundation's going to streak clear off my face. And my mascara will give me raccoon eyes."

"You'll match your mother-in-law," Maddie said with a giggle.

"Oh, just go ahead and kill me if I ever get circles like hers," Merrick said. "You know what I suspect? I suspect she paints them on. She's one of those people who like to look sick. She's always trotting off to her doctor and of course he tells her she's fine but when she comes back she says, 'Well, he *thinks* I'll be all right . . .'"

"Will he be at the wedding?" Pixie asked.

"Will who be at the wedding?"

"That Dane person."

"Oh. I don't know. Will Dane be at the wedding?" Merrick called down the porch to Abby.

Abby said, "He wasn't invited."

"He wasn't? Well, feel free to bring him if you like."

"Oh, you two go together?" Pixie asked Abby.

Abby gave a half shrug, hoping to imply that they did go

together but that she could take him or leave him, and Pixie heaved a theatrical sigh of disappointment.

"Now, here is the sixty-four-dollar question," Merrick said. "My curlers."

"What about them?" Maddie asked.

"You see how big and bobbly they are. I've been going to bed in these since I was fourteen years old. My hair is straight as a stick otherwise. What am I going to do on my wedding night, is the question."

"Ask me something hard," Maddie said. "You go to bed without them, silly. Then early, early in the morning you wake up before Trey does and you sneak off to the bathroom and put your curlers in and take a hot shower. Don't actually wet your hair; just steam it. Then get under the hair dryer—you'll have to slip your hair dryer into the bathroom the night before—"

"I can't bring my hair dryer on my honeymoon! It needs its own huge suitcase."

"Then buy yourself one of those new kinds that you can hold in your hand."

"What, and electrocute myself like that woman in the paper? Besides, you don't know how stubborn my hair is. Two minutes of steam won't have any effect at all."

Pixie said, "You should do your hair like her."

"Like who?"

"Her," Pixie said, poking her chin in Abby's direction. She was wearing a little smirk. "Abby."

Merrick didn't bother responding to that. "If I could just

327

get away from Trey for a couple of measly hours," she said. "If there was a beauty parlor in the hotel and it opened at five in the morning—"

The chainsaw roared up again, drowning out the rest of her words. Landis walked over to a dogwood tree and bent for a hoop of rope. Dane started up the hill toward where he'd left his axe.

Before the men came in for lunch they ducked their heads under the faucet at the side of the house, and so they walked in dripping wet, squeegeeing their faces with their hands. Earl actually shook himself all over, like a dog, as he took his seat.

Mr. Whitshank sat at the head of the table, Mrs. Whitshank at the foot. Abby sat between Dane and Landis. She and Dane were a good eighteen inches apart, but he slid his foot over so that it was touching hers. He kept his eyes on his plate, though, as if he and she had nothing to do with each other.

Mr. Whitshank was holding forth on Billie Holiday. She had died a couple of days before and Mr. Whitshank couldn't see why people were so cut up about it. "Always sounded to me like she couldn't hold on to a note," he said. "Her voice would go slippy-slidey and sometimes she'd mislay the tune." He had a way of rotating his face slowly from one side of the table to the other as he spoke, so as to include all his listeners. Abby felt like some sort of disciple hanging on her master's every word, which she suspected was his purpose. Then she altered her vision—she was good at that—and imagined she was sitting at a table of threshers or corn pickers or such, one of those old-time harvest gatherings, and this cheered her up. When she had a home of her own, she wanted it to be just as expansive and welcoming as the Whitshanks', with strays dropping by for meals and young people talking on the porch. Her parents' house felt so closed; the Whitshanks' house felt open. No thanks to *Mr.* Whitshank. But wasn't that always the way? It was the woman who set the tone.

"Now, the kind of music I favor myself," Mr. Whitshank was saying, "is more on the order of John Philip Sousa. I assume you all know who I'm talking about. Redcliffe, who am I talking about?"

"The March King," Red said with his mouth full. He was deep in a leg of fried chicken.

"March King," Mr. Whitshank agreed. "Any of you recall *The Cities Service Band of America*?"

No one did, apparently. They hunkered lower over their plates.

"Program on the radio," Mr. Whitshank said. "No kind of music but marches. 'Stars and Stripes Forever' and 'The Washington Post' march, my favorite. I like to had a fit when they took it off the air."

Abby searched for any trace in him of the wild boy from Yancey County. She could see why some might call him good-looking, with that straight-edged face of his and not a sign of a paunch even in his fifties or maybe sixties. But his clothes were so proper, almost a caricature of properness (he had corrected the wayward lapel by now), and his eyes had a disenchanted droop at the outside corners. There were gnarly purple veins on the backs of his hands and distinct black dots of whiskers stippling his chin. Oh, let Abby not ever get old! She pressed her left ankle against Dane's ankle and passed the biscuits on to Landis.

"My father thinks Billie Holiday's the greatest," Dane offered. He took a swig of his iced tea and then leaned back, clearly at ease. "He says Baltimore's biggest claim to fame is, Billie Holiday used to scrub front stoops downtown for a quarter apiece."

"Well, I and your father will have to agree to disagree," Mr. Whitshank said. Then he gave a quick frown. "Who *is* your father?"

"Dick Quinn," Dane said.

"Quinn as in Quinn Marketing?"

"None other."

"Will you be going into the family business?"

"Nope," Dane said.

Mr. Whitshank waited. Dane stared back at him pleasantly.

"I would think that would be a fine opportunity," Mr. Whitshank said after a moment.

"Me and Pop tend not to see eye to eye," Dane told him. "Besides, he's ticked off because I got fired from my job."

He seemed perfectly comfortable volunteering the

information. Mr. Whitshank frowned again. "What'd they fire you for?" he asked.

"Just didn't work out, I guess," Dane said.

"Well, I tell Redcliffe, I say, 'Whatever you do in life, do your best. I don't care if it's hauling trash, you do it the best it's ever been done,' I say. 'Take pride in it.' Getting fired? It's a black mark on your record forever. It'll hang around to haunt you."

"This was at a savings and loan," Dane said. "I have no plans to make my career in savings and loans, believe me."

"The point is, what reputation you get. What opinion your community has of you. Now, you may not feel that a savings and loan is your be-all and your end-all . . ."

How could this man have been the hero of Mrs. Whitshank's romance? Whether you found it dashing or tawdry, at least it *had* been a romance, complete with intrigue and scandal and a wrenching separation. But Junior Whitshank was dry as a bone, droning on relentlessly while the other diners ate their food in dogged silence. Only his wife was looking at him, her face alight with interest as he discussed the value of hard labor, then the deplorable lack of initiative in the younger generation, then the benefits conferred by having lived through the Great Depression. If young folks today had lived through a depression the way *he* had lived through a depression—but then he broke off to call, "Ah! Going out with your buddies?"

It was Merrick he was addressing. She was crossing the

hall, heading toward the front door, but she stopped and turned to face him. "Yup," she said. "Don't wait supper." Her hair had become a mass of bubbly black curls that bounced all over her head.

"Merrick's fiancé, now; he's gone into *his* family's business," Mr. Whitshank told the others. "Doing a fine job too, I gather. Course we couldn't call him a practical fellow—doesn't know how to change his own oil, even; can you believe it?"

"Well, toodle-oo," Merrick said, and she trilled her fingers at the table and left. Her father blinked but then picked up his thread—the "spoiledness" of the rich and their complete inability to do for themselves—but Abby had stopped listening. She felt suddenly hopeless, defeated by his complacent, self-relishing drawl, his not-quite-right "I and your dad" and his trying-too-hard Northern *i*'s, his greedy attention to the details of class and privilege. But Mrs. Whitshank went on smiling at him, while Red just helped himself to another slice of tomato. Earl was stacking biscuits three high on the rim of his plate, as if he planned to take them home. Ward had a shred of chicken stuck to his lower lip.

"All of which," Mr. Whitshank was saying, "shows why you would never. Ever. Under any circumstances. Knuckle under to these people. I'm talking to *you*, Redcliffe."

Red stopped salting his tomato slice and looked up. He said, "Me?"

"Why you would not kowtow to them. Butter them up.

Soft-soap them. Tell them, 'Yes, Mr. Barkalow,' and, 'No, Mr. Barkalow,' and, 'Whatever you say, Mr. Barkalow. Oh, we wouldn't want to *discommode* you, Mr. Barkalow.'"

Red was cutting into his tomato slice now, not meeting his father's eyes or even appearing to hear him, but his cheekbones had a raw, scratched look as if they'd been raked by someone's fingernails.

"'Oh, Mr. Barkalow,'" Mr. Whitshank said in a simpering voice. "'Is this mutually *agreeable* to you?'"

"We got that trunk down, boss," Landis said. "Got her just about flat to the ground."

Abby wanted to hug him.

Mr. Whitshank was preparing to say more, but he paused and looked over at Landis. "Oh," he said. "Well, good. Now all's we have to do is wait for Mitch to finish lunch at his durn mother-in-law's."

"I wouldn't hold my breath, boss. You ever met his mother-in-law? Woman is a cooking *fiend*. Seven children, all of them married, all with children of their own, and every Sunday after church they all get together at her house and she serves three kinds of meat, two kinds of potato, salad, pickles, vegetables . . ."

Abby sat back in her chair. She hadn't realized how tightly she had been clenching her muscles. She wasn't hungry anymore, and when Mrs. Whitshank urged another piece of chicken on her she mutely shook her head.

*

"Another thing," Red said.

He had paused next to Abby as the men were leaving the dining room. Abby, collecting a fistful of dirty silverware, turned to look at him.

"If you're thinking you shouldn't come to the wedding because it's too short of a notice," he said, "that wouldn't be a problem, I promise. A lot of people Merrick invited are staying away. All those friends of Pookie Vanderlin's, and their moms and dads too—they've mostly said no. We're going to end up with way too much food at the reception, I bet."

"I'll keep that in mind," Abby told him, and she gave him a quick pat on the arm as if to thank him, but what she really meant to convey was that she had already put his father's tirade out of her mind and she hoped that he would do the same.

Dane, waiting for Red in the doorway, sent her a wink. He liked to poke fun at Red's devotion sometimes, referring to him as "your feller." Usually this made her smile, but today she just went back to her table clearing, and after a moment he and Red walked on out to join the others.

She set the silverware next to the kitchen sink where Mrs. Whitshank was washing glasses, and then she returned to the dining room. There stood Mr. Whitshank, scooping a gooey chunk of peach cobbler from the baking dish with his fingers. He froze when he saw Abby, but then he lifted his chin defiantly and popped the chunk into his mouth. With showy deliberation, he wiped his fingers on a napkin.

Abby said, "It must be hard to be you, Mr. Whitshank."

His fingers stilled on the napkin. He said, "What's that you say?"

"You're glad your daughter's marrying a rich boy but it irks you rich boys are so spoiled. You want your son to join the gentry but you're mad when he's polite to them. I guess you just can't be satisfied, can you?"

"Missy, you've got no business taking that tone with me," he said.

Abby felt as if she were about to run out of breath, but she stood her ground. "Well?" she asked. "Can you?"

"I'm proud of both my children," Mr. Whitshank said in a steely voice. "Which is more than *your* daddy can say for *you*, I reckon, with that disrespectful tongue of yours."

"My father is very proud of me," she told him.

"Well, maybe I shouldn't be surprised, considering where you come from."

Abby opened her mouth but then closed it. She snatched up the cobbler dish and marched out to the kitchen with it, her back very straight and her head high.

Mrs. Whitshank had left off washing dishes to start drying some of those that were sitting on the drain board. Abby took the towel from her, and Mrs. Whitshank said, "Why, thank you, honey," and returned to the sink. She didn't seem to notice how Abby's hands were shaking. Abby felt bitterly triumphant but also wounded in some way—cut to the quick.

How dare he say a word about where she came from?

He of all people, with his shady, shameful past! Her family was very respectable. They had ancestors they could brag about: a great-great-grandfather, for instance, who had once rescued a king. (Granted, the rescue was merely a matter of helping to lift a carriage wheel out of a rut in the road, but the king had nodded to him personally, it was believed.) And a great-aunt out west who'd gone to college with Willa Cather, although it was true that the great-aunt hadn't known at the time that Willa Cather existed. Oh, there was nothing lower-class about the Daltons, nothing second-rate, and their house might be on the smallish side but at least they got along with their neighbors.

Mrs. Whitshank was talking about dishwashing machines. She just didn't see the need, she was saying. She said, "Why, some of my nicest conversations have been over a sinkful of dishes! But Junior thinks we ought to get a machine. He's all for going out and buying one."

"What does *he* know about it?" Abby demanded.

Mrs. Whitshank was quiet a moment. Then, "Oh," she said, "he just wants to make my life easier, I guess."

Abby fiercely dried a platter.

"People don't always understand Junior," Mrs. Whitshank said. "But he's a better man than you know, Abby, honey."

"Huh," Abby said.

Mrs. Whitshank smiled at her. "Could you check out on the porch, please," she asked, "and see if there's any dishes?"

Abby was glad to leave. She might have said something she'd be sorry for.

No one was sitting on the porch. She picked up Merrick's cereal bowl and her spoon, and then she straightened and surveyed the lawn. At the moment, both chainsaws were silent. The air seemed oddly bright; evidently that naked trunk had made more difference than she had suspected. It was lying flat now, pointing toward the street, and Landis was untying a length of rope that had been looped around its circumference. Dane had paused for a cigarette, Earl and Ward were loading the wheelbarrow, and Red was standing next to the sheared-off stump with his head bowed.

From his posture, Abby thought at first that he was brooding about what had happened at lunch, and she turned away quickly so he wouldn't know she had seen. But in the act of turning, she realized that what he was doing was counting tree rings.

After all Red had been through today—the grueling physical effort and the din and the punishing heat, the altercation with the neighbor and the painful scene with his father—Red was calmly studying that stump to find out how old it was.

Why did this hearten her so? Maybe it was the steadiness of his focus. Maybe it was his immunity to insult, or his lack of resentment. "Oh, *that*," he seemed to be saying. "Never mind that. All families have their ups and downs; let's just figure the age of this poplar."

Abby felt buoyed by a kind of airiness at her center, like the airiness of the lawn once that trunk had been felled. She stepped back into the house so lightly that she made almost no sound at all.

"What's going on out there?" Mrs. Whitshank asked. She was wiping a counter; the last of the pots and pans had been dried and put away.

Abby said, "Well, they got the trunk down, but Mitch hasn't shown up yet. Dane is taking a cigarette break, and Ward and Earl and Landis are clearing the yard, and Red is counting tree rings."

"Tree rings?" Mrs. Whitshank asked. Then, perhaps imagining that Abby had no knowledge whatsoever of the natural world, she said, "Oh! He must be guessing its age."

"He was just standing there, after all that fuss, wondering how old a poplar was," Abby said, and all at once she felt on the verge of tears; she had no idea why. "He's a good man, Mrs. Whitshank," she said.

Mrs. Whitshank glanced up in surprise, and then she smiled—a serene, contented, radiant smile that turned her eyes into curls. "Why, yes, honey, he is," she said.

Then Abby went out to the porch again and settled in the swing. It was the prettiest afternoon, all breezy and yellow-green with a sky the unreal blue of a Noxzema jar, and in a minute she was going to tell Red she'd like to ride with him to the wedding. For now, though, she was saving that up—hugging it close to her heart.

She nudged a porch floorboard with her foot to set the swing in motion, and she swung slowly back and forth, absently tracing the familiar, sandy-feeling undersides of the armrests with her fingertips. Her eyes were on Dane now; she watched him with a distant feeling of sorrow. She saw how he dropped his cigarette, how he ground it beneath his heel, how he picked up his axe and sauntered over to a branch. What a world, what a world. And then the line that came after that one: "Who would have thought," the witch had asked, "that a good little girl like you could destroy my beautiful wickedness?"

But Abby stood up from the swing, even so, and started walking toward Red, and with every step she felt herself growing happier and more certain.

PART THREE

A Bucket of Blue Paint

10

Every ground-floor rom but the kitchen had double pocket doors, and above each door was a fretwork transom for the air to circulate in the summer. The windows were fitted so tightly that not even the fiercest winter storm could cause them to rattle. The second-floor hall had a chamfered railing that pivoted neatly at the stairs before descending to the entrance hall. All the floors were aged chestnut. All the hardware was solid brass—doorknobs, cabinet knobs, even the two-pronged hooks meant to anchor the cords of the navy-blue linen window shades that were brought down from the attic every spring. A ceiling fan with wooden blades hung in each room upstairs and down, and out on the porch there were three. The fan above the entrance hall had a six-and-a-half-foot wingspan.

Mrs. Brill had wanted a chandelier in the entrance hall—a glittery one, all crystal, shaped like an upside-down wedding cake. Silly woman. Junior had dissuaded her by pointing out the impracticality: any time the tiniest cobweb was spotted trailing from a prism, he would need to send a workman over with a sixteen-foot stepladder. (He failed to disclose that for another client, he had once designed an ingenious cable-and-winch lift system to raise and lower a chandelier at will.) His main objection, of course, was that a chandelier would not have been in keeping with the house. This was a plain house, in the way that a handcrafted blanket chest is plain—simple, but impeccably built, as Junior, who had built it, should know. He had overseen every detail, setting his hand to every part of it except those parts that somebody else could do better, like the honeycombing of tiny black-and-white ceramic tiles in the bathroom, laid by two brothers from Little Italy who didn't speak any English. The stairway, though, with the newel posts running clean through the hand-cut openings in the treads, and those pocket doors that glided almost silently into their respective walls: those were Junior's. He was a brash and hasty man in all other areas of life, a man who coasted through stop signs without so much as a toe on the brake, a man who bolted his food and guzzled his drinks and ordered a stammering child to "come on, spit it out," but when it came to constructing a house he had all the patience in the world.

Mrs. Brill had also wanted velvet-flocked wallpaper in the living room, fitted carpets in the bedrooms, and red-and-blue stained glass in the fanlight above the front door. None of which she got. Ha! Junior won just about every argument. Mostly, as with the chandelier, he cited impracticalities, but when he needed to he was not averse to bringing up the issue of taste. "Now, I don't know why, Mrs. Brill," he would say, "but that is just not done. The Remingtons didn't do that, nor the Warings, either"— naming two families in Guilford whom Mrs. Brill especially admired. Then Mrs. Brill would retreat—"Well, you know best, I suppose"—and Junior would proceed as he had originally intended. This was the house of his life, after all (the way a different type of man would have a *love* of his life), and against any sort of logic he clung to the conviction that he would someday be living here. Even after the Brills moved in and their cluttery decorations choked the airy rooms, he remained serenely optimistic. And when Mrs. Brill started talking about how isolated she felt, how far from downtown, when she went to pieces after she found those burglar tools in the sunroom, he heard the click of his world settling into its rightful place. At last, the house would be his.

As it had been all along, really.

Sometimes, in the weeks when he was sprucing the place up before he installed his family, he drove over in the early morning just to take a walk-through, to relish the thrillingly empty rooms and the non-squeaking floorboards and the sturdy faucet handles above the bathroom sink. (Mrs. Brill had wanted handles she'd seen in a Paris hotel, faceted crystal knobs the size of Ping-Pong balls. In Junior's opinion, though, the only sensible design was a chubby white porcelain cross—easiest to turn with soapy fingers—and for once Mr. Brill had spoken up and agreed with him.)

He liked to gaze up the stairs and imagine his daughter sweeping down them, an elegant young woman in a white satin wedding gown. He envisioned the dining-room table lined with a double row of grandchildren, mostly boys, his son's boys to carry on the Whitshank name. They would all have their faces turned in Junior's direction, like sunflowers turned to the sun, listening to him hold forth on some educational topic. Maybe he could assign a topic each night at the start of the meal—music, or art, or current events. A ham or perhaps a roast goose would sit in front of him waiting to be carved, and the water would be served in stemmed goblets, and the salad forks would have been refrigerated ahead of time as he had observed the maid doing in the Remingtons' house in Guilford.

Everything till now had been makeshift—his ragtag upbringing, his hidey-hole courtship, his limping-along marriage, and his shabby little rented house in a rundown neighborhood. But now that was about to change. His real life could begin.

Then Linnie Mae had to go and interfere with the porch swing.

In the Brills' time, the porch swing had been an ugly white wrought-iron affair featuring sharp-edged curlicues that gouged a person's spine. Its rust-pocked figure-eight hooks made a screechy, complaining sound, and the heavy chains could seriously pinch your fingers if you gripped them wrong. But Mrs. Brill had swung in that swing as a little girl, she'd told Junior, and it was clear from the lingering way she spoke how fondly she looked back on that little girl, how she cherished the notion of her cute little childhood self. So Junior had had to allow it.

When the Brills moved out, they left behind all their porch furniture because they were going to an apartment. Mrs. Brill told Junior, in a sad little voice, to be sure and look after her swing, and Junior said, "Yes, ma'am, I'll certainly do that." The moment they were gone, though, he climbed up on a ladder and unhooked the swing himself. He knew what he wanted in its stead: a plain wooden bench swing varnished in a honey tone, with a row of lathed spindles forming the back and supporting each armrest. It should hang by special ropes that were whiter and softer than ordinary ropes, easier on the hands, and when it moved there should be no sound at all, or at most just a genteel creak such as he imagined you would hear from the sails on a sailboat. He had seen such a swing back home, at Mr. Muldoon's. Mr. Muldoon managed the mica mines, and his house had a long front porch with varnished floorboards, and the steps were varnished as well, and so was the swing.

Junior couldn't find this swing ready-made and he had to commission one. It cost a fortune. He didn't tell Linnie how much. She asked, because money was an issue; the down payment on the house had just about ruined them. But he said, "What difference does it make? There's not a chance on this earth I would live in a place with a white lace swing out front."

It arrived raw, as he'd specified, so that it could be finished to the shade he envisioned. He had Eugene, his best painter, see to that. Another of his men spliced the ropes to the heavy brass hardware, a fellow from the Eastern Shore who knew how such things were done. (And who whistled when he saw the brass, but Junior had his own private hoard and it was not *his* fault there was a war on.) When the swing was hung, finally—the grain of the wood shining through the varnish, the white ropes silky and silent—he felt supremely satisfied. For once, something he'd dreamed of had turned out exactly as he had planned.

Up to this point, Linnie Mae had barely visited the house. She just didn't seem as excited about it as Junior was. He couldn't understand that. Most women would be jumping up and down! But she had all these quibbles: too expensive, too hoity-toity, too far from her girlfriends. Well, she would come around. He wasn't going to waste his breath. But once the swing was hung he was eager for her to see it, and the next Sunday morning he suggested taking her and the kids to the house in the truck after they got back from church. He didn't mention the swing because he wanted it to kind of dawn on her. He just pointed out that since it was only a couple of weeks till moving day, maybe she'd like to carry over a few of those boxes she'd been packing. Linnie said, "Oh, all right." But after church she started dragging her heels. She said why didn't they eat dinner first, and when he told her they could eat after they got back she said, "Well, I'll need to change out of my good clothes, at least."

"What do you want to do that for?" he asked. "Go like you are." He hadn't brought it up yet, but he was thinking that after they'd moved in, Linnie should give more thought to how she dressed. She dressed like the women back home dressed. And she sewed most of her clothes herself, as well as the children's. There was something thick-waisted and bunchy, he had noticed, about everything that his children wore.

But Linnie said, "I am not lugging dusty old boxes in my best outfit." So he had to wait for her to change and to put the kids in their play clothes. He himself kept his Sunday suit on, though. Until now their future neighbors, if they ever peeked out their windows (and he would bet they did), would have seen him only in overalls, and he wanted to show his better side to them.

In the truck, Merrick sat between Junior and Linnie while Redcliffe perched on Linnie's lap. Junior chose the prettiest streets to drive down, so as to show them off to Linnie. It was April and everything was in bloom, the azaleas and the redbud and the rhododendron, and when they reached the Brills' house—the Whitshanks' house!—he pointed out the white dogwood. "Maybe when we're moved in you could plant yourself some roses," he told Linnie, but she said, "I can't grow roses in that yard! It's nothing but shade." He held his tongue. He parked down front, although with all they had to unload it would have made more sense to park in back, and he got out of the truck and waited for her to lift the children out, meanwhile staring up at the house and trying to see it through her eyes. She *had* to love it. It was a house that said "Welcome," that said "Family," that said "Solid people live here." But Linnie was heading toward the rear of the truck where the boxes were. "Forget about those," Junior told her. "We'll see to them in a minute. I want you to come on up and get to know your new house."

He set a hand on the small of her back to guide her. Merrick took his other hand and walked next to him, and Redcliffe toddled behind with his homemade wooden tractor rattling after him on a string. Linnie said, "Oh, look, they left behind their porch furniture."

"I told you they were doing that," he said.

"Did they charge you for it?"

"Nope. Said I could have it for free."

"Well, that was nice."

He wasn't going to point out the swing. He was going to wait for her to notice it.

There was a moment when he wondered if she *would* notice—she could be very heedless, sometimes—but then she came to a stop, and he stopped too and watched her taking it in. "Oh," she said, "that swing's real pretty, Junior."

"You like it?"

"I can see why you would favor it over wrought iron."

He slid his hand from the small of her back to cup her

waist, and he pulled her closer. "It's a sight more comfortable, I'll tell you that," he said.

"What color you going to paint it?"

"What?"

"Could we paint it blue?"

"Blue!" he said.

"I'm thinking a kind of medium blue, like a . . . well, I don't know what shade exactly you would call it, but it's darker than baby blue, and lighter than navy. Just a *middling* blue, you know? Like a . . . maybe they call it Swedish blue. Or . . . is there such a thing as Dutch blue? No, maybe not. My aunt Louise had a porch swing the kind of blue I'm thinking of; my uncle Guy's wife. They lived over in Spruce Pine in this cute little tiny house. They were the sweetest couple. I used to wish my folks were like them. My folks were more, well, you know; but Aunt Louise and Uncle Guy were so friendly and outgoing and fun-loving and they didn't have any children and I always thought, 'I wish they'd ask if *I* could be their child.' And they sat out in their porch swing together every nice summer evening, and it was a real pretty blue. Maybe Mediterranean blue. Do they have such a color as Mediterranean blue?"

"Linnie Mae," Junior said. "The swing is already painted."

"It is?"

"Or varnished, at least. It's finished. This is how it's going to be."

"Oh, Junie, can't we paint it blue? Please? I think how best to describe that blue is 'sky blue,' but by that I mean a *real* sky, a deep-blue summer sky. Not powder blue or aqua blue or pale blue, but more of a, how do you say—"

"Swedish," Junior said through set teeth.

"What?"

"It was Swedish blue; you had it right the first time. I know because every goddamn house in Spruce Pine had Swedish-blue porch furniture. You'd think they'd passed a law or something. It was a *common* shade. It was common and low-class."

Linnie was looking at him with her mouth open, and Merrick was tugging his hand to urge him toward the house. He wrung his fingers free and charged on up the walk, leaving the others to follow. If Linnie said one more word, he was going to fling back his head and roar like some kind of caged beast. But she didn't.

The main thing he needed to do before they moved in was add a back porch. All the house had now was a little concrete stoop—one of the few battles with the Brills that Junior had lost, although he had pointed out to them repeatedly that their architect had provided no space for the jumble of normal life, the snow boots and catchers' masks and hockey sticks and wet umbrellas.

Junior always made a spitting sound when someone mentioned architects.

He didn't have men to spare these days because of the war. Two of them had enlisted right after Pearl Harbor, and one had gone to work at the Sparrows Point Shipyard, and a couple more had been drafted. So what he did, he took Dodd and Cary off the Adams job and set them to roughing out the porch, after which he finished the rest on his own. He went over there in the evenings, mostly, using the last of the natural light for the outside work and after that moving inside (the porch was enclosed at one end) to continue under the glare of the ceiling fixture his electrician had installed.

He liked working by himself. Most of his men, he suspected—or the younger ones, at least—found him stern and forbidding. He didn't set them straight. They'd be talking woman troubles and trading tales of weekend binges, but the instant he showed himself they would shut up, and inwardly he would smile because little did they know. But it was best they never found out. He still did some hands-on work; he wasn't too proud for that, but generally he did it off in some separate room—cutting dadoes, say, while the rest of them were framing an addition. They'd be gossiping and joking and teasing one another, but Junior (usually so talkative) worked in silence. In his head, a tune often played without his deciding which one—"You Are My Sunshine" for one task, say, and "Blueberry Hill" for another—and his work would fall into the tempo of the song. One long week, installing a complicated staircase, he found himself stuck with "White Cliffs of Dover" and he thought he would never finish, he was moving so slowly and mournfully. Although it did turn out to be a very well made staircase. Oh, there was nothing like the pleasure of a job done right—seeing how tidily a tenon fit into a mortise, or how the proper-size shim, properly shaved, properly tapped into place, could turn a joint nearly seamless.

A couple of days after he took Linnie to visit the house, he drove over there around four p.m. and parked in the rear. As he was stepping out of the truck, though, he saw something that stopped him dead in his tracks.

The porch swing sat next to the driveway, resting on a drop cloth.

And it was blue.

Oh, God, an awful blue, a boring, no-account, neither-here-nor-there *Swedish* blue. It was such a shock that he had a moment when he wondered if he was hallucinating, experiencing some taunting flash of vision from his youth. He gave a kind of moan. He slammed the truck door shut behind him and walked over to the swing. Blue, all right. He bent to set a finger on one armrest and it came away tacky, which was no surprise because up close, he could smell the fresh paint.

He looked around quickly, half sensing he was being watched. Someone was lurking in the shadows and watching him and laughing. But no, he was alone.

He had the key out of his pocket before he realized the back door was already open. "Linnie?" he called. He stepped inside and found Dodd McDowell at the kitchen sink, blotting a paintbrush on a splotched rag.

"What in the *hell* do you think you're doing?" Junior asked him.

Dodd spun around.

"Did you paint that swing?" Junior asked him.

"Why, yes, Junior."

"What for? Who told you you could do that?"

Dodd was a very pale, bald-headed man with whitish-blond eyebrows and lashes, but now he turned a deep red and his eyelids grew so pink that he looked teary. He said, "Linnie did."

"Linnie!"

"Did you not know about it?"

"Where did you see Linnie?" Junior demanded.

"She called me on the phone last night. Asked if I would pick up a bucket of Swedish-blue high-gloss and paint the porch swing for her. I thought you knew about it."

"You thought I'd hunt down solid cherry, and pay an arm and a leg for it, and put Eugene to work varnishing it in a shade to look right with the porch floor, and then have you slop blue paint on it."

"Well, *I* didn't know. I figured: *women*. You know?" And Dodd spread his hands, still holding the brush and the rag.

Junior forced himself to take a deep breath. "Right," he said. "Women." He chuckled and shook his head. "What're you going to do with them? But listen," he said, and he sobered. "Dodd. From now on, you take your orders from me. Understand?"

"I hear you, Junior. Sorry about that."

Dodd still looked as if he were about to cry. Junior said, "Well, never mind. It's fixable. Women!" he said again, and he gave another laugh and then turned and walked back out and shut the door behind him. He just needed a little time to get ahold of himself.

She was the bane of his existence. She was a millstone around his neck. That night back in '31 when he went to collect her from the train station and found her waiting out front—her unevenly hemmed gray coat too skimpy for the Baltimore winter, her floppy, wide-brimmed felt hat so outdated that even Junior could tell—he'd had the incongruous thought that she was like mold on lumber. You think you've scrubbed it off but one day you see it's crept back again.

He had considered *not* going to collect her. She had telephoned him at his boardinghouse, and when he heard that confounded "Junie?" (nobody else called him that) in her stringy high voice he'd known instantly who it was and his heart had sunk like a stone. He'd wanted to slam the earpiece onto the hook again. But he was caught. She had his landlady's phone number. Lord only knew how she'd gotten it.

He said, "What."

"It's me! It's Linnie Mae!"

"What do you want?"

"I'm here in Baltimore, can you believe it? I'm at the railroad station! Could you come pick me up?"

"What for?"

There was the tiniest pause. Then, "What *for*?" she asked. All the bounce had gone out of her voice. "Please, Junie, I'm scared," she said. "There's a whole lot of colored folks here."

"Colored folks won't hurt you," he said. (They didn't have any colored back home.) "Just pretend you don't see them."

"What am I going to do, Junior? How am I going to find you? You have to come and get me."

No, he did not have to come and get her. She didn't have the least little claim on him. There was nothing between them. Or there was only the worst experience of his life between them.

But he was already admitting to himself that he couldn't just leave her there. She'd be as helpless as a baby chick.

Besides, a little sprig of curiosity had begun to poke up in his mind. Someone from home. Here in Baltimore!

The fact was, there weren't a whole lot of people he knew to talk to in Baltimore.

So, "Well," he said finally. "You be waiting, then."

"Oh, hurry, Junie!"

"Wait out front. Go out the main door and watch for my car out front."

"You have a car?"

"Sure," he said. He tried to sound offhand about it.

He went back upstairs for his jacket. When he came down again, his landlady cracked her parlor door open and poked her head out. She had hair of a peculiar gold color with curls he couldn't quite understand: each as round and flat as a penny, plastered to her temples. "Everything all right, Mr. Whitshank?" she asked, and Junior said, "Yes, ma'am," and crossed the foyer in two strides and was gone.

Now, Junior's belongings back then wouldn't have filled a decent-size suitcase, but he did own a car of sorts: a 1921 Essex. He'd bought it off another carpenter for thirty-seven dollars when they all lost their jobs at the start of hard times. He'd justified the expenditure on the grounds that a car would help in his hunt for work, and that had turned out to be the case although he hadn't bargained on its many crotchets and breakdowns. It crossed his mind, as he was coaxing the cold engine to life, that he could have told Linnie to take a streetcar instead. But he knew that would have been beyond her. Streetcars were foreign to her. She'd have bungled it somehow. He couldn't even picture her making that train trip by herself, because she would have had to transfer in Washington, D.C., he knew, not to mention a whole lot of smaller stations before then.

He lived in the mill district, north of the station—a good distance north, in fact. To go south he cut east to St. Paul and then chugged between the rows of dimly lit houses, leaning forward from time to time to wipe the fog of his breath off the windshield. At length he passed the train station and turned right, onto the paving that crossed in front of its important-looking columns. He spotted Linnie immediately—the only person out there, her white, anxious face swiveling from side to side. But he didn't stop for her. Without consciously deciding to, he gathered speed and drove on. He took another right onto Charles Street and headed for home, but halfway up the first block he started picturing how her forehead would have smoothed when she caught sight of him, how relieved she would have looked, how experienced and knowing he would have seemed arriving in his red Essex. He circled back around and passed the important columns again, and this time he veered into the pickup lane. Slowing to a stop, he watched as she snatched up her cardboard suitcase and hurried to open the passenger door.

"Did you drive past me once before?" she demanded as soon as she was seated.

Just like that, he lost his advantage.

"I was getting ready for bed," he said, and his voice came out sounding whiny, somehow. "I'm half asleep."

She said, "Oh, poor Junie, *I'm* sorry," and she leaned across her suitcase to kiss his cheek. Her lips were warm, but she gave off the smell of frost. Also, underneath, another smell, one he associated with home: something like fried bacon. It weighed down his spirits. But after he started driving, putting the Essex through its gears, he began to feel in control again. "I don't know why you're here," he told her.

"You don't know why I'm *here*?" she said.

"And I don't know where I'm going to take you. I don't have the money to put you up in a hotel. Unless *you* have money."

If she did, she wasn't letting on. "You're taking me home with you," she told him.

"No, I'm not. My landlady only rents to men."

"You could slip me in, though."

"What: slip you into *my* room?"

She nodded.

"Not on your life," he said.

But he kept driving in the direction of the boarding-house, because he didn't know what else to do.

They reached an intersection, and he braked and turned to look at her. Five years, just about, hadn't changed her in the least; she might still be thirteen. Her face still seemed drawn too tight, as if she didn't have quite enough skin to go around, and her lips were still thin and colorless. It was as if she had frozen in time the day he left. He didn't know why he had ever found her attractive. But clearly she couldn't tell what he was thinking, because she smiled and ducked her chin and looked up at him sideways and said, "I wore those shoes you like so much."

What shoes could those be? He didn't remember any shoes. He glanced down at her feet and saw dark, high-heeled pumps with ankle straps, so blocky and oversized that her shins looked as slender as clover stems.

"How did you find out where I was?" he asked her.

She stopped smiling. She straightened and stood her big purse on the tip end of her knees.

"Well," she said, and she gave a sharp nod. (He'd forgotten how she used to do that. It said, "Down to business." It said,

"Let *me* handle this.") "Four days ago was my birthday," she said. "I'm eighteen years old now."

"Happy birthday," he said dully.

"Eighteen, Junie! Legal age!"

"Legal age is twenty-one," he told her.

"Well, for *voting*, maybe . . . and I already had my suitcase packed; I already had my money saved. I earned it picking galax every fall since you left. But I laid low till I was eighteen, so nobody could stop me. Then the day after my birthday, I had Martha Moffat drive me to the Parryville lumberyard and I asked the fellows there if they could say where you'd gone off to."

"You asked the whole yard?" he said, and she nodded again.

He could just picture how *that* must have looked.

"And this one fellow, he told me you might could have headed north. He said he remembered you coming in one day, wondering if anyone knew where this carpenter was they called Trouble, on account of his name was Trimble. And they told you Trouble'd gone to Baltimore, so maybe that's where *you* went, this fellow said, looking for work. So I got Martha to ride me to Mountain City and I bought a ticket to Baltimore."

Junior was reminded of those movie cartoons where Bosko or someone steps off a cliff and doesn't even realize he's standing on empty space. Had Linnie not grasped the *chanciness*? He could have moved on years ago. He could be living in Chicago now, or Paris, France.

It seemed to him all at once a kind of failure that he was not; that here he still was, all this time afterward. And that she had somehow known he would be.

"Martha Moffat's name is Shuford now," Linnie was saying. "Did you know Martha got married? She married Tommy Shuford, but *Mary* Moffat's still single and it's like to kill her soul, you can tell. She acts mad at Martha all the time about every little thing. But then they never did get along as good as you'd expect."

"As well," he said.

"What?"

He gave up.

They were traveling through downtown, with the buildings set cheek to jowl and the streetlights glowing, but Linnie barely glanced out the window. He had thought she would be more impressed.

"When I got off the train in Baltimore," she said, "I went straight to the public telephone and I looked for you in the book, and when I couldn't find you I called everybody named Trimble. Or I would have, except Trouble's first name turned out to be Dean and that came pretty soon in the alphabet. And he said you *had* looked him up, and he'd told you where you might could find work, but he didn't know if they'd hired you or not and he couldn't say where you were living, unless you were still at Mrs. Bess Davies's where a lot of workingmen board at when they first come north."

"You should get a job with Pinkerton's," Junior said. He wasn't pleased to hear how easy he'd been to find.

"I worried you had moved by now, found a place of your own or something."

He frowned. "There's a depression on," he said. "Or haven't you heard?"

"It's fine with *me* if you live in a boardinghouse," she said, and she patted his arm. He jerked away, and for a while after that she was quiet.

When they reached Mrs. Davies's street he parked some distance from the house, at the darker end of the block. He didn't want anyone seeing them.

"Are you glad I'm here?" Linnie asked him.

He shut off the engine. He said, "Linnie—"

"But my goodness, we don't have to go into everything all at once!" Linnie said. "Oh, Junior, I've missed you so! I haven't once looked at a single other fellow since you left."

"You were thirteen years old," Junior said.

Meaning, "You've spent all the time since you were thirteen never having a boyfriend?"

But Linnie, misunderstanding, beamed at him and said, "I know."

She picked up his right hand, which was still resting on the gearshift knob, and pressed it between both of hers. Hers were very warm, despite the weather, so that his must have struck her as cold. "Cold hands, warm heart," she told him. Then she said, "And so here I am, about to spend the first full night with you I've ever had in my life." She seemed to be taking it for granted that he had decided to slip her in after all.

"The first and *only* night," he told her. "Then tomorrow you're going to have to find yourself someplace else. It's risky enough as it is; if Mrs. Davies caught wind of you, she'd put us both out on the street."

"I wouldn't mind that," Linnie said. "Not if I was with you. It would be romantic."

Junior withdrew his hand and heaved himself out of the car.

At the foot of the front steps he made her wait, and he opened the front door silently and checked for Mrs. Davies before he signaled Linnie to come on in. Every creak of the stairs as he and Linnie climbed made him pause a moment, filled with dread, but they made it. Arriving on the third floor—the servants' floor, he'd always figured, on account of its tiny rooms with their low, slanted ceilings—he gave a jab of his chin toward a half-open door and whispered, "Bathroom," because he didn't want her popping in and out of his room all night. She wriggled her fingers at him and disappeared inside, while he continued on his way with her suitcase. He left his door cracked a couple of inches, the light threading out onto the hall floorboards, until she slipped inside and shut it behind her. She was carrying her hat in one hand and her hair was damp at the temples, he saw. It was shorter than when he'd first known her. It used to hang all the way down her back, but now it was even with her jaw. She was breathless and laughing slightly. "I didn't have my soap or a facecloth or towel or *anything*," she said. Even though she was whispering, it was a sharp, carrying whisper, and he scowled and said, "Ssh." In her absence he'd stripped to his long johns. There was a small, squarish armchair in the corner with a mismatched ottoman in front of it—the only furniture besides a narrow cot and a little two-drawer bureau—and he settled into it as best he could and arranged his winter jacket over himself like a blanket. Linnie stood in the middle of the room, watching him with her mouth open. "Junie?" she said.

"I'm tired," he said. "I have to work tomorrow." And he turned his face away from her and closed his eyes.

He heard no movement at all, for a time. Then he heard the rustle of her clothing, the snap of two suitcase clasps, more rustling. The louder rustle of bedclothes. The lamp clicked off, and he relaxed his jaw and opened his eyes to stare into the dark.

"Junior?" she said.

He could tell she must be lying on her back. Her voice had an upward-floating quality.

"Junior, are you mad at me? What did I do wrong?"

He closed his eyes.

"What'd I do, Junior?"

But he made his breath very slow and even, and she didn't ask again.

11

What Linnie had done wrong:

Well, for starters, she'd not told him her age. The first time he saw her she was sitting on a picnic blanket with the Moffat twins, Mary and Martha, both of them seniors in high school, and he had just assumed that she was the same age they were. Stupid of him. He should have realized from her plain, unrouged face, and her hair hanging loose down her back, and the obvious pride she took in her new grown-upness—most especially in her breasts, which she surreptitiously touched with her fingertips from time to time in a testing sort of way. But they were such *large* breasts, straining against the bodice of her polka-dot dress, and she was wearing big white sandals with high heels. Was it any wonder he had imagined she was older? Nobody aged thirteen wore heels that Junior knew of.

He had come with Tillie Gouge, but only because she'd asked him. He didn't feel any particular obligation to her. He picked up a molasses lace cookie from the picnic table laden with foods, and he walked over to Linnie Mae. Bending at the waist—which must have looked like bowing—he offered the cookie. "For you," he said.

She lifted her eyes, which turned out to be the nearly colorless blue of Mason jars. "Oh!" she said, and she blushed and took it from him. The Moffat twins became all attention, sitting up very straight and watching for what came next, but Linnie just lowered her fine pale lashes and nibbled the edge of the cookie. Then, one by one, she licked each of her fingers in turn. Junior's fingers were sticky too—he should have chosen a gingersnap—and he wiped them on the handkerchief he drew from his pocket, but meanwhile he was looking at her. When he'd finished, he offered her the handkerchief. She took it without meeting his eyes and blotted her fingers and handed it back, and then she bit off another half-moon of cookie.

"Do you belong to Whence Baptist?" he asked. (Because this picnic was a church picnic, given in honor of May Day.)

She nodded, chewing daintily, her eyes downcast.

"I've never been here before," he said. "Want to show me around?"

She nodded again, and for a moment it seemed that that might be the end of it, but then she rose in a flustered, stumbling way—she'd been sitting on the hem of her dress and it snagged briefly on one of her heels—and walked off beside him, not so much as glancing at the Moffat twins. She was still eating her cookie. Where the churchyard met the graveyard she stopped and switched the cookie to her other hand and licked off her fingers again. Once again he offered his handkerchief, and once again she accepted it. He thought, with some amusement, that this could go on indefinitely, but when she'd finished blotting her fingers she placed her cookie on the handkerchief and then folded the handkerchief carefully, like someone wrapping a package, and gave it to him. He stuffed it in his left pocket and they resumed walking.

If he thought back on that scene now, it seemed to him that every detail of it, every gesture, had shouted "Thirteen!" But he could swear it hadn't even crossed his mind at the time. He was no cradle robber.

Yet he had to admit that the moment when he'd taken notice of her was the moment she had touched her own breasts. At the time it had seemed seductive, but on second thought he supposed it could be read as merely childish. All she'd been doing, perhaps, was marveling at their brand-new existence.

She walked ahead of him through the cemetery, her skinny ankles wobbling in her high-heeled shoes, and she pointed out her daddy's parents' headstones—Jonas Inman and Loretta Carroll Inman. So she was one of the Inmans, a family known for their stuck-up ways. "What's your first name?" he asked her.

"Linnie Mae," she said, blushing again.

"Well, I am Junior Whitshank."

"I know."

He wondered *how* she knew, what she might have heard about him.

"Tell me, Linnie Mae," he said, "can I see inside this church of yours?"

"If you want," she said.

They turned and left the cemetery behind, crossed the packed-earth yard and climbed the front steps of Whence Cometh My Help. The interior was a single dim room with smoke-darkened walls and a potbellied stove, its few rows of wooden chairs facing a table topped with a doily. They came to a stop just inside the door; there was nothing more to see.

"Have you got religion?" he asked her.

She shrugged and said, "Not so much."

This caused a little hitch in the flow, because it wasn't what he'd expected. Evidently she was more complicated than he had guessed. He grinned. "A girl after my own heart," he said.

She met his gaze directly, all at once. The paleness of her eyes startled him all over again.

"Well, I reckon I should go pay some heed to the gal I came here with," he said, making a joke of it. "But maybe tomorrow evening I could take you to the picture show."

"All right," she said.

"Where exactly do you live?"

"I'll just meet you at the drugstore," she said.

"Oh," he said.

He wondered if she was ashamed to show him to her

family. Then he figured the hell with it, and he said, "Seven o'clock?"

"All right."

They stepped back out into the sunlight, and without another glance she left him on the stoop and made a beeline for the Moffat twins. Who were watching, of course, as keen as two sparrows, their sharp little faces pointing in Junior and Linnie's direction.

They had been seeing each other three weeks before her age came out. Not that she volunteered it; she just happened to mention one night that her older brother would be graduating tomorrow from eighth grade. "Your *older* brother?" he asked her.

She didn't get it, for a moment. She was telling him how her younger brother was smart as a whip but her older brother was not, and he was begging to be allowed to drop out now and not go on to the high school in Mountain City the way their parents were expecting him to. "He's never been one for the books," she said. "He likes better to hunt and stuff."

"How old is he?" Junior asked her.

"What? He's fourteen."

"Fourteen," Junior said.

"Mm-hmm."

"How old are *you*?" Junior asked.

She realized, then. She colored. She tried to carry it off,

though. She said, "I mean he's older than my *other* brother."

"How old are you?" he said again.

She lifted her chin and said, "I'm thirteen."

He felt he'd been kicked in the gut.

"Thirteen!" he said. "You're just a . . . you're not but half my age!"

"But I'm an *old* thirteen," Linnie said.

"Good God in heaven, Linnie Mae!"

Because by now, they were doing it. They'd been doing it since their third date. They didn't go to movies anymore, didn't go for ice cream, certainly didn't meet up with friends. (What friends would those have been, anyhow?) They just headed for the river in his brother-in-law's truck and flung a quilt any old which way under a tree and rushed to tangle themselves up in each other. One night it poured and it hadn't stopped them for a minute; they lay spread-eagled when they were finished and let the rain fill their open mouths. But this wasn't something he had talked her into. It was Linnie who had made the first move, drawing back from him in the parked truck one night and shakily, urgently tearing open her button-front dress.

He could be arrested.

Her father grew burley tobacco, and he owned his land outright. Her mother came from Virginia; everyone knew Virginians thought they were better than other people. They would call the sheriff on him without the least hesitation. Oh, Linnie had been so foolish, so infuriatingly brainless, to meet him like that at the drugstore in the middle of her hometown wearing her dress-up dress and her high-heeled shoes! Junior lived over near Parryville, six or eight miles away, so maybe no one who had seen them together in Yarrow knew him, but it couldn't have escaped their notice that he was a grown man, most often in shabby clothes and old work boots with a day or two's worth of beard, and it wouldn't be that hard to find out his name and track him down. He asked Linnie, "Did you tell anybody about us?"

"No, Junior, I swear it."

"Not the Moffat twins or anyone?"

"No one."

"Because I could go to jail for this, Linnie."

"I didn't tell a soul."

He made up his mind to stop seeing her, but he didn't say so right then because she would get all teary and beg him to change his mind. There was something a little bit hanging-on about Linnie. She was always talking about this great romance of theirs, and telling him she loved him even though he never mentioned love himself, and asking him if he thought so-and-so was prettier than she was. It was because it was all so new to her, he guessed. God, he'd saddled himself with an infant. He couldn't believe he had been so blind.

They folded the quilt and they got in the truck and Junior drove her back to town, not saying a word the whole ride although Linnie Mae chattered nonstop about her brother's upcoming graduation party. When he drew up in front of the drugstore, he said he couldn't meet her the following night because he'd promised to help his father with a carpentering job. She didn't seem to find it odd that he would be carpentering at night. "Night after that, then?" she said.

"We'll see."

"But how will I know?"

"I'll get word to you when I'm free," he said.

"I'm going to miss you like crazy, Junior!"

And she flung herself on him and wrapped her arms around his neck, but he pulled her arms off him and said, "You'd better go on, now."

Of course he didn't get word to her. (He didn't know how she had thought he would do that, seeing as he'd said they couldn't tell anyone else.) He stayed strictly within his own territory—two acres of red clay outside Parryville bounded by a rickrack fence, in the three-room cabin he shared with his father and his last unmarried brother.

As it happened, the three of them did have work that week, replacing the roof on a shed for a lady down the road. They would set out early every morning in the wagon, with a tin bucket of buttermilk and a hunk of cornpone for their lunch, and they'd turn their mule loose in Mrs. Honeycutt's pasture and go up on the roof to work all day in the blazing sun. By evening Junior would be so bushed that it was all he could do to force supper down. (His brother Jimmy had taken over the cooking after their mother died—just fried up whatever meat they'd last killed, using the half-inch of white grease that waited permanently in the skillet on the wood stove.) They'd be in bed by eight or eight thirty, workingmen's hours. Three days in a row they did that, and Junior didn't give more than a thought or two to Linnie Mae. Once Jimmy asked if he wanted to go into town after supper and see if they could find any girls, and Junior said, "Nah," but it wasn't on account of Linnie. It was just that he was too beat.

Then they finished with the roof, and they didn't have anything else lined up. Junior spent the next day at home, but he was bored out of his mind and his father was acting ornery, so he figured maybe the next morning he would walk on down to the lumberyard and look for work. They were used to having him come and go there; they could generally use a hand.

He was sitting out on the stoop with the dogs, smoking a cigarette—the twilight still at that stage where it's transparent, the fireflies just beginning to turn on and off in the yard—when a car he didn't know pulled in, a beat-up Chevrolet driven by a fellow in a seed-store cap. And a girl jumped out the front passenger door and walked over to him, saying, "Hey, Junior." One of the Moffat twins. The dogs raised their heads but then settled their chins on their paws again. "Hey back," Junior said, not using a name because he didn't know which one she was. She handed him a piece of white paper and he unfolded it, but it was hard to read in the dusk. "What's this?" he asked.

"It's from Linnie Mae."

He held it up to the faint lantern-light that was coming through the screen door. "Junior, I need to talk to you," he read. "Let the Moffats give you a ride to my house."

He got a lump of ice in his chest. When a girl said she needed to talk . . . oh, Lord. Part of him was already trying to figure out where to run, how to get away before she delivered the news that would trap him for life. But the Moffat twin said, "You coming?"

"What: now?"

"Now," she said. "We'll ride you over."

He stood up and stepped on his cigarette. "Well," he said. "All right."

He followed her to the car. It was a closed car with four doors, and she got into the front and left him to settle in the rear beside the other twin, who said, "Hey, Junior."

"Hey," he said.

"You know our brother Freddy."

"Hey, Freddy," he said. He didn't recall ever meeting him. Freddy just grunted, and then shifted gears and pulled out of the yard and set off down Seven Mile Road.

Junior knew he should make conversation, but all he could think about was what Linnie was going to tell him and what he was going to do about it. What *could* he do about it? He wasn't such a bastard as to pretend it hadn't been him. Although it did cross his mind.

"Linnie's folks are throwing a party for Clifford tonight," the first twin said.

"Who's Clifford?"

"Clifford her brother. He's finished eighth grade."

"Oh."

It seemed to him kind of funny to make such a fuss about eighth grade. When *he* had finished eighth grade, the big to-do was over why on earth he was set on going on to high school. His father had had it in mind to put him to work, while Junior was thinking that there were still some things he hadn't learned yet.

Linnie surely didn't expect him to come to the party, did she? Even she couldn't be that dumb.

But the twin said, "She'll be able to slip out of the house easy, being as there's family around. They'll never notice she's gone."

"Oh," he said, relieved.

That seemed to use up all their conversational topics.

They cut over on Sawyer Road instead of driving on into Yarrow, so he supposed the Inmans' farm must lie to the north of town. The smell of fresh manure started drifting through his open window. Sawyer Road was just gravel, and every time the Chevrolet hit a bump the headlamps flickered and threatened to die. It made him nervous. Shoot, *everything* made him nervous.

He wondered if this was a setup, if they'd have the sheriff ready and waiting at the house. Junior wasn't liked by the sheriff. As a boy he'd caused a near-accident when he and some friends of his were riding on the back of a wagon and they signaled to the car behind that it was okay to pass. And there'd been a few other situations, over the years.

Freddy turned left where Sawyer Road butt-ended into Pee Creek Road, which was paved and gave a much smoother ride. Some distance after that he turned right, onto a dirt driveway. The house looked big to Junior. It was painted white or light gray and all the windows were lit. A few cars and trucks were parked at different angles on the grass out front. Freddy drove around to the rear, though, where Junior could make out the silhouettes of several dark sheds and barns. "*Here* we are," the first twin said.

A shadow moved away from the nearest barn and turned into Linnie, wearing something pale. As she approached the car, Junior asked the Moffats, "Are you-all going to wait for me, or what?"

Before they could answer, Linnie stepped up to his window and whispered, "Junior?"

"Hey," he said.

She leaned in close, although she couldn't be thinking he would do anything soft in front of these people, could she? He fended her off by opening his door, nudging her backward. "You-all wait here," he told the Moffats. "I'm going to need a ride home."

Linnie said, "Thanks, Freddy. Hey, Martha; hey, Mary."

"Hey, Linnie," the twins said in chorus.

Junior stepped out of the car and shut the door behind him, and immediately Freddy shifted into reverse and started backing up. "Where're they going?" Junior asked Linnie.

"Oh, off somewheres, I guess."

"How am I getting home?"

"They'll be back! Come on."

She was leading him toward the barn she'd come out of, gripping him by the hand. He resisted. "I'm not going to be but a minute," he said. "They should have stayed."

"Come *on*, Junior. Someone will see you!"

He gave up and followed her into the barn, which was pitch-dark once she had shut the door behind them. "Let's go up in the loft," she whispered.

But that didn't feel right. You could be cornered, in a loft. "We can talk down here," he said. "I can't stay long. I need to get home. Are you sure the Moffats know to come for me? Why'd you tell them about us? You swore you wouldn't tell a soul."

"I didn't! Just the twins. They think it's romantic. They're real happy for us."

"Good God, Linnie."

"Let's go up in the loft, I mean it. It's more comfortable there; it's got hay."

He ignored her and headed for the rear of the barn, across creaky, straw-littered floorboards. She said, "I don't know why you're being so contrary." She reached out in the dark, feeling for something and then yanking, and an overhead bulb lit up and pained his eyes. These people had electricity even in their outbuildings. He saw that he was standing next to a rusted plow. A thin slant of trampled-down hay was piled in the corner beyond. Linnie's face looked all crinkly in the sudden brightness, and his did too, he supposed. She was wearing a dress that seemed a mite low in the neck to him. He was surprised her mother had allowed it; Linnie always made out that her mother was so strict. He could see the two mounds of her breasts swelling above the fabric, but it didn't affect him. He pulled his Camels from his shirt pocket. "What'd you want to talk about?" he asked.

"You can't smoke in here!"

He put the Camels away.

"Go ahead and say it," he said.

"Say what?"

"Say what you brought me here to tell me."

She drew herself up straight. "Junior," she said, "I know why you've stopped meeting me. You're thinking I'm too young for you."

"What? Wait."

"But age is just a date on a calendar. You aren't being fair. You're going by something I can't help. And you can see that I'm a woman. Haven't I *acted* like a woman? Don't I *feel* like a woman?"

She took one of his hands and laid it above the U of her neckline, where the swelling began. He said, "That's what you wanted to tell me?"

"I want to tell you that you're being narrow-minded."

"Shoot, Linnie," he said. "You're not in trouble?"

"In trouble! No!"

He didn't know why she sounded so shocked; they hadn't always been careful. But he felt such a weight lifting off him that he laughed aloud, and then he bent to set his lips on hers and his hand slid lower on her neckline, down inside it, where it didn't seem she was wearing a brassiere although she surely could have used one. He squeezed, and she drew a sharp breath, and he pressed her back toward the corner of the barn and laid her down on the hay, not once taking his lips away. He kicked his boots off, somehow. He got free of his overalls and his BVDs all in one move. Linnie was struggling out of her drawers, and just as he reached to help her he heard . . . not words but a sort of bellow, like the sound a bull makes, and then, "Great God Almighty!"

He rolled over and scrambled to his feet. A skinny little stick of a man was lunging toward him with both hands outstretched, but Junior stepped aside. The man landed against the plow and hastily righted himself. "Clifford!" he roared. "Brandon!"

Junior had the confused impression that the man was trying out different names on him, but then from the direction of the house he heard another voice call, "Daddy?"

"Get out here! Bring a gun!"

"Daddy, wait, you don't understand," Linnie said.

But he was too busy trying to clamp his hands around Junior's throat. Junior thought he should be given a moment to get his overalls back on; it put him at a disadvantage. He pried Mr. Inman's fingers loose without much difficulty, but when he spun toward where his clothes lay the man grabbed hold of him again. Then, "Freeze!" somebody shouted, and he turned his head to find two boys standing in the doorway training Winchesters on him.

He froze.

"Hand me that," Mr. Inman ordered, and the younger boy stepped forward and passed him his rifle.

Mr. Inman backed up just far enough to put the length of the rifle between himself and Junior, and then he cocked the lever and told Junior, "Turn around."

Junior turned so he was facing the two boys, who seemed more interested than angry. They had their eyes fixed on his crotch. Junior felt the cold, perfect circle of the rifle muzzle in the dead center of the back of his neck. It prodded him. "Forward," Mr. Inman said.

"Well, if I could just—"

"Forward!"

"Sir, could I just get my clothes?"

"No, you cannot get your clothes. Could he get his clothes! Just go. Get out of my barn and get off of my land and get out of this *state*, you hear? Because if you're not two states over by morning I will set the law on you, I swear to God. I've half a mind to do it anyhow, except I don't want the shame on my family."

"But, Daddy, he's half nekkid," Linnie said.

"You shut up," Mr. Inman told her.

He jabbed the rifle harder into the back of Junior's neck and Junior lurched forward, sending a last desperate glance toward the crumple of his clothes in the hay. The toe of one boot was poking out from underneath them.

It was dark in the yard, but the bulb above the back door of the house lit him clearly, he could tell, because the people

crowding out on the stoop all gasped and murmured—
women and a couple of men and a whole bunch of children,
all ages, their eyes as round as moons, the little boys nudging
one another.

It was a blessing to leave the circle of light and step into
the deep, velvety blackness just beyond. With one last jab
of the rifle muzzle, Mr. Inman came to a halt and let Junior
stumble on by himself.

He hadn't walked barefoot since he was in grade school.
Every stob and pebble made him wince.

Next to the Inmans' yard it was woods, the scrubby kind
thick with briers to snatch at his bare skin, but that was
better than the open road, where headlights could pick him
out at any moment. He found himself a middling-size tree
that he could stand behind, close enough that he could
still see pieces of the Inmans' lighted windows through the
undergrowth. He was hoping for Linnie Mae to come out
eventually with his clothes.

Gnats whined in his ears and tree frogs piped. He shifted
from foot to foot and swatted away something feathery, a
moth. His heartbeat got back to normal.

Linnie didn't come. He supposed they had locked her up.

After some time he took his shirt off and tied the sleeves
around his waist with the body of the shirt hanging down in
front like an apron. Then he stepped out from behind the
tree and made his way to the road. The ground alongside it
was stony, so he walked on the asphalt, which was smooth
and still faintly warm from a day's worth of sun. With every

step, he listened for the sound of a car. If it was the Moffats' car, he would need to flag it down. He could already picture how the twins would snicker at the sight of him.

One time he heard a faint hum up ahead and he saw a kind of radiance on the horizon. He ducked back into the bushes just in case and kept a watch, but the road stayed empty and the radiance faded. Whoever it was must have cut off someplace. He returned to the pavement.

If the Moffats did come, would he recognize their car in time? Would he mistake another car for theirs and get caught by strangers without his pants on?

This was the kind of fix that the men he worked with told jokes about, but when he tried to imagine talking about it ever, to anybody, he couldn't. To begin with, the girl was thirteen. Right there that put a different light on things.

Sawyer Road took so long to show up, he started worrying he had passed it. He could have sworn it was closer. He crossed to the other side of the pavement so he'd be sure not to miss it, although the other side was low-growth fields and he would be easier to spot there. He heard a fluttering overhead and then the hoot of an owl, which for some reason struck him as comforting.

Much, much later than he had expected, he came across the narrow pale band of Sawyer Road and he turned onto it. The gravel was vicious, but he had stopped bothering to mince as he walked. He trudged heavily, obstinately, taking a peculiar pleasure in the thought that the soles of his feet must be cut to ribbons.

He hoped Linnie had found a way out of the house by now and was standing in the yard calling "Junior? Junior?" and wringing her hands. Good luck to her, because she was never going to lay eyes on him again as long as she lived. If only she hadn't noticed that he'd been caught without his overalls on, he might have been able to forgive her, but "Daddy, he's half nekkid!" she'd said, and now whatever little feeling he might have had for her was dead and gone forever.

He didn't know what time it was when he finally hit Seven Mile Road. He walked in the very center, where the asphalt was smoothest, but his feet were so shredded by then that even that was torture. When he reached home the sky was lightening, or maybe he'd just turned into some kind of night-visioned animal. He nudged a sleeping dog aside with his foot, opened the screen door and stepped into the close, musty dark and the sound of snoring. In the bedroom, he shucked off the shirt tied around his waist and felt his way to the chifforobe and dug out a pair of BVDs. Stepping into them was the sweetest feeling in the world. He sank onto the rumpled sheets next to Jimmy and closed his eyes.

But not to sleep. Oh, no. His whole walk home he had been longing for sleep, but now he was thoroughly, electrically awake, watching vivid pictures flash past. The party guests gawking on the stoop. His skinny white legs with no pants on. Linnie's witless face and her dropped jaw.

He's half nekkid!

He hated her.

*

During his first months in Baltimore, those pictures could make him wince and snap his head violently to one side, trying to shake them out of his brain. Gradually, though, they grew fainter. He had other things to think about. Just making his way in the world, for instance. Figuring out how it all worked. Adjusting to the unsettling look of the horizon in these parts—the jumble of low, close buildings wherever he turned, the lack of those broad-shouldered purple mountains rising in the distance to give him a sense of protection.

At some point, it occurred to him that it was highly unlikely Mr. Inman would have set the law on him. As the man had said himself, he didn't want to shame his family. All Junior would have needed to do was keep out of the way for a while, and maybe partake in a fistfight or two if he chanced to be in the wrong place. But this realization did not cause him to pack up and go home. For one thing, he found it surprisingly easy to put his family behind him. His mother was the one he had cared about, and she had died when he was twelve. His father had turned mean after that, and Junior had never been close to his brothers or his sister, who were all considerably older. (Had he, in fact, just been looking for any excuse to get away from them all?) But what was even more important: by then he had discovered work. *Prideful* work, the kind that makes you eager to get out of bed every morning.

When he'd asked after Trouble's whereabouts in the

lumberyard that day, it had been in the back of his mind that maybe he'd get a job with him. Trouble had always struck him as interesting. He took his wood so seriously. In fact, his nickname was no accident: the mere appearance of his truck in the lumberyard would bring good-natured groans from the men, because they knew he would want to study each and every board as if he were looking to marry it. It shouldn't have any knotholes, any chewed-off ends or unsightly grain. (That was the word he used: "unsightly.") He built fine furniture, was why. He used to work at a factory in High Point but he quit in disgust and set up in Parryville, where his wife's people were from. And he'd more than once told the men in the lumberyard that he'd a good mind to strike out from Parryville, too, and go up north where there was more of a market for his kind of product.

So when Junior walked over to his brother-in-law's house the morning he left home (wearing his lace-up church shoes that made his battered feet hurt even worse), he asked if they could stop by the lumberyard on their way out of town. All he got at the lumberyard was a mention of Baltimore, but that would have to suffice. He climbed back into the truck and they drove to the gas station on Highway 80. "Tell the family I'll send them a postcard once I know where I'm at," he said when he got out. Raymond lifted one hand from the steering wheel and then pulled back onto the road, and Junior went into the station to look for somebody heading north.

He had a paper sack with two sets of clothes inside and a razor and a comb, and twenty-eight dollars in his pocket.

But he should have realized Trouble wouldn't want to hire him. Trouble liked to work alone. (And probably lacked the money for a helper, anyhow.) After Junior had spent two days tracking his shop down, the man didn't offer him so much as a drink of water, although he was civil enough. "Work? You mean lumberyard work?" he asked, all the while keeping his eyes on the drawer-front he was beveling.

Junior said, "I had in mind something that takes some skill. I'm good at making things. I'd like to make something that I could be proud of afterwards."

Trouble did pause in his beveling, then. He looked up at Junior and said, "Well, there's a house builder in these parts who seems to me real particular. Clyde Ward, his name is; I sometimes make cabinets for him. I might could tell you where you would find him." He also suggested Mrs. Davies's boardinghouse as a dwelling place, which Junior was glad to hear about because he'd been staying at a sailors' hotel down near the harbor where they expected him to sing hymns every evening.

After that, he never saw Trouble again. But he rented a room at Mrs. Davies's, in her three-story house in Hampden that must once have belonged to a mill owner or at least a manager, and he went to work for Clyde Ward, the most exacting builder he had ever come across. It was from Mr. Ward that he learned the great pleasure of doing things right.

He did send his family a postcard, eventually, but they never wrote him back and he didn't send another. That was okay; he didn't even think about them. He didn't think about Linnie Mae, either. She was a tiny, dim person buried in the back of his mind alongside that other person, his past self—that completely unrelated self who went out carousing every weekend and spent his money on cigarettes and fast girls and bootleg whiskey. The new Junior had a plan. He was going to be his own boss someday. His life was a straight, shining road now with a clear destination, and he supposed he ought to thank Linnie for setting his feet upon it.

12

Linnie's first act in Baltimore was to get them both evicted.

During the night, Junior had awakened twice—the first time with his heart racing because he sensed the presence of somebody else in the room, but then he found himself in the armchair and thought, "Oh, it's only Linnie," which came as a relief, under the circumstances; and the second time when he was jolted upright from what he believed was a dreamless sleep by the sudden realization that when Linnie had said she was of legal age now, she had probably meant legal marrying age. "She's like a . . . like one of those monkeys," he thought, "twining her arms tight around the organ grinder's neck." That time, he hadn't been able to go back to sleep for hours.

Even so, he rose early, both out of natural inclination and because there was always a rush for the bathroom in the mornings. He dressed and went to shave, and then he came back to the room and tapped the sharp peak of Linnie's shoulder. "Get up," he said.

She rolled over and looked at him. He had the impression that she had been awake for some time; her eyes were wide and clear. "You can't stay here while I'm at work," he told her. "You have to go out. There's a girl comes upstairs to clean in the mornings."

"Oh," she said. "Okay." And she sat up and drew back the covers and swung her feet to the floor. She was wearing a nightgown that would have worked better in the summer, a thin white cotton petticoat-thing that barely covered her knees. It was the first time he had seen her out of her winter wraps, and he realized she had changed more than he had first thought. She might still be too thin, but she had lost her coltish gawkiness. Her calves and her upper arms had more of a curve to them.

When she stood up he turned away from her so as not to see her dressing, and he went over to the bureau. A tin oatmeal canister sat on top; he opened it and took out the loaf of store bread that he kept shut away from the mice. Then he raised the window sash and reached for the milk. "Breakfast," he told Linnie.

"That's your breakfast? Doesn't your landlady give you breakfast?"

"Not me. Some of the others, they can afford to get their three squares here but I can't."

He shut the window and uncapped the milk bottle and took a swig. (It was something of a pleasure to show off how handily he dealt with adversity.) Then he held the bottle toward Linnie, still carefully not looking at her, and he felt her lift it out of his grasp. "But what about in hot weather?" she asked. "How'll we keep the milk from souring when it's hot?"

We? He felt that organ-grinder panic again, but he answered levelly. "In hot weather I switch to buttermilk," he said. "Can't much go wrong with that."

The milk bottle jogged his elbow and he took it and passed her a slice of bread in exchange, keeping his face set stubbornly toward the window where the smoke stood up from the chimneys outside as if it were too cold to drift. Tonight he should bring the milk in; he didn't want it freezing solid.

Linnie Mae was unclasping her suitcase now, by the sound of it. Junior folded his own slice of bread into quarters to get it over with quicker, and he took a large bite and chewed doggedly, listening to the rustles behind him. Then he heard the click of the door lock and he wheeled around. She was grasping the doorknob to turn it; he lunged past her and threw himself in front of her. It startled her, he could tell. She drew back as if she thought he might hit her, which he wouldn't have, but still, it was just as well she knew he meant business.

"Where do you think you're going?" he asked her.

"I need to use the bathroom."

"You can't. Someone'll see you."

"But I need to pee, Junior. *Bad.*"

"The café down the street has a bathroom," he said. "Get your coat on; we're leaving. I'll show you where the café is." She was wearing what looked like a summer dress, belted and short-sleeved. Didn't they have winter back home anymore, or what? And on her feet were those same high-heeled shoes. "Put on warmer shoes, too," he said.

"I didn't bring any warmer shoes."

How on earth did her *mind* work? "Come on the way you are, then," he said. "It's too risky to use the bathroom here; it's six men deep in the mornings."

She took her coat from the closet and put it on so painstakingly that it seemed she was bound and determined to irk him, and then she lifted her purse down from the closet shelf. Meanwhile, Junior set the milk back outside, and then he hunched himself into his jacket and went over to the bed. The suitcase lay there wide open, brazen as you please, and he closed it and bent to slide it underneath the bed, way back toward the wall. After one last look around the room, he said, "Okay. Let's go."

He peeked out the door first, making sure the hall was empty. He motioned her out ahead of him and locked the door behind them, and they walked the length of the hall and down the two flights of stairs without encountering anyone. They crossed the foyer, which was the most dangerous part, but the parlor door stayed shut. Junior heard the clink of china and he smelled coffee. He wasn't one for coffee himself but the smell always made him long for some—or just for people eating breakfast together, a slant of morning sunlight across the tablecloth.

Out on the sidewalk, the cold air at first seemed a blessing. (The third floor always collected the heat.) Junior came to a stop and pointed toward the intersection with Dutch Street, where the sign for the café was plainly visible. "But what if it's not open yet?" Linnie asked him. She was no longer bothering to keep her voice down, although they were standing right under Mrs. Davies's parlor window.

"It'll be open. This is a workingmen's neighborhood."

"And after that, what? Where will I go?"

"That's *your* business," he said.

"Can't I come with you to where you work? I could help out, maybe. I know how to hammer and saw some."

"That is a bad idea," he said.

"Or just wait in your car, then! I can't stay out in the cold all day."

She was standing too close to him, lifting her face to him. He could actually feel her warm foggy breath and smell the sleepy smell of it. Her hair had a frowsy, uncombed look and her nose was pink.

"You should have thought of that before you came," he said. "Go sit in the train station or something. Ride the streetcar up and down. I'll meet you out front of the café a little after five."

"Five!"

"Then we'll talk about your plans."

He could tell from the way her forehead cleared that she

thought he meant *their* plans. He didn't bother setting her straight.

The work he was doing that week was for an elderly couple in Homeland, flooring an unfinished attic and changing a louvered attic vent into a window. He had found it the way he found most work these days: driving out to one of the better-off neighborhoods and knocking on people's doors. In his glove box he kept the letter of reference Mr. Ward had written for him when Ward Builders had had to shut down, but people generally took Junior's word for it that he knew what he was doing. He made a point of wearing clean clothes and shaving daily and speaking respectfully and trying his best to watch his grammar. Then once he had a job lined up, he would drive off for whatever materials he needed; he had a credit arrangement with a builders' supply in Locust Point. He would return with the Essex loaded down like an ant beneath an oversized breadcrumb. Best decision he'd ever made was buying that Essex. Lots of workmen had to transport their materials on the streetcar— pay the extra fare for their lengths of pipe or lumber and enlist the conductor's help in roping them to the outside of the car—but not Junior.

This particular job wasn't very interesting, but it was a good deal more useful than the hand-carved mantels and built-in knickknack shelves of his days with Mr. Ward. The couple's grown daughter was moving back home with her four children and her husband, who had lost his job, and the attic was where the children would sleep. Besides, Junior knew that sooner or later, things were bound to get better. Folks in these parts would be wanting their mantels and their knickknack shelves once again, and then his would be the name that came to mind.

People in Homeland could often be clannish, but this couple acted friendlier and some days the wife called up from the bottom of the attic staircase to say that she was leaving a little something for his lunch. Today she left an egg sandwich cut on the diagonal, and he ate one half but he wrapped the other half in his handkerchief to take back to Linnie. Even though he was desperate to get shed of her, it wasn't all bad knowing that somebody somewhere was waiting for him.

Junior hadn't had much luck with girls in Baltimore, to tell the truth. Girls up north were just harder. Harder to figure out and harder-natured, both.

So he knocked off from work a tiny bit early, more like four thirty than five.

He found a parking spot just half a block past Mrs. Davies's—one advantage of getting home at this hour. As he was maneuvering into it he chanced to look back toward the boardinghouse, and what should he see but that floppy old-fashioned felt hat and Linnie Mae beneath it, wrapped in a huge denim jacket, sitting on Mrs. Davies's front steps as bold as brass. He didn't know which was more upsetting: that she'd show herself in public like that or that she'd managed to get hold of her hat, which she had not been wearing that morning, and the jacket that hung in the back of his closet waiting for warmer weather. How had she *done* that? Had she gone back to the room? Had she picked his lock, or what?

He slammed the car door getting out, and she looked his way and her face lit up. "It's you!" she called.

"What in hell, Linnie?"

She stood up, clutching the jacket tighter around her. She was wearing her coat underneath. "Now, Junie, don't get mad," she said as soon as he was closer.

"You were supposed to wait at the corner."

"I *tried* to wait at the corner, but there isn't any place to sit."

Junior took hold of her elbow, not gently, and steered her away from the steps to stand in front of the house next door. "How come you're wearing my jacket?" he asked her.

"Well," she said, "it's like this. First I went into the café to use the bathroom, but they said I couldn't on account of I hadn't bought anything. So I told them I'd be buying a hot chocolate after, and then I sat with that chocolate and *sat* with it; I'd take a little sip only every thirty minutes or so. But they were real inhospitable, Junior. After a time, they said they needed my stool. So I left, and I walked a long ways, and this one place I found a slat bench and I sat a while, and this old lady and me got to talking and she told me there was a breadline three streets over; I should come with her because she was going; you had to get in line early or they would run out of food. It was not but ten or ten thirty but she said we should go right then to hold our places. I said,

'Breadline!' I said, 'Charity?' But I went with her because I figured, well, anyhow it would be someplace warm to sit. So we stood in that line it seems like forever; all these people stood with us, and some of them were children, Junior, and I lost all feeling in my feet; they were like two blocks of ice. And then when time came for the place to open, you know what? They wouldn't let us inside. They just came out on the stoop and handed each of us a sandwich wrapped in wax paper, two slices of bread with a hunk of cheese in between. I asked the old lady with me, I said, 'Don't they let us sit down anywhere?' 'Sit down!' she said. 'We're lucky enough to have something to put in our stomachs. Beggars can't be choosers,' she said. And I thought, 'Well, she's right. We're beggars.' I thought, 'I have just stood in a breadline to beg my lunch from strangers,' and I started crying. I left the old lady and walked I-don't-know-where-all eating my sandwich and crying, and I didn't have a notion where I was anymore or where the café was that I was going to meet up with you in front of, and that sandwich was dry as sawdust, let me tell you, and I wanted a drink of water and my feet felt like knives. And then I looked up and what did I see? Mrs. Davies's boardinghouse. It looked like home, after all I'd been through. And I thought, 'Well, he told me the girl came to clean in the mornings. And it's not morning anymore, so—'"

Junior groaned.

"—so I walked right in, and it was so warm and toasty in the foyer! I walked up the stairs with no one to see me and I went to your room and tried to open the door but it was locked."

"You knew that," Junior said. "You saw me lock it."

"Did I? Well, I don't know; I must have been distracted. You hurried me out of there so fast . . . 'Well,' I thought, 'okay, I'll just sit in the hall and wait. At least it's warm,' I thought, and I sat right down on the floor in front of your bedroom door."

He groaned again.

"And next thing I knew, it was 'Awk!' I think I must have fallen asleep. 'Awk!' I heard, and there was this colored girl standing over me, eyes as big as moons. 'Miz Davies! Come quick! A burg-ular!' she screeches. When she could clearly see I was dressed nicely. And Mrs. Davies heard and came running, came clattering up the stairs out of breath and 'Explain yourself!' she says. I was thinking since she was a woman, maybe she'd have a kind heart. I threw myself on her mercy. 'Mrs. Davies,' I said, 'I'll be straight with you: I'm up from down home to see Junior because the two of us are in love. And it's so cold outside, you wouldn't believe, so blessed cold and all I've had all day is a little hot chocolate and a breadline sandwich and one sip of milk from Junior's windowsill and a slice of his store-bought bread—' "

"Lord God, Linnie," Junior said in disgust.

"Well, what *could* I say? I figured since she was a woman . . . wouldn't you think? I thought she might say, 'Oh, you poor little thing. You must be chilled to the bone.'

But she was ugly to me, Junior. I should have guessed it, from that dyed hair. She said, 'Out!' She said, 'You and him both, out! Here I was thinking Junior Whitshank was a decent hardworking man!' she says. 'Why, I could have got way higher rent from someone who'd take his meals here, but I let him stay on out of Christian spirit and this is the thanks I get? Out,' she says. 'I'm not running a brothel,' and she flips up this ring of keys hanging on her belt and unlocks your door and says, 'Pack all your things, yours and his both, and get out.'"

Junior gripped his forehead with one hand.

"Then she stood right there like I was some sort of criminal, Junior, watching every move while I packed. Colored girl standing next to her with eyes still big as moons. What did they think I would steal? What would I *want* to steal? I couldn't find any suitcase for you and so I asked real polite, I said, 'Mrs. Davies,' I said, 'do you think I might borrow a cardboard box if I promised to bring it back later?' But she said, 'Ha! As if I'd trust you!' Like a little old cardboard box was something precious. I had to pack your things in a tied-up pair of your overalls, for lack of anything better."

"You packed all I owned?" Junior asked.

"All in this big lumpy tied-up hobo bundle. And then I had to—"

"You packed my Prince Albert tin?"

"I packed every little thing, I tell you."

"But did you pack my Prince Albert tin, Linnie."

"*Yes*, I packed your Prince Albert tin. Why're you making such a fuss about it? I thought you smoked Camels."

"I don't smoke anything nowadays," he said bitterly. "It costs too much."

"Then why—?"

"Let me get this clear," he told her. "I don't have a place to live anymore, is that what you're saying?"

"No, and me neither. Can you believe it? Would you ever think that she could act so ugly? And then I had to carry all those things down the street—my suitcase and that great knobby bundle and your canister with the bread inside and—oh! Junior! Your milk bottle! I forgot your milk bottle! I'm so sorry!"

"*That's* what you're sorry about?"

"I'll buy us another. Milk was ten cents at this store I went past. I've got ten cents, easy."

"You are telling me I'm sleeping on the street tonight," Junior said.

"No, wait; I'm getting to that. There I was, toting all our worldly goods, walking down the street and crying, and I was looking for a ROOM TO LET sign but I didn't see nary a one so finally I just knocked on some lady's door and said, 'Please, my husband and I have lost our home and we've got no place to stay.'"

"Well, *that* would never work," Junior said. (He didn't bother dealing just now with the "husband" part.) "Half the country could say *that*."

"You're right," Linnie said cheerfully. "It didn't work a bit, not with her nor with the next lady either nor the lady after that, though all of them were real nice about it. 'Sorry, honey,' they said, and one lady offered me a square of gingerbread but I was still full from the charity sandwich. By then I was way down Dutch Street. I'd turned left at the café and of course I didn't bother asking *there*, not after how they'd treated me. But the next lady said that she would take us in."

"What?"

"And it's a nicer room, too. It's got a bigger bed, so you won't have to sleep on a chair. No bureau, but there's a nightstand with drawers, and a closet. The lady let me have it because her husband's been laid off work and she's been thinking for a while now, she said, that maybe their little boy should move in with his sister so they could rent his room out for five dollars a week."

"Five dollars!" Junior said. "Why so steep?"

"Is that steep?"

"At Mrs. Davies's I pay four."

"You do?"

"Is this with meals?" Junior asked.

"Well, no."

Junior looked longingly toward Mrs. Davies's house. For one half-second, he contemplated climbing her steps and ringing the doorbell. Maybe he could reason with her. She'd always seemed to like him. She had asked him to call her Bess, even, but that would have felt impertinent; she had to be in her forties. And just this past Christmas Eve she had invited him down to her parlor for a glass of something special (as she called it) that she had bought at the paint store, but that had been sort of uncomfortable because even though Junior missed having people to talk to, somehow with Mrs. Davies he hadn't been able to think of a single thing to say.

Maybe he could make like he had come to return his key, and then he would happen to mention that he barely knew Linnie Mae (which was true, in fact), that she was nothing to him, merely a girl from home in need of a place to stay, and he had taken pity on her.

But right while he had his eyes on the house, a little gap in the parlor curtain closed with an angry snap, and he knew there was no use trying.

He set off toward the Essex, and Linnie walked beside him with a bounce to each step, almost as if she were skipping. "You're going to like Cora Lee," she said. "She comes from West Virginia."

"Oh, she's 'Cora Lee' already, is she."

"She thinks we're just real cute and adventurous to be up here on our own so far away from our families."

"Linnie Mae," he said, stopping short on the sidewalk, "how come you claimed I was your husband?"

"Well, what else could I tell people? How would anyone give us a room if they didn't think we were married? Besides: I *feel* married. It didn't even feel like I was telling a story."

" 'Lie' is what they call it up here," he told her. "They don't pussyfoot around calling it a 'story.' "

"Well, I can't help *that*. Down home it's rude to say 'lie,' as you very well know your own self." She gave him a little poke in the ribs, and they started walking again. "Anyhow," she said, "neither one applies, not 'lie' nor 'story' neither. I honestly feel like you and I have been husband and wife forever, from a time before we were born, even."

Junior couldn't think where to begin to argue with that.

They had reached his car now and he walked around to the driver's side and got in and started the engine, leaving Linnie Mae to open the passenger door herself. If it weren't that she was the only one who knew where all his earthly belongings were, he would gladly have left her behind.

The new room was not nicer than the old one. It was even smaller, in a millworker's squat clapboard house about five blocks south of Mrs. Davies's. The bed was a single with a sunken-in mattress, admittedly wider than the cot at Mrs. Davies's but not by much, and there was a water stain on the ceiling near the window. But Cora Lee seemed pleasant enough—a plump, brown-haired woman in her early thirties—and almost her first words as she was showing him the room were, "Now, I want you to tell us if anything's not right, because we've never taken in roomers before and we don't know just how it's done."

"Well," Junior said, "in the old place, I was paying four dollars. We were paying four dollars."

But from the way Cora Lee's face suddenly lurched

and froze, he could tell she had set her heart on five. A cannier man might have argued even so, but Junior didn't have it in him and he changed the subject to the bathroom arrangements. Cora Lee looked happy again. Now that her husband wasn't working, she said, Junior was welcome to take first turn at the bathroom in the mornings. Linnie, meanwhile, was bustling around needlessly straightening the bedspread. Plainly she found money talk embarrassing.

Once Cora Lee had left them on their own, Linnie came to stand in front of him and wrap her arms around him as if they were honeymooners or something, but he freed himself and went to check the closet. "Where's my Prince Albert tin?" he asked.

"It's in with your shaving things."

He reached down a wrinkled paper bag from the closet shelf. Sure enough, there was the tin, and his roll of bills was still folded inside it. He put it back. "We need to buy something for supper," he said.

"Oh, I'm taking us out for supper."

"Out where?"

"Did you see that place on the corner? Sam and David's Eatery. Cora Lee says it's clean. Tonight's special is the meatloaf plate, twenty cents apiece."

"Forty cents total, that means," he said. "One of those tall cans of salmon from the grocery store is not but twenty-three cents, and it lasts me half a week."

Although it wouldn't last *both* of them half a week, he

realized, and he felt something close to fear at the thought of having to feed two instead of one.

"But I want us to celebrate," Linnie said. "It's our first real night together; last night didn't count. And I want me to be the one that pays."

He said, "How much money have you got, anyhow?"

"Seven dollars and fifty-eight cents!" Linnie said, as if it were something to brag about.

He sighed. "You're better off saving it up," he told her.

"Just this once, Junie? Just on our first night?"

"Could you *please* not call me Junie?" he said.

But he was already putting his jacket back on.

Out on the street Linnie was jubilant, hanging on to his arm and chattering away as they walked. She said Cora Lee had offered them half a shelf in the icebox. "The refrigerator," she corrected herself. "They have a Kelvinator. We could keep our milk there and some cheese, and then when I know her better I'll ask to use her stove one time. I'll clean up after myself real good so she lets me use it again, and next thing you know it will be like the kitchen's our own. I know just how to work it."

Junior could well believe it.

"Also I'm getting a job," she said. "I'm finding me one tomorrow."

"Now, how are you going to do that?" Junior asked. "It's not like a thousand grown men aren't pounding these same streets hunting any work they can hustle up."

"Oh, I'll find something. Just wait."

He drew away and walked separate from her. He felt he was caught in strands of taffy: pull her off the fingers of one hand and then she was sticking to the other. But he had to play his cards right, because he needed that room she had got them. Assuming he couldn't somehow persuade Mrs. Davies to take him back.

Sam and David's was tiny, with its specials listed in whitewash on the steamy front window. The twenty-cent meatloaf plate included bread and string beans. Junior let Linnie tug him inside. There were four small tables and a counter with six stools; Linnie chose a table although Junior would have felt easier at the counter. The customers at the counter were lone men in work clothes, while those at the tables were couples.

"You don't have to have the meatloaf," Linnie told him. "You can get something pricier."

"Meatloaf will be fine."

A woman in an apron came out and filled their water glasses, and Linnie beamed up at her and said, "Well, hey there! I am Linnie Mae, and this here is Junior. We've just moved into the neighborhood."

"Is that so," the woman said. "Well, I am Bertha. Sam's wife. I bet you're staying at the Murphys', aren't you."

"Now, how did you know that?"

"Cora Lee stopped by and told me. She was just real tickled she'd found such a nice young couple. I said, 'Honey, they're the ones should be tickled.' There's no finer people around than Cora Lee and Joe Murphy."

"I could tell that," Linnie said. "I could tell straight off. I took one look at that sweet smiling face of hers and I could tell. She's just like the people back home."

"We're all like the people back home," Bertha said. "We all *are* the people back home. That's what Hampden's made up of."

"Well, aren't we lucky, then!"

Junior studied the price list on the wall behind the counter until they were finished talking.

Over the meatloaf, which turned out to taste better than anything he'd eaten in a good long while, Linnie told him she had a plan to lower their room rent. "You will keep your eyes open for some little thing that needs fixing," she said. "Some loose board or saggy hinge or something. You'll ask Cora Lee if it would be all right if you saw to it. Don't mention money or nothing."

"Anything," he said.

She clamped her mouth shut.

"You've got to stop talking so country if you want to fit in here," he told her.

"Well, and then a few days later you will fix something else. This time don't ask; just fix it. She'll hear the hammering and come running. 'I hope you don't mind,' you tell her. 'I just noticed it and I couldn't resist.' Of course she'll say she doesn't mind a bit; you can see from that leak in our ceiling that her *husband's* not going to do it. Then you'll say, 'You know,' you'll say, 'I've been thinking. Seems to me you want someone around to keep this house repaired, and it's occurred to me that we might could work something out.'"

"Linnie, I think they need the cash," he told her.

"Cash?"

"They'd rather let the house fall apart and go on *eating*, is what I'm saying."

"Well, how could that be? They still need a roof over their heads! They still need a roof that doesn't leak."

"Tell me: are people not having hard times in Yancey County?" Junior asked.

"Well, sure they're having hard times! Half the stores are closed and everyone's out of work."

"Then why don't you understand about the Murphys? They're probably one payment away from losing their house to the bank."

"Oh," Linnie Mae said.

"Nothing's the same anymore," he said. "No one's in any position to cut us a deal. And no one can give you a job. You'll use up your seven dollars and that will be the end of it, and I can't afford to support you even if I wanted to. Do you know what's in my Prince Albert tin? Forty-three dollars. That's my entire life savings. It used to be a hundred and twenty before things changed. I've gone without for years, even in better times—given up smoking, given up drinking, eaten worse than my daddy's dogs used to eat, and if my stomach felt too hollow I'd walk to the grocery store and buy a pickle from out of the barrel for a penny; a sour dill pickle can really kill a man's appetite. I was Mrs.

Davies's longest-lasting roomer, and it's not because I liked fighting five other men for the bathroom; it's because I had ambitions. I wanted to start my own business. I wanted to build fine houses for people who knew to appreciate them—real slates on the roofs, real tiles on the floors, no more tarpaper and linoleum. I'd have good men under me, say Dodd McDowell and Gary Sherman from Ward Builders, and I'd drive my own truck with my company's name on the sides. But for that, I'd need customers, and there aren't any nowadays. Now I see it's never going to happen."

"Well, of course it will happen!" Linnie said. "Junior Whitshank! You think I don't know, but I do: you went all the way through Mountain City High and never made less than an A. And you've been carpentering with your daddy since you were just a little thing, and everyone at the lumberyard knew you could answer any question that anybody there asked you. Oh, you're *bound* to make it happen!"

"No," he said, "that's not the way it works anymore." And then he said, "You need to go home, Linnie."

Her lips flew apart. She said, "Home?"

"Have you even finished high school? You haven't, have you."

She raised her chin, which was answer enough.

"And your people will be wondering where you are."

"It's all the same to *me* if they're wondering," she said. "Anyhow, they don't care. You know that me and Mama have never gotten along."

"Still," he said.

"And Daddy has not spoken to me in the last four years and ten months."

Junior set his fork down. "What: not a word?" he asked.

"Not a single word. If he needs me to pass the salt, he tells Mama, 'Get her to pass me the salt.'"

"Well, that is just spiteful," Junior said.

"Oh, Junior, what did you imagine? I'd get caught with a boy in the hay barn and next day they'd all forget? For a while I thought you might come for me. I used to picture how it would happen. You'd pull up in your brother-in-law's truck as I was walking down Pee Creek Road and 'Get in,' you'd tell me. 'I'm taking you away from here.' Then I thought maybe you'd send me a letter, with my ticket money inside. I'd have packed up and left in a minute, if you'd done that! It wasn't only my daddy who didn't speak to me; not much of anyone did. Even my two brothers acted different around me, and the girls who were nicey-nice at school were just trying to get close, it turned out, so that I'd tell them all the details. I thought when I went on to high school they wouldn't know about it and I could make a fresh start, but of course they knew, because the kids from grade school who came along with me told them. 'There's Linnie Mae Inman,' they'd say; 'her and her boyfriend paraded stark nekkid through her brother's graduation party.' Because that's what it had grown into, by then."

"You act like it was my fault," he told her. "You're the one who started it."

"I won't say I didn't. I was *bad*. But I was in love. I'm still in love! And I know that you are, too."

He said, "Linnie—"

"Please, Junior," she said. She was smiling, he didn't know why, but there were tears in her eyes. "Give me a chance. Can't you please do that? Don't let's talk about it just now; let's enjoy our supper. Isn't our supper good? Isn't the meatloaf delicious?"

He looked down at his plate. "Yes," he said, "it is."

But he didn't pick his fork up again.

On the walk home, she began asking him about his day-to-day life: how he spent his evenings, what he did on weekends, whether he had any friends. Even though he'd drunk nothing but water with his meal, he started to get that elated feeling that alcohol used to give him. It must have come from spilling all the words that he had kept stored up for so long. Because the fact was that he *didn't* have any friends, not since Ward Builders shut down and he'd lost touch with the other workmen. (To be social, a person needed money—or men did, at any rate. They needed to buy liquor and hamburgers and gas; they couldn't just sit around idle, chitchatting the way women did.) He told Linnie he did nothing with his evenings, he'd often as not spend them washing his clothes in the bathtub; and when she laughed, he said, "No, I mean it. And weekends I sleep a lot." He was past shame; he told her straight out, not trying to look popular or successful or worldly-wise. They climbed the steps of the Murphys' house and let themselves in the front door, passing the closed-off parlor where they could hear a radio playing—some kind of dance-band music— and the sound of two children good-naturedly squabbling about something. "You peeked; I saw!" "No I didn't!" Even though it wasn't Junior's parlor and he had never met those children, he got a homey feeling.

They climbed the stairs and went to their room (no lock on *this* door), and right away Junior started worrying about what next. On his own, he would have gone to bed, since he always got such an early start in the mornings, but that might give Linnie the wrong idea. She might have the wrong idea even now; he sensed it from the demure way she took her coat off, and the care she took hanging it up. She removed her hat and placed it on the closet shelf. Her hair was in disarray and she patted it tentatively with just the tips of her fingers, keeping her back to him, as if she were getting ready for him. Something about the pale, meek nape of her neck, exposed by the accidental parting of her hair at the rear of her head, made him feel sorry for her. He cleared his throat and said, "Linnie Mae."

She turned and said, "What?" And then she said, "Take your jacket off, why don't you? Make yourself comfortable."

"See, I'm trying to be honest," he said. "I'd like to get everything clear between us."

The beginnings of a crease developed between her eyebrows.

"I feel bad about what you've been through back home," he said. "I guess it wasn't much fun. But when you think about it, Linnie, what have we really got to do with each other? We hardly know each other! We went out together less than a month! And I'm trying to make it on my own up here. It's hard enough for one; it's impossible for two. Back home, at least you've got family. They'd never let you starve, no matter how they feel about you. I think you ought to go home."

"You're just saying that because you're mad at me," she told him.

"What? No, I'm not—"

"You're mad I didn't tell you how old I was, but why didn't you *ask* how old I was? Why didn't you ask if I was in school, or whether I worked someplace, or how I spent all the time that I wasn't with you? Why weren't you *interested* in me?"

"What? I was interested, honest!"

"Oh, we both know what you were interested in!"

"Hold on," he said. "Is that fair? Who was the first to start taking her clothes off, might I remind you? And who dragged me into that barn? Who made me put my hand on her? Were *you* interested in how I spent *my* time?"

"Yes, I was," she said. "And I asked you. Only you never bothered answering, because you were too busy trying to get me on my back. I said, 'Tell me about your life, Junior; come on, I want to know everything about you.' But did you tell me? No. You'd just start unbuttoning my buttons."

Junior felt he was losing an argument that he didn't even care about. He had wanted to make an entirely different point. He said, "Shoot, Linnie Mae," and jammed his fists hard in his jacket pockets, except something in his left pocket stopped him and he pulled it out and looked at it. Half a sandwich, wrapped in a handkerchief.

"What's that?" she asked him.

"It's a . . . sandwich."

"What kind of sandwich?"

"Egg? Egg."

"Where'd you get an egg sandwich?"

"Lady I worked for today," he said. "Half I ate and half I brought home to give to you, but then you were all set on us going out for supper."

"Oh, Junior," she said. "That's so sweet!"

"No, I was just—"

"That was so nice of you!" she said, and she took the sandwich out of his hand, handkerchief and all. Her face was pink; she suddenly looked pretty. "I love it that you brought me a sandwich," she said. She unwrapped it, reverently, and studied it a moment and then looked up at him with her eyes brimming.

"It's squashed, though," he said.

"I don't care if it's squashed! I love it that you thought about me while you were away at work. Oh, Junior, I've been so lonely all these years! You don't know how lonely I've been. I've been so all, all alone all this time!"

And she flung herself on him, still holding that sandwich, and started sobbing.

After a moment, Junior lifted his arms and hugged her back.

She didn't find a job, of course. That part of her plan didn't work out. But her kitchen-sharing plan did. She and Cora Lee got to be friends, and they cooked together in the kitchen while they talked about whatever women talk about, and before long it just made more sense for Junior and Linnie to eat their meals with Cora Lee and her family. Then when the weather turned warm the two women hatched a plot to buy fruits and vegetables from the farmers who rolled into Hampden on their wagons, and they'd spend all day canning, blasting the kitchen with heat; and later Linnie would be the brave one who went around hawking their products to the neighbors. They didn't make much money, but they made some.

And Junior actually did fix up a few things around the house, just because otherwise they would never have gotten done, but he didn't charge anything or try to get a deal on the rent.

Even after times improved and Junior and Linnie moved into the house on Cotton Street, Linnie and Cora Lee stayed friends. Well, Linnie was friends with everybody, it seemed to Junior. Sometimes he wondered if those years of being an outcast had left her with an unnatural need to socialize.

He'd come in after work and find wall-to-wall women in the kitchen, and all their mingled young ones playing in the backyard. "Don't I get supper?" he would ask, and the women would scatter, rounding up their children on the way out. But he wouldn't say Linnie was lazy. Oh, no. She and Cora still had their little canning business, and she answered the phone for Junior and saw to the billing and such as he began to have more customers. She was better with the customers than he was, in fact, always willing to take time for a little small talk, and adept at smoothing over any problems or complaints.

By then he had his truck—used, but it was a good one—and he had a few men working for him, and he owned a fine collection of tools that he'd bought from other men here and there who were down on their luck. These were really solid tools, the old-fashioned, beautifully made kind. A saw, for instance, with an oiled wooden handle that was carved with the most delicate and precise etching of a rosemary branch. It was true that the sweat that darkened the handle had not been his forebears' sweat, but still he felt some personal pride in it. He always took excellent care of his tools. And he always went to lumberyards where he could choose his own lumber board by board. "Now, fellows, I know anything you might take it into your heads to put over on me. Don't give me anything with dead knots, don't give me anything warped or moldy . . ."

"What if I had been married?" he thought to ask Linnie

years later. "What if you'd come up north and found me with a wife and six children?"

"Oh, Junior," she said. "You would never do that."

"What makes you so sure?"

"Well, for one thing, how would you get six children inside of just five years?"

"No, but, you know what I mean."

She just smiled.

She acted older than he was, in some ways, and yet in other ways she seemed permanently thirteen—feisty and defiant, and stubbornly opinionated. He was taken aback to see how easily she had severed all connection with her family. It implied a level of bitterness that he had not suspected her capable of. She showed no desire to shed her backwoods style of speech; she still said "holler" for "shout," and "tuckered" for "tired," and "treckly" for "directly." She still insisted on calling him "Junie." She had an irritating habit of ostentatiously chuckling to herself before she told him something funny, as if she were coaching *him* to chuckle. She pressed too close to him when she wanted to persuade him of something. She plucked at his sleeve with picky fingers while he was talking to other people.

Oh, the terrible, crushing, breath-stealing burden of people who think they own you!

And if Junior was the wild one, how come it was Linnie Mae who'd caused every single bit of trouble he'd found himself in since they'd met?

He was a sharp-boned, narrow-ribbed man, a man

without an ounce of fat who had never had much interest in food, but sometimes when he came home from work in the late afternoon and Linnie was out back gabbing with her next-door neighbor he would stand in front of the refrigerator and eat all the leftover pork chops and then the wieners, the cold mashed potatoes, the cold peas and the boiled beets, foods he didn't even like, as if he were starving, as if he had never gotten what he really wanted, and later Linnie would say, "Have you seen those peas I was saving? Where are those peas?" and he would stay stone silent. She had to know. What did she think: little Merrick craved cold peas? But she never said so. This made him feel both grateful and resentful. Lord it over him, would she! She must really think she had his number!

At such moments he would run his mind back through that long-ago trip to the train station, this time doing it differently. Down the dark streets, turn right past the station, turn right again onto Charles Street and drive back to the boardinghouse. Let himself into his room and lock the door behind him. Drop onto his cot. Fall asleep alone.

13

Junior had Eugene take the porch swing down to Tilghman Brothers, an establishment near the waterfront where Whitshank Construction sent customers' shutters when they were so thick with paint that they resembled half-sucked toffees. Evidently the Tilghman brothers owned a giant vat of some caustic solution that stripped everything to the bare wood. "Tell them we need the swing back in exactly a week," Junior told Eugene.

"A week from today?"

"That's what I said."

"Boss, those fellows can take a month with such things. They don't like to be hurried."

"Tell them it's an emergency. Say we'll pay extra, if we have to. Moving day is two Sundays from now, and I want the swing hanging by then."

"Well, I'll try, boss," Eugene said.

Junior could see that Eugene was thinking this was an

awful lot of fuss for a mere porch swing, but he had the good sense not to say so. Eugene was an experiment—Junior's first colored employee, hired when the draft had claimed one of the company's painters. He was working out okay, so far. In fact, last week Junior had hired another.

Linnie Mae had been worrying lately that Junior would be drafted himself. When he pointed out that he was forty-two years old, she said, "I don't care; they could raise the draft age any day now. Or you might decide to enlist."

"Enlist!" he said. "What kind of fool do you take me for?"

He had the feeling sometimes that his life was like a railroad car that had been shunted onto a side track for years—all the wasted, wild years of his youth and the years of the Depression. He was lagging behind; he was running to catch up; he was finally on the main track and he would be damned if some war in Europe was going to stop him.

When the swing came back it was virgin wood—a miracle. Not the tiniest speck of blue in the least little seam. Junior walked all around it, marveling. "Lord, I hate to think what-all they must have in that vat," he told Eugene.

Eugene chuckled. "You want I should varnish it?" he asked.

"No," Junior said, "I'll do that."

Eugene shot him a look of surprise, but he didn't comment.

The two of them carried it out back and set it upside down on a drop cloth, so that Junior could varnish the underside first and give it time to dry before he turned it over. It was a warm May day with no rain in the forecast, so Junior figured he could safely leave it out overnight and come back the next morning to do the rest.

Like most carpenters, he had an active dislike of painting, and also he was conscious that he wasn't very good at it. But for some reason it seemed important to accomplish this task on his own, and he worked carefully and patiently, even though this was the part of the swing that wouldn't show. It was a pleasant occupation, really. The sunlight was filtering through the trees, and a breeze was cooling his face, and "Chattanooga Choo Choo" was playing in his mind.

> *You leave the Pennsylvania Station 'bout a quarter to*
> *four,*
> *Read a magazine and then you're in Baltimore . . .*

When he was done, he cleaned his brush and put away the varnish and the mineral spirits, and he went home for supper feeling pleased with himself.

The next morning he came back to finish the job. The swing was dry, but a fine dusting of pollen was stuck to the underside of the seat. He should have foreseen that. No wonder he hated painting! Cursing beneath his breath, he dragged the drop cloth toward the back porch with the swing along for the ride. Then he spread another drop cloth inside the enclosed end of the porch and hauled the swing in and set it right side up. This was going to be done properly, by God. He tried to forget how the lower surfaces of the armrests had rasped against his fingertips when he grabbed hold of them.

Eugene had painted the back porch interior earlier in the week, and the smells of paint and varnish combined to make Junior feel slightly light-headed. He drew the brush along the wood with dreamy strokes. Wasn't it interesting how the grain of the wood told a story, almost—how you could follow the threads and be surprised at how far they traveled, or where they unexpectedly broke off.

He wondered if someday Merrick would be proposed to in this swing, if Redcliffe's children would swoop back and forth in it so raucously that their mother would seize the ropes to slow it down.

After Junior learned how a man could feel about his children, he had conceived a deep and permanent anger toward his father. His father had had six sons and a daughter, and he'd let them loose easier than a dog lets loose of her pups. The older Junior got, the harder he found it to understand that.

He made a quick, sharp, shaking-away motion with his head, and he dipped his brush again.

This varnish was the color of buckwheat honey. It drew out the character of the wood and added depth. No more of those eternal Swedish-blue swings of home! No more raggedy braided rugs and rusted metal gliders; no more baby-blue porch ceilings that were meant, he supposed, to suggest the sky; no more battleship-gray porch floors.

Linnie was going to start up the walk on moving day, and at the foot of the porch steps, "Oh!" she would say. She would be staring at the swing; one hand would fly to her mouth. "Oh, why—!" Or maybe not. Maybe she would conceal her surprise; she might be crafty enough. Either way, Junior himself would climb the steps without breaking stride. He wouldn't give a sign that anything was different. "Shall we go in?" he would ask her, and he would turn to her and gesture hospitably toward the front door.

There was a satisfaction to imagining this scene, and yet he felt something was lacking. She wouldn't fully realize all that lay behind it: his shock at what she had done and his outrage and his sense of injustice, and his hard work to repair the damage. Eugene's trip to Tilghman Brothers, the exorbitant fee they had charged for the expedited service (exactly double their regular fee), Junior's two separate trips to apply the varnish and the final trip he would make Friday morning to screw the eyebolts back in and reattach the ropes on their figure eights and hang the swing from the ceiling: she would have no idea of any of that. It echoed the pattern of their lives together—all the secrets he had kept from her despite his temptation to tell. She would never know how deeply he had longed to free himself all these years, how he had stayed with her only because he knew she would be lost otherwise, how onerous it had been to go on and on, day after day, setting right what he had done wrong. No, she had absolute faith that he had stayed because he loved her. And if he told her otherwise—if he somehow managed to convince her of his sacrifice—she would be crushed, and the sacrifice would have been for nothing.

He circled each spindle with his brush, smoothing varnish into each joint, tracing the crevices of the lathing with tender, caressing strokes.

> *Dinner in the diner,*
> *nothing could be finer*
> *Than to have your ham 'n' eggs in Carolina . . .*

On Friday when he went back to hang the swing he took along more boxes from home and a few small pieces of furniture—the play table from the children's room and the little chairs that went with it. Might as well haul as much as possible over ahead of time. He parked in the rear and carried everything in through the kitchen and up the stairs. While he was up there, he indulged himself in a survey of his new property. He stood at the hall railing to admire the gleaming entrance hall below, and he stepped into the main bedroom to gloat over its spaciousness. His and Linnie's beds were already in place—twin beds, like those the Brills had had, delivered last week by Shofer's. Linnie couldn't understand why they didn't keep on sharing their old double, but Junior said, "It just makes more sense, when you think about it. You know how I'm always tossing and turning in the middle of the night."

"I don't mind you tossing and turning," Linnie said.

"Well, we'll just try this out, why don't we. We're not throwing the double away, after all. If we change our minds we can always move it back in from the guest room."

Although privately, he had no intention of moving it back. He liked the *idea* of twin beds—their Hollywood-style glamour. Besides, he'd spent enough of his childhood sharing a bed with various brothers.

In the far corner of the bedroom stood the Brills' armoire, which he also considered glamorous. It made his cheeks burn, though, to remember that he had first understood it to be called a "more."

"Mrs. Brill," he had said, "I hear you're not taking your more to the new place. You think I could buy it off you?"

Mrs. Brill's eyebrows had knotted. "My—?" she said.

"Your more in the bedroom. Your boy said it was too big."

"Oh! Why, certainly. Jim? Junior was just wondering if he could buy our armoire."

It wasn't till then that Junior had realized his mistake. He was furious at Mrs. Brill for witnessing it, even though he had to admit that she had behaved very tactfully.

In a way, it was her tact he was furious at.

Oh, always, always it was us-and-them. Whether it was the town kids in high school or the rich people in Roland Park, always someone to point out that he wasn't quite measuring up, he didn't quite make the grade. And it was assumed to be his own fault, because he lived in a nation where theoretically, he *could* make the grade. There was nothing to hold him back. Except that there *was* something; he couldn't quite put his finger on it. There was always some little tiny trick of dress or of speech that kept him on the outside looking in.

Nonsense. Enough. He owned a giant cedar-lined closet now that was meant for storing nothing but woolens. The wallpaper in this bedroom came all the way from France. The windows were so tall that when he stood at one, a person down on the street could see from the top of Junior's head almost to his knees.

But then he noticed a patch of blistered paint at the corner of one sill. The Brills must have left that window open during a rainstorm. Or else it was the result of condensation; *that* would not be good.

Also, the wallpaper underneath it was showing its seam too distinctly. In fact, the seam was separating. In fact, where the paper met the sill it was actually curling up from the wall a tiny bit.

Saturday was the day he went around giving estimates; that was when the husbands were home. So he didn't stop by the new house. He wrapped up his appointments early, because tomorrow they were moving and there was still some packing to do. He got home about three o'clock and walked on through to the kitchen, where he found Linnie pulling cleaning supplies from the orange crate under the sink. She was kneeling on the floor, and the soles of her bare feet, which were facing him, were gray with dirt. "I'm home," he told her.

"Oh, good. Could you reach down that platter from up top of the icebox? I clean forgot about it! I like to walked off and left it."

He reached for the platter on the refrigerator and placed it on the counter. "I've half a mind to take another load to the house before it gets dark," he told her. "It would make things that much easier in the morning."

"Oh, don't do that. You'll wear yourself out. Wait for tomorrow when Dodd and them get here."

"I wouldn't take the heavy stuff. Just a few boxes and such."

She didn't answer. He wished she would get her head out of the orange crate and look at him, but she was all hustle-bustle, so after a minute he left her.

In the living room, the children were piling up empty cartons to build something. Or Merrick was. Redcliffe was still too little to have any plan in mind, but he was thrilled that Merrick was playing with him and he staggered around happily, dragging boxes wherever she told him to. The rug had been rolled up for the move and it gave them an expanse of bare floorboards. "Look at our castle, Daddy," Merrick said, and Junior said, "Very nice," and went on back to the bedroom to change out of his good clothes. He always wore his suit when he was giving estimates.

When he returned to the kitchen, Linnie was packing the cleaning supplies in a Duz carton. "Mrs. Abbott's husband said no to half the features she was wanting," Junior said. "He went straight down the list: 'Why's *this* cost so much? Why's this?' I wished I had known he would do that way before I went to all that trouble with my figures."

"That's a shame," Linnie Mae said. "Maybe she'll talk to him later and get him to change his mind."

"No, she was just going along with it. 'Oh,' she said, all sad and mournful, each time he crossed something off."

He waited for Linnie to comment, but she didn't. She was wrapping a bottle of ammonia in a dish towel. He wished she would look at him. He was starting to feel uneasy.

Linnie Mae wasn't the type to shout or sulk or throw things when she was mad about something; she would just stop looking at him. Well, she would look if she had some cause to, but she wouldn't *study* him. She would speak pleasantly enough, she would smile, she would act the same as ever, and yet always there seemed to be something else claiming her attention. At such times, he surprised himself by his urgent need of her gaze. All at once he would realize how often she did look at him, how her eyes would linger on him as if she just purely enjoyed the sight of him.

He couldn't think of any reason she would be mad at this moment, though. He was the one who should be mad— and *was* mad. Still, he hated this feeling of uncertainty. He walked over to stand squarely in front of her, with only the Duz carton between them, and he said, "Would you like to eat at the diner tonight?"

They seldom ate at the diner. It had to be a special

occasion. But Linnie didn't look at him, even so. She said, "I reckon we'll have to, because I took everything in the icebox over to the house today."

"You did?" he said. "How come?"

"Oh, Doris was keeping the children so I could get some packing done, and I just thought, 'Why don't I visit the new house on my own?' You know I've never done that. So I packed up two bags of food and I caught the streetcar over."

"We could have put the food on the truck tomorrow," Junior said. His mind was racing. Had she seen the revarnished swing? She must have. He said, "I don't know why you thought you had to lug all that by yourself."

"I just figured I was going anyhow, so I might as well carry something," she said. "And this way we can have breakfast there tomorrow, out of the way of the men."

She was focusing on the canister of Bon Ami that she was setting upright in one corner of the carton.

"Well," he said, "how'd the place look to you?"

"It looked okay," she said. She fitted a long-handled scrub brush into another corner. "The door sticks, though."

"Door?"

"The front door."

So she had definitely gone in through the front. Well, of course she had, walking from the streetcar stop.

He said, "That door doesn't stick!"

"You push down the thumb latch and it won't give. For a moment I figured I just hadn't unlocked it right, but when

I pulled the door toward me a little first and *then* pushed down, it gave."

"That's the weather stripping," Junior said. "It's got good thick weather stripping, is why it does like that. That door does not stick."

"Well, it seemed to me like it did."

"Well, it doesn't."

He waited. He almost asked her. He almost came straight out and said, "Did you notice the swing? Were you surprised to see it back the way it was? Don't you have to agree now that it looks better that way?"

But that would be laying himself open, letting her know he cared for her opinion. Or letting her *think* he cared.

She might tell him the swing looked silly; it was a trying-too-hard copy of a rich person's swing; he was pretending to be someone he was not.

So all he said was, "You'll be glad to have that weather stripping when winter comes, believe me."

Linnie fitted a box of soap flakes next to the Bon Ami. After a moment, he left the room.

Walking to the diner in the twilight, they passed people sitting out on their porches, and everyone—friend or stranger—said "Evening," or "Nice night." Linnie said, "I hope the neighbors will say hey to us in the new place."

"Why, of course they will," Junior said.

He had Redcliffe riding on his shoulders. Merrick

scooted ahead of them on her old wooden Kiddie Kar, propelling it with her feet. She was way too big for it now, but they couldn't buy her a tricycle on account of the rubber shortage.

"That Mrs. Brill," Linnie said. "Remember how she'd talk about 'my' grocer and 'my' druggist? Like they belonged to her! At Christmastime, when she'd drop off our basket: 'I got the mistletoe from my florist,' she'd say, and I'd think, 'Wouldn't the florist be surprised to hear he's yours!' I surely hope our new neighbors aren't going to talk like that."

"She didn't mean it like it sounded," Junior said. Then he took two long strides ahead of her and turned so that he was walking backwards, looking into her face. "She probably just meant that *our* florist might not carry mistletoe, but hers did."

Linnie laughed. "*Our* florist!" she echoed. "Can you imagine?"

But her eyes were on old Mr. Early, who was hosing down his steps, and she waved to him and called, "How you doing, Mr. Early?"

Junior gave up and faced forward again.

The longest she'd ever stopped looking at him was when she wanted to have a baby and he didn't. She'd wanted one for several years and he had kept putting her off—not enough money, not the right time—and she had accepted it, for a while. Then finally he had said, "Linnie Mae, the plain truth is I don't *ever* want children." She had been stunned. She had cried; she had argued; she had claimed he

431

only felt that way on account of what had happened with his mother. (His mother had died in childbirth, taking the baby with her. But that had nothing to do with it. Really! He had long ago put that behind him.) And then by and by, Linnie had just seemed to stop savoring the sight of him. He had to admit that he had felt the lack. He'd always known, even without her saying so, that she found him handsome. Not that he cared about such things! But still, he had been conscious of it, and now something was missing.

He had been the one to give in, that time. He had lasted about a week. Then he'd said, "Listen. If we *were* to have children . . ." and the sudden, alerted sweep of her eyes across his face had made him feel the way a parched plant must feel when it's finally given water.

Over supper he talked to Merrick and Redcliffe about how they would have their own rooms now. Redcliffe was busy squeezing the skins off his lima beans, but Merrick said, "I can't wait. I hate sharing my room! Redcliffe smells like pee every morning."

"Be nice, now," Linnie Mae told her. "You used to smell like pee, too."

"I never!"

"You did when you were a baby."

"Redcliffe is a baby!" Merrick teased Redcliffe in a singsong.

Redcliffe popped another lima bean.

"Who wants ice cream?" Junior asked.

Merrick said, "I do!" and Redcliffe said, "I do!"

"Linnie Mae?" Junior asked.

"That would be nice," Linnie Mae said.

But she was turned in Redcliffe's direction now, wiping lima-bean skins off his fingers.

It was their custom to listen to the radio together after the children had gone to bed—Linnie sewing or mending, Junior reviewing the next day's work plan. But the living room was a jumble now, and the radio was packed in a carton. Linnie said, "I guess maybe I'll head off to bed myself," and Junior said, "I'll be up in a minute."

He spent a while packing his business papers for the move, and then he turned out the lights and went upstairs. Linnie had her nightgown on but she was still puttering around the bedroom, putting the items on top of the bureau into drawers. She said, "Are you going to need the alarm clock?"

"Naw, I'm bound to wake on my own," he said.

He stripped to his underthings and hung his shirt and overalls on the hooks inside the closet door, although as a rule he would have just slung them onto the chair since he'd be wearing them tomorrow. "Our last night in this house, Linnie Mae," he said.

"Mm-hmm."

She folded the bureau scarf and laid it in the top drawer.

"Our last night in this bed, even."

She crossed to the closet and gathered a handful of empty hangers.

"But I can still *visit* you in your new bed," he said, and he gave her rear end a playful tap as she walked past him.

She made a subtle sort of tucking-in move that caused his tap to glance off of her, and she bent to fit the hangers into the bureau drawer.

"Junior," she said, "tell me the truth: where did that burglar's kit come from?"

"Burglar's kit? What burglar's kit?"

"The one in Mrs. Brill's sunroom. You know the one I mean."

"I don't have the slightest idea," he said.

He got into bed and pulled the covers up, turned his face to the wall and closed his eyes. He heard Linnie cross to the closet again and scrape another collection of hangers along the rod. Outside the open window a car passed—an older model, from the putt-putt sound of it—and somebody's dog started barking.

A few minutes later he heard her pad toward the bed, and he felt her settling onto her side of it. She lay down and then turned away from him; he felt the slight tug of the covers. The lamp on her nightstand clicked off.

He wondered how she had reacted when she first saw the revarnished swing. Had she blinked? Had she gasped? Had she exclaimed aloud?

He had a vision of her as she must have looked trudging up the walk with her two bags of food: Linnie Mae Inman in her country-looking straw hat with the wooden cherries on the brim, and her cotton dress with the cuffed short sleeves that exposed her scrawny arms and roughened elbows. It made him feel . . . hurt, for some reason. It hurt his feelings on her behalf. All alone, she would have been, threading up the hill beneath those giant poplars toward that wide front porch. All alone she must have figured out the streetcar, which was one she hadn't taken before—she only ever went down to the department stores on Howard Street—and she'd decided which way to turn at the corner where she got off, and she had no doubt tilted her chin pridefully as she walked past the other houses in case the neighbors happened to be watching.

He opened his eyes and shifted onto his back. "Linnie Mae," he said toward the ceiling. "Are you awake?"

"I'm awake."

He turned so his body was cupping hers and he wrapped his arms around her from behind. She didn't pull away, but she stayed rigid. He took a deep breath of her salty, smoky smell.

"I ask your pardon," he said.

She was silent.

"I'm just trying so hard, Linnie. I guess I'm trying *too* hard. I'm just trying to pass muster. I just want to do things the right way, is all."

"Why, Junior," she said, and she turned toward him. "Junie, honey, of course you do. I know that. I *know* you, Junior Whitshank." And she took his face between her hands.

In the dark he couldn't see if she was looking at him or

not, but he could feel her fingertips tracing his features before she put her lips to his.

Dodd McDowell and Hank Lothian and the new colored man were due to arrive at eight—Junior let his men start a little late when they worked on weekends—so at seven, he drove Linnie and the children to the house along with some boxes of kitchen things. The plan was that she would stay there unpacking while he went back to help load the furniture.

As they were pulling into the street, Doris Nivers from next door came out in her housecoat, carrying a potted plant. Linnie rolled down her window and called, "Morning, Doris!"

"I'm just trying not to bawl my eyes out," Doris told her. "The neighborhood won't feel the same! Now, this plant might not look to you like much, but it's going to flower in a few weeks and give you lots of beautiful zinnias."

"Zeenias," she pronounced it, in the Baltimore way. She passed the plant through the window to Linnie, who took it in both hands and sank her nose into it as if it were blooming already. "I won't say 'Thank you,'" she told Doris, "because I don't want to kill it off, but you know I'm going to think of you every time I look at it."

"You just *better* had! Bye, kiddos. Bye, Junior," Doris said, and she took a step backward and waved.

"So long, Doris," Junior said. The children, who were

still in a just-awakened stupor, merely stared, but Linnie waved and kept her head out the window till their truck had turned the corner and Doris was out of sight.

"Oh, I'm going to miss her so much!" Linnie told Junior, pulling her head in. She leaned past Redcliffe to set the plant on the floor between her feet. "I feel like I've lost my sister or something."

"You haven't *lost* her. You're moving two miles away! You can invite her over any time you like."

"No, I know how it will be," Linnie said. She blotted the skin beneath her right eye and then her left eye with an index finger. "Suppose I ask her to lunch," she said. "I ask her and Cora Lee and them. If I give them something fancy to eat they'll say I'm getting above myself, but if I give them what I usually do they'll say that I must not think they're as high-class as my new neighbors. And they won't invite me back; they'll say their houses wouldn't suit me anymore, and bit by bit they'll stop accepting *my* invitations and that will be the end of it."

"Linnie Mae. It is not a capital crime to move to a bigger place," Junior said.

Linnie Mae reached into her pocket to pull out a handkerchief.

When he drew to a stop in front of the house, she asked, "Shouldn't we park around back? What about all we've got to carry?"

"I thought we'd have a bite of breakfast first," he said.

Which made no sense, really—they could eat breakfast

just as well if he had parked in back—but he wanted to give their arrival the proper sense of occasion. And Linnie might have guessed that, because she just said, "Well. See there? Now you're glad I brought that food over."

While she was gathering herself together—hunting her purse on the floor and bending for her plant—he came around and opened the door for her. She looked surprised, but she passed Redcliffe to him, and then she stepped down from the truck. "Come on, kids," Junior said, setting Redcliffe on the ground. "Let's make our grand entrance." And the four of them started up the walk.

Under the shelter of the trees the front of the house didn't get the morning sun, but that just made the deep, shady porch seem homier. And the honey-gold of the swing, visible now through the balustrade, gladdened Junior's heart. He had to stop himself from saying to Linnie, "See? See how right it looks?"

When his eyes caught a flash of something blue, he blamed it on the power of suggestion—a crazy kind of aftereffect of all that had happened before.

Then he looked again, and he froze.

A trail of blue paint traveled down the flagstones—a scattered explosion of blue starting directly in front of the steps and then collecting itself to proceed in a wide band down the walk, narrowing to a trickle as it approached his shoes. It was so thick that it almost seemed he could peel it up with his fingers; it was so shiny that he instinctively drew back his nearest foot, although on closer inspection he saw that it had dried. And anyone—or was it only Junior?—could tell from the briefest glance that it had been flung in anger.

Linnie, meanwhile, had disengaged her hand from his and gone ahead, calling, "Slow down, Merrick! Slow down, Redcliffe! Your daddy needs to unlock the door!"

It would take his men days to remove this. It would take abrasives and chemicals—offhand, he wasn't even sure what kind—and scrubbing and scraping and grinding; and still, traces of blue would remain. Really the blue would never come off, not completely. There would be microscopic dots of blue in the mortar forever after, perhaps unnoticed by strangers but evident to Junior. He could see his future unreeling before him as clearly as a movie: how he would try one method, try another, consult the experts, lie awake nights, research different solutions like a man possessed, and no doubt end by having to dig the whole thing up and start over. Failing that, the walk would be marked indelibly, engraved with Swedish blue for all time.

And meanwhile Linnie Mae was heading up the walk with her spine very straight and her hat very level, all innocent and carefree. Not even a glance backward to find out how he was taking this.

Why had he worried for one second about abandoning her at the train station? She would have done just *fine* without him! She would do just fine anywhere.

She had set out to snag him and succeeded without half trying. She had weathered five years of public scorn entirely on her own. She'd ridden who knows how many trains on who knows how many branch lines and tracked him down without a hitch. He saw her craning her neck by the pickup lane; he saw her ringing strange ladies' doorbells with her suitcase and her hobo bundle; he saw her laughing in the kitchen with Cora Lee. He saw her yanking his whole life around the way she would yank a damp sweater that she had pulled out of the washtub to block and reshape.

He supposed he should be glad of that last part.

Redcliffe stumbled but righted himself. Merrick was running ahead. "Wait," Junior called, because they were nearing the steps now. They all stopped and turned toward him, and he walked faster to catch up. Birds were singing in the poplars above him. Small white butterflies were flitting in the one patch of sun. When he reached Linnie's side he took hold of her hand, and the four of them climbed the steps. They crossed the porch. He unlocked the door. They walked into the house. Their lives began.

PART FOUR

A Spool of Blue Thread

14

Years ago, when the children were small, Abby had started a tradition of hanging a row of ghosts down the length of the front porch every October. There were six of them. Their heads were made of white rubber balls tied up in gauzy white cheesecloth, which trailed nearly to the floor and wafted in the slightest breeze. The whole front of the house took on a misty, floating look. On Halloween the trick-or-treaters would have to bat their way through dia-phanous veils, the older ones laughing but the younger ones on the edge of panic, particularly if the night was windy and the cheesecloth was lifting and writhing and wrapping itself around them.

Stem's three little boys clamored to have the ghosts put up this year the same as always, but Nora said it couldn't be done. "Halloween isn't till Wednesday," she told them. "We'll be gone by then." They were vacating the house on Sunday—the earliest date that Red was allowed into his apartment. The plan was for all of them to be resettled by the start of the work week.

But Red overheard, and he said, "Oh, let them have their ghosts, why don't you? It'll be their last chance. Then our men can haul them down for us when they come in on Monday morning."

"Yes!" the little boys shouted, and Nora laughed and flung out her hands in defeat.

So the ghosts were brought forth from their paper-towel carton in the attic, and Stem climbed up on a ladder to hang them from the row of brass hooks screwed into the porch ceiling. Up close, the ghosts looked bedraggled. They were due for one of their periodic costume renewals, but nobody had the time for that with everything else that was going on.

Jeannie and Amanda's chosen items had already been moved out by the two Hughs in Red's pickup. Stem's items were consolidated in a corner of the dining room. Denny's one box was in his room, but he said he couldn't take it with him on the train. "We'll UPS it," Jeannie decided.

"Or just, maybe, one of *you* keep it," he said. And that was how it was left, for the moment.

There were still a few things in the attic, still a few things in the basement—most of them to be discarded. The rest of the house was so empty it echoed. One couch and one armchair stood on the bare floor in the living room, waiting to go to Red's apartment. The dining-room table had been sent to a consignment shop and the kitchen table stood in its place, ridiculously small and homely, also to go with Red. The larger pieces of furniture had had to be carried out through the front door, because maneuvering them through the kitchen was too difficult; and each time that happened, someone had to scoop up the long trains of the two center ghosts on the porch and anchor them to either side with bungee cords. Even so, Stem and Denny—or whoever was doing the carrying—would be snared from time to time in swags of cheesecloth, and they would duck and curse and struggle to free themselves. "Why on earth these damn things had to be strung up *now* . . ." one would say. But nobody went so far as to suggest taking them down.

The whole family had been commenting on how helpful Denny had been lately, but then what did he do? He announced on Saturday evening that he'd be leaving in the morning. "Morning?" Jeannie said. The Bouton Road contingent was eating supper at her house, now that their pots and dishes were packed, and she had just set a pork roast in front of Amanda's Hugh for carving. She plunked herself down in her chair, still wearing her oven mitts, and said, "But Dad's moving in the morning!"

"Yeah, I feel bad about that," Denny said.

"And Stem in the afternoon!"

"What can I do, though?" Denny asked the table in general. "There's supposed to be a hurricane coming. This changes everything."

His family looked puzzled. (The hurricane was all over the news, but it was predicted to strike just north of them.) Jeannie's Hugh said, "Usually people head *away* from a hurricane, not toward it."

"Well, but I need to make sure things are battened down at home," Denny said. There was a pause—a stunned little snag in the atmosphere. "Home" was not a word the family connected with New Jersey. Not even Denny, as far as anyone had known until this moment. Jeannie blinked and opened her mouth to speak. Red looked around the table with a questioning expression; it wasn't clear that he had heard. Deb was the first to find her voice. She said, "I thought your things were all packed up in a garage, Uncle Denny."

"They are," Denny said. "They're in my landlady's garage. But my landlady's on her own; I can't just tell her to fend for herself, can I?"

Stem asked, "Couldn't you at least stay till we get Dad moved?"

"The Weather Channel is saying Amtrak might stop the trains by tomorrow afternoon, though. Then I'd be stuck here."

"Stuck!" Jeannie said, looking offended.

"They're talking about cutting service to the whole Northeast Corridor."

"So . . ." Red said. He drew a deep breath. "So, let's see if I've got this straight. You plan on leaving in the morning."

"Right."

"Before I'm in my new place."

"'Fraid so."

"The thing of it is, though," Red said, "what about my computer?"

Denny said, "What about it?"

"I was counting on you to set up my Wi-Fi. You know I'm not good at that stuff! What if I can't connect? What if my laptop goes all temperamental on account of being relocated? What if I try to log on and get nothing, just one of those damn 'You are not connected to the Internet' screens? What if I get a whirling beach ball that goes on and on and on, and I can't get out of it, can't make contact, can't hook up anywhere?"

He was asking not only Denny but all of them, sending a wild, scattered gaze around the table. Denny said, "Dad. Amanda's Hugh knows *way* more about computers than I do."

But Amanda's Hugh said, "Who, me?" And Red just kept staring into one face and then another. Finally Nora, who was seated next to him, set a hand on top of his. "We will take care of all that, I promise, Father Whitshank," she said.

Red peered at her for a moment, and then he relaxed. No one pointed out that Nora didn't even have her own e-mail address.

"Well, this is just great," Jeannie told Denny. She stripped off her oven mitts and slammed them down next to her plate. "You waltz on out whenever you like; everything stops for Lord Denny. Everyone's just thankful you stayed as long as you did; everyone's falling all over themselves because it's such a rare and exalted privilege when you honor us with your presence."

"The prodigal son," Nora said contentedly, and she smiled across the table at Petey. "Isn't it?" she asked him.

But Petey had his mind on the hurricane. He said, "What if you get picked up in the air, Uncle Denny, like the mean neighbor lady in *The Wizard of Oz*? Do you think that might could happen?"

"You never know," Denny said, and he chose a roll from the bread basket and gave it a jaunty upward toss before setting it on his plate.

Sunday dawned cloudy and ominous, which was no surprise. Even without a direct hit, the hurricane was bound to spread a swath of wind and rain and electrical glitches throughout the city. Before things could get any worse, therefore, Jeannie and Amanda dropped off their husbands to help with the heavy lifting, and then Amanda collected the three little boys and the dog and took them back to her house so they would be out from underfoot. Jeannie's assignment was to drive Red to his apartment, along with a small load of kitchen items, and start settling him in. No point making him witness the final dismantling of the house, was everybody's reasoning. But he kept dragging his heels. Ordinarily a man who hated to impose, he had peevishly refused Nora's offer of cold cereal for breakfast and requested eggs, although the eggs were packed in a cooler by then and the skillet was in the bottom of a carton. "Dad—" Stem had begun, but Nora had said, "That's all right. I can fix him eggs in a jiffy."

Then Red took so long to eat them that he was still at it when Jeannie arrived. She had to wait, barely hiding her impatience, while he slowly and methodically forked up tiny mouthfuls, chewing in a contemplative way as he watched Stem and the two Hughs pass back and forth through the dining room with boxes for Jeannie's car. "She's always telling me she should have known what kind of person I was when she found out I didn't recycle," Amanda's Hugh was telling Stem, "but how about what *I* should have seen, from the note she wrote to complain about it?"

Jeannie jingled her car keys and said, "Dad? Shall we hit the road?"

"Last night I dreamed the house burned down," he told her.

"What, this house?"

"I could see all the beams and uprights that hadn't been exposed since when my father built the place."

"Oh, well . . ." Jeannie said, and she made a sad little secret face at Nora, who was rewrapping the skillet in newspaper. "That's understandable, really," she said. Then she asked, "Did Denny get off okay?"

"No," Red said, "I think he's still in bed."

"In bed!"

Nora said, "I knocked on his door a while ago and he

said he was getting up, but maybe he went back to sleep."

"He was the one who couldn't wait to leave!"

"Calm yourselves," Denny said. "I'm up."

He was standing in the doorway, already wearing his jacket, with a canvas duffel bag hanging from each shoulder and a third, much larger bag at his feet. "Morning, all," he told them.

Jeannie said, "Well, finally!"

"I see we've beaten the rain, so far."

"Only through pure blind luck," she said. "I thought you were in such a hurry!"

"I overslept."

"Have you missed your train?"

"Nah, I've still got time." He looked over at his father, who was single-mindedly pursuing a stray bit of egg white with his fork. "How're you feeling, Dad?" he asked.

"I'm okay."

"Excited about your new place?"

"No."

"There's coffee," Nora told Denny.

"That's all right. I'll get some at the station." He waited a beat. "Should I call a cab?" he asked. "Or what?"

He was looking at Jeannie, but Nora was the one who answered. "I can take you," she told him.

"Seems like you've got your hands full."

He looked again at Jeannie. She flung back her ponytail with an angry snap and said, "Well, *I* can't do it. My car's packed to the gills."

"It's no trouble," Nora said.

"Ready, Dad?" Jeannie asked.

Red set his fork down. He wiped his mouth with a paper towel. He said, "It seems wrong to just walk off and let other folks do the work."

"But we're going to work at the new place. You're the only one who can tell me where you want your spatulas kept."

"Oh, what do *I* care where my spatulas are kept?" Red asked too suddenly and too loudly.

But he heaved himself to his feet, and Nora stepped forward to press her cheek to his. "We'll see you tomorrow evening," she told him. "Don't forget you promised to come to our house for supper."

"I remember."

He lifted his windbreaker from the back of his chair and started to put it on. Then he paused and looked at Denny. "Say," he said. "That guy with the French horn, was that *your* doing?"

Denny said, "What?"

"Did you arrange it? I can just about picture it. Paying a guy good money, even, just so we'd all start missing you."

"I don't know what you're talking about."

Red gave a shake of his head and said, "Right." He chuckled at himself. "That would be too crazy," he said. He shrugged into his windbreaker and settled the collar. "Still, though," he said. "How many guys in tank tops listen to classical music?"

Denny looked questioningly at Jeannie, but she was ignoring him. "Got everything, Dad?" she asked.

"Well, no," he said. "But the others are going to bring it, I guess." Then he walked over to Denny and set a palm on his back in a gesture that was halfway between a clap and a hug. "Have a good trip, son."

"Thanks," Denny said. "I hope the new apartment works out."

"Yeah, me too."

Red turned from Denny and left the dining room, with Jeannie and Nora trailing behind. Denny picked up the bag at his feet and followed.

"See you in a while," Red told the two Hughs in the front hall. They were just coming in for another load, both of them slightly winded.

Jeannie's Hugh asked Jeannie, "Are you leaving now? I think we can maybe fit one more box in."

"Never mind that; just put it on the truck," she said. "I want to get going." And she shouldered past him and hurried to catch up with Red, as if she feared he might try to escape. They threaded between the tied-back swags of cheesecloth on the porch; Stem stood aside to let them pass. "We should be over there in an hour or so," he told Red. Red didn't answer.

At the bottom of the steps, Red paused and looked back at the house. "It wasn't a dream per se, as a matter of fact," he told Jeannie.

"What's that, Dad?"

"When I had that dream the house burned down, it wasn't an actual *dream* dream. It was more like one of those pictures you get in your head when you're half asleep. I was lying in bed and it came to me, kind of—the burnt-out bones of the house. But then I thought, 'No, no, no, put that out of your mind,' I thought. 'It will do okay without us.'"

"It will do just fine," Jeannie said.

He turned and set off down the flagstone walk, then, but Jeannie waited for Denny and Nora, and when they had caught up she reached across Denny's burden of bags to give him a hug. "Say goodbye to the house," she told him.

"Bye, house," he said.

"The last time I missed church, I was in the hospital having Petey," Nora told Denny as she was driving.

"So, does this mean you're going to hell?"

"No," she said in all seriousness. "But it does feel odd." She flicked on her turn signal. "Maybe I'll try to make the evening prayer service, if we're finished moving in by then."

Denny was gazing out his side window, watching the houses slide past. His left hand, resting on his knee, kept tapping out some private rhythm.

"I guess you'll be glad to get back to your teaching," she said after a silence.

He said, "Hmm?" Then he said, "Sure."

"Will you always just substitute, or do you want a permanent position someday?"

"Oh, for that I'd have to take more course work," he said. He seemed to have his mind elsewhere.

"I can imagine you'd be really good with high-school kids."

He swung his eyes toward her. "No," he said, "the whole thing got me down, it turns out. It was kind of depressing. Everything you're supposed to teach them, you know it's only a drop in the bucket—and not all that useful for real life anyhow, most of the time. I'm thinking I might try something else now."

"Like what?"

"Well, I was thinking of making furniture."

"Furniture," she said, as if testing the word.

"I mean, work that would give me something . . . visible, right? To show at the end of the day. And why fight it: I come from people who build things."

Nora nodded, just to herself, and Denny returned to looking out his side window. "That thing about the French horn," he said to a passing bus. "What *was* that, do you know?"

Nora said, "I have no idea."

"I hope he's not losing it."

"He'll be all right," Nora said. "We'll make sure to keep an eye on him."

They had reached the top of St. Paul Street now. It would be a straight shot south to Penn Station. Nora sat back in her seat, her fingers loose on the bottom of the wheel. Even driving, she gave the impression of floating. She said, "I would just like to say, Denny—Douglas and I would both like to say—that we appreciate your coming to help out. It meant a lot to your mom and dad. I hope you know that."

He looked her way again. "Thanks," he said. "I mean, you're welcome. Well, thank *you* both, too."

"And it was nice of you not to tell about his mother."

"Oh, well, it's nobody's business, really."

"Not to tell Douglas, I mean. When he was younger."

"Oh."

There was another silence.

"You know what happened?" he asked suddenly. There was something startled in his tone, as if he hadn't intended to speak until that instant. "You know when I was mending Dad's shirt?"

"Yes."

"His dashiki kind of thing?"

"Yes, I remember."

"I was thinking I would never find the right shade of blue, because it was such a *bright* blue. But I went to the linen closet where Mom always kept her sewing box, and I opened the door, and before I could even reach for the box this spool of bright-blue thread rolled out from the rear of the shelf. I just cupped my hand beneath the shelf and this spool of thread dropped into it."

They were stopped for a red light now. Nora sent him a thoughtful, remote look.

"Well, of course that can be explained," he said. "First of

all, Mom *would* have that shade, because she was the one who had made the dashiki in the first place, and you don't toss a spool of thread just because it's old. As for why it was out of the box like that . . . well, I did spill a bunch of stuff out earlier when I was sewing on a button. And I guess the rolling had to do with how I opened the closet door. I set up a whoosh of air or something; I don't know."

The light turned green, and Nora resumed driving.

"But in the split second before I realized that," he said, "I almost imagined that she was *handing* it to me. Like some kind of, like, secret sign. Stupid, right?"

Nora said, "No."

"I thought, 'It's like she's telling me she forgives me,'" Denny said. "And then I took the dashiki to my room and I sat down on my bed to mend it, and out of nowhere this other thought came. I thought, 'Or she's telling me she knows that *I* forgive *her*.' And all at once I got this huge, like, feeling of relief."

Nora nodded and signaled for a turn.

"Oh, well, who can figure these things?" Denny asked the row houses slipping past.

"I think you've figured it just right," Nora told him.

She turned into Penn Station.

In the passenger drop-off lane, she shifted into park and popped her trunk. "Don't forget to keep in touch," she told him.

"Oh, sure. I'd never just disappear; they need me around for the drama."

She smiled; her two dimples deepened. "They probably do," she said. "I really think they do." And she accepted his peck on her cheek and then gave him a languid wave as he stepped out of the car.

The clouds overhead were a deep gray now, churning like muddy waters stirred up from the bottom of a lake, and inside the station, the skylight—ordinarily a kaleidoscope of pale, translucent aquas—had an opaque look. Denny bypassed the ticket machines, which had lines that wound back through the lobby, and went to stand in the line for the agents. Even there some ten or twelve people were waiting ahead of him, so he set down his bags and shoved them along with his foot as the line progressed. He could sense the anxiety of the crowd. A middle-aged couple standing behind him had apparently not thought to reserve, and the wife kept saying, "Oh, God, oh, God, they're not going to have any seats left, are they?"

"Sure they are," her husband told her. "Quit your fussing."

"I knew we should have called ahead. Everybody's trying to beat the hurricane."

"Hurkeen," she pronounced it. She had a wiry, elastic Baltimore accent and a smoker's rusty voice.

"If there's not any seats for this one we'll catch the next one," her husband told her.

"Next one! Watch there not *be* a next one. They'll stop running them after this one."

The husband made an exasperated huffing sound, but Denny sympathized with the wife. Even with his own reserved seat, he didn't feel entirely confident. What if they shut down the trains before his train arrived? What if he had to turn around and go back to Bouton Road? Stuck in his family, trapped. Ingrown, like a toenail.

The man in front of him was called to a window, and Denny shoved his bags farther up. He was going to get the elderly agent with the disapproving face; he just knew it. "Sorry, sir . . ." the agent would say, not sounding sorry in the least.

But no, he got the cheery-looking African-American lady, and her first words when he gave her his confirmation number were "Aren't *you* the lucky one!" He signed for his ticket gladly, without his usual muttering at the price. He thanked her and lugged his bags to the Dunkin' Donuts to buy coffee and, on second thought, a pastry as well, to celebrate. He was going to make it out of here after all.

The few tables outside the Dunkin' Donuts were occupied, and so were all the benches in the waiting room. He had to eat standing against a pillar with his bags piled at his feet. More passengers were milling around than at Christmas or Thanksgiving, even, all wearing frazzled expressions. "*No*, you can't buy a candy bar," a mother snapped at her little boy. "Stick close to me or you'll get lost."

A mellifluous female voice on the loudspeaker announced

the arrival of a southbound train at gate B. "That's B as in Bubba," the voice said, which Denny found slightly odd. So did the young woman next to him, apparently—an attractive redhead with that golden tan skin that was always such an unexpected pleasure to see in a redhead. She quirked her eyebrows at him, inviting him to share her amusement.

Sometimes you glance toward a woman and she glances toward you and there is this subtle recognition, this moment of complicity, and anything might happen after that. Or not. Denny turned away and dropped his paper cup in the waste bin.

The train at gate B-for-Bubba was traveling to D.C., where nobody seemed to want to go, but when Denny's northbound train was announced there was a general surge toward the stairs. Denny thought of what Jeannie's Hugh had said the night before; shouldn't all these people be heading *away* from the hurricane? But north was where home was, he'd be willing to bet—drawing them irresistibly, as if they were migratory birds. They pressed him forward, down the stairs, and when he reached the platform he felt a twinge of vertigo as they steered him too close to the tracks. He pulled ahead, making his way to where the forward cars would board. But he didn't want the quiet car. Quiet cars made him edgy. He liked to sit surrounded by a sea of anonymous chatter; he liked the living-room-like coziness of mixed and mingled cell-phone conversations.

The train curved toward them from a distance, almost the same shade of gray as the darkened air it moved through, and a number of cars flashed past before it shrieked to a stop. There didn't appear to be a quiet car, as far as Denny could tell. He boarded through the nearest door and chose the first empty seat, next to a teenage boy in a leather jacket, because he knew he had no hope of sitting by himself. First he heaved his luggage into the overhead rack, and only then did he ask, "This seat taken?" The boy shrugged and looked away from him, out the window. Denny dropped into his seat and slipped his ticket from his inside breast pocket.

Always that "Ahh" feeling when you settle into place, finally. Always followed, in a matter of minutes, by "How soon can I get *out* of here?" But for now, he felt completely, gratefully at rest.

People were having trouble finding seats. They were jamming the aisle, bumbling past with their knobby backpacks, calling to each other in frantic-sounding voices. "Dina? Where'd you go?" "Over here, Mom." "There's room up ahead, folks!" a conductor shouted from the forward end.

The train started moving, and those who were still standing lurched and grabbed for support. A woman arguably old enough to be offered a seat loomed above Denny for a full minute, and he studied his ticket with deep concentration till another woman called to her and she moved away.

Row houses passed in a slow, dismal stream—their rear windows drably curtained or blanked out with curling paper shades, their back porches crammed with barbecue grills and garbage cans, their yards a jumble of rusty cast-off appliances. Inside the car, the hubbub gradually settled down. Denny's seatmate leaned his head against the window and stared out. As imperceptibly as possible, Denny slid his phone from his pocket. He hit the memory dial and then bent forward till he was almost doubled up. He didn't want this conversation overheard.

"Hey, there. It's Alison," the recording said. "I'm either out or unavailable, but you can always leave me a message."

"Pick up, Allie," he said. "It's me."

There was a pause, and then a click.

"You act like saying 'It's me' will make me drop everything and come running," she said.

Another time, he might have asked, "And didn't it?" Three months ago he might have asked that. But now he said, "Well, a guy can always hope."

She said nothing.

"What're you up to?" he asked finally.

"I'm trying to get ready for Sandy."

"Who's Sandy?"

"*What* is Sandy, idiot. Sandy the hurricane; where have you been?"

"Ah."

"On the news they're showing people laying sandbags across their doorways, but where on earth do you buy those?"

"I'll see to that," he told her. "I'm already on the train."

Another pause, during which he held very still. But in the end, all she said was "Denny."

461

"What."

"I have not said yes to that yet."

"I realize you haven't," he said. He said it a bit too quickly, so she wouldn't retract the word "yet." "But I'm hoping that the sight of my irresistible self will work its magic."

"Is that right," she said flatly.

He squinched his eyes almost shut, and waited.

"We've already talked about this," she told him. "Nothing's changed. No way am I going to let things go on like they were before."

"I know that."

"I'm tired. I'm worn out. I'm thirty-three years old."

The conductor was standing over him. Denny sat up straight and thrust his ticket at him blindly.

"I need somebody I can depend on," she said. "I need a guy who won't change jobs more often than most people change gym memberships, or take off on a road trip without any notice, or sit around all day in sweat pants smoking weed. And most of all, someone who's not moody, moody, moody. Just moody for no reason! Moody!"

Denny leaned forward again.

"Listen," he said. "Allie. You're always asking what on earth is wrong with me, but don't you think I wonder too? I've been asking it all my life; I wake up in the middle of the night and I ask, 'What's the *matter* with me? How could I screw up like this?' I look at how I act sometimes and I just can't explain it."

The silence at the other end was so profound that he wondered if she had hung up. He said, "Al?"

"What."

"Are you there?"

"I'm here."

He said, "My dad says he remembers my mom's gone even while he's asleep."

"That's sad," Allie said after a moment.

"But I do, too," he said. "I remember *you're* gone, every second I've been away."

All he heard was silence.

"So I want to come back," he said. "I want to do things differently this time."

More silence.

"Allie?"

"Well," she said, "we could take it day by day, I guess."

He let out his breath. He said, "You won't regret it."

"I probably will, in fact."

"You won't, I swear to God."

"But this is a trial run, understand? You're only here on approval."

"Absolutely. No question," he said. "You can kick me out the first mistake I make."

"Oh, Lord. I don't know why I'm such a pushover."

He said, "Are my things still in your garage?"

"They were the last time I looked."

"So . . . I can move them back into the house?"

When she didn't answer immediately, he took a tighter

grip on the phone. "I'm not saying I have to," he said. "I mean, if you tell me I have to live above the garage again, just to start with, I would understand."

Allie said, "Well, I don't know that we would need to go *that* far."

He relaxed his grip on the phone.

The two young girls just behind him could not stop laughing. They kept dissolving in cascades of giggles, sputtering and squeaking. What did girls that age find so funny? The other passengers were reading, or listening to their music, or typing away on their computers, but these two were saying "Oh, oh, oh" and gasping for breath and then going off in more gales of laughter.

Denny glanced toward his seatmate, half expecting to exchange a look of bafflement, but to his horror, he discovered that the boy was crying. He wasn't just teary; he was shaking with sobs, his mouth stretched wide in agony, his hands convulsively clutching his kneecaps. Denny couldn't think what to do. Offer sympathy? Ignore him? But ignoring him seemed callous. And when someone showed his grief so openly, wasn't he asking for help? Denny looked around, but none of the other passengers seemed aware of the situation. He transferred his gaze to the seat back in front of him and willed the moment to pass.

It was like when Stem first came to stay, when he slept in Denny's room and cried himself to sleep every night and

Denny lay silent and rigid, staring up at the dark, trying not to hear.

Or like when he himself, years later in boarding school, longed all day for bedtime just so he could let the tears slide secretly down the sides of his face to his pillow, although not for any good reason, because God knows he was glad to get away from his family and they were glad to see him go. Thank heaven the other boys never realized.

It was this last thought that told him what to do about his seatmate: nothing. Pretend not to notice. Look past him out the rain-spattered window. Focus purely on the scenery, which had changed to open countryside now, leaving behind the blighted row houses, leaving behind the station under its weight of roiling dark clouds, and the empty city streets around it, and the narrower streets farther north with the trees turning inside out in the wind, and the house on Bouton Road where the filmy-skirted ghosts frolicked and danced on the porch with nobody left to watch.

www.vintage-books.co.uk